Reborn

By SARA MACK

Reborn (Book 3 in The Guardian Trilogy)

ISBN-13: 978-1494227937
ISBN-10: 1494227932

Cover art by Breena Slayton & S.M. Koz
Edited by Abbie Gale Lemmon

Dedicated to
My family, immediate and extended

Your support amazes me.
I love you to the moon and back.

Table of Contents

Prologue

Do you dream in color or black and white?

The last few nights have brought me brilliant, prismatic dreams. I've never dreamt like this before. My hope is that the odd images will continue and reveal the missing pieces of my past. I need to know what I've been told is true by seeing it for myself with my mind's eye. It will be easier for me to accept my new reality through my memories because right now things are just...

Unbelievable.

Garrett says the blast from The Allegiant's hand should have killed me. He owes my survival to the charm I wear around my wrist; a bracelet given to me by someone I don't remember. I play with it now, turning it around and around, as the airplane descends. After three days of living with complete strangers in a foreign place, I'm almost home. The familiarity of it beckons me. I keep telling myself I'll be able to think clearly – remember more – surrounded by what I know.

As the wheels of the plane touch down, relief courses through my body. I'm here; I made it. I can pick up where my life left off and things will make sense again.

I hope.

Chapter 1

"Where do you want this?"

I turn around and reach for my suitcase. "I told you I could carry that."

Dane moves it out of my reach. "It's not a problem. Where do you want it?"

I sigh and gesture down the hallway. "In the bedroom."

He walks around me and disappears. I know he'll only be gone a minute – he hasn't let me out of his sight since I came to. It's both reassuring and overbearing at the same time.

I set my backpack on the floor and look around the living room. Everything is as I remember it: television remote on the coffee table, cat toys in the corner. Blanket puddled in the center of the couch. I stare at it, remembering the last night I spent here. I fell asleep in that very spot.

"You have to admit I have good taste," Dane's voice makes me jump.

I'm confused. "How do you mean?"

"I sent that for your birthday." He follows my stare and walks over to run his hand along the couch. He then eyes the television. "Where's the flat screen?"

I shake my head. "What flat screen?"

He frowns. "The other half of your gift."

"I don't know what you're talking about."

His expression falls. "Right." He moves to sit down and bounces on the couch, testing the cushions. "At least it's comfortable," he says. "I won't throw my back out."

Yeah, about that...I look down. His staying here makes me uneasy. "Listen." I meet his eyes. "I'm sure you would be happier at your own place. I don't need a babysitter."

He looks at me like I'm crazy. "I'm not leaving you."

"Garrett and James will be back in a day or two. They'll be right next door; I'll be fine."

He makes a face. It's the same expression he had when this plan was first discussed. "I'm staying until they get here," he says, then adds "maybe longer" under his breath.

I hold out my hands. "I don't want you to feel obligated to stay. I remember this; I remember everything except Guardians."

"And everyone associated with them," he quietly reminds me.

No one knows the fall-out of what happened last week. The boys are concerned that I may run into someone I don't remember. If Dane stays with me he can steer me clear until James and Garrett arrive. "Still," my shoulders sag, "I don't want to inconvenience you."

"It's not an inconvenience," he says then stands. "Besides, being here gives us some time to get reacquainted." He pauses. "Without an audience."

I give him a wary look. I know we have a past, but I don't know how strong our relationship was.

After we established what I did and did not remember, James, Garrett, and Dane filled me in on everything Guardian – who they are, that James once was, that Garrett was, too. They told me about The Allegiant and the Intermediate, and about the strangers that came to help. But, they glossed over the relationships. When James began to explain how he and I were involved, it garnered a harsh look from Dane. That resulted in a snide comment from James after which Garrett stepped in and told them to hold off on the more personal stuff, for now.

I'm not ready to delve into my past just yet, so I turn toward my room. "I'm going to unpack."

"Well, I'm hungry," Dane says and shrugs out of his jacket. "Where do you go to eat around here?"

I decide to be difficult. "The kitchen."

He smiles. "There she is. I was wondering when the real you might return."

I roll my eyes. "There are some take out menus in the drawer under the microwave. Take your pick."

He heads to the kitchen as I enter my bedroom. I find my suitcase on the bed and his propped against the wall. This is so weird. I take off my coat and get to work.

Unzipping the bag, I pull out my stuff, making a pile of the clean clothes and throwing the dirty ones into a heaping pile on the floor. I mentally remind myself that I have a test tomorrow in Stats, and I should email my instructors to let them know I've returned. I immediately scratch the email idea. I'll just talk to them tomorrow in person. I do have to call my parents and lie to them about the fake accident that ended my fake trip abroad. I shake my head as I continue to sort. I hate lying. That hasn't changed.

"Hey."

"Geez!" I jump in surprise as Dane interrupts my thoughts.

One side of his mouth quirks up as he leans against the doorframe. He holds out two menus. "Chinese or pizza?"

"Pizza," I answer without hesitation.

"Mushroom, green pepper, and ham?"

I frown. "How do you know what I like?"

He smirks. "I know a lot about what you like."

The look he gives me insinuates he's not talking about food. "Go order it then," I say, irritated. "Tell me how much I owe you."

He scoffs and pulls his phone from his pocket. "Like I'd let you pay."

I shoot him a look. Was he always this annoying? At the airport he wouldn't take my money to get his car out of the parking lot. "I will pay for what I eat," I say adamantly.

"Oh, okay," he says as he brings his phone to his ear. "The cost of two slices will surely break me. I'll really need that $2 later."

I open my mouth to respond to his sarcasm, but the pizza place answers and he walks away. I stare at my unpacked clothes while he orders from the living room. These next couple of days could be a challenge.

Once the contents of my suitcase are organized, I head to grab my backpack and catch Dane putting on his jacket.

"Where are you going?"

"To the store we passed at the corner," he says. "You have nothing to drink."

I feign shock and bring my hand to my chest. "You're actually going to leave me alone?"

He gives me a dry look and opens the door. "Yes. Now would be a good time to call your parents if you'd like some privacy."

I would like some privacy, but more than just a trip to the store in length.

"You remember what to tell them, right?"

I close my eyes and nod. "It rained in Ireland. I was walking on cobblestones, slipped, and hit my head. The fall messed with my old concussion, and I have some short-term memory loss. My advisor sent me home. The end." I open my eyes.

"Very good," Dane tells me. "I'll be back before dinner's delivered."

"Yes Mom, I'm fine. I promise."

"Emma, I swear to God you're trying to give me a heart attack," my mother says through the phone. "When did this happen?"

My finger traces the pattern on my comforter. "Yesterday," I lie.

"Why didn't you call us? Why didn't someone call us? I'm going to have a word with that school!" she threatens.

"No, Mom, don't. I didn't even pass out. My memory is just a little hazy and the school didn't want to risk my staying overseas in case it got worse. I thought you would be glad I'm home." I know I am.

"I'm relieved, actually," she sighs. "So, what don't you remember? Did the doctors say your memory would come back?"

"It's hit or miss," I say. It's probably the most truthful thing I will tell her about this whole experience. "At first I couldn't remember the date or where I was. I couldn't recognize some of the people in my group." Especially the Three Musketeers hovering over me when I awoke.

"But it got better?"

"It's getting there. Everything is back except..."

"Except what?"

From what James and Dane told me, the two of them are sure to come up in conversation with my parents. Apparently I've known James since we were kids, and Dane helped save me from an attack I don't remember. "There are some pictures in my phone of people I don't recognize."

"What do they look like?" my mom asks. "Do the names Matt and Shel ring a bell?"

"Oh, I remember them," I say and it's not a lie. Matt and Shel are my best friends.

"Then what do the strangers look like?"

"One has light brown hair and really blue eyes and the other..."

Her sharp intake of breath stops my speech. "Oh, honey," she says with real concern. "You don't remember James?"

"Who's James?" Maybe she will tell me what Garrett wouldn't allow discussion of earlier.

"Sweetie, I'm coming out there. I can't tell you this over the phone; I don't know how you will react."

"It's that bad?"

"It could be," she says. "I'm heading out first thing in the morning."

I shake my head. She can't find Dane here. "No, how about this weekend? I want to get caught up now that I'm back in classes."

"Are they going to allow you to do that?"

"I hope so," I lie again. I'm already caught up. "I need to talk with everyone and see."

The buzzer from the front door of my building rings. It's either the pizza man or Dane.

"What's that?" she asks.

"Dinner," I say as I walk toward the door. "Pizza guy."

"All right, I'll let you eat," she says. "Go to bed early and get some rest. Expect me on Saturday."

I smile into the phone. "I can't wait. I love you. Tell Dad I love him, too."

"Will do. See you soon."

I hang up the phone and move to the intercom that connects to the front door. "Hello?"

"It's me. Let me in."

I can't help but smile at the irony in this. Dane wants to monitor my every move yet he is locked outside. "No," I say back to him.

He buzzes again. "You're not funny. Unlock the door."

"Make me," I laugh. When is the last time I laughed?

"Emma, I swear..."

I release the button, so I can't hear him anymore. I picture him outside cursing which makes me grin. He pushes the buzzer again, but I don't answer. After a second or two, he holds the button down, so the buzzer rings continuously. It's loud and I can only take the sound for about a minute before it grates on my nerves. It's like fingernails on a chalkboard. I begrudgingly leave my apartment to let him in.

When I open the door he looks at me exasperated. "What was that?"

"*That* was fun."

"It's cold out here," he complains. He hands me a two-liter of Coke. "Paybacks are hell you know."

I don't feel threatened. "Whatever. You won; I let you in."

He picks a case of beer up off the ground and walks past me.

"Expecting a party later?"

"I need this to put up with you," he says as we walk down the hall. "The next few days could be rough."

"You're so funny," I say sarcastically, even though I was thinking the same thing earlier. I shut the door to my apartment behind us, and Dane stops midway to the kitchen, turning to face me.

"What?"

He tilts his head. "Have you remembered anything yet?"

I blink. I've been home all of five minutes. "No. Why?"

He stares at me for a moment then turns toward the kitchen. "Just asking."

Twenty minutes later the pizza is delivered, and I make myself comfortable in the living room to eat. I sit cross-legged at one end of the couch while Dane takes the other. We must be starving because we don't speak, our mouths too full of food for anything else.

After finishing my second piece I find myself contemplating a third. Instead, I reach for my glass. "I wonder when James and Garrett will get here," I muse. The two of them had to take the long way back by renting a car and driving to Michigan once they got off the island. James may be human again, but he has no ID to fly.

"Why?" Dane frowns, mid-chew.

"I'd like to see my cat again." I take a drink. "I wonder if LB has missed me."

"I'm sure she has," he says and polishes off his fourth slice. He reaches for his beer and tips it back. "Did you talk to your parents?"

"Yeah. My mom's concerned, of course. I talked her out of coming here immediately, but she'll be here Saturday."

"Your parents are good people." He leans back against the couch. "I wish I could say the same for mine."

"You don't get along with your parents?"

He gives me a blank look.

"Let me guess. We've discussed this before?"

He nods. "My dad and stepmother own Bay Woods. You remember your summer job, right?"

"I do. I worked there with Shel until she went out of state." I pause, trying to open up my memory bank. Things get foggy after that memory until another face emerges. "Then I worked with Leslie."

He shakes his head. "No, you worked with me. You worked with Leslie for, like, two weeks."

My eyebrows shoot up. "Really?" My brain seems to remember a whole lot of Leslie. I frown as I realize how much I am missing. I know everything Guardian is gone, but it's not just the people. It's every interaction, every emotion, every moment. Suddenly, I want to know. The unease I felt before at discovering my past is replaced by curiosity. "How long would it take you to fill me in about...us?"

He regards me, takes a long pull from his bottle, and finishes it. "Hours," he says seriously. He stands, reaching for my plate. "You want me to take that?"

"Thanks." I hand it over, but eye him suspiciously. "Are you avoiding my question? I thought you wanted to get reacquainted?"

"I do," he says. "I'll be right back."

He takes the plates and the pizza box into the kitchen and disappears. I uncross my legs and stretch and then rearrange myself on the couch. I glance at the clock; it's nine. I have class in the morning at ten.

Dane returns from the kitchen with a beer in each hand. Is our past that rough? Should I be inebriated, too? "Is one of those for me?"

He looks surprised. "You want one?"

I think I do. "Yeah."

He hands me a bottle as he sits, holding it out by the neck. "You don't typically drink beer."

"I know." I twist off the cap and take a sip. It's cold and tastes bitter, but for some reason I want it. "Okay, start talking."

"I think you should ask me some questions."

"How about you hit the highlights? Tell me what you want me to know."

He looks doubtful. "I'm not sure we should go there just yet."

"I'm not going to flip out or anything." At least I think I won't. I take another drink to enhance my confidence.

"You're killing me," he says. "Just ask me something."

"Just tell me something."

"God, you're impossible!"

"You make it too easy." I smile. "Have we always bickered like this? Like an old married couple?"

He laughs, but then his grin fades into a small smile. He looks at the drink in his hand, clearly remembering something, and then shakes his head to clear the thought as he raises the bottle to his lips.

"What is it?" I ask then pause as a thought strikes me. "We're not married are we?"

He almost chokes on his beer. "No." He clears his throat. "But I did take you on my honeymoon."

I sit up straight. "Say again?"

He looks me in the eye. "Might as well air the dirty laundry first." He shifts his body, so he's facing mine. "I was engaged to someone named Teagan. I had the trip booked before I broke up with her. You needed a place to hide, so St. Thomas was it."

That sounds logical. "Did I know this when we were there?"

"You found out when we arrived."

"About Teagan?" I ask in surprise.

"No, about the honeymoon. You knew all about her."

"Oh. That's better." I was thinking I went with him without knowing he had a fiancée. "So you and Teagan are through? How come?"

"That's a long story."

I look at the clock and take another drink. "The night's young."

He sighs. "I don't love her anymore."

This is like pulling teeth. "Because?"

"Because I love you."

17

I freeze. I was not expecting that answer. He loves *me*? "I thought you didn't want to go there just yet."

"That's not what I was referring to."

My face flushes. There's more? I decide to play it off. "I know I saved your life, but you don't have to lie."

He sets his beer on the table and moves closer to me. "I fell in love with you before you tried to kill yourself," he says. "Which, by the way, I will never forgive you for. If you hadn't jumped in front of me you wouldn't be in this situation."

"But you'd be dead." I frown. "It worked out. I'm alive and you're alive. It's all good."

"Is it? You have no memory of us. It took so long for you to realize your feelings for me. Now they're gone."

"Maybe they'll come back," I say. I feel bad I can't reciprocate what he feels. It's obvious he means what he says.

"I hope so because James is human again. He's going to fight for you."

My face twists. What is this? Some sort of turn of the century battle for the maiden's hand? I've never been the girl everyone wants; I've never dated. Well, I thought I'd never dated. I clutch the bottle in my hands. "James and I were serious?"

He scoffs. "That's the understatement of the year."

"How serious?"

"You've been together since you were seventeen."

What? We were together five years? Why can't I remember that? I should remember that! "And then he died and came back?"

Dane nods.

I take another drink as I mull things over. Maybe my subconscious knew I'd need this beer. "When did things end between James and me?"

Dane sighs. "I don't think they officially did. Can we not talk about him anymore?"

What does that mean? I was seeing two guys at the same time? I wouldn't do that; I know I wouldn't. "Fine. How serious were you and I?"

"Very."

I give him a sarcastic look. He's not being very forthcoming. "That's vague. Just tell me. I'm a big girl."

Concern clouds his features. "Are you sure?"

"Jesus!" I sit ramrod straight, so I'm looking directly at him. "I'm not some fragile little flower! I got blasted by a supernatural being and survived for Christ sake! Do you want me to know about us or not? Just tell me!"

Dane looks shocked by my outburst. I take it I wasn't prone to shouting prior to my mind wipe? He accepts my challenge however and leans closer to me. "You're serious? You want to know right now?"

I meet his eyes. "Yes."

"We slept together," he says without an ounce of regret. "We slept together and you told me you loved me."

All the blood drains from my face. Of all the things.... Call me naïve, but I was expecting a kiss or two, maybe second base. But sex? With him? I mean, look at him! How can I not remember *that?!* "When?" I ask, blindsided.

"Last week."

For the love of all that is holy. I tip my bottle up and drain it in three swallows.

"You okay?" Dane asks.

I nod and hand him my empty bottle. "Can I have another, please?"

Chapter 2

My bed shakes. "Emma, wake up."

"Nooo," I moan and grab the pillow, folding it over my head.

"You have to get up. You're going to miss class."

"No, I'm not. The alarm didn't go off."

I flinch as the pillow disappears from my face. "It's gone off six times! Don't make me pull you out of there."

I open one eye. Dane is standing over me with my pillow is his hands. "You're really here," I say stupidly.

A slight smile dances across his lips. "Where else would I be? Now get up."

I try, but my arms feel weak and my head pounds. "I thought I dreamt last night."

"You wish you dreamt last night." He tosses the pillow at the foot of the bed and leans over me with a smirk on his face. "You're hung over."

"I am not," I say and try to sit up again. It's not working.

"Are too. I should never have listened to you; five was too many."

"I never asked for five!" I groan. "You kept feeding me drinks hoping to score – again." My late night drunken debauchery is a direct result of his revelation. I guess I couldn't handle it without some liquid courage.

"Now why didn't I think of that?" He pretends to ponder. "Oh, yeah, because that's not what I was doing." He pulls off the covers. "Get. Up."

Cold air rushes over my legs, so I instinctively pull them to my chest for warmth. "Give me my blankets back!" I whine. "I just need ten more minutes."

"Ten minutes won't cure what you have," Dane says. "Do you have some Tylenol?"

"In the bathroom."

He leaves and I hear him rummaging around for aspirin. I look at my alarm. I am going to be late. I pull the covers over me and roll, winding myself inside them. My instructors think I'm out of town, my Stats teacher can continue to do so. I'll see him on Thursday...

My eyes spring open. I have a test!

Shit.

I unwrap myself, scoot to the edge of the bed, and drag myself to my dresser. I pull out a pair of jeans and slide them on under my sleep shirt.

"Whoa," Dane says as he reenters my room. "Did you have a miraculous recovery?"

"No, I have a test," I grumble and yank open the next drawer to find a top. I settle for my old Western sweatshirt then dig around for a bra in my top drawer. No luck. How can they all be dirty? I look on the floor and find the one I wore yesterday. I bend over to pick it up and feel every pulse of blood my heart pushes through my veins. My head wants to explode. I wish I had time to shower.

Dane notices my pain, probably because I have my eyes smashed shut. "Do you need help?"

"Yes." I snag my underwear with my finger. "Get out so I can get dressed."

"Why don't you take your test online?" he asks and sets a glass of water on the bedside table.

I shoot him an incredulous look. "You're the one who woke me up to get to class!"

"You're the one who insisted on going!" He takes a few steps toward me. "Don't you remember? Last night you kept talking about seeing your instructors, picking up where you left off, things making sense again. You made me pinky swear to get you up this morning."

"I did?" That sounds so immature.

"Yes, so make up your mind. Take your test online or move your ass."

My eyes instinctively narrow. "I am moving my ass." I hold on to my clothes and step around him, headed for the bathroom. Once inside, I shut the door, dress, and brush my teeth. I quickly pull a comb through my hair and tack it up in a messy ponytail. I forego my traditional lip gloss routine and throw some Chapstick in my pocket.

When I throw open the door Dane is waiting. He hands me two pills and the glass of water. I take them and swallow.

"Ready?" he asks.

"As ready as I'm going to be." I brush past him, grab my bag and jacket from the bedroom, and then head toward the front door. I yank it open.

"Wait," he says from behind me. "I'll drive you."

I turn around and watch him search for his coat, just now noticing that he's fully dressed. How early did he get up? He lifts the blankets from his makeshift bed on the couch then eyes his coat tossed across the back of the chair. He grabs it and then picks his wallet and keys off the table. "Lead the way."

I look him over suspiciously.

"What?"

"If I wanted to walk would you let me?"

"Absolutely not," he says and nudges me out the door.

That's what I thought.

Unfortunately, I have three classes on Wednesdays which does nothing to cure my aching head. I think I did okay on my test though, which surprises me. Maybe the key to my understanding Stats is alcohol; although, I don't care to test that theory. All of my instructors seemed pleased to have me back due to the lie I told them about a family emergency. After I woke up on the island, I stumbled across the email I sent to my professors explaining my sudden absence. The guys were putting the rental house back together and wouldn't let me help. It was frustrating, and I spent a lot of time on my laptop as a distraction.

Since my last class let out early, I pull out my phone and text Dane.

Pick me up.

After a minute he responds. *Pick me up what?*

I roll my eyes. *Pick me up PLEASE.*

As he drove me to class this morning, we got into a discussion about manners. He stated I was being ungrateful for his services, and I could at least cut the attitude after I gave him crap about not allowing me to walk to class. I told him I'm an adult and I'm perfectly capable of getting myself around; although, secretly, I don't want to walk in the cold weather. It's the principle of the thing. Without the memories of anyone taking care of me I'm having trouble accepting his assistance. I've always been self-sufficient. Or at least I thought.

My phone vibrates. *That's better.*

I lean against the side of the building and decide to text Shel. With getting back, and all of last night's confessions, it slipped my mind to let my best friend know I'm home. Okay, I'm sure the drinking didn't help, but learning what I did threw me. On top of all the Guardian stuff, I have to come to terms with the fact that I had two relationships – serious ones – that I have no recollection of having. It's disturbing. In a way I feel violated, but in another I feel, I don't know, fortunate? Smug? James and Dane aren't hard on the eyes and in my limited time with them I know they are genuinely nice guys. In my world, if someone told me to identify them from a lineup of potential suitors, I'd epically fail.

I finish my message to Shel. *Hey! I'm home. Trip got cut short. I hit my head; long story. Call me when you have time!*

My cell vibrates within seconds. *No way! I've SO missed you! Will you be around tonight? I'm at the hospital now.*

She must have picked up some additional volunteer hours. *Absolutely. Call me whenever :)*

I put my phone in my coat pocket and pull out one of two granola bars I bought earlier. I nibble on it as I wait for Dane. My stomach accepts the food, but it's hungry for more. I'm going to have to eat when I get home.

"Emma?"

I turn around. My housemate from upstairs, Samantha, is headed my way. I wave.

"I haven't seen you in forever!" she gushes. "Where have you been?"

I swallow and smile. "Out of town." I only remember hanging out with Samantha once, but the memory is hazy. "How are things?"

She sighs in an exaggerated way. "Todd and I broke up."

As I recall, I didn't like her boyfriend much, but I say "I'm sorry" anyway.

"I'm not." She flips her blonde hair over her shoulder. "I wasted far too much of my time on that jerk."

I nod, because I remember Todd. "So things are good then?"

"They could be better." She smiles and steps closer to me. "I'm glad I ran into you because I've been meaning to ask...are you and Garrett together?"

I look at her dazed. "Um, no."

"You guys aren't dating?"

"Why would you think that? No, we've never dated." I think. A miniature version of myself appears in my head and starts rummaging through imaginary files. I can't find anything on Garrett and me as a couple. But then again, he's a former Guardian, and I don't remember those.

"Yay!" She claps her hands which embarrasses me. I look around to make sure no one is watching our exchange.

"I so want to ask him out, but he hasn't been around, and then you weren't around, so I figured you two were together, because you seemed really close and..."

I block her out as she babbles. Garrett and I were close? How close? My stomach starts to feel like lead. He mentioned he was my neighbor and James' mentor; a Guardian becoming human. But that's it. I couldn't possibly have been involved with him too. Right?

"...so do you know where he is?"

I snap back to Samantha. "Yes. I mean no. I mean he should be back tomorrow."

She notices my odd response. "You don't mind if I ask him out do you? Is he seeing someone?"

"No." I shake my head. "I don't think he's seeing anyone."

She beams. "Good!"

My eyes are distracted as Dane pulls to a stop along the curb in front of us. "There's my ride," I tell her as I push myself away from the wall. I can't help but notice how wide her eyes get as she takes in his gray Camaro. "Good luck with Garrett," I offer as the passenger door swings open from the inside. I start to make my way to the curb and she follows.

"Who's your friend?" she asks.

I reach the open door and peer inside to find Dane leaning across the center console expecting me. "This is Dane," I say as she crouches down and sticks her head in the car.

"Hi! I'm Samantha," she eagerly introduces herself. "I live upstairs from Emma."

Dane smiles. "Nice to meet you."

"Same here!" She turns to me and pretends to whisper. "You should really bring your friends around more often."

What?

She faces Dane again. "How long have you known Emma?"

My expression twists behind her back. Is that really any of her business?

"Awhile," he says and looks at me, his eyes lighting up.

"*Really*," she draws out the word. "Are you guys together?"

I scowl. What's it to her?

"If she'll have me."

My mouth falls open at Dane's honest response.

She glances back to give me a sour look then turns to give Dane a flirty one. "I can't imagine why she wouldn't!"

I picture her offering her services if things don't work out with me, so I decide to end this conversation. "Well, it was good seeing you," I say, pushing myself forward and forcing her back. I slide past her and into the seat, reaching for the door handle. "Let me know how it goes with Garrett." Like I care.

"Totally." She flashes her smile more for Dane's benefit than mine. "If it works out we should double."

I give her a sarcastic smile and slam the door. Dane snickers and tries to hide his amusement by biting his lower lip.

"What's so funny?"

He laughs as he pulls away from the curb. "If you can't figure it out I'm not telling you."

"What? You like her flirting with you?"

He shrugs. "She's cute."

I groan. "Just a FYI: her eyes aren't blue and her boobs aren't real."

Dane's eyebrows shoot up. "Not that I could see her, ah...chest, but how do you know?"

I recall the one time we hung out together at the bar when she revealed she wore color contacts. I remember thinking her hair and her body were just as fake for some reason. "I don't," I concede. "Just a guess."

"You shouldn't spread rumors about people," he chastises me. "It's not nice."

"And you shouldn't keep private jokes."

He sighs. "I was amused by your reaction, okay?"

I frown. "What reaction? I didn't say anything."

He shakes his head. "Actions speak louder than words. Think about it."

My confused expression melts as the light dawns. He thinks I cut off the conversation because I was jealous. I open my mouth to dispute his thoughts, but then close it immediately. Samantha was annoying me and I want to go home to get rid of this headache. But, was jealousy my true motivation? I decide to change the topic.

"Samantha said something that bothered me." I cross my arms.

"What's that?"

"She asked if Garrett and I were dating. I told her we never did, but she said we were close." I look at Dane. "I was never involved with Garrett, right? Please say I wasn't."

Dane smiles. "No, you weren't involved with Garrett. As a matter of fact you texted me once – and I quote – "*Garrett is not hot.*""

"Why would I discuss that with you?"

"It was a mistake. You thought I was Shel."

Hmmm. I didn't think Garrett was hot? I conjure up a picture of his face and wonder why. I mean, I guess he's not *hot,* but he's a good-looking guy.

Dane interrupts my thoughts. "I know you two were friends and he helped you a lot with Guardian stuff. Other than that, I have no idea."

I uncross my arms. "Well, that makes me feel better. I was starting to think I had personality amnesia. I can't imagine myself attracting two guys let alone three."

Dane shoots me a look. "You underestimate yourself."

I choose to ignore him.

He turns into the parking lot for my apartment building and cuts the engine. I reach for my bag then the door handle.

"Hold on." He grabs my arm. "I have something I want to run by you."

I give him a questioning look.

"This afternoon, I was thinking about your memory and how to bring it back."

I scoff. "Nothing good on TV?"

He lets go of my arm and moves his hand to my wrist where the bracelet I was given hangs outside of my coat sleeve. I have yet to take it off, and he hooks his finger beneath it. "I need you to remember," he says as he stares at it. "I don't think you understand how important it is."

My face falls. "Of course I understand. Huge chunks of my life are gone; I'd like to have those back."

"Do you understand how important your memories are to me, though?" He meets my eyes. "There's so much we've shared I can't possibly relay every detail. You would believe everything I tell you if you experienced it again."

"I don't think you're lying to me if that's what you're worried about," I say. "I trust you." I don't know why I trust him, but I do. I have since I met him again.

"Well, that's something," he says and pulls his hand away from my wrist.

He looks melancholy, which I don't like, and I decide to entertain his thoughts. "Did you come up with anything good?" I ask. "To resurrect my past?"

"One thing," he says quietly. "But you have to be open to it."

Um, okay. I'm not sure I'm comfortable with how this sounds. He reaches for my hand and I allow him to take it, but I don't grasp it back.

He prefaces his idea. "Don't be mad..."

I'm not sure I'm going to like this.

"...but I think we should kiss."

Evidently, I was holding my breath because I let it out in a rush. "That's it?" I ask, relieved.

"Well, yeah. What did you think I was going to suggest?"

Blood rushes to my face. "I don't know. The way you were talking...something more serious."

He cocks an eyebrow and smiles. "Really? No, I wasn't going there. Although, if you want to I wouldn't say no..."

I smack his arm with my free hand. "No! I don't want to."

He laughs. "I thought kissing you might unlock something. You know, shake some memories loose."

I wrinkle my nose as Snow White and Sleeping Beauty jump to mind.

He frowns. "You don't like the idea?"

"It's not that." I shake my head. "I just had a Disney moment. Have you been watching fairytales?"

He smiles and releases my hand to bring his to my face. He traces my jaw and then gently holds my chin as he brings his mouth to mine.

"Wait," I say, stopping him in his tracks. "You're going to kiss me here? In the car?"

He leans back. "Why not? We've kissed here before. I thought a familiar location might help."

Of course we've kissed in his car. What haven't we done? I make a face.

He drops his hand. "What's the matter?"

"It's just... I don't remember kissing anyone. It's like this is my very first kiss *ever*. I don't know what to do; I'm out of practice."

"You weren't out of practice last week," he says and cradles my face again. "It's like riding a bike."

"A bike I don't remember."

He leans forward and my heart begins to race. My throat constricts and my mouth goes dry. "Listen..." I stop him again.

"What?" He holds his face inches from mine.

"What if it's not the same as before?" I'm grasping at straws. "What if it's terrible and..."

"You're stalling," he says and brings his mouth down on mine.

I don't know what to do, so I tense up and allow him to kiss me without much participation. Seconds pass and I begin to relax; as his mouth molds mine I follow his lead. *Okay*, I think, *this isn't so hard*. No memories flash behind my closed eyes, so after a minute or two, I decide to make new ones. According to my brain this *is* my first kiss after all. Feeling more confident, I lean into his hold and press myself forward, reaching out to lay my hand against him, at his collar. Warmth radiates up my arm when I feel his skin beneath mine and spreads through my body. He realizes my hesitation is gone and his kiss becomes more urgent. Was this how it was before? Because this is pretty good.

Dane pulls his lips from mine just far enough to speak. "Anything?" he breathes.

I shake my head and try to find his mouth again.

BAM! BAM! BAM!

Three loud knocks on the car window startle us, and we spring apart. My head snaps to the right, and I see James standing outside my door, clearly pissed off. I glance quickly to Dane's side and see Garrett.

My face flushes from embarrassment. Guess who's back early?

Chapter 3

Why do I feel like a child who's been caught by her parents?

I meet Dane's eyes. He feels something as well, but it's not shame. Its more disappointment mixed with irritation. The first thing that comes to mind slips out. "What do we do?"

He sighs. "Get out of the car."

I reach for my bag and catch James staring at us with his arms crossed. "Can't we just drive away?"

Dane looks out the windshield. "The curb's kind of high..." He turns to me and smirks. "But, it's the thought that counts."

I make a face and reluctantly push the door open. James steps back as I emerge, but then walks forward as I stand. He fixes his clear blue eyes on me and asks, "Has your memory returned?"

I frown and shake my head. His eyes immediately shoot daggers at Dane who stands opposite us with Garrett. "We had a deal," he snaps.

"What deal?" I ask.

"That he wouldn't try anything unless you remembered us."

"It was an experiment." Dane rounds the car. "I asked if she would be open to the idea and she agreed."

James gives me a puzzled look. "Why would you kiss someone you barely know?"

"It seemed logical." I shrug. "I want my memory back. I'm willing to try anything."

His eyebrows shoot up. "Anything?"

"Well, not *anything*," I concede. "Kissing Dane just made sense."

His forehead pinches. "How does that make sense?"

"Because she's done it before," Dane defends me and stops to stand beside us. "I thought it might release something."

"Well, she's kissed me too," James says sarcastically. "Should we try that next?"

Dane's eyes flash then narrow.

Is this seriously happening? These two are acting like babies. "I have an idea," I say as I step between them. "I should kiss Garrett."

That shuts them up. All three of them regard me with shocked expressions, especially Garrett, as I walk toward him. "I've been told we were close," I say. I wink at him to let him know I'm not serious then whisper, "Play along."

He smiles. "Oh no. I'm not getting in the middle of this. We *were* close but only in a friendly way." He places his hands on my shoulders and says, "Give them a break, okay?" He turns me around to face James and Dane. "And give her a break too, would you? We just got back."

"Speaking of," I step away from him, "where's LB?"

"In the car." He gestures to the opposite end of the parking lot. "We literally pulled in seconds after you."

Dang. If I had let Samantha flirt a little longer we could have foregone all this. Thinking of her reminds me of our conversation, and I change the subject. "Someone is looking for you," I tell Garrett over my shoulder as I head to my car.

He follows me. "Who?"

"Samantha. She wants to ask you out."

He looks confused. "What happened to Todd?"

"Apparently she got smart or he got smart, one of the two. They broke up."

As we pass James and Dane he asks, "You remember them?"

"She does," Dane pipes up. "She also remembers that her eyes aren't blue and her chest is fake."

I shoot him an annoyed look.

"It's true." He shrugs.

"So, you remember small details," Garrett observes, intrigued.

"I told you. I remember everything but you guys."

We reach my car and I pause, looking over my white Grand Am. I've had this car since I graduated high school. I remember everything about her: the summer I got her, how much she cost, how my dad haggled with the guy we bought her from. She's the first car I've ever owned.

"Is something wrong?" Garrett asks. "I promised I would take good care of your things."

"No, I was just thinking. I have a lot of memories wrapped around this car." I open the door and find LB's carrier on the floor in the back seat. "LB? Are you in there?"

I hear a quiet mew and my face breaks into a grin. I'm really excited to have her back; I can't wait to snuggle her. I lift the carrier and shut the door to see that James has joined Garrett at the trunk to unload. I notice James with a bag of LB's things, and I reach to grab it. "I can take that."

"I've got it," he says and places it in the empty litter box along with a few other cat items. He reaches for a small duffle bag and swings it over his shoulder, then picks up LB's stuff. "Let's go," he says and starts to make his way toward the building.

I match his step, and we pass Dane as we walk to the front door. He's leaning against his car with his arms crossed, observing us. Is this how things are going to be? Dane watching James, James watching Dane. Both of them watching me. It makes me uncomfortable. I'm not used to being under constant scrutiny.

We round the corner and make it to the door. I set LB down as I fish for my keys.

"I'm sorry."

I pause and look at James. "For what?"

"For making you anxious."

I blink. How does he know I'm anxious? "It's all right," I put him off and open the door. "There's just a lot to take in right now."

He follows me inside, and we enter my apartment where I immediately drop my backpack and crouch down to open LB's carrier. She springs from the cage and takes off only to stop mid-stride. She looks around, appearing to notice she's back home.

"Hey, Booger," I say in a baby voice and she turns to sprint back to me. She rubs her head against my knee and purrs loudly as I scratch behind her ears. "I've missed you," I tell her and pick her up, holding her on her back like an infant. I rub her belly and she purrs louder.

I stand and notice James smiling at us. "She's happy," he says and reaches out to pet her too.

I find myself studying him as he scratches LB. I think back to what little Dane told me about us. We dated since we were seventeen. He died and came back. We never officially called it quits. Suddenly, I'm overwhelmed by the significance of him being here. By all accounts he shouldn't be and for more reasons than one.

He catches me staring. "What?"

"It's going to take us a while to catch up, isn't it?"

He gives me a tiny smile. "Yeah."

"How long do you think?"

He shrugs. "I couldn't say. Days? Weeks?"

"Months?" I offer.

"Maybe so." He pulls his hand away from LB and studies my eyes. "Would that be a bad thing?"

To my surprise my heart picks up under his stare. "No."

His face relaxes and his fingers move and twist into a piece of my ponytail that sits on my shoulder. "You don't know how bad I want to kiss you right now," he says quietly. "It's all I've thought about since we left the island."

Wow. How do I respond to that?

LB squirms and rights herself, jumping from my arms and breaking our tense moment. I step away from James and he releases my hair. I scramble to find something else to discuss. "Do you still plan on living with Garrett?" I ask.

"He does," Garrett says, surprising me from the doorway. "But, I might have to kick him out if he doesn't carry his weight."

James shoots him a look. "What's the problem?"

"Come help me carry the rest of this stuff."

James sighs and heads out the door. Garrett looks at me before closing it. "I hope you don't have any plans. After we're settled we all need to talk."

About an hour later my phone chimes. *Welcome back! Check your email.*

I read the cryptic text from Matt as Dane lounges on my couch flipping channels. He hasn't said much since our neighbor's arrival, and I can tell he's trying to relax, but failing miserably. I feel bad for him and want to make it better. Why does his being upset bother me? He's practically a stranger.

Yet you kissed him.

My conscience appears and my ears turn red. What was I thinking? I replay our kiss and my rebellious side thumps my conscience on the head. *It was a good idea, dummy.* I bite my lip as I study Dane, recalling his mouth on mine. How I can make that happen again?

"Who's on the phone?"

Dane's question breaks my train of thought. "Um, Matt," I say quickly as I redirect my attention and open my email. "He sent me a message."

His note is the first in my inbox.

Em –

Glad to hear you're back! Attached are the forms required for the internship you asked about. My dad signed off on everything. I would have sent them sooner, but I didn't know when you would be back in the States. I hope you're still thinking about working for us. I don't make a great receptionist and Sheila is about to explode! Let me know your decision when you get a chance.

We'll have to get together soon!

Matt

My memory reels back to my last day at Western. I recall the overwhelming need to move back home, but don't remember what set it off. I re-live the conversation with my advisor, Mrs. Andrews. I remember talking to Matt about interning at his dad's veterinary clinic in lieu of classes; I remember falling asleep content with my plans for the future. Then I remember waking up with my world turned upside down.

I read over Matt's email again and a calm feeling settles over me. I still like this idea a lot. Moving back home sounds amazing.

I hear a knock on the door then see it crack open. "Are you busy?" It's Garrett.

Dane sighs and turns off of the television. "Do we have a choice?"

Garrett and James enter my apartment, and I push Matt's message to the side for now. I readjust myself in the living room chair as Garrett takes a seat opposite Dane. James chooses to stand, leaning against the wall. It's times like this that I really need a dining table.

"Do you want to sit?" I ask James and start to unfold my legs.

He shakes his head. "Standing doesn't bother me." He gives me a small smile. "I'm still getting used to being human."

Oh. Right.

"Now that things have calmed down, we need to have a serious discussion," Garrett says.

Dane frowns. "About what?"

"For one, the likelihood of Kellan's return. He's not going to easily forgive what happened."

Dane scowls as I recall who Kellan is. He's the one who nearly killed me, but somehow took my memories instead.

Garrett takes a heavy breath. "Obviously we've lost all ties to the Intermediate. We have no idea what's taking place. We can only assume Kellan returned with Lucas after he blasted Emma, given that humanity isn't in chaos. Kellan needs Lucas to maintain order; two of the four Allegiant are dead. He's probably forcing Lucas to carry on as usual and biding his time until he can devise his revenge."

"We haven't heard from Thomas or Meg or any of the others," James says. "It's probable that they're still captive."

Who are Meg and Thomas again?

"If only I could get a hold of Jack," Garrett mutters. "It would really help."

"Jack is?" I ask.

"My brother," Garrett answers. "My twin."

Yes. I'd forgotten.

Dane leans forward. "So you're worried about Kellan coming back? I understand he's pissed that your friends killed his buddies, but shouldn't he take it out on them?"

"I'm afraid he will, but he still has a score to settle with me," Garrett says. "He didn't get to exact his punishment and now that you and Emma are involved...we're all at risk."

James turns to Dane. "You know Kellan was gunning for you."

Dane sighs. "Yes, you've made that clear."

"Why?" I ask. "What did Dane do that was so wrong?"

Garrett eyes the bracelet on my wrist. "He placed that on you."

"So?"

Garrett shares a knowing look with James that raises my suspicions. "That's another thing we need to talk about," he says. "Do you remember me telling you about Madeline and Ash? The people that showed up to help us?"

I nod.

"James and I stopped to speak with them briefly before coming here. We asked if they could help us understand what happened, why the bracelet protected you in some ways, but not in others. They told us it was because you are Lost."

My face pinches. "I'm what?"

James moves closer. "All humans are supposed to have a Guardian. I was yours."

"Yes, you told me."

"When The Allegiant restored my humanity, my duty vanished. You no longer have a Guardian." He pauses and eyes

Garrett. "Emma," he says seriously, "there's no one in the Intermediate to assign you. You are unprotected. You're what we call Lost."

I give him a wary look. "And that's a bad thing?"

"For an ordinary human it's a very bad thing," Garrett says. "But you're better off. Until we know how much protection the bracelet offers you, one of us will need to be near you at all times."

I hesitate trying to process the information. "So, you're saying I need a babysitter."

Garrett shifts his weight to the edge of his seat. "It'll be more like having a bodyguard. We'll need to know your schedule, where you plan to be, and with who."

This is really awkward and my expression twists. Will I ever have privacy? "I do have some common sense; you can't spend all your time hovering over me."

Garrett agrees. "You're right. We'll need to take shifts and the more help we have the better. That's why we –" He pauses. "I mean that's why *I* would like Dane to help as well." He turns to look at him. "Will you consider it?"

Dane doesn't even think twice. "I'm in."

What? These three can't just integrate themselves into my life! "Hold on a minute," I protest. "You can't monitor my every move!"

James tries to reassure me. "It won't be that weird. Garrett and I will be right next door."

Matt's email flashes through my mind and I snort. "Not for long. I'm moving after the semester ends."

James face falls. "Where? Why?"

My eyes dart to Garrett and Dane and they are equally surprised. "I got permission to take an internship during the winter semester. I'll be working for Matt's dad and living with my parents."

I can't help but notice the smile Dane tries to hide. Clearly he's pleased, but why?

James moves to crouch in front of me. "Emma, I can't follow you there. Your hometown is mine too; I can't be seen by people who knew me. You have to stay here."

Ah. That's why.

"I'm sorry, but this is *my* life," I say adamantly. "My decision. I'm moving."

James opens his mouth to dispute me, but Garrett interrupts. "It's okay," he says and directs his attention to James. "We can make this work; we can move. Lucas gave me money, and I believe he gave Emma some too."

I have money?

"That's if you're willing to share," Garrett quickly amends and gives me an apologetic smile. "We can live outside of town and James can escort you when it's safe for him to do so."

I narrow my eyes. Damn! I need some time to myself!

"Actually, this might work better," Garrett muses and turns to Dane. "You have to return home eventually. It will be more convenient with Emma closer to you."

I tap my fingers impatiently against my knee. They're all so great at planning my life. "How long is this going to last? You can't possibly take me everywhere. What if I need to go to the gynecologist?"

All three of them blanch and I smirk. "See?"

I can visualize the wheels turning in Garrett's head. "We'll have to take each situation as it comes and stay behind the scenes if necessary," he says and looks to James and Dane. "The main point is that we are near Emma should she need us."

They all nod and I curse under my breath. Am I even here? Does my opinion matter? I get it; I'm at risk without a Guardian and Kellan seeks to hurt me. But wait...why is he mad at me again? So Dane put a bracelet on my wrist and I'm somewhat protected. Big deal.

"Can someone explain why Kellan hates me?" I ask. "Because I don't get it."

Garrett and James exchange another knowing glance. I'm starting to hate those.

"Madeleine and Ash will be here in a few days to explain," Garrett says. "My knowledge of The Larvatus is limited. I'd rather you hear it from them."

"The who?"

"The Larvatus. Translated it means Charmed."

"Madeline and Ash are charmed?"

"Yes," Garrett says. He pauses and looks at his hands then back at me. "And from what little I understand, now you may be charmed too."

Chapter 4

There was too much testosterone in my apartment, so I kicked them out.

All of them.

After I locked the door, I threw myself on the bed and put my head under the pillow to block out what Garrett said. *"From what little I understand, you may be charmed, too."* Just what is that supposed to mean?! I don't want to be anything, but me!

Emma Lynn.

Twenty-two year old daughter of Dale and Marlene.

Sister of Mike. Best friend to Matt and Shel. Mother of LB.

Soon to be college grad.

It's getting hard to breathe with my nose flattened against the mattress, so I roll over and toss the pillow aside. Garrett said Madeline and Ash would arrive in a few days to explain. Thoughts of their visit send sarcastic thoughts searing through my mind. I sure hope they show up on Saturday – that would be perfect! That's when my mother is supposed to be here. I can imagine our conversation:

Hey Mom! Great to see you!

Who are these strange people?

I have no idea, but apparently I'm one of them.

How did that happen?

I was in the Caribbean instead of Ireland like you thought. I saved Dane's life by jumping in front of a powerful Guardian's death beam.

What were you and Dane doing in the Caribbean?

Sleeping together. Aren't you proud?

I close my eyes, inhale deeply, and then exhale slowly. There's nothing I can do about any of this, and I'm starting to feel helpless. I open my eyes and lift my wrist to stare at the bracelet I wear. The thin leather band is knotted and it holds a shiny silver amulet in the center. I bring it closer to my face to scrutinize the charm and realize that it is forged to look like a tree with leafy branches and exposed roots. Intertwined against the trunk, I find the shape of a crescent moon on one side and a blazing sun on the other. It really is a beautiful piece. I concentrate on it, tilting it back and forth, so it catches the light. Suddenly, a rainbow of color shimmers across the metal and disappears. I blink rapidly. Did I just see that? I try to do it again but nothing happens. My mind must be playing tricks on me due to the dull ache that still resides in my temples. I lower my arm to the bed and sigh.

LB jumps up next to me and starts to knead the comforter to make herself a cozy spot. She turns around twice then lies down, pressing her body against mine when I raise my arm.

"You're an animal LB," I say. "You're supposed to sense things, right?"

She looks at me as she purrs.

"Can you tell if I've changed into something freaky?"

She stares at me for a moment then decides to clean herself, licking her paw and pulling it over her ear and across her face.

"So I take it that's a no?"

My question doesn't interrupt her grooming.

I start to absentmindedly pet her as I consult the time on my alarm clock. James will be back in an hour to stay the night since he won the coin toss. I stare at the ceiling and grit my teeth. If I'm not going anywhere I shouldn't need a sitter.

I close my eyes and take advantage of the silence. Maybe I can nap, get rid of this headache, and wake up in a better mood.

My brief slumber helped, but a hot shower sealed the deal. After James arrived, I left him in the living room and retreated to the bathroom to wash away this day. The ache in my head went down the drain with the water, which left me slightly more optimistic about my evening.

"This is kind of weird," James says when I eventually join him, handing over the blankets that Dane used last night. "I've never spent a night here that wasn't in your bed."

I shoot him a look. "This is weird for you? Try being me." I cross my arms. "If you can't get comfortable here you're more than welcome to go back to Garrett's."

He gives me half a smile. "You'd like that wouldn't you?"

"I don't need supervision."

"You think so?"

"I know so."

He pauses, regarding me. "And what if Kellan returns for you?"

I sigh. "He wouldn't know where to look."

"Yes, he would," James says. "Meg and Thomas, Jenna and Joss. They've all been here."

My eyebrows shoot up. "All of the Guardians who are being held have been in my apartment?"

He nods emphatically.

"What was this? Guardian central?"

He smiles. "Something like that. Especially with Garrett next door." He turns away from me and places the blankets on the couch. "Besides," he says, "don't you think it's fair that you get to know me again, too?"

I had a feeling this was about more than just some peeved Allegiant. I move my hands to my hips. "That's not what I was saying."

He faces me. "So what are you saying?"

"Normal people get to know each other by going out on dates. Not living together immediately."

"Our circumstances are slightly different." He smiles and takes a step back, allowing himself to fall against the couch. "Consider this our first date."

I eye his sweatpants and t-shirt. "I'm so glad you dressed up for the occasion."

He shrugs. "I don't mind what you're wearing."

I immediately wrap my arms around myself, although my yoga pants and Henley shirt leave plenty to the imagination. "Don't start with that crap."

He looks confused. "What crap?"

I give him a sarcastic look as I walk around the table to sit in the chair.

"What? You can't sit next to me?" he asks.

"I..." I hesitate. I guess I can, I wasn't really thinking about it. I push myself off the chair and move to the opposite end of the couch. "Better?"

"Much," he says and leans forward. His eyes lock on mine, and he doesn't say anything. His expression softens, and it looks as if he's seeing me for the first time.

After a few uncomfortable seconds I ask, "Everything okay?"

"There was a time when we would have killed for this moment," he says. "It was our plan to live in this apartment. To finish school and start the rest of our lives together."

I swallow.

"But, my accident changed everything. When I think of what I put you through..." He closes his eyes. "I'm so sorry."

It upsets me to see him sad. "Hey." I scoot closer and face him, crossing my legs in front of me. "What's done is done. The accident was just that. An accident. You didn't kill yourself on purpose. Even I realize that and I don't remember any of it."

He opens his eyes and reaches for my hand, which I allow him to take. "I'm grateful," he says as he runs his thumb across my knuckles. "There are things I'm glad you can't remember." He looks into my eyes again. "But so much more I wish you did."

I sense a kiss is imminent and my stomach knots. How inappropriate is this? Hours ago I kissed Dane! Granted it was an experiment, but...

I create a diversion. "Tell me something you want me to remember," I say and sit up straight, putting another inch of distance between us. "Something good."

"There's a lot."

I tilt my head in thought. "You said to consider this our first date. What was our real first date like?"

He smiles. "It was prom."

I frown. "I thought we've known each other since we were kids?"

"That's right."

"And you waited until prom to ask me out?"

He laughs. "I didn't even do that." He turns his body to face mine and takes my other hand. "We'd been good friends for years and did practically everything together. We went to the movies, did homework, just hung out, you name it. I came and went at your house and you did so at mine. Everyone thought we were together, but we weren't, and I was comfortable with that. But, by junior year, I started to get *un*comfortable and realized I'd waited long enough to make things official. The only problem was I had no idea if you felt the same about me. I asked you to the dance under the guise of going as friends."

I stare at him. "And I fell for it?"

He shrugs. "I would say so. You seemed pretty shocked when I kissed you on the dance floor."

My mouth falls open a little. "I hope I got the message after that."

He grins. "Yeah, you did."

"Huh." I smirk as I dig for memories of prom. They're fuzzy. I remember Shel and me spending a lot of time together dancing. That's about all.

James releases one of my hands and touches my face, running his fingers from my temple to my chin. "You looked so beautiful," he says quietly.

My skin tingles under his touch, taking me by surprise. "Uh..." What do I say? Thank you?

"Not that you don't every day." He drops his hand and collects mine again.

This feels so awkward. I search for something to say. "I'm sure you looked pretty good yourself." I squeeze his hands. "I wish I could remember."

"Me too."

I concentrate on our entwined fingers. "Tell me something else. Another memory."

James twists his mouth in thought. After a moment his eyes light up and he laughs to himself. "This is a good one. The day I left Ferris."

"What were you doing at Ferris?"

"They gave me a scholarship to play hockey out of high school," he explains. "I went there first, then came here after..." He pauses and gives me a wary look. "Do you remember someone named Patrick?"

Patrick? I think back. "He was my lab partner, right?" Yep, I remember him. "He was nice enough, but he started to creep me out a little. Then he left school."

James looks concerned. "That's all you remember?"

Hmmm. Something is up with Patrick. Great. "Is there more?"

"A lot more." James' eyes flash and his jaw tenses, his grip on my hands tightening. "He attacked you this summer. He's the cause of your concussion."

What? I was told I had a concussion to aid in my "I-was-really-in-Ireland" excuse, but I don't know how I got it.

James can tell I'm confused. "Three years ago he started harassing you. Following you around, taking all the same classes. It made you nervous, so I came here to ask him to back off. We ended up getting into a fight."

"A physical fight?"

"A bad one," he confirms. "He disappeared after that, but I left Ferris and transferred here to be with you. Just in case he came back."

My stomach starts to feel queasy. "So what happened?"

"When I hit him I really messed up his face. I partially blinded him in one eye, which I never meant to do. In his messed up mind he blamed you instead of me, convinced himself that you put me up to it while in reality all you had asked me to do was talk to him. When he found out I died he started to stalk you; he ended up confronting you at your house." James shudders. He looks into my eyes, his filling with pain. "He tried to force himself on you..."

Oh, this is bad. "Stop," I say. I don't want to remember this if I don't have to. "He didn't, did he?"

"No. You fought back. But he hurt you."

I reach up and rub my forehead. Why don't I remember this? Patrick has nothing to do with Guardians.

"Dane saved you," James says, "and I was there, too. We both took care of Patrick, although Dane was able to do a lot more than me."

My mind scrambles to wrap around what he's telling me. I was almost raped and James and Dane stopped it. Thank God for the both of them. "What would I have done without you?" I ask. Impulsively, I lean forward and hug James, wrapping my arms around his neck and setting my chin on his shoulder. "Thank you so much," I whisper.

I feel his arms circle my waist then move up my back, pressing me to him. "No thanks necessary," he says quietly.

As we stay wrapped around one another his heartbeat falls in rhythm with mine. I know this because I can feel it beating through his chest. It feels comfortable and safe here, and I close my eyes as I relax into his arms. One of his hands brushes up my back to move my hair away from my neck, and he turns and plants a soft kiss against it.

My eyes pop open and I lean back, so we're inches apart. "What are you doing?"

"What I've always done," he says and searches my face.

I place my hands on his shoulders and push myself back to where I was. "I don't know if I'm ready for what we've always done."

He looks alarmed. "I didn't mean to make you uncomfortable," he says, even though his hands have fallen from my waist and linger on my knees. "I couldn't help myself. You feel so *good*."

I arch an eyebrow. "Come again?"

He absentmindedly rubs my knee. "I only regained my humanity a week ago. I haven't truly felt anything in months," he says. "You don't know how long I've waited to feel the real you beneath my hands again and not just your temperature."

The sincere way he looks at me almost makes me wish I didn't have a conscience. I grab his hands and lace my fingers through his. "Will this do for now?"

"I'll take whatever you can give me," he says and tightens his grip around mine.

I study our hands. "So what was the good memory you had about the day you left Ferris?"

He chuckles. "You were helping me get settled into my dorm and helping me unpack. Let's just say the idea of us living so close after a year of driving back and forth got the better of us."

"Really?" I purse my lips. "Your good memory is of us getting it on?"

He gives me a sly smile. "I have lots of those. This particular time was interesting."

"How so?"

"We were carrying boxes down the hallway. We were almost to my room when I looked at you and you looked at me. Without a word we both dropped the boxes and started making out."

"In the hall?"

He nods. "You pushed me up against the wall..."

My jaw drops. "I pushed you?"

"...and things started to get a little out of hand. You reached around me and ended up pulling the fire alarm." He grins. "The whole building had to be evacuated."

My face flushes even though I recall none of this. "Did they find out it was me?"

James laughs. "No, we got out of there pretty quick."

I can't help but laugh with him as I picture the scene. I stare at him for a moment, realizing we have countless memories together, and smile. "Keep talking."

Hours later I try to hold my eyes open. It's well past one a.m. and James has been filling me in all night. I want to hear more, but I'm so tired.

"Why aren't you sleepy?" I yawn.

"This turning human thing has left me with some lingering Guardian traits," he says. "It's weird. I've only slept twenty four hours since it happened."

"Is that normal?"

He shrugs. "The same thing happened to Garrett, but he's turning gradually. He thinks all of my human traits should have returned by now because of the way I was Reborn."

"All of your traits? What else are you missing?"

"Hunger. I eat maybe once a day."

Nice. I wish I had that problem. I remove my hand from his and flex my fingers; they're cramped. "Anything else?"

"I've only used the bathroom twice since last week."

I make a face. "Okay. I don't need to know anymore."

He smirks. "I do shower and brush my teeth if that's what you're worried about."

I raise my hand to cover my mouth as I yawn again.

"Come here," he says and tugs on the hand he still holds. He scoots back into the corner of the couch, shifts his legs, and pulls me to lie down beside him with my back to his chest. "Do you think you could sleep here? With me?"

It feels so good to lie down; I stretch out and bury myself against the cushions beneath me. "Umm hmm," I mumble.

James grabs the blankets that sit on the back of the couch and covers us with them. He rests his arm over my side. "What time do you have to be up tomorrow?" he asks.

"Not until ten."

"Go to sleep," he says and pulls me against him. "I'll wake you when it's time."

I lean against him knowing that this is exactly where I'd be if his accident had never happened. It feels odd, but it feels good, too. I allow myself to fall asleep, relaxed and content. Maybe this bodyguard thing isn't so bad after all.

Chapter 5

"Surprise!"

I almost lose my balance as Shel launches herself forward and hugs me tightly. "What are you doing here?" I ask, grinning over her shoulder.

"I thought you might want to see a friend," my mother says as she follows her through the door.

I squeeze Shel tight then step back. Instantly we start laughing for no reason. God it feels good to see her! I feel like it's been eons.

My mom walks around Shel to hug me as well. She rocks me side to side for a second and then steps back, holding me at arm's length and inspecting me.

"What?" I smile.

"You look great," she says. "Have you been tanning?"

I frown. "Why would I go tanning?" I would never pay to sit under artificial cancer-causing light.

"You look different," Shel says coming forward. "You must have picked up some color in Ireland. Was it sunny? I thought it mostly rained there."

Shoot! I've only been back from the Irish Caribbean for five days; I didn't think about having a tan! I race for an explanation. "We had a week of unnaturally warm weather," I lie. "I spent as much of it outside as I could. Maybe I did get a tan." I lift my arm pretending to inspect it. "I really didn't notice."

"Oooo, what's that?" Shel asks and reaches for my wrist, noticing my bracelet. "Did you get this over there?"

53

"Yep," I lie again. "Do you like it?"

She lifts my wrist higher to get a better look. "It's so intricate," she says and spins it around. "I love it."

My mother takes a turn to eye it as well, nodding her approval. "It's pretty."

"Well, come in and sit down," I say, backing up.

"Where's LB?" Shel asks as she takes off her coat and tosses it over the back of the couch.

"On my bed."

She takes off to bother her as my mom takes a seat. "Give me that." I reach for her coat and place it next to Shel's. I wish I had somewhere to hang them. "I guess I could use a coat rack, huh?"

My mom smiles. "I'll remember that; Christmas is coming. You should make a list."

I shake my head. "You've started shopping, haven't you?" My mom always starts her holiday shopping in October, I swear.

"You know I shop year round," she says and starts to dig through her purse. I sit down next to her as she pulls out a small beat up pocket calendar and pen. She flips to the back and writes down *coat rack*. "What else do you need for this place?"

"About that..." I drift off. I've been saving my big moving home secret until now. "Shel!" I call into the bedroom. "Get in here!"

She reappears holding LB. "What's up?"

"I emailed Matt this morning," I tell her. "My advisor signed off yesterday."

She breaks out into a beaming smile. "Yay!"

"What's going on?" my mom asks, confused.

I turn toward her, excited. "I won't be living here next semester."

She narrows her eyes at me. "Emma Lynn. What are you up to now? Where will you be?"

"Home." I smile. "I'm moving back home."

It takes a minute for my revelation to register. I see her let out a breath of relief. "How?"

"I have three classes left," I explain as Shel sits next to me. "I talked to my advisor, and I can complete an internship in place of two. Based on my friend's brilliant suggestion," I look at Shel, "I'll be working at Mr. Randall's clinic. The other class I'll take online."

My mom takes my hand and clutches it. She has tears in her eyes.

"Don't cry!" I say, panicked. "I thought you'd be happy!"

"I am." A tear escapes and she quickly wipes it away. "I've been worried about you. Especially after this last incident with your head..." She holds my hand in both of hers. "I'm ecstatic."

I lean forward and give her another hug, this one harder than the last. Since James shared the Patrick incident with me I have a better understanding of her worry. "I can't wait to be home," I say into her shoulder.

"When will you need dads truck?" she asks when she releases me.

"Classes end in two weeks. Would that weekend be okay?"

"Absolutely," she says. She leans around me to look at Shel. "We should celebrate."

"Hecks yeah, we should!" Shel lets LB jump from her arms. "What should we do?"

"Shopping?" my mom suggests. "Isn't there a mall near here?"

"Crossroads," I confirm. "It's about fifteen minutes away." Normally shopping isn't something I enjoy, but for some reason it sounds so fun right now. I would do anything to spend time with these two.

"Then let's go," Shel says and stands.

"I'll drive," I volunteer.

"Wait." My mom looks Shel in the eye. "I think we should talk about James first."

Oh, I really don't want to do that. I mean, I want to at some point, but I know so much more about him now. I look at Shel suspiciously. "That's why you're here, isn't it?"

She gives me a sheepish smile and sits down. "Yes. But, I wanted to see you regardless."

My mom takes my hand again. "I thought it would be best if we were both here to explain James to you."

How can I make this go away? I want to have fun. "It's okay. Things have been coming back. I remember James."

"What do you remember?"

I tick what I know – and can say in front of my mother – off on my fingers. "That he was my boyfriend. We went to prom together. We were friends since we were kids. He went to school here with me, and he died in April."

Concern is etched across Shel's face. "You don't sound sad about that."

Damn. I should have thrown in some unsteady breaths or something. I shrug. "I guess all the emotions haven't returned?"

Her eyes jump to my mom for a moment then back to me. "Emma, you were completely wrecked when James died. Your parents asked me to stay with you over the summer to pull you out of your depression."

I was depressed? I remember a happy summer with Shel visiting.

"Honey, you scared us," my mom says. "She had to force you out of the house."

My eyes grow wide. She did? "But we worked at the golf course." I turn to Shel. "You made me do that?"

She nods. "I also kind of pushed you into doing a few other things."

"Like what?"

She looks shy again, which is rare for Shel. "Visiting the cemetery."

"And?"

"Going to Matt's for his Memorial Day party."

"And?"

"I think that's all. You weren't as depressed after that. Especially after you met Dane. Now, I did push you into a few things with him, but you've already forgiven me for those." She smiles as if my forgiveness should extend to her other prodding.

Wait, what? She pushed me into things with Dane? Man, this sucks! I can't ask her about that. She doesn't know I don't remember him either.

"I guess we should be glad you've forgotten such a sad time," my mother says. "But, James was a very special person in your life." She places a flash drive in my hand. "I downloaded some pictures of the two of you. I thought it might help."

I look at the drive for a moment then at her, touched by the gesture. "Thank you. I'm sure it will. It's not like I don't want to remember him."

Shel and my mom look at me with sympathetic expressions. I don't want them to be sad for me because I'm not. "What do you say we don't dwell on this?" I suggest and carefully place the flash drive on the coffee table. "Let's go enjoy ourselves and have a fun afternoon."

Shel tilts her head. "I like your way of thinking, even though it's completely unexpected."

"What do you mean?"

"You're not acting like post-accident Emma."

I smirk. "There's a post-accident Emma? What am I acting like then?"

She smiles. "Pre-accident Emma." She leans into me and whispers, "I like it."

I elbow her playfully in the arm. "Then let's go."

We all stand, and as my guests get their coats, I leave the room to find mine. I grab my purse, give LB a kiss, and head toward the door.

"By the way," Shel asks, "have you talked to Dane lately? He's been out of town and Matt's barely been able to get a hold of him. Have you two made up yet?"

I stare at her puzzled. Made up? Did we have a fight?

And then, as if on cue, the door to my apartment opens and Dane steps inside. "Emma? Are you decent? I left my toothbrush..."

OH. MY. GOD. I didn't lock the door! How could he forget I was expecting my mother today?

Dane freezes wide-eyed as he takes in my mom and Shel, and my eyes bounce between the three of them. Shel's mouth hangs open and my mom only blinks. Dane quickly rearranges his features to be more relaxed. "Hey." He smiles and steps further inside. "I guess Emma didn't tell you I was visiting."

They all look at me. "I-I was getting to that," I stutter. I try to shoot him a subtle look. What now?

"I was headed home from my business trip and decided to stop by," he says. He walks over to Shel and gives her a one-armed hug. He looks at my mom and flashes his mega-watt grin. "Mrs. Donohue."

"Dane," she says.

Shel glances between us then shoots me a look. It's not just any look, either. It's the Shel Inquisition Look. Her jaw tenses. "How long has he been here?" she asks.

I say "Not long" as Dane says "A day or so."

My face flushes. We're not doing a very good job. I attempt to clarify. "He's been here about a day which isn't a long time."

Shel crosses her arms and widens her stance. "Is that so?"

"Yes." I try not to look at the floor, but it's hard. Curse my horrible lying abilities!

"So," Dane interrupts, "where are you ladies off to?"

"The mall," my mother says and adjusts her purse over her shoulder. "Care to join us? I would hate to invade on your time with Emma."

My mouth falls open as I catch my mom's eye. She gives me a knowing smile. What in the world is going on here?

Dane holds his hands out in front of him. "Oh no, I'll leave that up to you. I don't think I could keep up," he tries to joke. His eyes fall on mine. "I'll be with Garrett watching the game." He backs toward the door. "Just let me know when you get back."

"What about your toothbrush?" Shel asks with her eyebrows raised. "Weren't you looking for that?"

"Ah..." Dane hesitates. "Yeah. It's not a big deal. I'll just come back later."

"No, I think you should get it now," Shel presses.

What is she up to?

Dane gives her a wry smile. "You know what? You're right." He confidently walks past us and into my bathroom. I watch him, so I don't have to look at Shel or my mom. He appears seconds later, toothbrush in hand. As he passes Shel he waves it inches from her face. "Got it," he says and grabs the door handle. "It was nice to see you again," he says to my mother. "Have fun shopping." To Shel he says, "Tell Matt I'll give him a call."

"Oh, I will," she says, her eyes narrow.

He blasts her with his smile then exits quickly. The sound of the door closing causes my tense body to jerk. I'm in for it now.

"Well, wasn't that interesting?" my mom asks, turning to me.

"He just stopped by after his work trip." I try to act casual. "So, yes," I turn to Shel, "I have talked to him."

"It's a lucky thing you were home from Ireland," she says. "He would've missed you."

"No." I make my way to the door. "He knew where I was. We've been texting."

"Really?" She raises her brows again. "Why didn't I know about this?"

"Because I don't tell you everything." I grab a hold of the doorknob and pull. "Are we shopping or would you rather interrogate me?"

"Shopping," my mom pipes up.

Bless her. She knows I'm uncomfortable.

My mother walks out the door, and I take a step to follow her. Shel grabs my arm, pulling me back. "We. Need. To. Talk."

"Later," I whisper.

"Of course later. But don't think you're getting out of it."

I roll my eyes.

Outside, I study the ground as we head to the car. What kind of believable lies can I come up with before we get back? As I slide into my seat and adjust the rearview mirror, I catch Garrett heading to Dane's Camaro. He unlocks the door and glances my way before getting in. His eyes lock on mine and he gives me a small nod. I sigh.

Looks like we have a shadow.

I pull a sweater over my head and adjust the cowl neck. My mother has convinced me that I need some professional clothes if I'm going to be working a real job in a real office. She's right; I own next to nothing that is workplace appropriate. So far, I've settled on a black skirt, a pair of brown dress pants, and two tops, one with long sleeves. I turn in the mirror and pull the sweater down over my backside; it's long and lands mid-thigh. This would look good with leggings...

"Can you help me?" Shel asks from outside the changing room curtain.

"Yep." I sweep the fabric aside to let her in. "What's up?"

"I think I'm trapped in this dress," she says and turns around. "Can you unzip me?"

I laugh and pull on the zipper. It's tight at the top, but then slides down easily. "Planning a night out?" I ask.

"Every girl needs a little black dress." She turns and faces me. "Do you have one?"

I shake my head.

"You should get one, especially if you're seeing Dane." She points at me. "His father's important; you might have to attend a dinner or two."

I sigh. "It's not like that with me and Dane."

She snorts. "*Riiight.* He left his toothbrush at your place." She gives me a condescending look. "You're sleeping with him."

My face registers complete shock. "I am not!" Well, not right now anyway.

She puts her hands on her hips. "You expect me to believe that?"

"Yes!" I say adamantly. "We are *not* sleeping together." I turn away from her and lift the sweater over my head to put it back on the hanger. I need to avoid her gaze for a minute.

She inhales sharply. "What the...!"

I spin around. "What? What's wrong?"

She crosses her arms and her face twists into a sour expression. "You have tan lines," she almost growls.

My face pinches. "What? No, I..." I look over my shoulder at my back in the mirror. Shit. I do have tan lines. I look at Shel.

"Where were you?" she asks through gritted teeth.

What can I say? Suddenly my ears feel like they're on fire.

We stare at each other; Shel in her unzipped dress and me in my underwear. I might as well be naked and purple for the way she looks at me. After a moment her tense jaw goes slack and her eyes get as wide as saucers.

"What?" I whisper.

"You were with Dane," she says slowly. "His skin is as dark as yours."

How could she know that? I think back to what he was wearing when he came by. He wore a white t-shirt; the kind guys typically wear under their clothes. She saw his arms. I look down and twist my fingers together.

"Emma, where were you?" she asks me again, softer this time.

My throat feels dry. There's not one lie I could possibly tell her that she would believe. I give her a pleading look. "St. Thomas."

"With Dane?"

"Yes. You cannot tell anyone."

Her arms fall and she takes a step toward me. "Not even Matt?"

"Let me ask Dane first," I tell her and reach for my jeans. I'm starting to shiver, although I'm not particularly cold.

She looks bewildered. "How did this happen? I mean I'm thrilled it did; I'm happy for you. But why all the secrecy? What's going on?"

"It's a long story," I manage to say, buttoning my pants. I reach for my shirt and pull it on. "Can we discuss it when we get back?"

She nods then steps forward and wraps her arms around me, pinning mine to my sides. I stand there immobile.

"This is awesome," she says, but when she steps back she pouts. "I'm not happy you lied to me though."

"I'm sorry. It was necessary. Believe me."

She regards me for a moment. "I do."

My phone rings and I turn to grab it out of my purse. It's my mom. "Hello?"

"Are you two done yet? I'm at the restaurant; I'm starving."

"We're on our way," I tell her and hang up. "Mom's at the Steak and Potato."

"Good." Shel rubs her belly. "I'll be dressed in a sec."

She steps out of the dressing room, and I let out a heavy breath. How more complicated can things get? Shel knows I wasn't in Ireland and Dane wasn't out of town on business. Not to mention Garrett is following us around the mall like some sort of creeper. I'm surprised she hasn't noticed him given her super sleuth skills. I sigh and reach for my shoes, but stop. I pick up my phone and text Dane instead.

When I get back I need you.

As I'm tying my laces my phone chimes.

It's about time.

Haha. *I'm serious. We have a problem.*

What?

Shel's on to us.

Chapter 6

"You quit your job?"

"I didn't have a choice."

This is news to me too, but I try to keep my face emotionless in front of Shel. She assumes I know everything Dane is telling her.

We sit side by side as he attempts to explain our rendezvous in the Caribbean. Shel is opposite us, perched on the edge of the chair. My mom left about an hour ago to drive home before it got too dark.

"Teagan was pressuring you that much?" She frowns.

"She had her father on her side. He told me he'd fire me if I didn't change my mind about the engagement. I was out of a job regardless; it was easier to make a clean break."

My eyebrows shoot up and I quickly lower them. This Teagan sounds like a piece of work.

"I was upset about it," Dane says and looks at me. "I called Emma to talk. She told me how overwhelmed she was feeling, too." He gives me a tiny smile. "I suggested we go away for awhile. To clear our heads."

Shel leans forward. "So you two ran away together. That's not a bad thing." She pauses. "But why not say so? It's not a crime to need a vacation."

"Do you think my parents would've been okay with my running off?" I ask. "In the middle of the semester? With a guy? Come on."

Shel's expression twists. "You know your parents love Dane."

63

They do? That would explain my mom's lack of concern regarding his toothbrush.

"It was better if no one knew," Dane explains. "We wanted to be left alone. I didn't want to tell my dad I quit, and I didn't want Teagan knowing where I was. Neither of us wanted to answer a ton of questions." He gives Shel a pointed look.

"Fine," she sighs and sits upright, then eyes me. "What about your memory? Did you really forget James or is that a lie, too?"

"No." I shake my head. "I did forget."

"Emma hit her head on the side of the pool," Dane says. "I was worried about her, so I brought her home."

I look at him out of the corner of my eye. He's so good at lying. Should that worry me?

"Have you seen a doctor?" Shel asks, concerned. "Head injuries are no joke."

"Yes," I fib. "On the island. I had a CT scan and everything."

Dane shoots me an impressed glance.

Shel's shoulders relax. "Well, it's about time you two got your act together. I'm happy for you." She looks at Dane. "Are you living here now?"

He almost laughs. "Um, no."

"I told you things weren't like that." I give her an exasperated stare.

"Whatever!" She nearly jumps out of her seat. "You mean to tell me you two escaped to paradise and *nothing* happened? Give me a break!"

Dane gets defensive. "She didn't say that." He deliberately takes my hand. "We're working on it, okay? Did we have a great time in St. Thomas? Yes. Does that mean it continues here in the real world? Maybe. Both of us are just out of serious relationships. We don't want to screw this up."

Wow. Nicely put. I'll have to congratulate him later.

Shel holds her hands up in surrender. "Okay, okay. I just want to see you guys happy, that's all."

"Believe me," Dane holds my hand tight, "we want that, too."

Shel gives us a long stare then pulls out her phone to consult the time. "Well, I guess I'd better get going," she says and stands. "I have an early volunteer shift tomorrow."

I remove my hand from Dane's and stand with her. She walks around the table and gives me another super tight hug. "Promise me you'll fill me in from now on? I worry about you."

I speak into her shoulder. "I promise."

She releases me and we head to the door. She turns and gives Dane a small wave. "I'll see you around," she says and smiles. "Give Matt a call and tell him where you are, would you?"

He returns her smile. "Will do."

"Okay." She faces me. "Now that you're back, and break is coming up, we'll have to get together. Sound good?"

"Sounds perfect," I say.

I usher her out and lock the door, then turn and lean against it. "Geez," I say to the ceiling with relief.

Dane walks toward me. "I think it went well," he says. "She has no reason not to believe us. Everything we said was the truth."

I look at him. "You quit your job because your fiancées father threatened you?"

"Yes."

"You called me to talk about it?"

"Yes."

"I told you I was overwhelmed here?"

"No." He stops in front of me. "You said that to your mother when you gave her the Ireland excuse."

Oh. Well, that makes sense. "We really dodged a bullet today." I look him in the eye. "Can you imagine if James had walked in instead of you? What would we have done?"

He takes another step closer. "You're right. We need a better system."

"How about knocking first?" I say sarcastically and cross my arms. "You don't own the joint, you know."

"I'm sorry," he says. "I forgot about your mom's visit."

"Obviously."

"Hey, even if I had knocked you would've asked who it was. I would have said my name and we still would have been caught."

I bite my lip. "You're right. Maybe you guys should call before coming over. You never know who might be here."

Dane frowns. "Who else are you expecting?"

I shrug. "I don't know. Maybe one day I'll have a hot date and won't want to be interrupted."

Dane raises an eyebrow and gives me half a smile. "Would you like to have a hot date?"

Here we go. "Shut up. You know what I mean."

"Do I?" he asks.

It's just now that I realize how close he's standing. "Why are you in my space?" I ask. "Back up." I pull myself away from the door which only brings us closer.

"Now you're in my space." He smiles. "You back up."

"Please." I stand my ground. I try to change the subject from the topic of our proximity. "Who's on guard tonight?" I casually ask.

"Yours truly."

Ooookay. Is it getting warm in here or is it just me? "Well, bodyguard, can you move?"

He tilts his head. "Why? Does this bother you?"

"No. You're in my way."

"Then go around."

How impossible is he being? I huff and take two steps to the side.

Suddenly, he grabs me around the waist and lifts me off the ground. "AH!" I yelp and lock my hands around his forearms. "What are you doing?"

"Guarding your body," he laughs.

"Put me down!" I kick.

He sets my feet on the floor, but doesn't let go. He slides his hands to my rib cage and starts to tickle me mercilessly.

"Stop!" My knees buckle as I burst into a fit of laughter. I try to free myself by writhing beneath his hands, but it doesn't work.

As I shrink to the floor to get out of his grip, I grab his leg just above his knee and press down hard.

"Hey!" He reflexively steps back. His hold loosens enough for me to slip away and I take off, putting the coffee table between us.

"Serves you right!" I laugh and try to catch my breath.

His eyes light up as he stalks me around the table. "I'm going to catch you." He grins.

"I'm *so* scared."

He darts to his left, and I jump to my right. He calculates the distance and decides to step *over* the table. I leap onto the couch and throw one leg over the back, trying to get away. Just as I'm about to swing the other leg over, he grabs my ankle.

"No!" I laugh and shake him loose. I fling myself off the back of the furniture and the force sends my body flying.

"There's a wall there," he snickers as I bounce off it.

I glare at him as I rub my shoulder.

"Where are you going to go?" he challenges me.

"Away," I say as my eyes roam the room. Where can I go? I make a split second decision and sprint for the bedroom. If I can get there before him I can shut the door.

He leaps off the couch and is behind me in two strides. He's so close that I let out an "Eeep!" as we cross through the doorway. LB takes one look at us, immediately jumps off the bed, and hightails it out of there. I run to the opposite side of the room, and Dane stops with the bed between us.

"Do you give up?" I smile. "You haven't caught me yet."

He grins back. "Never."

He steps up on the bed to come across it and at me. I take off the way I came and he switches direction mid-mattress, leaping off and blocking my path. Damn it! We stare each other down.

"Looks like you're trapped." He smirks. "Any last words?"

"Before what?" I make a face. "I'm so winning this."

He looks confused, but then starts to advance. "What are you going to do?"

I raise my eyebrows and barrel straight for his mid-section, wrapping my hands around his waist and tickling him as hard as I can.

He laughs and twitches under my fingers, but that doesn't stop him from finding my sides and torturing me again. Pretty soon I'm reaching for whatever I think might be ticklish – under his chin, his armpits, his sides, even his knees. We're a hysterical tangle of arms and legs, both of us trying to gain an advantage over the other. At some point he gets a hold of my leg and takes me out, causing me to fall on my backside with an "Ooof!"

He laughs as he stands over me. "I think I win," he pants.

"Not so fast!" I wrap myself around his leg and pull. He topples to the side with a "Whoa!" landing next to me on the floor.

Side by side we lay there laughing, both of us bitten by some sort of tickle fight bug. I wipe the tears from my cheeks. "That was fun," I tell him even though my shoulder hurts from hitting the wall.

"Yeah," he says and props himself on his elbow. "I still claim victory though."

"What? How?"

He smiles. "You fell first."

"Whatever," I say sarcastically. "I thought it was the first one caught not the first one to fall."

"In that case," he says and swings his body up and over mine, so he's straddling my waist. He does it so fast that I don't have time to react before he scoops up my wrists and pins them next to my head. "I win."

Oh no, he doesn't. My expression twists. "You're a terrible cheater."

"How am I a cheater?" He leans forward to get in my face. "I. Win."

His cocky attitude challenges me and my heart begins to pound. The fact that he's sitting over me doesn't help either. How can I flip this? Ah ha! "Let go of my hands," I say in a deadly serious tone.

I think he feels I'm offended, so he does as I ask. I reach for his waist and slowly slide my hands over his chest, then push against his shoulders to move out from underneath him. As I bring myself to kneel, he sits back on his heels and gives me a curious look. I methodically wrap one hand around his neck and press the other against his chest. I can feel his heartbeat pick up through his shirt as I move forward and hold my lips centimeters from his. He closes his eyes.

"What!"

I throw myself at him with all my might, causing him to fall backward and to the side. I quickly scramble up his body, throw my leg over his waist, and gather his wrists like he did mine. He stares at me wide-eyed as I grin. "Now that's how you cheat. I win."

"You're rotten." He narrows his eyes at me. "You know I can get out of this and make you pay."

My bravado gets the best of me. "Please do."

In one easy motion his lips are on mine. I release his wrists and try to sit up, but he uses his freedom not to claim victory, but to wrap one hand around my waist and run the other into my hair. His palm cradles my head and presses my mouth down on his. Instinctively, my hands turn into fists, clutching his shirt beneath them.

I swear time stops. His mouth invades mine and my mind races. My first kiss with him was just a few days ago! Yes, it was nice, but this is way more intense. How will I know what to do? Suddenly, I'm nervous and it shows. My lips still and he pulls away.

"I thought you wanted me to make you pay," he breathes.

I do. I don't want him to stop, but I don't want to look like an idiot either. "I didn't know what you were charging. This is new for me."

His eyes grow dark and lock on mine. "Do you trust me?"

Why do I nod yes? It's an involuntary motion. I mean, he's never given me a reason not to trust him and I have done this before, right?

He slowly catches my mouth with his and kisses me softly. This I can handle. After a minute or two an unfamiliar – yet welcome – feeling starts to build in my belly. I like this. I can't explain why, I just do. My pulse accelerates and one hand travels to wind my fingers in his hair while the other stays pressed against his chest. When I feel his hands trace my spine, my body tells me he's ready to up the ante.

He holds me tighter, and I press myself against him. The intense kiss from earlier returns and this time I'm ready for it. I allow him to mold my mouth with his as my confidence grows. My insides continue to knot telling me we're doing something right. My body remembers things my mind cannot, and I find myself pulling my mouth from his and following his jaw until I reach his ear. My teeth graze it – where did that come from? – and he makes a sound low in his throat. The realization that I caused his response makes me smile. I decide to work my way along his neck, leaving a trail of kisses to his shirt collar. Suddenly, my skin feels electric as one of his hands slides across my waist under my clothes while the other moves to my behind. My nerves completely evaporate. Even though I don't quite understand where this is coming from, I know I don't want it to stop. But how far am I willing to go? How far will he let it?

My question is soon answered. He lifts the bottom of my shirt with both hands, pulling it up and clearly wanting it off. Immediately, I feel overheated and want that too. I push myself to sit and help him remove it by pulling one arm out and lifting it over my head. I lean back over him as he slides it down my other arm, but it gets hung up on my bracelet. He gives it a good yank, pulling it off and taking the bracelet with it.

Blinding light scorches my eyes.

I slam them shut and press my forehead into his shoulder, screaming as I do.

"Emma? Shit! What's wrong?" he panics.

Images flash before me. Teagan dressed as Dorothy from the Wizard of Oz. Dane tossing me into a swimming pool. A crazed woman calling me a whore. James kissing my forehead with Meg by his side. Dane holding my hand as we sit in a golf cart.

"Emma?" I feel my body shake and then move. I pry open one eye to find him sitting and holding me against his chest. "What's going on?"

My fingers clutch at his shoulder as the pain and the images keep coming. James telling me he loves me for the first time. My finger swirling a pattern in the dirt. Patrick leering above me. Dane lifting his shirt to expose stitches. James lying beside me and playing with my hair.

"Damn it! Talk to me!"

A man telling me his name is Lucas. Patrick licking my neck. James telling me that he is my Guardian. Dane helping me out of a flowerbed.

"Emma!"

I peel my eyes open again and attempt to speak. "Brr...." is all I can get out. My eyes sting and my thoughts are scattered; I can't fill my lungs with enough air to form words.

"What?" Dane asks. "B what?"

More pictures. Angry James slamming a door. Dane kissing me while he carries me up stairs. James rolling into a wall as I kiss him. My fingers sliding off a casket as I'm pulled away.

I lift my wrist in an attempt to explain. It feels heavy, as if it's tied with weights. "Brr....."

He understands. Still holding me with one arm, he leans over and grabs my shirt, ripping the bracelet from the sleeve. He grabs my arm and roughly slides the jewelry over my hand.

Instantly, the pain is gone. My eyes clear and there is no bright light. The images disappear.

Dane takes my face in both of his hands. "Are you okay?" he asks, his eyes crazed. He kisses me again to get some sort of response.

I sag against his chest and he wraps his arms around me tight. "What just happened?"

A tear finds its way out of the corner of my eye and trails down my face.   My breathing is erratic and my throat feels swollen, but I can speak.

"I found my memories," I whisper.

Chapter 7

From across the kitchen table, three sets of eyes stare at me. I feel like I'm being interrogated in an old black and white detective film.

"Tell me again what you saw," Garrett says.

I cross my arms in annoyance. "Maybe you should take notes."

This will be my third time rehashing what happened, and I really don't care to. I want to go back to my place and process my memories alone. The physical and emotional pain I felt recalling them has left me raw.

"We need to be clear when Madeleine and Ash arrive." Garrett sits back in his chair. "Maybe they can explain this."

"Where is the all-knowing duo?" I ask sarcastically. Man, I'm in a mood.

James notices. "Em, we're just trying to help."

"I don't need your help." I point to the bracelet. "As long as I'm wearing this, I'm fine."

Garrett tips his head. "How did it come off again?"

My eyes dart to Dane, and he clears his throat. He's been fairly silent through this whole ordeal. "I took it off," I sigh for a third time.

"Why would you do that?"

I give Garrett a stale look. "In case you haven't noticed, I don't wear jewelry. No earrings, no necklaces, no bracelets, no rings." I wave my fingers at him. "I've been wearing it for days; I wanted it off."

He frowns at me.

"What?" I ask, exasperated.

"Nothing compelled you, did it? I mean, you didn't get a sudden urge or hear a voice or anything like that?"

What kind of urge is he referring to? "N-no," I stutter. "Why?"

"I wonder if Kellan isn't using some sort of trick." Garrett strokes his chin. "He didn't want you to have the bracelet; he knows it's important. What if he's trying to get to you subliminally?"

James steps forward. "You might be right."

Leave it to them to jump to that conclusion! The bracelet came off by accident. If Garrett and James think Kellan is making a move they'll step up patrol. This is the last thing I need. What can I say without revealing what happened with Dane?

I shake my head adamantly. "I didn't feel or hear anything. There's no danger."

"Yes, but..." Garrett grimaces, unsure.

"We should take extra precautions just in case," James says. "These two can spend the days with you and attend your classes. I can handle the nights."

Oh no. This is so not happening! "Stop. I'm safe. Really."

Garrett looks at me with concern. "Emma, I think its best..."

"Can I talk to you for a minute?" Dane interrupts and taps Garrett's shoulder. "In private?"

Garrett gives Dane a puzzled look, but stands to follow him anyway. They walk past me and out of sight.

James frowns. "What's that all about?"

I shrug. "Beats me."

He walks around the table and leans against the edge, his face filling with concern. "Are you okay?"

"I'm fine."

"You remembered my mother calling you a whore. You saw my funeral again." He looks into my eyes. "Are you sure?"

"Honestly?" I ask. "I haven't had a minute to think about anything. I've been here since it happened."

He looks at my wrist then runs his finger over the amulet. "I hate that this hurts you. I thought it kept you safe."

I follow his finger with my eyes. "I still think it does."

"By blocking your memory?"

I grumble. "If Madeline and Ash get here this century I'll ask. What's taking them so long?"

"They're in mourning," James says. "Claire was Madeline's mother."

"Claire?" I think back to prior conversations. She was the Larvatus that died in St. Thomas; the one who gave me the bracelet. Now I feel bad. Here I am acting all moody about their lack of presence when they have every right to take care of themselves first. "That's really sad," I say. "I'm sorry. I didn't know."

"How could you?" he says and leans closer. "We'll get this straightened out. I don't want you in danger – from anyone or *anything*." He wraps his hand around my wrist and the leather band. "You're too important."

I'm not. At least not in my mind. I'm just a normal girl who's been thrown into abnormal circumstances.

"So," Garrett and Dane return to the kitchen. "Dane seems to think you're not in any immediate danger." He raises an eyebrow at me.

I glance between the two of them cautiously. "I agree."

James stands. "Why? What makes him the expert?"

"I explained what I saw when Emma took off the charm." Dane crosses his arms. "She wasn't coerced."

"We don't have to take any extra precautions just yet." Garrett moves toward the refrigerator. He opens the door and pulls out a two liter. "You guys thirsty?"

James looks at me and back to Garrett again, irritated. "No. Why are you changing the subject? What did you two talk about?"

"We discussed backing off and giving Emma some space," Dane interjects. "I know it's something she wants." He hesitates. "And something you don't."

I can see James' body tense. "You pulled him aside to gang up on me?"

"Kinda."

James stares at Dane, his eyes boring into him.

"Is there something you want to say?" Dane asks.

"Yeah." James steps forward. "I really don't like you."

Dane is not intimidated. "The feeling is mutual."

James clenches his hands into fists. "So we're clear?"

Dane stares him down. "Crystal."

The tension in the room is palpable. My heart wants to beat out of my chest. Are they going to fight right here?

"Guys." Garrett steps between them. "Enough. I'm handy, but not that handy."

What? I give Garrett a questioning look.

"Living with these two is like living with Jekyll and Hyde. I've already patched two holes in the wall from flying fists. I still have one to go."

"Are you kidding?" I look around the room. I see no broken drywall here.

"Living room." Garrett glances over his shoulder.

My expression twists. Fighting? Seriously? "How old are you?" I snap.

All three of them look at me.

"You're throwing punches?" I ask incredulously. "Why? What's worth that?"

Silence.

I meet each of their stares. James looks justified. Dane's hard expression softens. Garrett looks apologetic. I want to yell at them for their ludicrous behavior, at James and Dane for acting like children, and at Garrett for putting up with it. "You...how...so stupid!" I'm unable to form a sentence. I stand, frustrated, and head for the door.

"You're leaving?" James asks.

"What do you think?"

Dane brushes past Garrett and to my side.

"Where are you going?" I ask.

"With you," he says, confused. "It's my night."

"I thought I got to have more space."

"Yeah, but..." Dane looks at me like I've lost it. "I got you out of 24 hour supervision. Not the regular stuff."

"I want out of the regular stuff." I put my hands on my hips. Suddenly, I feel like a mother punishing her kids. "You're going to act immature? So can I."

"Em, come on." James steps beside Dane. "It was one fight."

"Two," Garrett coughs.

"You're not helping," James mutters.

I eye my two exes. "This is because of me, right?"

More silence.

I assess the three men before me. Garrett's place is getting trashed because of me; James and Dane hate each other because of me. I realize they will never be friends, but can't they at least act civil? My eyes flash. "I will not be responsible for you hurting one another. If you can't get along for Garrett's sake or mine, I'm taking myself out of the picture."

"What does that mean?" Dane moves toward me.

"It means Garrett will be staying at my place." I glance at him and he looks surprised. "If that's okay."

"Um...sure," Garrett mumbles.

"Emma...what?" James looks confused.

"He doesn't need to put up with your crap and neither do I. I'm sure he'd like some peace."

James gives Dane a sidelong glance. "Em, we're not going to be friends."

Dane nods. "What do you expect us to do? Hold hands and sing kum-ba-yah?"

I shoot them a sardonic look. "No. I expect you to act like reasonable adults."

"So, what are you saying? We're grounded?"

I think it over. Some distance between us is probably long overdue. "Yeah, basically. From me, for a few days."

"You're being impossible." Dane crosses his arms. "What's the point?"

"The point," I stare at them, "is that I want you both in my life. If you want that too, you'll learn to get along without violence. I understand you don't like each other; I'm not saying you have to. But figure out a way to tolerate one another. Because if one of you gets hurt or removes the other from my life," I pause, "I'll remove myself from yours."

"That was kind of harsh, don't you think?"

"Not at all," I say defensively. "I'd be wrecked if one of them got hurt because of me. They need to know where I stand."

"Fair enough," Garrett concedes. "You do know they won't kill each other, right?"

"Yes," I sigh. Maybe that last part of my speech was a little over dramatic. "I wouldn't put it past them to sabotage one another, though. Dane used you against James."

Garrett raises his brow. "Did you really want one of us with you 24/7? He saved you from James' idea."

True. "What *did* he tell you?" I ask suspiciously.

Garrett tries to hide his smile, but fails. "He told me what happened."

"Which was?"

"He removed the bracelet."

Surely he didn't tell him *everything*. "It was an accident," I explain.

Garrett winks at me. "If you say so."

My face flushes crimson. "He told you?" That's just great! I press my palm against my forehead.

"Don't worry." He rubs my knee. "It wasn't a play by play."

Thank God. I peek at him. "I suppose you think I'm a terrible person?"

His forehead creases. "Why would I think that?"

I drop my hand. "Duh."

"You're trying to sort out your feelings and rediscover them," he says. "You have to test the water. How else will you know?"

78

I give him a surprised look. "Really? If you were trying to reconnect with a girl you loved would you be willing to share?"

He chews his bottom lip. "I'm not sure. Your situation isn't...normal."

"You've got that right." My shoulders sag. "I've only kissed Dane, honest."

He chuckles. "You don't have to defend yourself to me."

We fall silent and after a few seconds, Garrett offers his hand. I take it. His touch is reassuring in that I know he wants nothing more from me. He's a friend.

"They both love you," he says seriously. "I don't envy the choices any of you have to make. And for that I'm sorry."

I meet his eyes. "You didn't do anything. The James and Dane situation is my mess."

"You're wrong." He takes an unsteady breath. "It's my fault."

"How so?"

"If I hadn't listened to Lucas, hadn't listened to Jack...if I'd backed out of trying to be human like I was this close to doing," he holds his thumb and forefinger slightly apart, "none of this would have happened. James and I would still be Guardians and this disaster would never have affected you."

"I doubt that." I shake my head. "The minute James made the choice I was involved."

"Yes, but only in an ordinary way."

I smile, trying to make him feel better. "Nothing about Guardians is ordinary."

"I just...I want you to know that I'm sorry. For involving you and letting you down. You were my first human friend in over sixty years and I screwed it up."

My face twists. "Were? Aren't we still friends?"

"I hope so." He gives me half a smile. "We weren't before you lost your memory. You were furious; you kicked me out."

I did? "You know, maybe losing my Guardian memories isn't such a bad thing."

He gives me a questioning look.

"It's a fresh start," I realize. "I don't want to remember fighting with you. Or James. Or Dane."

He squeezes my hand. "But wouldn't it be easier if you could recall your past with them?"

"I used to think so." I grimace. "But after what happened today I'm not so sure."

"Why?"

"It hurt." I remove my hand from his and rub my temple. "Really bad. I don't think I want to go through that again."

Garrett wears a sympathetic expression. "If you want to learn more I can help." He taps the bracelet. "If you take this off I can take away the pain."

"You can? How?"

"Like this." He stands. He places his hands on either side of my head and a blast of cool air travels from my head through my toes leaving my body humming in its wake. "What was that?" I ask wide-eyed.

"You used to call it reiki," he says.

"You've done this to me before?"

"On occasion." He smiles.

My body tingles. I blink as my vision appears better; I can see the tiniest detail from across the room. I lift my hand and flex my fingers. They feel stronger somehow; I can sense every bone and ligament. I pause and take stock of the rest of my body. Every muscle feels energized; I want to leap off the couch. I can hear my blood rush through my veins with every exchange of breath. What is this? I'm so in tune with myself I want to look in the mirror to see if I'm glowing. "Was it always this way?" I ask in awe.

"Why? How do you feel?"

"Amazing." I stand. "Strong. Like I could crush concrete with my bare hands."

He scrutinizes me. "It relieved physical pain before. Rid you of nightmares. The method brings peace in whatever form necessary."

"So, I needed strength right now? And better vision?" I pause and tilt my head. I swear I can hear LB scratching in the next room. "And better hearing?"

"Hold on." Garrett raises his hand to silence me. His expression turns anxious. "Look at me and concentrate."

"Why?"

"Just do it."

I focus on his face. What am I supposed to concentrate on? He has nice eyes. They're almost completely changed now with just a hint of aqua blue. His brown hair looks recently cut; did I notice before how it curls a little on top? His nose is straight, his lips look kissable...wait! Did I just think that? Why? I immediately redirect my thoughts. He's average height; he's wearing a long-sleeved tee and distressed jeans...

"You want to kiss me."

I hear his voice loud and clear, but his mouth doesn't move. I try to keep a shocked expression off my face, but fail. No! That's not true!

"What did you hear?" he asks.

"Nothing." I look away. How embarrassing is this?

His eyes light up. "You heard my thoughts."

"M-maybe," I stutter.

"Emma," he smiles. "I was shouting. I had to say something you'd react to; I know you don't want me."

I let out my trapped breath, exasperated. "Couldn't you just have said hello?"

He laughs. "I wanted to have some fun."

"You're in an awfully good mood," I notice. "What happened to apologetic Garrett?"

"Don't you see what this means?" He reaches out and grasps the tops of my arms. What feels like an electrostatic spark zaps between us and I jump. He steps back, still smiling. "With training you can defend yourself."

"Would you tell me what's going on?" I'm starting to panic. I still feel strong and could quite possibly crush him if wanted to.

"You're one of them. I'm sure of it now."

"One of who?"

"The Larvatus."

My mouth drops open. "You're wrong."

He gets close to me again. "You can read minds. I'm not wrong."

What the shit is this? I've never been able to do that before! "Why now? It's probably just a freak reaction to your reiki."

"Maybe so." He pauses to think. "Or...."

"Or what?"

"It opened your mind to what you really are."

Chapter 8

This new found strength is driving me mad.

I execute another perfect handstand which is something I could never do before. I hold my body straight as an arrow and then slowly fall into a front walk over. I back up, get my bearings, and do it again. And again.

Garrett looks toward the ceiling for reprieve. "Please stop."

"I can't," I complain and start to pace. It's been two days since his "reiki" awakened this insanity inside my body. I could barely sit still during classes today; thank God I only have two weeks left. "I need to burn some energy."

"Go back to the gym," he suggests.

I consider it. The day after my awakening – that's what we're calling it – I almost went stir crazy. After getting precious little sleep due to my hyper-awareness, I went on a cleaning rampage in my apartment. My improved eyesight lent itself to finding every speck of dust and dirt. Garrett was impressed for awhile, but when I couldn't stop moving he suggested I use the gym privileges included in my tuition. Western has a recreation center full of fitness equipment that I never had the urge to try. We spent hours there; I worked muscles I didn't know I had. We also discovered I could bench press 300 pounds, roughly three times my body weight, which impressed us both.

That was yesterday. Today, all I've managed to do is go to class, fidget in my seat, and experiment with gymnastics in my living room. Going to the rec center is a good idea; if anything it will keep me away from my grounded neighbors. I can't complain;

Garrett says his place is in one piece and I haven't seen or heard from them in a day and a half. But, last night, when I couldn't sleep again, I let my mind wander to my recovered memories of James and Dane. I compared them with my new ones and realized I miss their company, overbearing as it is. I had half a mind to spring them this morning, but I still want to prove my point. I settled on releasing them tomorrow for good behavior before I finally dozed off.

"Let's go." I nudge Garrett's legs with my foot. They fly off the table where he had them propped, and he catches himself against the couch.

"Hey! Don't break me."

I roll my eyes. "Wuss."

He rights himself and rubs his calf, then stands. "I don't know how much I can do today. My muscles ache more than I expected."

I poke his belly. "That's because you're turning into a soft human."

He smiles. "I know."

"Let me change and we'll go. You can spot me."

He nods.

We spend four hours at the gym. I rotate through all the equipment and even lap the indoor track. I've never been able to run with any kind of stamina before and the feeling is exhilarating. Overnight, my body has turned into a finely-tuned machine; a machine that craves activity. As we walk back to my apartment – there's no way I'm driving with this much energy to burn – I notice the edge is taken off my need to move, but it's not completely gone. How will I keep this up? Will the urge ever wane?

"I'm starving," I tell Garrett. "Let's get some food."

"The lasagna I made wasn't enough?" he asks, surprised. "I've never seen you eat so much."

Yeah. I kind of ate a lot before I started with the handstands. My stomach growls. "I must have burned through it. Let's get ice cream."

"Ice cream?" He frowns. "It's December."

84

"So?"

"You want something cold?"

My eyes light up. "Yes. With hot fudge."

We stop at a small market near our apartments. "Do you want vanilla or chocolate or what?" I ask with my head stuck in the freezer. I'm feeling a Neapolitan concoction myself.

"Whatever you're having is fine," Garrett says holding the freezer door open for me. Under his arm he holds two cans of whip cream and the biggest jar of hot fudge I could find. We were out of luck when it came to the maraschino cherries, but I did spy some mixed nuts when we came in that I might have to buy.

I grab a carton of each flavor and back out of the freezer. "This should work."

He eyes get big. "Three gallons? Are we having a party?"

"Did I hear party?" a perky voice asks from behind.

I turn to find Samantha with her head tilted and a fake smile plastered on her face. I offer her a smile in return. She looks as if she's agitated and trying to hide it. Hmmm. I concentrate on her eyes. Garrett and I discovered I can only hear thoughts when I consciously try. Her voice slams into my brain.

"She said they weren't dating!"

Time to fix this scenario. "Hey! It's good to see you again."

"Sure." Her eyes dart to Garrett and she turns flirty. "How've you been? I haven't seen you in ages!"

"I can't complain," Garrett says.

"I told Garrett you were looking for him." I glance over my shoulder. "Didn't I tell you she was looking for you?"

His eyes lock on mine for an instant and I concentrate again. His voice sounds in my mind. *"Thanks a lot!"*

I give him a tiny shrug.

"Er...yes," he says to Samantha. "Emma mentioned she ran into you the other day."

She redirects her attention to me. "Speaking of, where's Dane?" *"Does he know about her other boyfriend?"* her smug thoughts echo in my head.

Wow. Really? Can't Garrett and I hang out without assumptions? "He's back at the apartment. We invited Garrett over for dessert."

"How nice." Her eyes light up. *"Can I come too?"* she thinks.

That sounds like a bad idea. Her annoying behavior may cause me to pummel her face, not to mention I would have to release Dane early from his "grounding." If I know her the way I think I do she'll find a way to invite herself. Garrett's going to hate me for this, but...

"Do you have plans tonight?" I ask.

She beams and then looks at Garrett from beneath her lashes. "No."

"Perfect!" I fake enthusiasm. "Weren't you saying you wanted to know Garrett better? Why don't you two hang out at your place? I'll split half this ice cream with you."

Her smile turns shy as she addresses Garrett. "What do you say?"

I can feel his eyes drilling into the back of my head. I risk a glance and he growls at me silently. *"You are in so much trouble."*

I know he won't be rude to Samantha; it's not in his genes. He hesitates. "Uh—sure."

"Great!" I say. "Let me go buy this." I turn to Garrett. "Give me those." I hold out my tower of cartons so he can balance the whip cream and hot fudge on top.

"No; I'll help you," he insists. "We'll be right back," he says to our neighbor.

I lead the way to the register.

"What are you doing?" Garrett whispers. "What am I supposed to do with her? And who's going to watch you?"

"I'll be fine. Super strength, remember?"

He gives me a condescending look.

"Besides, you'll be upstairs," I place my items on the counter, "and you could use some time for yourself. When's the last time you went on a date?"

It takes him a moment to answer. "1942."

86

"See?" The cashier rings up our sundae buffet. "A night out is long overdue. Who knows? You might enjoy yourself."

He reaches for his wallet. "Doubtful."

"That will be $18.51," the cashier says as she pops her gum.

Garrett tries to hand her a twenty. "Stop." I grab his wrist. "I set you up. My treat."

After we gather the bags, we meet Samantha by the door. "I drove if you'd like to ride back with me," she volunteers.

I smile, yet study her eyes. *"You get the backseat,"* she sends my way. Shouldn't she be grateful that I got her some time alone with Garrett?

The ride to our building in her yellow Volkswagen Beetle is short. Surprisingly, the interior of the car is pretty big. "There's a lot of room back here," I volunteer from the rear.

"Plenty," she says suggestively.

Garrett flashes me a look and I hear *"Help me"* in my head. I stifle a laugh.

Just inside our apartment entrance, I divvy up the dessert between the plastic bags. "Have fun!" I wave as I send them on their way. Samantha shoots me a smile as Garrett tries to mask a scowl. *"You know where to find me,"* he sends into my brain. *"Feel free to create an emergency."*

I give him a small wave and turn the key in my door. A fake emergency or otherwise is not likely to happen. When's the last time he kissed a girl? He may thank me later.

I flip on a few lights and rid myself of my coat. My stomach makes another unsettling noise, and I immediately head to the kitchen to create the most obnoxious sundae ever. Huge scoops of chocolate and strawberry ice cream – I gave the lovebirds the vanilla – drip with fudge. A mountain of whip cream sits on top. Oh yeah.

When midnight rolls around I turn off the TV and glance at the door. I kind of thought Garrett would be back by now. I'm starting to feel guilty about what happened. All I wanted to do was let Samantha know we weren't together and avoid involving Dane. I didn't mean to subject Garrett to hours of her company. Should I rescue him or is he having a good time? I wish I had his number; I'd send him a quick text.

Standing, I fold his blankets and pile them neatly on the couch. I should try to go to sleep. It may be an hour or two before I drift off, but I do have class tomorrow. I also get to spring my neighbors from Emma Restriction. At first I smile, but then it fades. I haven't heard from them in two days. Will they want to see me or have they reached the conclusion that I'm not worth the effort? Either they took what I said seriously or they're extremely pissed. How will I feel if it's the latter?

I push the question aside because I'll never sleep if I ponder it. I move around the room turning off lights, leaving one lamp on for Garrett, should he return. As I pass by the door, I pause. Would he *really* spend the night with Samantha? It has been awhile since he's done anything remotely romantic. The thought unsettles me and shake it away. He's a grown man; he can do whatever he pleases. He could fall in love with her if he wanted to. For some reason the thought makes me physically shudder. Why am I allowing his absence to nag me so much?

Minutes later, I find myself in bed with the sheets pulled to my chin and LB at my side. I occupy my thoughts with upcoming finals and my move back home. Eventually sleep takes me, but it's restless. I can't help but keep one ear tuned for the sound of my friend's return.

Alarms are the worst. Even though I'm partially awake I still loathe the sound. I slam my hand on the snooze button and rub my eyes. LB stretches and leaps from my bed which causes me to pause. Since Garrett's been here she sleeps with him; I think they bonded while they were in hiding. If she spent the night with me that can only mean...

He never came back.

I throw off the covers and spring from my bed. Sure enough the lamp still burns and the blankets on the couch haven't been touched. He stayed upstairs? This is unexpected. I thought he didn't want to spend time with our neighbor, let alone the night. A few hours together were enough to change his mind? What kind of mad seduction skills does she have?

Surprised, I make my way to the bathroom to ready myself for class. I run the shower and confusion clouds my thoughts. Something's not right. Is it possible Garrett's hormones took over? He doesn't seem the type, but what do I know? Just because he stayed with her doesn't mean anything happened. I almost laugh out loud. This is Samantha we're talking about.

By the time I've dressed and choked down some yogurt, I've made up my mind. I need to see him. Just to set my mind at ease. It's selfish, but I need to know he doesn't blame me; that he's not mad and he stayed out because he wanted to. Maybe he thought my set up was to get out from under his "protection."

I leave for class early and head upstairs to Samantha's apartment. Nervously, I knock on her door. Will they be awake? Technically Garrett has Intro to Ethics with me in a half hour not that he's been attending class. He could use it as an excuse to leave though, if he wanted to.

A moment later the door opens. Samantha's dressed and she's toweling her hair. "Oh, hey," she says. "What's up?"

My eyes search behind her. "I'm sorry to bother you." I refocus on her face. "But is Garrett here? We have class in, like, thirty minutes."

Her eyes get a somewhat dreamy look to them then she snaps out of it. She steps forward, almost through the doorway. "Thank you for last night," she says quietly. "Between us girls I owe you big time."

I concentrate on her eyes and her thoughts mirror her comments. No sarcasm this morning. I clear my throat uncomfortably. "I take it things went well?"

"I got one kiss. I had to work for it, but it was worth the effort." She smiles.

One kiss? That's all? So what's he still doing here? I fake an encouraging expression. "So, is he ready to go or…"

Samantha frowns. "I don't know. He left around 11:30."

"He's not here?"

"No. He said something about homework and left. He's not at his place?"

My pulse starts to accelerate. He could be there, but anxiety is building in my chest. "He must have left without me," I mumble. I need to get downstairs and fast. "I should go. Sorry to interrupt."

"It's okay." She steps back. "I'll see you around."

"Yeah."

I wait until she closes the door then break into a sprint down the stairs. I bypass my place and pound on Garrett's door, careful not to punch my fist entirely through. *Please be here, please be here, please be here,* I silently chant.

James opens the door. "Emma?"

"Tell me Garrett is here," I nearly plead.

He looks confused. "No. I thought he was with you."

My stomach drops to my toes.

"What's wrong?"

"He's gone," I barely say.

"What do you mean he's gone?"

"I don't know where he is."

James searches my face. He can see I'm upset and his expression turns anxious. I try to read his thoughts, but all I get is silence. Maybe it doesn't work when I'm worried?

He reaches out and pulls me over the threshold, closing the door. "What happened?"

I look over and see Dane frozen, holding a bowl of cereal with a spoonful midway to his lips. His forehead creases and I stare at him. His voice resonates in my brain, relieved. *"She's here."* Then it changes, concerned. *"What's going on?"* Apparently my mind-reader isn't broken.

I answer both their questions. "Garrett and I ran into Samantha last night. I read her mind; she thought Garrett and I were together. To set her straight I sent him with her for a few hours. He never came back." The guys know about my new found abilities. Garrett filled them in, excited that I was supposedly a Larvatus.

"He left you?" James asks, shocked. "Why would he do that?"

Guilt is written all over my face. "I made him. It was only supposed to be for a little while. I thought he should have some fun."

"Did he want to go?"

"Not really." I look down. This is all my fault.

Dane sets his bowl aside. "Where do you think he is?"

"Hell if I know," James responds. "He's not with Samantha?" he asks me.

"She said he left around 11:30."

James crosses his arms as Dane approaches us. I'm sure we're all thinking the same thing, but none of us want to say it. I meet Dane's eyes. *"11:30? That's when..."*

"Hey," he addresses James. "Isn't that when you got that headache?"

"It was more of a hum in my brain," he says. "Like when I was a Guardian."

That seals it for me. I guess I'll be the brave one and say what no one else will. "Garrett's been taken," I state matter-of-factly.

"You don't know that," James says. I think he's trying to set my mind at ease although he doesn't look like he believes his own words. I try to read his thoughts again. Nothing comes through.

"He wouldn't just leave," I protest.

"You're right."

A voice that sounds eerily like Garrett's sounds from across the room.

All three of us turn and my heart nearly bursts with relief. It's Garrett, but...it's not. The person is his mirror image dressed in army fatigues.

"Jack?" James blinks. "What are you doing here?"

"I'm here to help," he says as he steps toward us. "Kellan has Garrett."

Chapter 9

"It was too much not to know," Jack says, looking pensive. "I had to go back. I wanted to check with Lucas and find out what was happening."

Reality has hit me square in the chest. I know James and Garrett were once Guardians and I've seen others that I've forgotten. But Jack is the first I've encountered with new eyes. Dane sits next to me and I glance at him for the briefest of seconds. His thoughts echo in my mind. *"Holy hell."* You got that right.

"Were you able to speak to him?" James asks.

"Barely. I couldn't find him at our normal meeting locations, so I took a chance and went to Post. While the others were at Assembly, I appeared in Quarters."

"What?" Dane asks, puzzled.

"Post is where The Allegiant reside. You can't get in unless you're summoned," Jack hesitates. "Usually."

"Us rabble shy away from The Allegiant," James says. "The stigma is you don't go to them, they come to you. You don't dare manifest in their personal space. It's monitored."

"So how'd you get in?" I ask Jack.

"Garrett and I have been there before. Lucas was our Guardian before he became Allegiant. I'm familiar with the layout."

"What did you find?"

His expression turns pained. "I found Lucas. Bound and gagged and extremely weak. I never knew The Allegiant could be subdued; I'd thought they were omnipotent."

James frowns. "Well, that's clearly not the case. Two of them were killed. I saw it with my own eyes."

"I believe you." Jack looks grave. "When I removed his gag, Lucas thanked the Great One that I'd returned and told me what had happened. He wouldn't allow me to release him; he asked me to locate Kellan, get as much information as I could, and report back instead." He pauses and looks at each of us. "That's when I found Garrett with the others."

James gets animated. "You saw Meg? Thomas and Joss? How are they?"

"Tired. Angry. Ready for revenge."

Guilt weighs heavy on my heart for Garrett's capture. I should never have pushed him to spend time away from us. "Is your brother okay?" I ask.

"For now," Jack says. "Part of him is still Guardian, but he has human needs too. He can't stay in the Intermediate indefinitely. The longer he's without food and water he'll die."

I close my eyes and my stomach feels like lead. Could he have said anything worse?

"Not that I want anyone hurt," James says, "but why hasn't Kellan disposed of Garrett and Lucas already? You know, pick us off one by one."

"Lucas told me Kellan is using him to accomplish tasks that cannot be done alone, like creating more Allegiant. Lucas knows Kellan will kill him when he's no longer needed."

"Wait." James stands. "The Allegiant create others? I thought the Gift was bestowed by God."

Jack's expression twists. "Apparently not."

James regards him in disbelief. "What's he keeping Garrett around for?"

"Bait." Jack grimaces. "Kellan wants to lure you into a fight."

Adrenaline surges in my veins. It must register on my face because Dane wraps his hand around mine. I meet his eyes with a questioning look. None of us deserves to be hurt by this psycho, and I immediately begin to strategize. We need to prepare.

"When?" I ask.

Jack shakes his head. "I didn't get all the details; I had to move to avoid being seen. I do know Kellan has begun to rally his troops, and he's forced Lucas to create at least one other Allegiant. Lucas said he didn't want to because the person wasn't worthy."

James begins to pace. "So why didn't you free him? He could be helping us right now."

"Yeah," Dane says, perturbed. "We're sitting ducks."

Jack looks him in the eye. "That's why I'm here. Lucas has a plan."

I have to stop myself from letting out a sarcastic laugh. It doesn't appear that Lucas' plans have panned out so far. I manage to prevent myself from rolling my eyes, but can't help the smart words that slip from my lips. "Really? You trust this guy? He lied to you. He's trapped and weak. What makes you think his plan will work?"

Jack is surprised by my sarcasm and he shoots me an irritated glance. I concentrate on his eyes. *Who does she think she is?* he asks. His eyes find my hand wrapped around Dane's and his look turns questioning. *What? No more love for James? That'll clear the way for Meg.* His words are condescending.

I don't know what that's supposed to mean, but I don't appreciate his tone. I pull my hand from Dane's and lean forward. "For your information *who I think I am* is a Larvatus. I can read your thoughts and I can kick your ass, so you might want to watch your silent commentary."

James' eyes widen and he tries to hide a smile. It turns into a lopsided smirk, and I wish I could hear what he's thinking.

"Well." Jack raises his brow. "Lucas wasn't kidding when he said the game has changed. He mentioned the Charmed."

I cross my arms. "And I assume we're part of his grand plan?" It's amazing how quickly I've claimed this group as my own. Do I truly have their power? Will they even want me? All I know is I have some serious energy coursing through my veins and my friend's lives have been threatened. Bring it on, Jack. Tell me what you've got.

"Yes," he says, annoyed. "Lucas wants us to work with The Larvatus to free him and the others when the time is right. With me as your spy, we can take Kellan by surprise before he acts." He gives me a superior look. "Although convincing your kind to work with an Allegiant might be difficult."

My kind? I feel the need to defend these people I know nothing about. "Madeline and Ash are Garrett's friends. If for nothing else they'll do it for him."

"You know that for sure?"

He's got me there. I've never met The Larvatus that I can remember. "No," I say stubbornly.

His expression turns smug.

"Then let's get them here," James says. "The sooner the better."

Jack stands. "That's my next stop."

"You know where to go?"

"Hope Mills, North Carolina. Garrett said I'd hardly recognize our home town."

"We'll be here waiting."

"Are you sure?" Jack looks over his shoulder. "It might be hard to contain Miss Know-It-All over there. Maybe the three of you should talk about your roles while I'm gone. We're only going to get one shot at this."

Is he insinuating I'm going to screw things up? I jump to my feet to question him, but he vanishes before I can utter a word.

James' eyes light up. "You certainly got under his skin."

I scowl. "He should keep his snide remarks to himself."

"You read his mind?"

I nod.

"To be fair he didn't know he wasn't keeping his thoughts to himself," James says. "What did he say?"

"He thinks my feelings for you have changed. He said the way is clear for Meg."

James tries to look unaffected, but he swallows nervously as Dane muffles a snicker. This deserves an explanation. "Care to fill me in?" I ask.

His eyes dart to Dane and I turn to see what he's looking at. Dane wears a self-satisfied grin. "You heard the lady."

"Like you have room to talk," James says approaching us. "Why don't you tell her your fiancée has been blowing up your phone since Saturday?"

"Teagan?" I ask.

"Ex-fiancée," Dane corrects James. "At least she knows about her. What have you told her about Meg?"

My eyes shoot back to James. What is going on here? I have one memory of Meg; I know what she looks like. Other than that her name has only come up in conversation about his captured friends. As I recall her face I don't have any feelings of jealousy aside from the fact that she's incredibly pretty. What don't I know?

James scowls at Dane then looks at me. "We used to fight about Meg. I told you we were friends, but you thought she wanted more."

I eye him. "Did she?"

He lets out a heavy sigh and runs his hand through his hair. "Yes. She kissed me right before you left for St. Thomas. I didn't have a chance to tell you, I swear."

I stare him confused. "You kissed Meg?"

He nods.

Why doesn't this bother me? I mean it bothers me a little, but not nearly as much as I'm sure it would if I had all my memories. I turn to Dane and his thoughts ring in my ears. *"Should I bring up Rebecca?"*

Who is that? In lieu of what's going on with Garrett, I don't feel like finding out right now. I tuck the information away for another time. "What about you?" I ask Dane. "What does your ex want?"

He stands. "She's worried about her dad. He's been missing for over a week and they've filed a police report. She has a right to be upset. It looks like Lucas won't be coming home any time soon."

Okay, now I'm even more confused. "What does Lucas have to do with Teagan's dad?"

Dane looks between James and I. "Lucas *is* Teagan's dad."

"Are you serious?" I ask the two of them. "Did I know this before?"

He nods. "We found out on the island. He tracked me down to talk about the engagement and my job. The Allegiant followed. It's how we were caught."

Its times like these I wish I had taken Garrett up on his offer to "reiki" away the pain associated with removing the bracelet. There are so many things I don't remember.

"So The Allegiant are partly human?" I ask in surprise. "Lucas is leading a double life?"

"Apparently," Dane says. "And now his family and his business are suffering for it. Teagan wants me to come home and help with the company. She's temporarily taken over for her father; she wants to give me my job back."

I blink. "That's great news! You should do it."

He looks at me like I'm insane. "Are you crazy? She only wants to use me to get out of a bind. She's held my job over my head before; she'll do it again."

I cross my arms and try to talk some sense into him. "You need a job and you loved your old one. Teagan's hurting; she needs your help. You'd really leave her hanging?"

He stares at me in confusion.

"Just because you help her doesn't mean you'll marry her. You were friends once, right? She needs a shoulder. Offer her one."

Dane crosses his arms to match mine. "She'll misconstrue why I'm there."

"Then set her straight from the get-go. She needs help." Why is this so hard for him to understand? "Are you worried you'll fall for her again?"

His expression twists. "No! Never."

"Then you should go."

We stare at one another, and I recall Jack's last statement about our roles. Dane doesn't need to be here; the chances of him getting hurt are high.

"You want me to leave?" he asks, irritated.

"No," I tell him honestly. "But, we don't know what Kellan is planning, and I don't want you hurt. I saved your life once; I don't want to have to do it again. Besides, you need to live *your* life. Stop worrying about me and go back to your family. They must miss you."

Dane scowls. "Trust me they don't."

I sigh. "That's a lie and you know it."

"Do I? You know the history between my father and me. Oh, wait, that's right. You don't. Shall I enlighten you again?"

My eyes widen in surprise. "Are you getting sarcastic with me? I just want you to be safe, that's all." I turn to James. "You too. Maybe you should go into hiding together until this is over."

James grimaces. "I'd rather not." He looks at Dane. "No offense."

"None taken."

Well, this is an improvement in their relationship.

"Do you think you're invincible now?" James asks. "You don't think you need us? We're all on Kellan's hit list."

I take a step back from them. "Last time I checked you're both human. Am I wrong?"

Silence.

"How are you going to work against Kellan and who he brings? You told me what happened to the other Allegiant and to Claire. They all had supernatural powers and they died! I don't want that to happen to either of you."

"You're human too," Dane says quietly. "What makes you think you can fight them and not get hurt?"

"My chances are infinitely better. Garrett said with training I can defend myself."

"How?"

I thought he told them about my increased strength and improved senses. They know about the mind reading, maybe they have to see my strength to believe it. I look around the room. If Garrett were here I would promise to fix what I'm about to break.

I walk toward the wall and stop a few feet in front of it. With a swift kick I put my foot through the drywall once, then twice. Huge chunks of plaster fall to the floor exposing the wood studs and insulation underneath. I turn to them with a smirk.

They look slightly stunned, but not thoroughly convinced. "I could do that," James says. "Show us something else."

I pause to think. What's heavy around here? My eye catches the entrance to the kitchen and I march inside. The refrigerator ought to do. The guys follow me and I wrap my arms around the front of the appliance. Bending my knees I tighten my arms and lift. The fridge hovers about six inches off the ground. I set it back down and turn around.

Both of them look at me approvingly. "Not bad," James says. "But I think you can do better."

I give them an incredulous stare. "What? I'm 5'6 and it's awkward to hold! It's impossible to lift it any higher. I didn't even break a sweat!"

James and Dane look at each other, and Dane shrugs as if saying "Oh well, that's all she's got."

I look at the floor and think about what else I can do to prove my strength. My head snaps up. "Follow me."

I walk past them and out of the apartment. I head outside the building where snow flurries dance through the air. It's funny how the cold doesn't bother me anymore. Not that it's my favorite temperature, but I don't have a coat on and I'm only slightly uncomfortable. I make my way to the parking lot behind the building.

"Where are you going?" Dane asks.

"You'll see," I say over my shoulder.

I find Samantha's yellow Bug and head toward it. I stop behind the rear fender and eye the guys. Both of them have their arms wrapped around themselves to block the winter air. I give them a stern look. "This is the last thing I'm doing."

I place my hands beneath the fender, bend my knees, and lift. Because the front wheels are on the ground and I have a good grip, I'm able to raise the rear end of the car as high as my shoulders. I hold it there for a few minutes, feeling like Hercules, then set it down controlled and gentle. I brush my hands together ridding them of invisible dirt.

When I look at the guys both of their mouths are open, and I can't help but break out in a smile. I cross my arms and lean against the car. "Satisfied?" I ask arrogantly.

Neither of them speaks. I meet James' eyes and try to read his thoughts. Again nothing. Why can't I hear him? I shift my eyes to Dane.

"That was hot."

My face flushes. That's not the reaction I was going for, but I'm flattered nonetheless. I push myself off the car. "Let's go back inside."

Chapter 10

Madeline wraps me in a warm hug. "I'm sorry it took us so long to get here."

Instantly, I feel bonded to her like we are family reunited. When she steps back and holds me at arm's length, Ash sets his hand on my shoulder with a small smile. It's as if he's welcoming me into the fold and his touch radiates serenity. Their presence grounds my body and takes the edge off the energy coursing through it.

Madeline immediately pulls me to her side, wrapping her arm around my shoulders and leading me further into Garrett's living room. "We'll start with meditation," she says as we sit. "We can teach you to harness your energy, so it won't drive you nuts." She smiles.

I let out a relieved sigh. "Thanks. I was beginning to think I would have to spend half my life in the gym or running marathons."

She laughs and it mesmerizes me for a second. I've never heard such a melodic sound come from a person. I catch her eyes and they're a bright emerald green like mine. I've never seen anyone with the same shade; I always thought my color was a bit freakish. Her thoughts resonate in my head.

"They're not freaky. They're beautiful."

I blink at her unspoken comment. "You think so?"

She looks shocked. "You heard my thoughts?"

My face turns red. I should probably ask before I start reading random people's minds. "I'm sorry," I apologize. "I was studying your eyes and I slipped."

She looks at Ash as he rounds the couch to sit at my other side. He addresses Dane and James. "How long has she been like this?"

James shrugs and looks at me. "Two days?"

I nod. "Garrett triggered something when he demonstrated his reiki. At least that's what we think happened."

Ash gives me a confused stare. "His what?"

"Reiki. That's probably not the right word for it, but he was trying to show me how he can take away pain. He said he's done it before to help me with headaches and nightmares."

Ash looks at Madeline in surprise. "Really," he says to me while looking at her. Are they reading each other's thoughts?

Madeline grasps my hand. "Why were you in pain?"

My eyes dart to Dane and back to her again. "The bracelet came off. This crazy light blinded me and my lost memories began to play behind my eyes. The pictures and emotions were...a lot."

She looks to Ash again with concern. Inherently, I know they're having a silent discussion about me and I try to catch her eyes. She's avoiding me on purpose and it's frustrating. I'm right here, damn it.

"First things first," Ash says and stands. He removes a long duster to reveal a rather ordinary long-sleeve ringer tee and jeans. Other than his heavy boots he looks like he just stepped off campus. His wavy brown hair falls to his chin and catches in the stubble there. He brushes it away and I think that must get annoying.

"It does," he smiles and answers my question. "But Madeline likes it."

I quickly look down. I should have realized they could see into my mind! It's a good thing I wasn't thinking anything else.

Madeline follows Ash's lead and gets comfortable at the same time by removing her leather jacket. When she turns to place it over the back of the couch, I see her jet black hair is braided and falls past her waist. She wears grey leggings, a soft blue sweater, and the same type of boots as Ash. When she's settled she grasps my hand again, and the light catches her wrist. Her bracelet is identical to mine.

Ash rests his elbows on his knees and looks at Jack who has been hanging near the rear of the room. "You said The Allegiant want us to spend some quality time together."

"Not all of them. Just Lucas," he clarifies.

"In order to free him and Garrett?"

"And the other Guardians being held against their will."

Ash rubs his chin. "How many are we talking about?"

Jack pauses to count. "Six in total."

Ash frowns. "We don't make a habit of working *with* The Allegiant."

"Seeing as how you killed two of them that doesn't surprise me."

"Why is that exactly?" James asks our guests. "I mean, until you showed up in the Caribbean, I had no idea you existed."

Madeline scoffs. "I'm sure the Larvatus lesson was left out of Guardian training on purpose."

Ash nods, agreeing with her. "Centuries ago, an Allegiant named Xavier defected. He was ostracized by his brothers for voicing his progressive thoughts. It became so unbearable he left the Intermediate to complete his existence in human form. Our legend says he tried for years to live a normal life, but he found it impossible. His natural curiosity and Allegiant tendencies got the better of him, so he ended up creating the first of our kind. When his experimentation was a success the desire to prove his brothers wrong resulted in The Larvatus. He created us to rise against them."

Created us? My eyes grow wide. "How old are you?"

Ash smiles. "Madeline and I were not created by Xavier himself; he was long gone by the time we passed. I became a Guardian when I was 28 and a Larvatus sixty years later. That was in the seventies, so I guess in human years I'd be about 125."

My eyes swing to Madeline.

"I'm 118."

My mouth falls open. "You wear it well."

She laughs. "We age slowly."

That's a nice perk. My thoughts turn to her mother who passed. "But you can die?"

"We *will* die. We're mostly human with a mix of Guardian traits."

James crosses his arms. "How is that possible? Did you both assign your Wards like Garrett assigned me?"

Madeline's expression turns sympathetic. "If Garrett had known there was another way he would never have assigned you to Emma. He said he would have sought us out rather than hurt the two of you."

James frowns. "If The Allegiant know about your kind then why didn't Lucas tell him to find you in the first place?"

"Because he didn't know we still existed," Ash says. "You saw how surprised The Allegiant were when we crashed the party in St. Thomas." He pauses to readjust his weight on the couch. "After Xavier created the first Larvatus he started to seek out Guardians who were unhappy and wanted another chance at a human life. One Guardian led to another and another until they were defecting left and right. He thought he was helping those in need and proving his point to his brothers."

"Which was?"

"That Guardians who are denied eternity should get a second chance rather than stay miserably trapped. He thought the best way to protect humanity was from above and below. Maintain the Intermediate, but put some troops on the ground, so to speak."

I can see where that would make sense. If a Guardian is unhappy what good are they to their Ward? If they could have another chance at life *and* protect people on earth...

"That doesn't sound like a bad idea," I say. "Why were The Allegiant so against it?"

"They believe being Reborn is reserved for the elite."

Madeline sighs. "They think they're the only ones who deserve to live again. One of the benefits of becoming Allegiant is you get to lead a human life. Very few Guardians get that chance."

"Explaining the resurrection of the dead is also difficult," Ash says. "What would a person think if they saw their grandfather walking around town and he died ten years ago?"

Good point.

"So, I take it The Allegiant found out what Xavier was doing and got pissed," Jack says.

"Absolutely." Ash stands. "Once word got out that you could be human again there was an exodus. Guardians were leaving the Intermediate which left Wards alone and Lost. The Allegiant thought the more Guardians that defected the higher the potential for earthly chaos. They didn't bother to question if the Charmed on land were doing any good."

"Instead of working with Xavier to find a middle ground The Allegiant attacked." Madeline looks Jack squarely in the eye. "They didn't ask questions, they didn't hesitate. Many of them were killed, but they still decimated The Larvatus. When Xavier's brothers returned to the Intermediate they made sure to let the Guardians know how vile we were and that we had paid with our lives. They were told never to speak of us and threatened with banishment."

"The Allegiant thought they'd erased our existence," Ash says. "But a few escaped. Xavier was among them; although, he was wounded and wouldn't live long. He loathed his brothers for what they'd done and felt horrible guilt over the death of so many. Rather than risk the lives of the remaining Larvatus in another battle, he made them swear to a quieter uprising. Very slowly more Charmed were created so as not to draw attention. To this day, we carry on as Xavier intended albeit in a more controlled manner. We create more Larvatus when we find an unhappy soul. We work to prevent whatever wrong we can while we're here. And we work against The Allegiant by rebelling against what they believe in."

Our guests' history leaves us silent. Hearing these things makes me question so much, including my sanity. Rather than ask them if I'm headed for the loony bin, I settle on a safer topic.

"Why did you agree to help Garrett?" I ask. "Your existence is no longer secret."

"It was never really hidden," Ash turns to me. "The Allegiant who attacked us were so full of themselves they never bothered to follow up on their handiwork, and we never bothered to set them straight. The relevance of our existence has faded over the years as old Allegiant are replaced with new. We've never been a threat."

"Until now," Jack says.

"Wait," I interrupt. "The Allegiant that rule today are not the same ones that have ruled for all time?"

Madeline shakes her head. "When they grow tired of their duty they can leave it. They create another to take their place then choose eternity or a human existence."

"Oh," I say like that makes sense. Is there a handbook available so I can follow along?

In response to my thoughts, a tiny laugh leaves her. "And, just so you know, we agreed to help Garrett because we've been in his shoes. Our enemy is common. Once we found out you were all in hiding, fearful of The Allegiant, that's all it took. There was no question we would help when the time came."

"How did he find you guys?"

Ash smiles. "By accident. We stumbled upon each other in Hope Mills. I noticed his eyes and read his mind. I knew he was Reborn, but not one of us. I was curious."

Dane raises his hand as if he's in a classroom. He has yet to say anything, and I practically forgot he was here. Ash's attention lands on him and the others follow suit. His voice is flat as he asks his question. "What about Emma?"

Ash looks puzzled. "What about her?"

"She was never a Guardian. How is it that she's remotely like you?"

His tone hints that he's irritated. My eyes lock on his to find out what's bothering him and his thoughts echo in my mind. He's less than thrilled that I am associated with these people.

Madeline squeezes my hand. "She was Gifted."

"Excuse me?" I ask.

"My mother gifted you before she died." Wearing a tiny smile she runs a finger over the amulet that was once Claire's. "We can gift some of our abilities to humans we deem worthy. Garrett spoke highly of you," she lifts her gaze to meet mine, "and he wanted to keep you safe."

He did?

"Yes," she answers silently. *"Very much so."*

"What was she given exactly?" Dane presses.

Why is he so annoyed? I shoot him a look. *"I'm worried"* comes across loud and clear.

"Those Gifted inherit all of our traits save a few," Ash says and turns to me. "You know about the strength, heightened senses, and ability to read minds. Which, by the way, you've mastered quite quickly." He looks impressed. "What you don't know is the enchantment over you and within the bracelet allows you to travel to the Intermediate and elsewhere if Mad and I accompany you. Also, you're able to kill Allegiant – with training, of course."

Okay. That both frightens and excites me. "What can't I do?"

"You cannot perform what you called reiki and you can't manifest independently. You cannot create Larvatus or gift your abilities to anyone else."

I'm kind of glad I can't gift anything. Who wants that responsibility?

"Let me make sure I've got this," I say. "Besides the strength and the senses, I can travel to the Intermediate as long as I'm accompanied by you. I can kill Allegiant and I can read minds. All because of this?" I raise my wrist.

Madeline nods. "And because of the enchantment my mother bestowed upon you. Before she died she held your hand and said something, correct?"

"Respira," Dane says from across the room. "She said respira."

I'm glad he remembers because that memory is sure blocked.

Madeline smiles, wistful. "Of course. Respira means 'breathe again'. Her intent was to pull you to the life of the Charmed and protect you should you need it. The blast from Kellan killed you, but respira saved you from a full death."

I blink at her. "I'm sorry. Can you repeat that?"

"When you were hit by Kellan you died." She rubs my hand. "The enchantment brought you back."

Um, what?

"Think of it like this," Ash tries to explain. "Say you jump off a cliff without a bungee cord. You're certain to die, right? An enchantment is like an invisible rope that pulls you back before you hit the ground. It pulled you to life and to The Larvatus."

I'm stunned. "I thought the bracelet was what protected me from Kellan."

"It did to a degree. The bracelet is charged with protective qualities, but nothing that equals an enchantment. In order to Gift you, Claire had to bestow both because you're human."

Madeline looks at Dane. "It's a good thing you put the bracelet on her when you did. She became one of us at that moment."

"No wonder Kellan is angry with you," James says to Dane. "You helped create another Larvatus."

The look on Dane's face registers the shock that I feel inside. I died? Dane helped create me? Shit just got real.

"Speaking of the amulet," Madeline continues, "it's a conduit. Because you're Gifted your abilities flow through it. If you take the bracelet off everything leaves with it. Does that make sense?"

I nod slowly. "Your amulet doesn't do the same?"

She shakes her head and releases my hand. She removes her bracelet and nothing happens. She slides it back on. "Our abilities are inherent in us because we were created, not Gifted. We wear these for added protection and to identify ourselves to others."

"That must be why it hurt so much to remove it," I say. "But why is it blocking my Guardian memories? Do you know?"

Madeline looks at Ash. "That is something new to us. When you mentioned it before we were confused."

"Maybe the gifting didn't fully take," I say. "Maybe my dying screwed it up. I mean everything seems to work accept that and reading James."

Ash frowns. "I noticed that, too."

"You noticed I can't hear James?"

"No," he says. "I can't hear him either."

James looks confused. "Does that mean something?"

Ash eyes Jack. "How many Allegiant do you know exist?"

"Three. Kellan and Lucas and the one Lucas was forced to create."

"I assume that's you?" Ash asks James.

He looks baffled. "No. I'm human."

Ash holds his chin with his thumb and forefinger. "How was your humanity returned?"

"By The Allegiant. Right before you arrived on the island."

"Let me guess." Ash takes a step forward. "They stood side by side, each one touching the other?"

James starts to look worried. "Yes, but Lucas was immobile on the ground."

"Doesn't matter," Ash says. "You need at least two Allegiant to create another. Any more is just for show."

"But I'm human," James protests.

"So are they – when they want to be. Have you tried to *be* anything else?"

"No."

"When's the last time you ate?"

"Yesterday."

"Are you hungry now?"

James shakes his head.

"What about sleep? Do you sleep?"

"Barely."

Ash turns to me. "The only minds we can't hear are Allegiant." He looks around the room. "I believe our enemy numbers four."

"That's insane!" James steps toward Ash. "I'm no one's enemy. If I'm Allegiant why wouldn't I know it?"

"Because you were never enlightened to that fact. You want to be human therefore you remain in a human state."

James looks at Ash in disbelief. "That can't be possible!"

Ash sets his feet and crosses his arms. "Try to manifest."

"I can't."

"Try," Ash nearly growls.

James huffs. He clenches his hands into fists at his sides and closes his eyes.

And disappears.

Chapter 11

James is Allegiant.

I didn't see that coming.

A barrage of questions followed his reappearance. James, Jack, Madeline, and Ash converged on one another, speculating and tossing around insinuations. They interrogated each other in a tense way that was exhausting to watch. After some time Dane slipped from the room and moments later I managed to do the same. I found him leaning against the kitchen counter drinking a beer. Without a word he held the bottle out to me, and I gladly took it. He retrieved another from Garrett's refrigerator and we stood side by side nursing our drinks in silence. I didn't bother to read his thoughts. There was nothing to say that wasn't blatantly clear. How much more twisted can things get?

That was a week ago. Looking back, I think it was my last relaxed moment. Immediately, Madeline and Ash took up residence in my apartment and wanted to start training me to fight right away. I had to explain that I had classes and finals to conquer, as well as a move back home to prepare for. At first they couldn't understand how such mundane tasks could trump learning to battle the supernatural, but we eventually set a schedule, albeit one that is killing me.

After classes and studying, we spend at least four hours a night at the rec center. I have to admit by the time we get there I'm itching to work my muscles. After a long day of sitting I'm giddy at the thought of punching something or flipping someone. Ash holds nothing back when it comes to challenging me. At the end of each session Madeline insists we meditate to calm my energy for the next day. This is what's wearing me out. It's like a rollercoaster. The mornings start out simple and slow like the beginning of the ride. As the day progresses my energy climbs as if I'm going up a big hill. The workouts are the thrill of going over the top, and the meditation is the slow coast to the end of the track. Working my mind and body relentlessly like this exhausts me. I've been sleeping like a baby.

Needless to say, I don't have much time for anything else, my neighbors included. Not that I'm their activities coordinator, but I feel bad not spending any time with them. I don't feel as guilty about James because, while I'm in class, Madeline and Ash work with him to discover his Allegiant side. Yes, this goes against everything they believe in, but they understand James is on our team. He never intended to become an Allegiant, nor does he feel the way Kellan does. In a way he was betrayed too, and we all know how The Larvatus feel about that. James was turned and no one bothered to let him know. Way to make friends guys.

Dane is another story. He has nothing to do with his time. Sure, he replaced the drywall I ruined in Garrett's apartment and he has one more coat of paint to go. But that's all he's done. Watch paint dry. He does accompany me to the gym each night so we can run the track together as a warm up; he used to run cross country in high school. He leaves immediately afterward though, so Madeline and Ash can take over. It doesn't give us much time to visit, and he has to be lonely with Garrett gone and James busy. I've been tempted to read his thoughts to find out if he resents his time here, but I stop myself each time we're together. I mean, who wants someone in their head? I surely don't. I also don't want to abuse my newfound privilege.

Tonight, as we head to the rec center, I try to think of how to tell him to go home early without making it seem like I'm pushing him away. I only have four days left at Western before I move, so that's four days he could have of normalcy.

"What are you thinking about?" he asks.

I give him a tiny smile. "You."

114

He smirks. "Why?"

I stop walking and look at him. "I feel bad. You have to be so bored."

He shrugs and then takes my hands, winding is fingers through mine and holding them up. "Not right now. This is the highlight of my day."

I sigh. "You need to get out of here. Take Teagan up on her offer and get back to work."

He looks at our hands. "I know."

Wait. "You know?"

He gives me a lopsided smile. "What do you think I've been doing all week?"

I stare at him confused.

"I've had some time to think about what you said."

My eyes get big. "You're going to help her?"

He tightens his fingers around mine and pulls me closer. "Yeah, but with conditions. I start back on Monday."

"That's great!"

He looks doubtful. "Pre-charmed Emma wouldn't think so."

"Well, post-charmed Emma does. Why didn't you tell me?"

He hesitates. "I didn't want it to bother you."

I press his hands against his chest. "I meant what I said before. It doesn't bother me. It's actually a huge relief."

His expression falls, and I search his face. "What's wrong?"

One side of his mouth twitches. "You can't tell?"

"I'm not reading your thoughts."

"How come?"

"Because it's not fair. I do it on a need to know basis."

He smiles. "Is that a rule you learned in Jedi training?"

"No, it's my own rule." I squeeze his fingers. "So spill. What's the matter?"

He sighs. "I kinda wish it did bother you."

Okay, I'm confused. "You just said you didn't want it to bother me. Which is it?"

"It's just...I know you're overloaded right now, and I really don't want it to worry you. But on the other hand, a little jealousy would be nice."

I give him a wry smile. "You need an ego boost?"

"Wouldn't you?"

I blink at him.

"Never mind." He takes a step back.

"No, tell me." I hold on to his hands.

He groans. "Can you read my mind? It'd be easier."

I tilt my head. "*Please* tell me."

He takes a heavy breath. "It's hard not to feel insecure. You have these amazing abilities and so does James. It's only going to bring you two closer and I'm...I'm just me. I'll never be anything else."

The possibility of Dane feeling inadequate has never crossed my mind. I hate that he feels that way and concern clouds my features. I take a step closer as he continues.

"It would be nice if you were jealous of Teagan because it would mean you have feelings for me, that they're growing." He looks at our hands again. "I know it sounds messed up."

"It doesn't." What can I say to put his mind at ease? I do care about him, but are my feelings growing? Unfortunately, they haven't had a chance. The two of us have barely spent any time together.

"Listen," I say and his hazel eyes meet mine. "First of all, I would never put the words Dane and insecure in the same sentence. You're far from it."

He gives me a stale look.

"Second, so what you don't have crazy weird abilities. James and I are freaks! Have you considered that I need you to be normal? For my own sanity?"

He cocks an eyebrow. "The yin to your yang so to speak?"

"Maybe so." I smile then pause, thinking of how to word this. "I have feelings for you; honestly, I do. But, you're right. They haven't grown and that's not your fault or mine. We just haven't had any time to get to know each other like we once did."

He looks down.

"Here's what I propose." I step back. "The semester ends in two days; we'll be home in four. I'll have all kinds of time between training and interning at the clinic. You sir," I poke him in the chest, "are going to have to take me out on some real dates."

He gives me a sly glance. "I'm going to hold you to that."

"I want you to," I say emphatically.

He smiles and drops one of my hands. He raises the other to his lips, plants a quick kiss on the back, and pulls me in the direction of the rec center.

"Do you feel better now?" I ask as we walk.

He nods.

"Good. I don't like it when you're unhappy. Your face is too pretty to be sad."

He abruptly stops and I end up yanking his arm. "What?"

"You're killing me Grace."

"Grace?" My forehead pinches.

"It's my nickname for you," he says and resumes walking. "You had a rather ungraceful fall at Matt's last Fourth of July."

I remember. "I fell in the flowerbed."

He gives me a dazed look. "How...?"

"It was one of the memories that came back when you...you know..." My ears feel hot. We haven't discussed the whole bracelet-getting-caught-in-my-shirt thing.

He tries not to grin by biting his lip.

"Stop," I tell him. "I'm embarrassed enough as it is."

"What's there to be embarrassed about?" he asks. "I'm glad it happened. I'd like it to happen again."

My heart flips. I'd be lying if I said I hadn't replayed that night a million times. "You mean my screaming and crying into your shoulder wasn't a turn off?" Please. He should be heading for the hills.

He shakes his head. "Ah, no."

Regardless, safe and slow is probably our best course of action. "Even so, we should set some dating ground rules. Like leaving any and all clothing *on*."

117

"Awww." He frowns. "You're no fun."

I laugh and look up to see we've arrived at our destination. I reach out to open the door. "Ready to get your butt kicked?"

"As always. You think you could take it easy on me for once? Allow me a few shreds of manly dignity on the track?"

I scoff. "Not in this lifetime." We walk through the door and I dig through my bag for my student ID. "And don't worry. You're always manly." Yeah, I've noticed. He's the whole package. Only a blind woman could miss his tousled hair, toned body, and smoldering eyes.

I sign the two of us in then turn to see if he's following me to the locker rooms. He's wearing that all-knowing smirk of his.

"What now?" I ask, exasperated.

He steps to my side. "You just told me I'm pretty and manly in a matter of minutes."

"And?"

He winks. "I'm glad you think so."

After our warm up, Dane delivers me to a room the gym typically uses for classes like yoga and Pilates. Madeline and Ash are already there and, to my surprise, so is James. I take in Dane's grumpy expression. "Really?" I ask.

He looks startled. "I thought you said you weren't reading minds."

"I don't have to. It's written all over your face."

He shakes his head. "I'll see you tomorrow."

I carefully punch him in the arm. "Same time, same place."

He gives me half a smile and walks away.

Entering the room, I drop my bag on the floor and greet my trainers. "Hey guys."

Madeline turns and greets me with a warm smile. "Ready for something new?"

"No meditation?" I half-heartedly joke as I walk toward her. I know it's supposed to calm me, but it feels like I'm coming down off a sugar high.

"No. Ash thinks you and James are ready to practice with one another."

My eyebrows shoot up. Cool.

"Jack will be back tonight," Ash says. "We have no idea when the ideal time will be to advance. We need to get in as much training as possible."

He's right. We have a schedule established with Jack, so we know when to expect him with information from his covert ops. So far Kellan has only forced Lucas to create one other Allegiant, but he's been selectively choosing Guardians and bringing them in on what's going on. Our guess is that they will soon be Allegiant too, and Kellan will make his move.

James smiles and taunts me at the same time. "You ready for a little action?"

He's digging this training just as much as I am. I smirk and take a defensive stance. "Bring it."

"Hold on." Ash steps between us. "While your fighting styles are similar there is one important difference."

I stand up straight to listen.

"Physically you're closely matched. But watch this." He gestures toward James.

James gives him a curt nod and raises his arm in front of him. He holds his hand toward the wall, and a faint ray of light emanates from his palm. A water bottle sitting on the floor explodes, and I jump. How could I forget about the light beam of death?

"I thought you said we were physically matched!" I turn on Ash. "How am I supposed to work around that?"

He walks over and pats my shoulder. "I said you were closely matched, not evenly. And you guessed how. You work around it."

I shoot him a confused look.

"Bob and weave," Madeline says.

Bob and weave? Are these two insane?

"No," Ash says, reading my mind. "This is why we practice."

My expression twists.

"Just be lucky your minds are off limits to each other," Madeline says. "The Allegiant can do some nasty things to human and Guardian minds alike."

"Such as?"

James comes closer to us and there's pain behind his eyes. "I can hear thoughts and capture memories by touch. I can force people to speak the truth. And then there's Erasure," he says.

I'm familiar with the term. It's what Garrett thought happened to me when we learned of my faulty memory. But why does he look sad? "That didn't happen to me," I try to appease him.

"But Projection did."

"Projection?"

"The Allegiant can force images and feelings into the mind," Ash says.

"When you were found on the island, The Allegiant used you to find me," James says. "They needed me to track Garrett through our residual Guardian bond. In order to pull me to you they caused you pain which I felt. One of them projected images into your mind; he showed you something horrible. I never got the chance to ask you what it was. You don't remember, do you?"

I shake my head no.

"They did the same to me to break down my defenses and track Garrett through our bond. It was terrible. I wouldn't wish it on anyone. I hate that I have the ability."

I frown. "What did they show you?"

His eyes dart to Madeline and Ash. "I'd rather not say."

It's obvious he doesn't want to tell me in front of present company. I'll have to ask later. "So can you do anything that you like?"

He shrugs. "I can do that reiki thing, and what I just showed you is pretty cool. Whatever I want to happen occurs through the beam. If I want to immobilize you or cut off your senses or – "

"Kill me?" It's what Kellan tried to do after all.

James looks horrified. "I would never..."

I smile and grab his arm. "I'm kidding! Lighten up. I know you'll use your talents for good."

He gives me a wary look. "This isn't fun and games."

I sigh. "That was a poor attempt at humor. I'm sorry."

He gives me a weak smile.

Ash interrupts. "Let's get down to business, shall we?" He turns to Madeline and extends his hand. She places a weapon in his palm. It's a dagger.

"This," he holds it up, "is your answer to his defenses."

I examine it. It looks like the handle and the blade are one piece and crudely cut from stone. "Is that made out of rock?"

He nods. "We call it an anlace."

As I look closer I can see an almost invisible outline of the amulet I wear on the blade. "How does it work?"

"It's made of the earth and enchanted with the elements. When an Allegiant is struck it calls forth their human side and dispatches them."

Suddenly, I have some serious reservations about today's practice. I glance between James and Ash with a feeling of uncertainty. "I'm not sure I'm comfortable with this."

Ash hands the anlace back to Mad, and she replaces the dagger with another. "That's why you're practicing with this one," he says. "It's not enchanted. You'd feel awful if you killed him." He gives me a wry smile. "And I don't want you hurting yourself either."

I let out a heavy breath. "That can hurt me?"

"What it does to an Allegiant it does to us," Madeline says sadly. "Don't lose control of it."

I focus on her face. Her thoughts reveal her mother's death and my heart aches.

Ash holds out the anlace, and I tentatively take it. It feels oddly perfect in my hand seeing as how I've never held anything remotely this dangerous aside from a kitchen knife. "Now what?"

Ash motions for James and I to back away from each other. He grabs his own weapon and runs through a few moves with me;

although, right now we'll mainly focus on my dodging James' light beam.

"I want you to get the feel for moving with something in your hand," Ash says. "Up until now you've just used your body which isn't enough against a real Allegiant."

"Hey," James speaks up. "I am a real Allegiant."

Ash gives him a blank look. "I meant one that's trying to kill her." He backs away from us. "Look at me when you can," he addresses me. "I'll give you direction through my thoughts. That way James won't know what to expect."

Yikes. Am I ready for this? My body wants to jump into action, but my mind is playing tricks on me. Can I attack someone I used to love?

"Okay." He nods toward James. "Come at her."

Turns out I have no problem attacking my old boyfriend. I admit to holding back at first, but when it became obvious that James wasn't, my pride took over; I wasn't about to be bested. We relentlessly went at each other. James would try to immobilize me which, unfortunately, happened a few times. I'm proud to say he never took control of the anlace though, and he was trying in earnest. We'd dance around one another, dodging each other's defenses, until one of us worked ourselves close enough for physical contact. We'd roll, wrestle, and flip the other until one of us was pinned. Then we'd separate and do it again. I didn't rely on Ash's thoughts after the first few rounds which was a small victory for me. He and Madeline were extremely pleased with how the night went. Maybe this lifestyle is my true calling.

As we walk home, out of nowhere, James shoves my shoulder and I nearly fall. "Hey!" When I regain my balance, I ram his side. He stumbles and I laugh. "Didn't you get enough earlier?"

He smiles. "Tonight was the most fun I've had in months."

I nod in agreement. "It was cool to actually fight. Training with Ash and Madeline is very stop and go. This was a full on battle."

He glances forward. The Larvatus are way ahead of us, already at the next street corner. He threads his fingers through mine as we continue walking.

"Are you ready to manifest tomorrow?" he asks.

"Yes! Practicing teleportation? Are you kidding me?" Ash promised we would work on that next.

James laughs. "You're a natural at this."

I shrug. "I think it's more the bracelet than me, but I am enjoying it."

We're silent for a few seconds, our joined hands swinging back and forth between us. "What will you be working on tomorrow?" I ask.

"Finding a place to live. While you're in class the three of us will be snooping around our hometown for a place to stay."

Talk about being self-absorbed! I never gave a second thought to what James and The Larvatus would do when I moved this weekend. I guess I figured they stay at Garrett's place since they can all manifest wherever they want. "Why not stay here?"

He shoots me a look that says 'Don't be stupid.' "Like we'd be far from you and Dane. We need to stick together."

He squeezes my hand, and I get the feeling this is about more than that. "Strictly a business move then?"

He's silent for a few seconds, a tiny smile dancing across his lips.

"Something funny?"

He stops walking. "I never...who knew we would share this? It's..."

"Freaking awesome?" I finish.

"Yeah." He grins.

We don't move and the longer he stares at me, I find myself getting lost in his handsome face. His eyes are so *blue*. "You have amazing eyes," I say quietly.

His expression softens. "I could say the same about yours."

Instantly, I pout. "You could? Does that mean you won't?"

He lets out a small laugh. "No." He raises his hand and slowly trails his fingers down my cheek. "All of you is beautiful. Even these," he traces my lips with his thumb, "when they're not being sarcastic."

I narrow my eyes to calm my pounding heart. "They'd have nothing to do without sarcasm."

He leans into me. "I could occupy their time."

His mouth feels soft and gentle on mine; his kiss is much less demanding than Dane's. It's nice, but it feels like he's holding back; probably because he thinks I'm going to shove him away. Instead, I reach out, find his waist, and pull myself against him.

Shocked, he steps back. "You're okay with this?"

Apparently so. I should probably wonder what that means about my sanity. I scrunch up my face. "You're right. We're supposed to be mortal enemies."

He quickly moves to me again. "Forget what I said."

"Nope. You've done it now. The mood is ruined." I turn and walk away.

He groans and draws out my name. "Emmmma! Come back."

I shake my head and smile over my shoulder as I pick up the pace. He smirks and, before I know it, it's an all-out chase. It's a good thing it's nearly midnight and there aren't many people out. James and I blow past a few pedestrians on the sidewalk and even race past Madeline and Ash.

"So much for being inconspicuous," I hear Ash chastise as we run past.

Adrenaline pumping, I make it to my building first and fumble with my keys. Damn it! If I could manifest alone I could poof myself somewhere. Within seconds, James runs up behind me just as I turn the key in the lock. I push my way inside leaving the front door open and race to my apartment only to be stopped again. Ugh! Again with the keys! He wraps his arms around me from behind and sets his chin in the crook of my neck.

"Your resistance is futile."

Whatever. I move against him. "I can totally toss you and you know it." I manage to turn my key and kick the door open with my foot. It leaves a dent. Whoops. I end up pulling him inside with me as I break out of his arms. I spin around and drop my bag with a wide smile. "Now what?"

He closes the door and looks at me. I recognize that expression. He slowly steps forward and I place my hand against his chest to stop him from moving further. His heart is beating like crazy. Just like mine.

"I want a do over," he says.

The way he looks at me makes my insides melt even though my conscience has awakened. "Do you think that's wise?"

He doesn't hesitate. "Yes."

I'm at a loss for words.

He stares at me for a few brief seconds then moves to hold my face in his hands. He lowers his lips to mine and moves against me, firmly this time. I lose myself; the hand I had pressed to his chest slides around his neck while the other curls around his wrist. We pull each other closer; when our bodies meet that now-familiar anticipation starts to build in my belly. This feeling should be illegal. It causes all rational thought to leave my mind. How is it possible that two people can make me feel this way? That has to be wrong!

James releases my face and his hands travel over my shoulders and along the sides of my body as we consume one another in the matter of what feels like a minute. Things have escalated into some sort of frenzy similar to our fighting, but instead of dodging one another we can't get close enough. He winds his arms around my waist, pressing me hard against him. His mouth leaves mine and appears under my ear, then travels down my throat.

My cell screams from the floor, startling us. Hello reality! I freeze but James doesn't. "Ignore it," he says against my neck.

"I can't." I try to lean away. "Who would call this late?"

He lets out a heavy sigh and rests his forehead on my shoulder. A second later he moves back, keeping one arm around my waist. I take the few steps toward my bag and remove my phone from the front pocket. I see it's my home number and my heart instantly stops beating.

"Hello?" I try not to sound panicked.

"Emma?" my mother asks. "Where are you?" She sounds flustered.

"At my place. Where else would I be?"

"I mean are you sitting down?"

Instantly, I drop to the floor. James follows and kneels beside me. "I am now."

"Em, your father and I are coming to get you. When are you finished with your last exam?"

"Thursday around eleven. Why are you coming early? You're freaking me out."

I hear her take a deep breath. "The police just left the house. Patrick escaped. They can't find him."

Chapter 12

Patrick disappeared this morning during a routine transfer to a less crowded facility. I thought that stuff only happened in the movies.

The police stated they were doing everything in their power to find him and in the meantime we needed to stay alert and call immediately if he surfaced. I managed to calm my mother by reassuring her that I'd seen no sign of him and that Dane was still here. She was further appeased when I offered no resistance to moving home a few days early. The only reason I was staying until Saturday was to give myself ample time to pack. I desperately wanted to tell her I can defend myself, not to mention I have some kick ass friends with supernatural powers. Instead, I had to settle for repeating that I wasn't scared and begging her not to worry. God help Patrick if he decides to mess with me now.

James went next door to inform Dane, and I filled The Larvatus in when they returned. The boxes I had been sporadically collecting for the move immediately appeared after that, and they all insisted on helping me gather my things. LB wandered around confused by the commotion until Madeline found a paper bag for her to play hide-n-seek in.

James angrily chucks my DVDs into a box. "I can't believe that asshole vanished."

"It's okay," I reply to try to calm him. Although, I know I'd feel a million times different if I could remember my attack. "I'm much stronger than I used to be. If he decides to show up I can take him." Actually, I would relish the opportunity.

He pauses from boxing my movies to smirk. "I would love to see that."

"Me, too," Dane agrees from across the room.

They make me smile. "Should I charge admission?"

"I'd pay to watch," Dane says. "I bet Matt and Shel and your family would, too."

I laugh. Maybe after this Allegiant crisis is over I should become a wrestler.

Movement in the center of the room catches my eye, and I turn to see Jack materialize. "Hey there," I greet him. It's funny how his manifesting doesn't faze me. I briefly wonder what it will feel like when I get to do it. "Ash!" I call toward the kitchen. "Jack is here."

Ash appears around the corner with Madeline right behind him. "Any news?"

Jack nods then looks confused. "What's with all the packing?"

"I'm moving earlier than expected," I explain. "Sayonara Western and hello home in two days."

He frowns. "Did anyone think to inform me? Unlike most people here I can't read minds."

I look around. No one mentioned the move to Jack? "Sorry," I apologize. "Will you need my address?"

"A general location will suffice." He crosses his arms.

James interjects to tell Jack where we're from and I sense Dane move to stand behind me. Over my shoulder he whispers, "How was practice?"

I look at him and whisper back. "Good."

"Did things get physical?"

I make a face. "Well, yeah. Why?"

"I didn't know making out was a defense tactic."

My eyes get wide. "Excuse me?"

He smirks and steps back, innocently rubbing the side of his neck with two fingers. Instantly my hand flies up to cover the same spot on my own. Shit! What does he see?

"We plan to look for a place of our own near Emma," I hear Ash tell Jack, "in order to continue training. Can you visit us tomorrow to learn the location?"

"Actually, some time among the living has become necessary. Turns out I'm a wanted man."

We all shoot Jack questioning looks and he grimaces. "Kellan read Garrett's mind; he knows I've visited. The good people of the Intermediate have been asked to keep an eye out for me."

James shifts his weight. "Then we can guarantee he's read Lucas' mind as well."

Jack nods. "I went to check on Garrett first. He stopped me before I said anything; he told me not to speak and simply said his thoughts weren't safe."

"And Lucas?"

"I avoided him entirely."

All eyes dart to Ash for guidance.

"It's too bad we won't be able to get more information from them," he says. "I'd hoped we would have a little more time. What did you learn otherwise?"

"They've created another Allegiant," Jack says. "Their number sits at four."

Concern flashes across James' face. "That evens us. We should act."

The thought of the big showdown happening so soon causes my breath to hitch. Am I ready for this?

"No." Ash purses his lips in thought. "We have three Larvatus, an Allegiant, and a Guardian on our side, not to mention countless other friends if I ask them." He gives James a reassuring glance. "We have time. I'm not going in unless I'm one hundred percent sure we're all coming out. You and Emma need as much practice as possible." He turns to Jack. "You'll continue to visit the Intermediate sporadically, yes?"

Jack looks offended. "Of course."

I let out a slow breath. I'm glad to hear Ash has our best interests at heart even though I never assumed any different.

"Then we will continue as planned." Ash takes a step back. "Now, I have a kitchen to pack. Care to help?"

Jack makes a face, but follows Ash just the same.

"I'll start on the bathroom," Madeline volunteers.

"No," I stop her. "I've got it." Now that we've been debriefed, I need a mirror. If I really wear evidence of James' kiss I need to do something about it.

As I make the short walk to the bathroom I pass Dane. "Where you headed?" he asks with fake innocence.

I shoot him a look. "To pee." I refuse to let him rile me any further as I'm sure a self-inflicted trip to Guilty Town is imminent.

I shut the door and examine my reflection. There's a small red splotch on the side of my neck, but nothing close to a hickey. This tiny thing drew Dane's attention? Does he inspect me with a microscope? I can't think of one person that would see this and assume I'd made out with someone! Nevertheless, I take my ponytail down and bring my hair over my shoulders to hide it. Now I'm self-conscious.

I use the facilities then leave to get a box to pack my stuff. Dane catches me before I can make a hasty retreat. "Find everything all right?"

"Barely," I say, annoyed.

He laughs at our private joke, but the humor doesn't reach his eyes. "I like your hair. Why'd you change it?"

"I was getting a headache."

"From having it up?"

"No, from you."

He chuckles.

"Have you finished interrogating me? Can I go pack now?"

"Sure." He smiles.

As I walk away I try to figure him out. Is he trying to get under my skin to make me feel bad? Because it's working. As I enter the bathroom, I toss the box on the counter and sigh. A restless night of thinking lies ahead of me. Guaranteed.

I have no regrets when it comes to my decision to leave campus. It's crazy to admit, but even simple things, like breathing, feel easier at home. I'm sure the end of the semester has a lot to do with how I feel, but I've noticed LB seems happier, too. True, my parents dote on her, but I'm sure she appreciates the laid back atmosphere. Compared to the string of guests constantly parading through our personal space at Western, I do too. My mind works better with occasional silence.

I smooth my sweater over my waistline and consult the mirror quickly. When I arrived home, and was confronted by a fully decorated tree and stockings hanging from the mantle, it hit me that Christmas is less than ten days away. I've done absolutely no shopping! Now that I've had time to think about buying gifts, today is the day to get it done. As I ready myself to head downstairs my cell vibrates against the dresser.

Busy?

It's James. Madeline and Ash bought him a phone in an effort to keep us connected since we can't simply walk next door and talk anymore. They didn't like the idea of him manifesting in my house, so they thought this was a better option.

Yep. Going shopping.

Seconds pass. *For what?*

Christmas.

I can't wait to see what you get me.

Aw, crap. Is he joking? Should I get him something? I was only planning on buying for my parents, my brother Mike, and his girlfriend Kate.

Are we celebrating??? I send back. I hope he says no. I have no idea what to get him.

Instead of texting back, my phone rings. "Hello?"

"Believe it or not, I could sense the panic in your message," James laughs. "I was kidding. You don't have to buy me anything."

I don't want to sound relieved, but I do. "Okay good. I'm already running low on time to find gifts for my family as it is."

"Maybe next year we could do Secret Santa," he muses.

I smile. "Is there something you needed?"

"The mats arrived today and Ash is installing them now. Practice is on for tonight. What time can you be here?"

Yes! With my move and The Larvatus needing a place to stay, we haven't been able to train for four days. My energy levels are crazy. I've been trying to meditate like Madeline taught me, but it's much easier when I'm with her.

"How does six sound? I should be back by then."

"Great. You should see the basement. It's even cooler than the rec center."

Madeline and Ash found a house to rent about fifteen minutes away from mine on a large piece of secluded property. It's on a private lake and sports roughly 6,000 square feet. It came furnished, but without a ready-made training facility; so it's taken a few days for The Larvatus to pull together a home gym. James loves it there; he's staying with them in what the realtor called the "guest apartment." He has his own separate entrance and everything. I suppose there's nothing like living in luxury if you're forced to stay away from your real home.

"I can't wait," I tell him and I mean it. Not only will I be able to work out, but I get see their place and all of them instead of merely talking on the phone.

"You still have the address right?" he asks.

"Yes. Let me get going, so I can be there on time."

"All right. See you later."

"Later." I hang up. It's hard to keep myself from skipping down the stairs.

"Where are you headed?" my father asks as I make a beeline for the back door.

"To the mall," I say as I shrug on my coat.

"Alone?" he asks, worried.

I try not to sigh. This has been the only point of contention since I returned to live under his roof. With Patrick still missing, my parents are hesitant to let me out of their sight, let alone go anywhere by myself.

"Yes." I give him a stern, yet please-let-me-do-this, look. "I have to Christmas shop and I can't have you or mom spying."

"Call up Kate and see if she's busy," he suggests.

"Dad," I say matter-of-factly. "I'm buying for her, too. That won't work."

A knock on the door interrupts us, and we look at each other confused.

"Stay put," he says and leaves the kitchen to answer it. Knowing him, I'm sure he suspects our visitor might be Patrick – like he'd be one to knock.

I finish zipping my coat and follow him with my eyes as he makes it to the door and pulls it open. "Well hello there!" he greets our guest.

"Hey, Mr. Donohue. Is Emma around?" It's Dane.

"She sure is. Come on in, come on in." He steps out of the way.

Dane catches my eye from the door as he stomps the snow from his shoes and gives me that damn perfect grin of his. I can't help it and give him a genuine smile in return. I haven't physically seen him since the move either. We've spoken on the phone, but I think we needed a few days apart, if only for the feeling of being out of each other's hair for a minute.

"What are you doing here?" I ask as I walk up to meet him.

"Bringing you this." He presents a silvery-gray glittered envelope. It's addressed to me in fancy calligraphy.

"Impressive." I lift my eyebrows. "What is it?"

"Open it and find out." He hands it over.

I take it, curious, and turn it around. I gently tear the flap, so as not to annihilate its prettiness.

"Today," Dane says impatiently.

I shoot him a look and pull out the heavy card stock to read an elaborate invitation to the annual Bay Woods employee holiday party.

"On New Year's Eve?" I ask.

He nods. "Normally, my dad and Lily have it on Christmas Eve, but this year they wanted to change it up, so people wouldn't be in such a rush to get home."

A huge grin breaks out on my face. "It's a masquerade ball." That sounds like so much fun.

"I know." He smiles. "Normally I dread these things, but this will be the first year I'll have someone there I want to see." He steps closer then realizes my dad is still standing behind him. He clears his throat. "Anyway, Shel's getting an invite too, so I figure she'll bring Matt and we can all celebrate the New Year together."

He stares at me and widens his eyes. We recently discussed this would be his signal to give me permission to read his mind. We got tangled in a conversation the other night about his purpose in pointing out I'd kissed James. I told him I felt he was trying to make me feel bad, and he was adamant that if I had just read his thoughts I would have known that wasn't his intent.

I concentrate on his eyes and hear *"Your dad makes me nervous."* I stifle a laugh. Then I hear *"I want to see you dressed up in a really bad way. Wear something tight please."*

I have to resist the urge to keep my mouth shut.

"Well, that's awfully nice of your parents," my father comments as he rounds us and peers over my shoulder to read the invite. I hold it out for him. "Is the party this big every year?"

"It is," Dane responds. "It's a bit ostentatious if you ask me."

My dad smiles. "I don't think so. It sounds like they care about their staff." He looks at me. "I take it you'll be needing a dress of some sort?" He reaches for his wallet. "Since you're headed to the mall maybe Dane can go with you and help pick something out."

I eye him suspiciously. Way to work my shopping trip into the conversation so I don't have to go alone! "No, Dad, I'm sure Dane has other things to do. Besides, I have my own money; put yours away." Little does he know I have around thirty grand, thanks to Lucas.

"Actually," Dane says, "I had nothing planned today other than the delivery of your invitation." He smiles. "I'll go with you if you want me to."

Again with the eyes. *"Spend time with me."*

My heart does a somersault. "Okay," I concede to both of them, but warn Dane. "I'm going Christmas shopping. It's going to be tedious and boring."

"Anything is better than sitting home watching the Lions lose. Did you see the game last week?" he asks my dad. "Terrible!"

My father groans. "No one can snag defeat from the jaws of victory like Detroit. They led the whole damn game to give it away in the last quarter!"

I walk toward the door as Dane and my dad follow. The sad state of our football team has been irritating my father since he was my age.

"Our last season was so much better," he continues to rant. "I should have known not to get my hopes up."

Dane laughs. "I hear you."

We step outside and say goodbye. I stop on the step and look at my dad before he shuts the door. He winks at me, clearly pleased I'm not leaving the house unattended. When I turn around I see Dane walking toward a car I don't recognize. "What happened to the Camaro?"

"She's seasonal," he says over his shoulder. "Now that I'm home I put her in storage." He reaches for the door handle. "This is my winter car."

I step to his side and appraise his "winter car." It's black and sleek and expensive. It's a Cadillac CTS. "Do you refuse to drive anything that costs less than forty grand?" I ask incredulously.

He smiles. "You don't like it?"

"I didn't say that. I just think it's a little pretty to subject to road salt. You are familiar with Michigan winters, right?"

He rolls his eyes and opens the door. "Get in the car."

I shrug and do as I'm told.

As we make our way to the expressway, I turn on him. "You're seriously nervous around my dad?"

"Of course," he says. "What guy isn't intimidated by a girl's father?"

"Don't be. He likes you."

He looks unsure. "You think? Have you read his mind?"

"No," I laugh. "I can just tell. Although, I'm sure he wouldn't appreciate your unclean thoughts. 'Wear something tight please'?" I mockingly quote him.

He takes my hand. "Can you blame me for wanting to dress the package?"

My eyes get wide. "Since when am I a gift? Do you think that means I'll let you unwrap me?"

He smirks. "One can only hope." He lifts my hand and plants a quick kiss on the back. "Maybe I should ask Santa?"

I pull my hand from his. "You know the rules. All clothes stay on."

"That's your rule not mine."

I give him an "oh please" look; although, I can't deny that my body responds to his words. I feel too warm in my coat all of a sudden. But, we've had this discussion. I can't do with him what I wouldn't do with James; my rules prevent all of us from getting hurt. A full month has yet to pass since I've met them again. If anything happens it needs to remain at first base.

"I have been a good boy." He pouts.

"Let it go already!"

He laughs and grasps my hand again, then turns serious. "You will come to the party right?"

A huge smile breaks across my face. "I wouldn't miss it."

Chapter 13

I catch a glimpse of the clock on the wall at Express. "Ugh!"
"What is it?"

"It's almost six!" I throw the sweater I was examining for Kate back on the rack. "I'm supposed to be at practice in ten minutes."

Dane makes a face. "You have fight club tonight?"

I nod vigorously as I dig for my phone. "The mats came today." Dane knows I've been waiting for the home gym to be complete.

"Why didn't you tell me?" he asks.

I shrug as I scroll through my contacts. "I was having so much fun I forgot." It's true; our time together has flown by. I select James' name and send him a quick message.

Completely lost track of time. On my way.

I toss my phone back in my purse and shift my shopping bags. "Looks like Kate's getting a gift card." I pluck one off a nearby rack and head to the registers.

"What a completely thoughtless gift," Dane chides me.

I stick my tongue out at him. I gave him the same spiel earlier when he tried to get away with purchasing the same thing for his father and stepmother. It took some time and convincing, but I managed to get him to put a little more effort into his gifts. He ended up with his and hers Burberry watches. Very nice. And very expensive. I tried to explain it's the thought that counts, not going broke, but he assured me the cost wasn't an issue. He then said they would probably faint at receiving something from him that wasn't redeemable.

As we wait to checkout, I peruse the displays near the counter. "Ah ha," I say and step to the side to grab a pair of hoop earrings. Three different shades of copper strands wind around each other to create delicate circles. "Thoughtful gift achieved. These are so Kate."

"I wouldn't know," he says. "I've never met her."

"I never introduced you?" She and my brother have been dating for, well, forever.

"I've only met your mom and dad." We move up in line.

Huh. "You should stop by the next time Kate and my brother are over."

"When will that be?"

I think about it. "Most likely Christmas Day. We always do gifts and dinner. You should come by after your family thing."

"We don't have a family thing," Dane says. "We usually host the staff party Christmas Eve and then kind of ignore Christmas Day."

"That's not fun," I tell him as we step up in line again. "Do you think it will be different this year? With the party on New Year's?"

He shrugs. "Don't know."

I feel bad for him. I still enjoy the holidays even though I'm well past believing in Santa Claus; although, I may want to revisit that belief. After all, there are Guardians and an Intermediate. Maybe the jolly red man does exist.

"Well, consider yourself invited to the Donohue Family Christmas," I say. "It's not fancy, but it's a good time. That is if you want to come."

At first he blinks at me like I've said something crazy. Then, a slow smile spreads across his face. He wraps his arm around my shoulders and plants a kiss on the top of my head. "I would love to come to your family Christmas."

I lean into him, but I'm confused. What was that about?

Before I can ask, we're next in line, and I purchase Kate's presents. After I drop nearly eighty bucks I turn to him. "I'm sorry I forgot about training. You don't mind driving me do you? If you want you can take me home and I'll jump in my car."

He fishes his keys from his pocket. "I do wish our day could stay free of the supernatural, but I am kind of curious to see this place where Madeline and Ash are staying."

"Me too." As we make our way out of the store and to the mall entrance my phone chimes. My hands are full, so I ask Dane to pull it from my purse. "Who is it?"

"James." He frowns and shows me the text.

Hurry up loser.

I laugh. "Here." I trade two of my bags for my phone and reply as we walk. *Well isn't that the pot calling the kettle black.*

Seconds pass and he responds. *Nope. I never lose.*

I text back. *Liar.*

Dane and I make it to his car and stow our packages. I pull up The Larvatus' new address on my phone as James sends another message.

If you ever get here I'll prove it.

I snort and start to reply.

"What is so fascinating?" Dane asks.

"James thinks he's better than me." I send my message.

Bring it on dork. You're going down.

The road on which Madeline and Ash are staying appears desolate in the dark. A few homes are scattered here and there, but they sit so far back from the dirt road you wouldn't know they existed if it wasn't for the mailboxes at the end of the driveways. When we come upon their address, we pass through an open gate flanked by brick columns. *Fancy,* I think to myself.

The drive to the house is long and curves to hug the lake it runs alongside. After several feet it straightens out leading us through a conglomeration of trees before delivering us to the front door.

And what a front door it is.

Dane lets out a low whistle. "How did they find this place again?"

I shrug. "James said something about a realtor."

Leaning forward, I look through the windshield at the house that looms before us. It appears modern, yet not. From here it looks to be at least three stories high with several large windows gracing the main floors. Smaller dormer windows sit at the very top. The outside is covered in rust colored brick except for three large sections, the middle and both ends, that are decorated with multi-colored stone. The house is symmetrical; the stone facades triangular in shape. The two on the ends resemble small towers. "Would you call that a turret?" I ask Dane, pointing up.

"Definitely."

He steps out of the car and I follow, tilting my head back to get the whole picture. I didn't know houses like this existed where I live. We're such a small Midwestern town. Soft light shines through most of the windows on the first floor leading my eye to the oversize main door. It looks heavy and made of a dark wood. A gorgeous light fixture hangs above the entrance appearing to be centuries old and three large circular steps made of stone radiate out from the porch.

We tentatively make our way up the stairs and find the doorbell. I almost expect a butler to answer, but instead we get James.

"Where's the dungeon?" I joke when he opens the door.

"Funny." He smiles. "It's actually a torture chamber."

"Let me guess," I step inside as he holds the door wide, "you're referring to the new gym?"

"Absolutely." His smile fades a little when he notices Dane is with me. "Hey."

"Hey," Dane says and explains his presence. "I'm playing chauffeur today."

James turns to me. "Something wrong with your car?"

I shake my head. "He stopped by as I was leaving to shop. We went together."

I can tell James is displeased that I brought a guest. To change the subject I look around the room. "Wow. Do we get a tour?"

"Tour first or practice?" he asks.

"Practice," Madeline answers for me, appearing from nowhere. She smiles and waves for us to follow her.

James, Dane, and I exit the foyer and pass under a balcony of sorts which is flanked on each end by a staircase. We walk through a great room that combines the living area and kitchen and pass a formal dining area off by itself, a game room, and what I assume is a guest bath. Madeline leads us to a closed door which she opens to reveal stairs. We follow her down to the basement where, when we turn the corner, I'm shocked. This place could rival any training facility in the United States.

"Are you kidding?" I look at Mad and James wide-eyed. All they do is smile.

I wander through the equipment running my hand over some of the machines. Treadmills, rowers, bikes, steppers, ellipticals, weight benches and free weights all fill the area. Further in I find a trampoline and then stop short when I see the entire back of the room has been transformed into a climbing wall with harnesses and ropes dangling from the ceiling. My mind registers the sound of dull thuds, and I turn to see Ash pounding away on a punching bag. He stops for a second to wave a gloved hand at me.

"Let me show you this." James grasps my wrist and leads me over a large open area of mats that I assume are for our training and meditation. Medicine balls, jump ropes, gloves, and other accessories line the walls we pass. James pulls me into another room which might have been a large bathroom or in home spa at one point.

"A hot tub?" I ask in awe.

"For aching muscles." He winks at me. "There's another one upstairs on the deck. Here's the sauna," he opens a cedar door, "and then there are two shower stalls around the corner."

"How did you guys do all of this in four days?" Dane asks skeptically.

"This room was pretty much like you see it," James says. "The bathroom was here, the tub, the sauna. All Ash added were the lockers."

He leads us further and we come across about ten lockers next to open shelves stacked with towels. James opens the door at the end. "This one is yours," he says to me. It's fully stocked.

I step forward and examine the contents. A stack of workout clothes sits neatly folded on the shelf and a pair of running shoes sits at the bottom. Everything has tags.

"Where did you get this?" I ask. "How much do I owe you?"

"They're from me and Ash," Madeline says from behind us. "I saved the receipts in case something doesn't fit."

I turn toward her. "Thanks, but you shouldn't have. Please let me pay you." Why are they buying me things? This feels awkward.

She smiles reading my mind. "You're one of us and we take care of each other. We want you to feel comfortable here."

"I'd feel comfortable regardless," I assure her. What could I possibly give them in return? Should I buy them Christmas gifts?

Madeline reaches out and takes my hand. "No," she says reading my thoughts again. "Your decision to participate in our way of life is gift enough for us."

I'm confused for a second. "I didn't think I had a choice."

"You always have a choice," she says. "You're Gifted, remember?" She taps the amulet at my wrist. "You take this off and your abilities go with it."

I did know that. I guess I pushed it to the back of my mind since I was enjoying my new talents so much, not to mention taking the bracelet off will bring me physical pain. "Well, it's still awfully generous of you," I tell her. "I will find a way to reciprocate." Maybe I can make them dinner.

She laughs and releases my hand as Dane asks, "So, are you expecting company?" He eyes the other lockers. "This is a lot of equipment for the four of you."

"There's no gym membership," Ash surprises us from the doorway. "You're welcome to join us anytime."

My eyes jump to James, and I notice his jaw tense.

"Actually, we do have some friends in the area," Madeline says. "One of them helped us find this place. We may have some visitors from time to time."

I raise my eyebrows. "Do you plan to live here permanently?"

"We're considering it," Ash says. "We have several homes; our main residence is in Hope Mills. When you're alive for one hundred-plus years it's nice to change up the scenery once and awhile."

I can't even fathom how wealthy they must be to keep up this lifestyle. "Are your houses all this big?" Suddenly, I feel terrible about them staying with me in my tiny apartment at Western. How crappy must that have been? Ash sleeping on the couch and Madeline sharing a bed with me.

"Not all of them, maybe two," Madeline says like it's no big deal.

"Are we going to practice or are we going to talk all night?" James asks, impatient. He nods toward my locker. "Get changed. We have some time to make up for."

"That's right." I cross my arms. "We wouldn't want your skills to get rusty now would we?"

He rolls his eyes as he follows Ash and Dane out into the main room.

"If you'd rather you can dress around the corner," Madeline says. "There's a stall next to the showers."

Of course they'd have a changing room too. "Did you guys think of everything?" I ask as I take off my coat.

"We were lucky with the setup down here. The previous owner designed the basement for her elderly mother-in-law who needed the open space to get around. The spa and sauna were for her physical therapy. That's why there's a separate entrance and a small kitchen off the other end."

A small kitchen? It must have been behind me when I came down the stairs.

"I can't imagine what a place like this costs," I say as I untie my shoes. "What do you...?" I stop myself. I was about to ask her what they do for money. Nosey much?

She laughs. "The Charmed look out for one another. I said the realtor was a friend? The owner of this place is too. We're all Larvatus. We're actually staying here for free."

I frown. "Why did I think you were renting?"

She shrugs. "Natural assumption?"

"I guess."

Madeline smiles. "To answer your question, we live by connections, odd jobs, and investments. Some of us manage to have inconspicuous careers, but most of us move from job to job. When you work at the same organization for years and haven't aged much rumors really start to fly around the office."

"I bet." I select a set of clothes and close the locker door. "Okay, I'll be out in a sec."

"Emma." She rests her hand on my arm. "Ash and I want you to know that you're more than welcome to stay here with us if you ever need to. We have more than enough space."

Her offer makes me feel all mushy inside like a Hallmark card. Who am I to make them care about me so much? "Thanks," I tell her sincerely. "I'm enjoying my time with my family, but I'll keep that in mind."

She smiles again and turns to leave. "I'm glad. I'll meet you out there."

It's nearly ten o'clock when we finish, and I'm leaning against the wall chugging bottles of water like I've been stuck in the Mojave for a week. Practice was great; it felt so good to move and stretch again. James and I managed to stay on an even keel tonight; neither of us can claim victory over the other due to the type of exercises Ash was having us perform.

"Next time Donohue," James threatens me.

"Whatever Davis." I brush him off with a smile.

I peel myself away from the wall and walk over to where Dane has been patiently observing us for the last four hours. "Do you want to check this out?" I ask him and present my anlace.

He eyes it warily and then runs his fingers across the blade.

"You can hold it." I push it toward him.

He takes it by the handle, testing the weight, and then gives it back to me. "Nice."

"All you have to say is nice?"

He looks up at me and widens his eyes. I hear his thoughts. *"This worries me on so many levels."*

Before I can ask him why, James appears behind my shoulder. "Ready for your tour?"

"Give me ten minutes to change."

I jump under the shower, wash off my sweat, and jump out in record time. Once I dress and rejoin everyone, we head up the stairs. When we get to the top it hits me.

"You have to work tomorrow!"

Dane turns to me. "Yeah. So?"

Talk about selfish. "It's late," I say. "Why didn't you say something? What time do have to be there?"

"Eight."

I look apologetically at The Larvatus and James. "Can we take a rain check on the tour? Dane needs to get home."

Dane frowns at me. "What am I, twelve? We can take the tour."

I push him toward the door. "I will not be responsible for your being late and or grumpy." I look at James. "Same time tomorrow?"

He nods, but looks disappointed.

"Really, Emma, it's not a big deal," Dane protests.

I continue to lead him to the door. "Don't make me carry you. You know I can."

He shoots me an exasperated look.

"I'll see you at six," I say to my friends as I open the door. "Thanks for everything. Tomorrow I'll bring snacks."

"I like chocolate," Ash says and it makes me laugh.

Madeline pipes up. "I like cheesecake."

"Chocolate cheesecake it is then."

Once we're inside his car Dane turns to me. "Why did you do that?"

I buckle my seatbelt. "I've taken up all your time tonight and you have an early morning. It's not fair."

He starts the engine. "And here I thought you wanted me all to yourself." He backs up the car and then turns us around. He pauses before he hits the gas. "It doesn't matter what time it is as long as I'm with you."

I give his hand a squeeze.

We make it to the end of the long drive and turn out on to the road. "What did you mean by you're worried on so many levels?" I ask.

He clutches the steering wheel. "I've never seen you fight before. And with a weapon no less. It's disturbing."

"Why? I'm good at it."

"Extremely good," he says. "I just hate to think of someone really trying to hurt you. It scares the hell out of me."

I don't know what to say. I don't want anyone attacking me either, but I'm confident in my abilities. It must look weird watching me wrestle James. Wait.

"This is about more than my fighting isn't it?"

He sighs. "You're right. Your boyfriend is a whole other level of worry."

Silence.

"Care to elaborate?"

"You're going to be spending a lot of time over there. He has his own space, a hot tub, and his hands all over you. Yeah, I'm concerned."

Does he think I'd throw caution to the wind and take up with James just because? "What do you think this is? Girls Gone Wild? I'm not going over there to go hot tubbing!"

Dane shoots me a look. "You know what I mean."

"That's why we have rules. Do you think I would break them?"

"I know I want you to break them with me. I'm sure he's thinking the exact same thing."

We sit in silence the rest of the way to my house which gives me time to think. When he pulls into the driveway and parks, I unfasten my belt and give him an apologetic look. "Listen, I'm sorry I worry you. It's not my intent, and I don't want to fight."

"Are we fighting?" he asks. "I thought we were having an honest discussion."

I give him a tiny smile of relief. "If you think it's better we don't hang out until this Kellan business is over I'd understand. I'm sure if the situation were reversed I wouldn't want you wrestling with Teagan."

He smirks. "Who says we won't be? Her dad's office is pretty big."

I give him an uncertain look and he makes a face. "Scratch that comment. It wasn't even remotely funny."

"No," I say. "What you choose to do with her is your business. I have no hold over you."

He leans across the console and looks into my eyes. When he moves closer, we end up kissing until I'm winded.

"When are you going to realize that's not true?" he whispers.

I bite my lip. "That kiss was pretty convincing."

"Was it?" He smiles. "Then we're making progress. I'm not giving up any of my time with you."

Chapter 14

"Ready?"

I nod and close my eyes. This will be my second manifestation. The first was three days ago, when The Larvatus helped transport me outside their house and on to the lawn. As Ash takes my right hand and Madeline my left, I concentrate on feeling weightless like they taught me. Today we're going somewhere new.

An effervescent tingle begins at my fingertips and travels up my arms toward my chest. It spreads throughout my body, making its way through my veins and causing them to feel like they're carbonated. The sensation builds and builds until suddenly it's gone. That's when I know we've arrived.

I open my eyes to find myself standing on an outcropping of rock that juts precariously from a tall bluff. A cool wind blows and tosses my hair around my face. As I tuck the strands behind my ears, I look out over a mountainous valley forested by trees that have lost their leaves for the winter season. Multiple shades of brown, tan, and evergreen pine interrupt the sprinkling of snow that covers the ground. The dreary colors contrast with the bright blue sky, and it's as if I can see forever in any direction. The sun decides to peek out from behind a random cloud and the view takes my breath away.

"Where are we?"

"Hawksbill Crag," Ash answers.

When I give him a questioning look he clarifies. "The Ozark Mountains."

The only thing I can think to say is "Get out!" I'm so eloquent.

Madeline's melodic laugh echoes around us. "The view is beautiful even in December."

"Amazing," I agree. I walk as far as I dare toward the edge of the rock and peer over the side. It's a long way down. I take a deep breath of fresh air and then exhale slowly. "Is this what you do for fun? Manifest yourselves around the globe?"

"And sometimes beyond."

Right. Despite knowing the purpose of the journey I'm still curious to see the Intermediate.

I wrap my arms around my body against the wind. Even though the view is pretty, it's cold up here. I turn to find Ash crouched down with one knee set against the rock, his elbow resting on the other, and his chin between his forefinger and thumb. He stares at the horizon deep in thought. "Jack said Garrett was looking rough," I say quietly. "How much time do you think we have?"

"Less than two weeks," he responds.

He sounds so sure I avert my gaze and stare at my shoes. Less than two weeks. On one hand, I'm excited to finally do this. Let's rescue some Guardians and put Kellan in his place already! But, I'd be lying if I said the thought of someone getting hurt or dying hadn't crossed my mind. If something happens to James, Madeline, or Ash how could I not bear some of the responsibility? And what if I'm the one who ends up mortally wounded? There's no coming back from death a second time.

Madeline either reads my mind or senses my concern because she's next to me in two strides. "You're ready," she says with confidence. "Any further practice is icing on the cake."

"Cheesecake?" I smile. I was true to my word and brought dessert that second night of training. For a little thing she sure can eat; although, I'm one to talk lately. My appetite has been insane which hasn't gone unnoticed. My mother actually cornered me yesterday to make sure I wasn't pregnant. Talk about awkward.

Madeline flushes. "My one and only weakness."

"I beg to differ," Ash chuckles and stands. He approaches Madeline and wraps his arms around her from behind. "I'd like to think I make you go weak in the knees."

She rolls her eyes and pats his arm. "Okay, I have two weaknesses."

He kisses her temple and it makes me smile. They love each other so much.

The wind picks up again, and I hold myself. Madeline notices. "Let's go back," she says to Ash. "Emma's cold."

"Sorry." I shrug. "I came unprepared. I didn't think to bring a man to keep me warm."

Ash snickers and Madeline elbows him.

"What?" I ask defensively.

Ash grins. "Which *coat* would you have brought?"

My mouth falls open, speechless.

"Ignore him," Madeline says. "I do." She removes herself from his embrace and clutches my hand. "Get over here," she chastises her man. "She can't do this without us."

Our return from Arkansas ends our practice for the day and, shortly after, I find myself roaming around James' apartment sipping hot chocolate. With Madeline and Ash's help, James has been busy making the space his own. In addition to the furniture that was already there, he's added two barstools under the counter that separates the dining area from the kitchen. In the living room, a new stereo system complete with surround sound speakers sits on the floor, fresh from its box. James kneels among the electronics, consulting instructions and pulling wires, trying to connect everything to the flat screen TV.

As I pass one of the side tables I notice another new addition. Pictures.

"Where did you get these?" I ask, curious.

"What?" He tears his eyes away from the blue and red cables.

"These pictures." I lean in close and study them. The first photo is of James and his family. He's standing between his parents at an ice rink somewhere, their arms wrapped around each other's waists. He wears all of his hockey equipment except his helmet, and his hair is plastered with sweat. It looks like they were caught in the middle of a hearty laugh; he must have just finished a game.

The second picture causes my heart to stop momentarily. It's of us at our high school graduation. We stand with our arms around one another clutching the fake diplomas they give out at the ceremony. We're wearing our black cap and gowns, honor cords and National Honor Society stoles slightly askew as we lean in to one another. We look deliriously happy.

"Damn it," he groans and rushes to my side. "You found your Christmas present."

I frown. "It wasn't exactly hidden. And why are you getting me a gift?"

James takes my drink from me and sets it on the table. He picks up the picture of us and turns it over, so all I can see is the back. On the white photo paper I see neat handwriting:

J & E – HS Graduation – June 2008

"I was going to wrap this," he says, disappointed. "I didn't mean to leave it out."

"That's okay," I say. "I'm the one invading your space and snooping around."

His blue eyes lock on mine. "I always want you to invade my space." He grasps my hand and leads me to the couch, gesturing for me to have a seat. I do and he sits beside me, wrapping his arm around my shoulders and pressing me to his side. He turns the picture over and holds it out in front of me. "Merry Christmas."

I give him a small smile and tentatively take it. "Thanks."

"I know we aren't exchanging gifts, but I wanted to give you something from our past." James traces the edge of the picture. "I wish I could have found something more sentimental, but my parents have packed my life away and hidden it in the armory that is their basement."

I looked at him in surprise. "You broke into your parent's house?"

"Not technically. I appeared inside while they were sleeping."

I smile. "How long did it take you to find this?"

"A minute," he sighs. "The only evidence of my existence is my senior picture that hangs on the living room wall. Besides that, my bedroom has been turned into a guest room and everything else has been boxed, sealed, and stowed."

My heart aches. Are his parents trying to forget him? I kiss his cheek. "I'm sorry."

He shrugs. "I know my mom was having a hard time handling things. I think this is her way of grieving. I mean, I didn't expect to find a James shrine or anything."

"But next to nothing?" I turn toward him. "That has to be hard. Your life should be celebrated, not forgotten."

He smiles. "I'm glad you think so."

I turn back toward his gift. "Tell me about this day."

"You remember most of it, don't you?"

"Well, yeah," I admit. "But not this." I wave the picture. "What did we do after this? I thought I went to Shel's house."

"You're right." He squeezes my shoulder. "*We* went to Shel's house. There was a ton of people there. Remember her mom was out of town and she left 'the plan' for Shel in case the police showed up?"

I laugh. "Yes! The 'toss-the-keg-out-the-back-door-and-down-the-hill' plan?"

"The very one," he laughs with me. "I'm glad we didn't have to do that; our blatant disregard for the law led to our one and only karaoke concert."

Oh lord. "Karaoke concert? As in we sang more than one song?"

He nods. "I think we started with "You Shook Me All Night Long," threw in some Black Eyed Peas, and ended with "Friends in Low Places."

I cringe. "You're making that up."

He smiles. "I'm not. Ask Matt and Shel."

I cover my eyes with my hand. Singing in front of people? That had to be the most ridiculous thing ever. "Why did you let me embarrass myself like that?"

His free hand trails across my belly and to my hip, pulling me closer. "Why wouldn't I? It was a spur of the moment thing. Besides, you can actually sing. I'm terrible."

We fall silent for a moment, and I contemplate what he's told me. It sounds like we had a ton of fun together. I touch his face on the photograph. "Thank you for this," I say sincerely. "We look happy."

His arm tightens around me. "We were."

My gaze shifts to him and he leans forward to kiss me softly. It feels relaxed and comfortable as I lean into him. After a minute he moves back and asks me, "What are you doing tomorrow?"

I sigh. "Shopping with Shel. We need to find dresses for the New Year's Eve party."

"What New Year's Eve party?"

"Oh." I straighten up. "The annual Bay Woods employee holiday party. It's a masquerade."

He face falls a little. "I take it Dane is your date?"

I swallow. "Yeah."

His hold on me relaxes. "What about Christmas? What are your plans?"

"You know. The same old, same old. Gifts and dinner with Mike and Kate." I hesitate. Should I mention Dane? Probably not.

He pulls the picture from my fingers, sets it back on the side table, and wraps his arms around me again. "I wish I could take you to the party. Or to anything for that matter."

I rest my head on his shoulder. "I don't get many invitations. It's no big deal."

"You're missing the point," he says against my hair. "I'll never be able to take you anywhere. Not as long as I stay around this town, anyway. Not to dinner, not to a movie, not even to the damn grocery store."

I slide my arms around his waist and hug him to let him know I understand. What he says is true. To avoid recognition, the safest thing for James to do is move out of state. And, if I want to be with him in any kind of normal sense, that means I would have to leave, too. The thought of us living in some sort of pseudo-hiding depresses me.

I change the subject and apologize to try and make things better. "I'm sorry I didn't get you a gift. Let me make it up to you. Name something you want. Anything."

He looks surprised. "You mean it?"

Mentally, I smack myself. That comment sounded much more innocent in my head. "Within reason," I elaborate. "Do you have a favorite movie? I'll get it and we'll watch it together. Or how about a favorite band? You could blend in at a concert."

After a few seconds gives me a tiny smile. "Stay the night with me."

I look at him uncertainly. "Like how do you mean?"

"Like this," he says and wraps his hand around my knee. He pulls it up, hooking my leg over his, and scoots as close to me as possible.

"Snuggled on the couch?" I ask.

"We'll probably get kinks in our necks," he says. "How about we move to the bedroom and make it more comfortable?"

"Emma?" My brother waves his hand in front of my face. "Where are you today?"

I blink and refocus. Yet again, my mind has traveled back to the night I spent with James. Don't get me wrong; all of my rules remain unbroken. We did nothing more than spend the time cuddled close, sharing an occasional kiss or two, and reminiscing about our past. It felt right, and I don't regret it.

So, how is it that I'm super excited to see Dane today? Shouldn't that feel wrong? Talk about confusing emotions. How twisted is it to want them both in my life? And when will they get fed up with me?

"Here." Mike thrusts a stocking into my hands. "Let's do this."

I stick my tongue out at my brother. "Pushy much?" What's his hurry anyway? Its Christmas morning. Let's make it last.

I glance around the room to see my parents and Kate have already started gutting their stockings, so I reach into mine. The first things I remove are two pair of fuzzy slipper socks. My mom knows those are my favorite. The next item is a package of hair bands as is standard every year. Further down, I discover a gift card for the local movie theater and another for a pedicure.

"Thanks!" I smile at my mom and dad. "How did you know my feet are gross?"

"With the amount you've been working out lately I figured they might need help," my mom says from her perch on the couch.

I've been covering up my Larvatus training sessions by lying. I told my parents I was taking a self-defense class which they allowed due to "Patrick the Outlaw."

I reach to the bottom of my stocking and discover some dark chocolate. Again, another favorite.

After our stockings are empty we tear into our presents. Kate loves the gift card and earrings I got her – score! – and my brother appreciates his long sleeved tees from American Eagle. Both of them went in together and got me the most gorgeous cashmere sweater. Talk about soft.

After my parents thank us for their gifts, my brother, Kate, and I are blown away when they present us with identically shaped boxes. They bought us all iPads. I think James probably heard our collective gasp of surprise the next town over when we opened them. How incredibly awesome are my mom and dad?

Once the paper is cleaned up, Kate and I head to the kitchen to start brunch. We've never been early risers, so it's brunch instead of breakfast. My brother stops us before we leave the living room though.

"Can you guys come back here for a minute?"

I turn to look at him, and he looks paler than pale. Upon further inspection he looks a little shaky, too. I glance at Kate, and I can tell she notices. Concern flashes across her face.

We step back into the living room and Mike reaches for Kate's hand, pulling her ahead of me. He stops in the center of the room, near where my dad is seated in his recliner. He takes a deep breath and drops to one knee.

Oh my God.

"Kate," he says, still holding on to her, "every minute of every day I love you more." He pauses and lifts his free hand. Pinched between his index finger and thumb is a sparkling diamond ring. "I think you know what this means but...will you marry me?"

Kate yanks her hand away from his to cover her mouth in surprise. Tears dance in her eyes as she stares at him. After a few seconds she utters a barely audible "Yes."

"What was that?" My brother leans forward with a hint of a smile.

"Yes!" She grins. She lowers her left hand to him, which is now shaking, and Mike slides the ring on to her finger. He beams up at her; I don't think I've ever seen him so happy.

He stands and Kate throws herself against him in huge hug. Immediately, my mom, dad, and I descend upon them. My mom wipes the tears from Kate's cheeks as they laugh and hug; my dad shakes Mike's hand and slaps him on the shoulder.

When I pull away from hugging Kate I snag her hand to study her ring. "Wow," I say and I mean it. My brother did an amazing job. A round diamond sits in the center of a platinum band, completely surrounded by smaller stones. The band itself has four diamonds that extend down each side and the entire ring shimmers. "It's beautiful."

I look at my brother, who I've never regarded as so grown up. Stepping forward, I gently punch him in the arm. "It's about time!"

He laughs as I wrap one arm around him in an awkward hug. Happy tears prick my eyes. "Seriously. Congratulations," I say into his shoulder.

He pats my back. "Thanks, Em."

Hours later, I lie on the couch playing with my Christmas gift. I've already downloaded two books, messed with the camera, and set up my email, so I can check it with one touch. I love my iPad.

Around five o'clock the only thing that could distract me from my new gift occurs which is a knock on the back door. I spring up to answer it.

"Ah. I see lover boy has arrived," Mike teases me.

I shoot him a look. "Please behave."

I pass through the kitchen, where my mom and Kate are busy talking, while dinner bakes. When I open the door to find Dane on the stoop I can't help but bust out in a huge smile. "Hey."

He grins at me. "Nice sweater."

"Thanks." I look down at myself. "Mike and Kate got it for me." I step back to let him inside and close the door behind him. "Want me to take your coat?"

"Sure." He hands me the gifts he's carrying which causes me to mentally frown. Why did he bring presents? He shrugs out of a black pea coat and then exchanges it for the packages. I turn and open the coat closet to hang it up. Surprisingly, he steps behind the door with me so we're blocked from the kitchen. I look at him, and he plants a quick kiss on my lips. "Merry Christmas," he says and smiles.

"Merry Christmas," I whisper. "Why are you kissing me in the closet?"

"Because I can't do it in front of your family."

I laugh.

"Dane's here," I announce as we enter the kitchen and my mom smiles his way.

"I'm glad you could join us," she says. "I hope you like ham."

"Thanks for having me," he responds politely then holds his stomach. "Of course I like ham."

"Dane, this is Kate. My brother's *fiancée*," I emphasize the word.

He raises his eyebrows. "Did this just happen?"

She grins and nods like a little kid.

"Congratulations," he says and extends his hand to shake hers. "It's nice to meet you."

"Likewise," she responds.

He juggles the gifts in his arms. "Do you want me to take those?" I ask. "Why did you bring presents anyway?"

"Because it's the polite thing to do," he says like I should know better. He smiles as he holds out a small rectangular bag to my mother. "This is for you and your husband."

She takes the gift reluctantly. "You shouldn't have." She sets it on the counter and pulls out a bottle of wine. She looks impressed and thanks him.

He smiles at her and then turns to me, holding the remaining gift out of reach. "I guess you don't want yours."

"Why did you get me something?" First James, now Dane? Someone could have filled me in on the gift-giving! I feel like an inconsiderate jerk.

"Because I wanted to surprise you," he says. His eyes widen. *"You might want to open this in private."*

Hmmm. Where could we go? "Let me introduce you to my brother and give you a tour," I say and grab his hand, leading him into the living room. My mom and Kate will think I merely wanted to change the subject.

"Dad? Mike? Dane's here."

Both my father and brother pull their eyes from the television to look at my guest. "Nice to see you again," my dad says. Mike simply waves.

I continue to lead Dane past them, toward the stairs. "Are you going to let me say hello?" he asks.

"Yeah. Where are you going?" Mike says as I step on the first stair.

"I'm showing him around the house," I say. "He's never been past the kitchen." I think.

As we ascend the stairs I hear Mike ask my dad, "You're going to let her take a boy to her room?"

Gah! What are we? Sixteen?! He's never cared before! "Shut up Mike!" I holler behind me.

I hear him laugh as Dane snickers. At the top of the stairs, I point out the rooms as we pass them. "Bathroom, Mike's old room, my room," I say as we enter.

He pauses as he studies the place I grew up. I admit it's kind of girly – all of my furniture is white, and my bed set is sage and ivory with a little pink around the edges. My clothes hamper overflows and LB's toys are scattered around the floor. A few boxes from the move still sit in one corner, and my closet door is ajar. Okay. It does look like a teenager lives here.

Dane's eyes finally land on me and they look amused.

"What?" I cross my arms. "I know it's a mess. I wasn't expecting to bring you up here."

"It's not that." He smiles. "I can just picture you growing up in this room. Protective older brother down the hall, loving parents in the kitchen. Running down the stairs on Christmas morning."

I eye him suspiciously. "Since when did you turn into a *Lifetime Original Movie?*"

He chooses not to answer me and presents his gift. "For you."

Warily, I take it. "Is this going to embarrass me?"

"It shouldn't."

I sit on the bed and set the box on my lap. Well, two boxes. There's a small one on top of larger one, wrapped in thick gold paper that looks like a tapestry. A stunning red bow made of fabric holds the two together. "Did you wrap this yourself?"

He takes a seat beside me. "I wish I could say I did, but no. I had help."

"Teagan?" I joke. She's been working him around the clock.

His expression twists. "No. Cynthia from Accounting."

I nod like I know who Cynthia is. I slide the bow off the present and set it aside. I pull the smaller box away from the first and carefully tear off the paper. When I remove the lid I'm speechless.

"I know you're not big on jewelry," Dane says and pulls the item from the box. "But this reminded me of you."

Draped over his finger is a delicate silver butterfly that sparkles in the light of my room. A thin, yet equally shiny, chain extends from the tip of each wing to form a loop. "It goes around your ankle," he explains. "I figured you could wear it and no one would know."

I slowly take it from him and stare at my palm. "Why did it remind you of me?"

"Because you're the same," he says. "When we first met you were wrapped in this protective shell. It took some time, but you broke free. And now look at you." He gives me a tiny smile. "All transformed and stretching your wings."

I stare at him in awe as tears jump behind my eyes. The thought he put behind this gift takes my breath away.

He looks at me, unsure. "Do you like it?"

Words escape me. Instead of speaking, I wrap my free hand around his neck and pull his mouth to mine. I try to convey how I feel through my kiss. I think it works. When we part, I manage to say, "I love it. I absolutely love it."

He grins. "Here," he takes the bracelet from me and places it back in the box, "open the next one."

I remove the paper from the next package and reveal a collector's edition of the game Clue.

"No way!" I exclaim and turn over the box, which is actually a metal tin. "The pieces look like real people!"

"And the weapons aren't plastic," he laughs.

"How did you know I love this game?"

"We played it in the Caribbean," he says. "I was Colonel Mustard and you were Miss Scarlet."

"We are *so* playing this after dinner," I say excitedly. "Thank you so much!"

"You're very welcome," he says and leans in to kiss me again.

"Guys!" my mother shouts up the stairs. "Dinner's ready!"

We laugh as we stop what we're doing. I stand and set my gift on the bed. "Let's go." I extend my hand.

"Wait," he says and stands with me. "One more thing."

"There's more?" I say in disbelief.

He reaches for his wallet, opens it, and produces a hot pink gift card. "I know how you feel about these, but I couldn't resist." He smirks and presents it to me.

It's from Victoria's Secret, and I immediately blush. I open the holder and see it's for an ungodly amount. "$500?!" I say in shock. "Why?"

"Trust me," he says. "I've seen the state of your underwear. You probably need more money than that."

I sock him in the arm. "This is too much. Take it back."

"No, it's not. Have you seen how much things cost there?"

"That's precisely why I own nothing from this store."

He wraps his arms around my waist. "You deserve it," he says. "Plus, it serves a double purpose."

"What's that?"

"Did you get me a gift?"

I look away, ashamed. "No. I'm sorry; I didn't know we were doing the gift thing."

"Then repay me one day," he says and kisses my forehead.

"How so?"

He leans forward and whispers in my ear. "Let me see what you buy. Deal?"

When he focuses on my face again, I shake my head. "You're incorrigible."

His eyes light up. "I'll take that as a yes."

Chapter 15

The dress I bought for New Year's Eve hangs over my closet door. As I stare at it I'm seriously second guessing my choice. What was I thinking? Black and lace are so not me!

Shel talked me into this one instead of the simple strapless I'd found. She did have a good point; I don't have the chest to pull off a strapless gown. She, on the other hand, will have no problem filling out hers.

"Emma! Get in here!"

I leave my bedroom and meet her in the bathroom where she's laid out a plethora of cosmetics. We've just returned from having our hair done which was a lot of fun. I wish I could hire someone to wash my hair all the time because it felt so good. Mainly it just felt great to spend time with Shel. Just us. No guys. No Guardian stuff. No lies.

She puts her arm around my shoulder and turns us to look at ourselves in the mirror. "We are going to rock this party tonight."

I smile back at our reflections. "You will. I'm going to look silly from the neck down."

"Um, I don't think so," she says. "That dress fits you like a glove. Besides, you need to show off all your hard work."

She thinks my newly toned body is due to my faux self-defense class. It's true my muscles are more defined and I'm not complaining. I can feel confident wearing a swimsuit while tossing some Allegiant.

She leans toward the mirror and inspects her hair. "You're sure you like this?"

"I love it," I repeat for the thousandth time. Her brown hair is swept completely off her neck and is tucked-in on itself in a loose contemporary twist. A few straight pieces of the shorter layers hang outside and frame her face.

"Your hair is getting really long," she says as she leans back and touches a piece of mine at the bottom. "It's nearly half way down your back."

"Yeah, it's a Larv..." I stop myself. I almost said it's a Larvatus thing. "It's been growing like crazy." It's also changing color. The auburn highlights that have always been there are taking over.

"I'm glad you decided to wear it down," she says. "It's pretty."

I didn't want to copy Shel and have my hair up, so half of it is pulled back and knotted at the crown of my head. The rest falls down my back in soft waves.

"Well," she picks up her phone and consults the time, "let's get to this, shall we?"

It's a good thing we started early. Two hours later we're still at it.

"Ow!" I complain as Shel pokes me in the eye. Again. "Are the fake lashes really necessary?"

"I bought them so we're wearing them," she says with determination.

"But they won't stick," I say. "I'd rather go without then have a dead caterpillar hanging off my face!"

"Fine," she huffs and tosses the lashes on the counter. "You're right. I give up."

"Finally," I grumble. I turn toward the mirror and peel off the other semi-stuck lash. Shel does the same to hers. I grab the eyeliner to fix what I messed up and then hand it off to Shel who does the same. I reach for the mascara and lay it on as thick as I dare without it getting goopy. Those makeup ads sure do lie. It's hard to keep it from clumping.

"There." I finish and look at her. "For never wearing makeup I think I did a darn good job."

She smiles at me. "You should wear it more often."

I grimace. "It takes too long. I'll save it for special occasions like this." I pluck a tube of lip gloss and a powder compact off the counter to put in my purse. "I'm going to get dressed."

"Be there in a sec," she says.

Once I'm in my bedroom, I put the makeup in my evening bag and pull my dress from its hanger. At least I'll be comfortable. It's made of a jersey material so it's soft and it moves. I lay it on the bed, undress, and then slide it on, pulling the one strap over my shoulder. There. That's it.

I walk to my closet to stand in front of the long mirror that hangs on the door and adjust the bodice. It gathers to the left at a sheer lace panel that wraps slightly around my side, but covers most of my back. The dress falls to the floor with a thigh high slit up the front which is very risqué for me. I turn and make sure the back of my shoulder strap isn't twisted and admire the lace panel that mirrors the one at my side. This one travels along the back of the dress from my knee to the floor.

Facing front again, I'm instantly grateful that all of my Caribbean tan hasn't disappeared. It's offset nicely against the black fabric and through the lace. I inhale and exhale. Dane requested tight and this dress hugs me to my hips. I don't think it will disappoint. I do, however, think I look like I'm trying to be something I'm not. Which is sexy.

When Shel enters the room I'm carefully buckling my strappy heels. They're open toed and I'm glad I had time to use my pedicure from Christmas. She moves past me and removes her dress from the garment bag she brought with her. After she pulls it on she asks me to help zip her up.

"Matt is going to bust something when he sees you in this," I say.

She grins. "I hope so."

Her dress is floor length too, with a small train. It's strapless and fits the top of her like a corset. The sheer overlay is encrusted with wavy lines of navy beading that trail to one side, and a nude underlay gives the appearance that she's wearing nothing beneath it. She shimmers.

As Shel pops diamond studs in her ears I grab our masks. Mine is gold with black swirls and made of tin; the eyes are outlined in gold glitter. At the top right corner a large flower blooms, also made of flexible steel, with tall leaves and black and gold petals. Shel's mask covers more of her face, coming down a little lower on her cheeks. It's ivory with a blue design and tall navy feathers that sprout from the forehead. Sprinkled in amongst the plumes are little blue flowers. She found both our accessories online.

I help put on her mask and then she helps me with mine. We find our bags and I start to head downstairs. The guys should be here in fifteen minutes.

"Wait," Shel says and pulls out her phone. "I want a picture."

We lean in close and she snaps one. We take a few more with funny faces and I ask her to send them to me. I turn to head out the door again.

"Em," she says. "Why are you still wearing that?" She focuses on my wrist. "It doesn't match your dress at all."

I glance at my bracelet. She's right. The brown leather and silver amulet look out of place with my black and gold ensemble. But I can't take it off. What do I tell her? I decide to lie.

"It's from Dane, remember? I never take it off."

She frowns. "Does he have a thing for bracelets?" She looks at my ankle.

I shrug and look down, too. The one around my ankle is so dainty it's barely noticeable. "I don't know. C'mon." I walk out the door, hoping she'll drop the subject.

When we make it downstairs my parents are watching television. My mom's jaw drops to the floor when she sees us. "You two look gorgeous!" she exclaims. "What happened to my baby girls?"

We laugh.

"I need a picture," she says and springs from her seat to get her camera. While she's gone, my dad rises from his recliner to give us each a peck on the cheek. "You look lovely," he tells us. "Just be sure your dates tell you the same. If not, you let me know."

I smile at him and squeeze his arm.

After we pose ridiculously for my mom – apparently we think we're in some kind of fashion magazine – Matt arrives to collect Shel. I was right; his eyes nearly pop out of his head when he sees her.

"Are you responsible for that dress?" he asks me as Shel finds her wrap.

"A little." I did influence her decision toward the blue instead of a red satin number.

"Thank. You." He enunciates each word.

"You're welcome." I smile.

He leans over my shoulder. "Dane is going to freak when he lays eyes on you."

"Thanks." I press my hands to my stomach. "I feel a little out of my element."

"Don't," he says and looks at my dress. "You own that."

I reach out and smooth his jacket sleeve. "You clean up pretty nice yourself, kid."

He needlessly straightens his bow tie and we laugh.

After Shel and Matt, leave I visit the restroom to fiddle with my hair. As I wait for Dane, I recall our conversation about tonight. I told him I could ride with our friends, but he wouldn't have it.

"I'm picking you up," he insisted. "I refuse to share you with them the entire night."

As I'm primping, I hear him arrive and exchange pleasantries with my parents. I pause and laugh at myself. I don't think I've ever used the word 'primp' before.

Exiting the bathroom, I find the three of them standing in the kitchen. They don't realize I'm there so I clear my throat to get their attention. When Dane turns around and finds me, his expression is indescribable. He blinks and his mouth opens and closes without making a sound. Does he like what he sees? Is he shocked or confused? Was he expecting more or less?

His eyes slowly sweep over me from head to toe and back again. It's when they focus on my face that I know it's just enough.

He steps forward and offers his hand with a lopsided smile. "You look amazing."

I place my hand in his and say, "You, too," and mean it. While Matt looked put together and dapper in his tux you could tell it was a rental and that he felt a little uncomfortable. Not Dane. I'm probably biased, but he looks as if he was made to dress this way. His tuxedo appears specifically tailored for him and everything from his hair to the way he's shaved today screams, 'I'm totally confident and used to this.'

"Where's your mask?" I ask.

"In the car. It's a little tough to drive in; plus, I look like an idiot."

"I doubt that," I say.

He helps me into an evening coat I borrowed from Kate, and we say our goodbyes. When we get to the car, he holds the door for me as I climb inside. I have to rearrange myself because my dress pulls to one side as I slide in. I bend my knees and scoot back in the seat which exposes my entire left leg due to the slit in my dress. I try to pull the pieces together to cover it, which doesn't work. There's a reason I don't do this very often.

When I'm as settled as I can be, he sprints around the car and takes his seat. He leans over to shut the door and ends up dropping his keys by my feet. Automatically, I reach down to grab them, and his hand flies out to stop me.

"I've got it."

He bends over and snags his key ring with one finger, but I feel the others at my ankle. Slowly his hand glides up my leg as he leans back, tracing my calf to my knee and then traveling up my thigh to the top of the slit in my dress. His touch leaves a trail of electricity behind it.

"Ahem." I raise my eyebrows. "We haven't even left the driveway."

"Do me a favor," he says. "Don't read my thoughts tonight."

"Why?"

He smiles. "Because I've seen you throw a right hook."

When we step over the threshold to his parents place I'm in awe. Their home is nowhere near as big as Madeline and Ash's mini castle, but it's still huge. Attendants take our coats in the foyer, and we are immediately approached by waiters carrying trays of champagne. Off to the right is an arched doorway, and, when I peer inside, I see several guests milling around a large sitting room with white furniture and an expansive fireplace. Christmas lights and garland drip off every surface and a massive tree sits in one corner; it must be twenty feet tall. A Baby Grand resides opposite the tree where a pianist plays a seasonal melody.

"Is that your living room?" I ask.

"Formal sitting room," he says like everyone has one. "Growing up I hung out in the den."

He places his hand against the small of my back and ushers me farther into his childhood home, saying hello to several guests. I recognize Katie, one of the girls I worked with this summer, and even spot Leslie and my manager Kris. Everyone is decked out in their finest attire, and I'm glad I blend in. I keep an eye out for Matt and Shel, but don't see them.

Dane leads me to a set of double doors that are thrown wide and steps inside. Tables upon tables of food line the perimeter of the room. On the center most table sits an ice sculpture of a sleigh and its seat is overflowing with shrimp. Chefs in white hats stand behind several stations frying, sautéing, and otherwise setting things on fire. People are gathered in small groups laughing, sampling, and flagging down wait staff that, I assume, are taking drink orders.

"Dining room?" I ask.

"The formal one, yes." He smiles. "I wanted you to know where the food was." He sets his hand against my belly, and I smack it away. I know I eat a lot, but damn! I'm not a vacuum!

He grabs my hand and pulls me around the rest of the first floor. After a brief stop at the den, which resembles a normal living room and is off limits to guests for the night, we pass through the kitchen which is doubling as a bar. French doors are thrown wide, exposing the backyard, where a large white tent has been resurrected to cover the heated patio. Beneath the tent is the dance floor for the evening; it's white and surrounded by round tables decorated for the New Year. Horns and confetti grace the center of each, and multicolored metallic streamers radiate from the center of the outdoor room at a mirror ball. They drape across the ceiling to the sides of the tent where they fall and puddle on the ground. A DJ plays from the far end of the dance floor and several people are already taking advantage of the music.

I turn to Dane. "Don't I get to see upstairs?"

"Maybe," he says and winds his hands around my waist. "If you're good."

"Son," a deep voice sounds to our left.

I turn to see an older man approach us, dressed in what appears to be a smoking jacket and holding a snifter glass. He's not wearing a mask and, when I focus on his face, I know what Dane will look like when he's older. Despite the gray at his temples and the laugh lines around his eyes he's the spitting image of his son.

"Dad." Dane extends his hand toward his father. Who shakes their parent's hand?

Mr. Walker takes it and pumps it twice. He has kind eyes, and they make me think that he'd rather give his son a hug.

When he regards me he asks, "Who is this radiant lady?"

Dane clears his throat. "This is Emma. Emma, Charles Walker."

He reaches for my hand and I give it to him. He simply squeezes my fingers and says, "It's a pleasure to meet you. You worked for me at the course this summer, yes?"

I nod. "In the concession area."

"I remember your name. I also seem to remember you taking a swim in my waterfall."

It's a good thing I'm wearing a mask because I don't remember this and it hides some of my confusion. "I'm..."

"It wasn't her," Dane interrupts. "I mean, she was there, but Matt and Shel were the ones actually in the water."

I let out a breath. What in the world were they doing?

Mr. Walker chuckles. "If my club manager had his way you would've been fired. It's a good thing Dane was there to save you."

What? "I'm so sorry," I apologize.

"Don't worry." He gives me a genuine smile. "It seems you two have a habit of saving each other from unpleasant things. Bad engagements, for example."

Heat rushes to my face, and I know my ears are flaming red.

"Dad!" Dane snaps at his father in a hushed tone.

"What?" he says innocently. "I've just met her and I already like her better."

"Dear." A woman approaches Mr. Walker from behind. "The Thompson's are here and Ken is looking for you."

Charles grimaces and turns to me. "Ken Thompson is a horse's ass."

I can't help it and let out a small giggle.

"Lily," Dane's dad makes a sweeping gesture with his hand, "have you met Emma? This is Dane's lovely date."

Dane's stepmother politely smiles, but her mind is elsewhere as she tries to steer her husband in the direction of Ken Thompson. She's not wearing a mask either – why the masquerade then? – and she wears a black velvet pencil dress with a matching cropped jacket embroidered with a gold pattern. Her brown hair is styled in a bob and streaked with gray in a classy way.

"Maybe we can talk later," she says as she pushes Charles away from us. "Enjoy yourselves."

When they're out of ear shot, I face Dane. He runs his hand nervously through his hair and exhales slowly.

"I like your dad," I say and step toward him, catching his hands in mine. "You look a lot like him and he's funny."

He smirks like he doesn't believe me and then takes advantage of how close we are to lower his lips to mine. "I've been dying to do that since I saw you tonight," he says.

I feel a hand around my arm and turn to face a smiling Shel. "There you are!" she says and starts to pull me in the direction of the music. "I need a dance partner."

I laugh and follow her, leaving Dane with Matt. They find a table at the edge of the dance floor as Shel and I take advantage of the music and the atmosphere.

After we've danced awhile, taken a break to eat, retrieved drinks from the bar, and danced some more, I realize I'm having a complete and total blast. I can't remember the last time I've laughed this much or felt so right. Sitting across Dane's lap with one arm wrapped around his shoulders seems like the most natural thing in the world.

A string of slow songs start and, by the second one, Dane lifts me off his legs and sets my feet on the floor. He stands and informs Matt and Shel that not only has he lost circulation in his limbs, but he wants my undivided attention. We dodge several couples on the dance floor before he finally decides to stop walking and gather me in his arms. It just so happens he's selected the furthest spot from our table to dance.

"Finally," he says as he leans in to me. He tries to rest his forehead on mine, but our masks rub uncomfortably against our skin.

"I'm taking this thing off," he says and removes his costume piece. His mask is plain black with a thin white line that traces the edge.

I push mine off my cheeks and up into my hair, wiggling my nose. "That does feel better." Apparently, Dane doesn't like where I leave it though, and he pulls it off my head entirely.

Turning, he sets both masks on a nearby chair. When he looks back at me, I notice a red line under his left eye. "Your mask left a mark." I smile and run my thumb across his skin.

He catches my wrist and gently kisses the inside of it. He continues up my bare arm, leaving a trail to my elbow, before placing my hand on his shoulder. As I try to breathe normally, I move my other hand to mirror the first and he wraps his arms around me, pulling me to him. We barely move to the music.

"We are in a public place you know," I say with my cheek pressed to his shoulder. "Maybe we should attempt to look like we're dancing?"

I feel his chest shake with laughter against mine and he turns us in a circle. "Better?"

I lift my head and nod. His hands move low on my hips and it takes only a second for his mouth to find mine. I feel self-conscious and lean away. *"Public place,"* I whisper.

The decision flashes in his eyes. He steps back and takes my hand, leading me off the dance floor, through the kitchen, and down a hallway we didn't explore before. We come upon a sliding glass door which he opens and pulls me through. As he closes it behind us and draws the shade, my line of vision is open to a glass room – a solarium. Soft light surrounds us along with a multitude of potted plants. A few chaise lounges and wicker chairs sit to our left, and to our right, the party tent butts up to where we're standing. I can hear the music clear as day.

"You grew up in the Boddy mansion," I say referencing the game of Clue.

He laughs and wraps one arm around me again. "I never thought of it that way." We start to dance and he brushes my hair away from my neck, zeroing in on my skin with his lips.

I tilt my head back and catch sight of the windows. "Um..." I stand up straight. "People can see us."

He frowns. "The only thing on that side of the house is a yard full of parked cars."

"Yeah, but if guests are leaving..."

He smirks. "I'm only kissing you. Unless you think something else might happen." His expression turns serious as he stares into my eyes. "I'll gladly remove more than your mask," he whispers.

My throat goes dry. "I thought you liked my dress."

"I do. Very much."

"But?"

He slides two fingers under my one strap and moves it an inch off my shoulder. "I've seen what's beneath it and I like that a lot, too."

I can't breathe and my knees nearly give out when I feel his mouth where my strap used to be. He's pushing boundaries he's never pushed before, and I need to stop this before things get out of hand. There's only one problem.

I don't want to.

"Emma."

When I hear my name it's as if a bucket of cold water has drenched me from head to toe. I quickly turn to see James standing a few feet from us, his arms crossed, and his expression serious. I step back from Dane and adjust my dress. "What is it?"

James takes me in, and I see his eyes widen at what I'm wearing. He blinks and refocuses. "It's time," he says. "Jack says Garrett is in serious trouble. We have to go."

"Now?" I take a step forward. I didn't bring anything with me. Not a change of clothes, not my anlace, nothing.

As if on cue The Larvatus appear beside him. In her hands Madeline holds a stack of clothes. She approaches me and hands over the garments. "We'll wait here."

My heart pounds. This is really happening. I turn toward Dane, and he looks as if the wind has been knocked from his lungs. Silently, he walks toward the sliding door and I follow. He leads me a short way down the hall to a bathroom where he flips the light switch. I step inside and before I can say anything he shuts the door behind me.

For a moment I stare at the back of the door speechless. I know he's unhappy and have no idea how to make it better. Instead of dwelling on it, I change clothes. Madeline has given me a pair of brown suede leggings, a plain white tank, and an olive green shift of some sort that belts at the waist. When I look in the mirror, I realize I'm wearing the exact same outfit she is. She's also given me boots to match hers.

I emerge from the bathroom and quickly make my way back to the solarium. Dane sits at the edge of one of the lounges with his elbows propped on his knees staring down at his hands. When he realizes I'm back, his head snaps up and he stands. James, Madeline, and Ash move toward me.

"Here." Ash pulls an anlace from his belt. "This one is enchanted. Don't forget."

I tilt the knife in the light to reveal the amulet symbol on the blade. I feel air brush the back of my neck and realize Madeline is behind me braiding my hair like hers. She completes it in a matter of seconds.

"How will I know when you've returned?" Dane's voice wavers. He pretends to cough to cover it up.

Ash opens his mouth to answer just as I hear the sliding door open. "Emma? What in the hell are you wearing?"

I whip around to see Shel step over the threshold into the glass room with Matt close behind.

"We were at the bar when I saw you come out of the bathroom." She frowns. "What is going –?"

She inhales sharply and reaches behind her to clutch at Matt's chest. He looks confused and grasps her hand as she twists his shirt in her fist. The blood drains from her face, and I've never seen her so pale. Matt follows her line of vision and I turn my head, too.

They've both seen James.

Chapter 16

"You're not dead."

Matt's voice is barely audible. He looks as if he can't decide whether to be overjoyed or scared shitless.

James gives him a defeated smile. "No. Not anymore."

Matt releases Shel's hand and she steps away from him cautiously, like if she moves too fast James will disappear. "Not dead," she repeats, her voice small. Her eyes dart from James to me. "Why aren't you freaking out?"

"Because I'm used to it," I say, almost ashamed. This is the biggest secret of secrets I've kept from her. With good reason of course, but still.

She shoots me a bewildered look and the tension in the room is suffocating. My heartbeat quickens and matches the rhythm of the party music next to us. It's steady and fast and growing faster. How can I explain this? Do I have time?

"Unfortunately no," Ash reads my thoughts and moves to my side. "Dane?" He looks over his shoulder. "Would you please escort your friends to our place? You have our permission to use whatever you need there. Explain things as best you can and we'll assist once we return."

Dane steps around Ash and reluctantly nods. Matt stares at him in disbelief. "You know about this?"

"He knows everything," I say quietly.

My gaze falls on Shel whose color has yet to come back. Actually, she's looking more and more green the longer she stares at us. I walk up to her and quickly gather her hands. "You have to trust me." I focus on her face. "You can ask Dane anything and he'll give you honest answers. When I get back you can interrogate me, too. This is it my very last secret. I have nothing else. I promise."

Her brow furrows. "Where are you going?"

I put it as simply as possible. "To save a friend."

"It's dangerous?" she asks and looks down at our hands. "You need a knife?"

I follow her gaze and realize I'm still holding my anlace, except now it's pressed between my palm and back of her hand. I swallow. "Yes. But James and Madeline and Ash will be with me."

She looks up and past my shoulder at the people behind us. "Am I losing my mind?"

"No." I shake my head. "You're completely sane."

She tries to smile, but it twists with confusion.

"Emma." Madeline nudges my arm to pull me back. "The sooner we go the sooner we'll return."

"Okay." I squeeze Shel's hands to reassure her, but now that my friends know I'm headed into dangerous territory I'm beginning to feel nervous. I step away from Shel to position myself between Madeline and Ash.

James takes a second to walk up to our friends. He hesitates in front of them, unsure of what to say. Matt tentatively extends his hand and when James takes it he looks astounded. He pulls James forward into a one-armed hug and pounds his back. "I can't believe this," he says into his shoulder. "You're fucking alive!"

James chuckles. "Yeah, I am."

When he removes himself from Matt he gently takes Shel's hand. "It's me. Don't be scared." He pauses and glances in my direction. "You know I'll take care of her."

She gives him a wary look. I think her years of medical studies have been negated in a matter of minutes.

Madeline and Ash take my wrists as James moves beside us. I close my eyes and try to feel weightless.

"Grace."

My eyes pop open and I find Dane. The look in his eyes is pleading.

"Come back to me."

I open my eyes to find myself in the shadows beneath a stone arch. I look both ways and see the sun reflecting off a paved path lined with trees and shrubbery. The wind blows and rustles the autumn leaves causing a few of them to float silently to the ground. I'm momentarily confused by the lack of fluffy clouds; it's how Heaven is typically depicted. Then I have to remind myself that this is not Heaven. This is the Intermediate.

"It's about time," Jack says as he rounds the corner.

James snorts. "Don't get your panties in a bunch. It didn't take us that long."

"You would've been here sooner if you didn't have to collect party girl over there."

I snap. "What's that supposed to mean?"

"It means that while you were celebrating some stupid tradition my brother is this much closer to death." He holds his thumb and forefinger an inch apart.

"You know we can't do this without Emma," Ash chastises Jack.

He huffs and I read his thoughts. *"If we're too late I'm holding her responsible."*

I arch an eyebrow. "Then let's get to it."

Ash clears his throat. "Across the street is the Allegiant headquarters. We're going to come at them on two fronts." He eyes Mad and I. "Jack will guide you two to where the Guardians are being held. Your goal is to release them and collect Garrett."

"Where will you be?" I ask.

"James and I will wait here until Jack delivers you. When he returns he will take us to Lucas. With any luck, we'll release our captives in roughly the same amount of time."

"And then what?" James asks.

"We rendezvous back here," Ash says. "With both Garrett and Lucas in tow, we'll your need help to manifest everyone back home."

"Understood."

"Jack will run interference between our two groups," Ash continues. "If some of us get into trouble he'll alert the others. This is Plan B. If you receive word that there's a problem, you will immediately abandon your mission to help the other team. I don't want any of us hurt or left behind. If we can't take care of this today we'll try another. Understand?"

Everyone nods. I lace my fingers and crack my knuckles. Let's go save some Guardians.

Jack walks away from us and toward the left side of the arch. Madeline and I follow and, when she passes Ash, she gives his arm a reassuring squeeze. I look to James and he wears an interesting expression. "You've got this," he says, but his eyes say something different. He's worried.

Risking Jack's wrath, I take an extra second to leave rank and wrap my arms around James. I give him the quickest hug imaginable and then sprint a few steps to catch up behind Madeline.

Next to the arch is a grassy hill dotted with the trees I spotted earlier. We make our way to the top and follow Jack alongside a paved street. Why the afterlife needs roads, I don't know.

"Walk next to me so it looks like we're friends," he whispers.

Madeline and I adjust our pace. As we walk we pass several people – Guardians – milling about alone or in groups. I glance from side to side and try not to look out of place. No one gives us a second thought, that I can tell. If a Guardian isn't speaking with someone they look lost in their own world or sit with their eyes closed. Connecting to their Wards, maybe?

It appears we're exiting a park of some kind because ahead of us sprawls what I can only describe as a metropolis. We reach the perimeter and continue across a large main street. I look up and catch the sign – Central Park West. Confused, I fall a step behind Jack as he leads us toward an impressive building where four white stone columns hug a multitude of stairs. At the top of the structure, and in between the columns, are the words Truth, Knowledge, and Vision etched in stone. In front of the stairs sits a bronze statue of a man riding a horse. I squint to concentrate my line of sight. According to the plaque the statue is of Theodore Roosevelt. I glance to my right and notice another sign. We're headed to the Museum of Natural History.

What the hell? I move to Madeline's side and bump her arm so she'll read my thoughts.

"Are we in New York City?"

She shakes her head. *"Only a replication. The Allegiant alter the Intermediate daily. Who wants to live for eternity in the same environment?"*

I nod in understanding. *"When we go inside will it look like a museum?"*

"No." She blinks. *"It's just a façade."*

Jack leads us along the street casually, near the edge of the sidewalk directly in front of the museum. We reach Teddy's statue and pass it. Was this not our destination?

Suddenly, he pulls us over and presses us back against the statues base, concealing us from view. "We need to manifest inside," he says to Madeline. "Let me guide the way."

Madeline takes my wrist and Jack grabs the other.

"We couldn't manifest in there to begin with?" I whisper. "Why risk being seen at all?"

Jack gives me an irritated look. "You need to know how to get back to the arch."

Oh. Right. "But, won't the others notice us with Garrett? If he's really that weak he won't be able to walk."

Madeline waves her fingers. "My reiki should be enough to get him there."

Okay. I'm going to shut up now.

The carbonated feeling builds inside my body until it disappears. Before I open my eyes, I feel a soft mist and hear what I think is the quiet rush of water. A moment later, I find that I'm correct; I am standing behind a waterfall. But this isn't a water-tumbling-over-rocks natural kind of waterfall. This looks like something out of a sci-fi movie.

Controlled water pours gently from above, out of an unknown source, arcing over us like a smooth curtain as far as I can see. It emanates a soft blue light which illuminates both Madeline and Jack. I look around. Is it lit from the other side? What does it fall into? Behind us is nothing but darkness and in front of us is a ledge. Where do we go from here?

Jack steps back and begins to feel along what must be a wall. I know he finds what he's looking for when his hands disappear from sight. There's a hidden entrance.

"This way," he says and vanishes.

Madeline and I give each other a wary look. We feel our way carefully along the invisible wall, mimicking Jack, until we locate the open space he found. I spread my arms wide when I step inside and trail my fingers along a smooth surface to both my right and my left. We must be in a hallway of sorts. It's pitch black though, and I feel as if I may step into nothingness at any moment.

"A little light would be nice," I mutter under my breath.

"Not when you want to keep something secret," Jack says ahead of me.

We're suspended in darkness for several feet until Jack's silhouette gradually comes into view. At a corner he stops and waits. When I reach him, I look toward the next leg of our journey. At the end of another dark hallway is a soft white light. It reflects off the smooth black walls, and I can't see anything beyond it.

Once Madeline joins us, Jack points. "Down there is where you'll find my brother and the others," he says quietly. "Once you release them you'll need to bring them back to where we arrived. None of us can manifest from any other point inside this area."

"Why?" I ask.

"These walls are made of coal."

"Coal?"

He looks impatient. "It binds us here like it traps souls in Hell."

My eyebrows shoot up. Good to know.

"When you get to the waterfall manifest outside with the Guardians help." He takes a step away from us. "Then get back to the arch. The faster we do this the better."

Madeline and I nod.

"I'm headed to Ash and James," he says. He turns on his heel and disappears the way we came.

Madeline focuses on my face and pulls her anlace from her belt. *"Ready?"*

This telepathic communication is great when you're trying to be stealthy. *"Yes."* I follow her lead and clutch my weapon.

She walks tentatively, yet defensively down the next hall, sweeping it with her eyes. After a few feet toward our destination, I choose to turn around and walk backward. It's probably best to keep an eye out behind us. Who knows who might show up? As far as I know, there's only one way in and out of here.

The closer we get to the light the brighter it grows. I have to squint even with my back turned. I sense Madeline stop walking so I do, too.

"Look at this," she says.

I turn around and shield my eyes. The light is seeping through a fissure in the ground that runs the width of the tunnel. It shines up the walls and hits the ceiling, essentially blocking our path like a door.

I look at her. *"I take it we go through?"*

Madeline shrugs. *"I suppose so. There's no other way."* She looks around then back at me. *"Jack could have been more specific."*

"He could be a lot more of things." I grimace.

She smiles. Carefully, she extends her free hand toward the light and gently pushes it through.

"Anything?" I ask her.

She shakes her head. *"It doesn't hurt."*

Good enough for me. I walk around her and step completely through the light.

And into a room of really surprised people.

"Emma?"

My eyes swing to an older gentleman with glasses, sandy brown hair, and a graying mustache. "Yes?"

He breaks out in a smile. "It's time, isn't it?"

"Time to get you out of here? Absolutely."

Three women who were sitting on the floor scramble to their feet. I recognize only one. Meg. When they stand they reveal Garrett laying the on ground. I immediately look over my shoulder to make sure Madeline has followed me inside. We lock eyes and then move toward him, causing the Guardians to step out of our way.

"Garrett?" I stow my anlace and kneel beside him, feeling his forehead. His eyes are closed and his skin feels clammy; he's practically translucent. My heart begins to race.

Madeline takes one of his hands and searches his wrist for a pulse. "It's there but it's weak," she says. "Move back." I scoot to the side and she places her hands on either side of his head.

"We tried that," a woman with black hair set in a bun says. Her voice is full of concern. "It's not working anymore."

Madeline gives her a reassuring smile. "My Pax is a little stronger."

My eyes meet hers. *"Pax?"*

"Reiki," she responds.

Madeline focuses and sends a wave of energy through Garrett's body. I can see it ripple over him like heat rising from hot pavement. After a moment, his eyes slowly open and he registers her face. "You're here," he croaks.

"Can you sit up?" She slides her hand under his shoulder and wraps the other around his arm to pull him forward. When he's a few inches off the ground, I place my hands against his back to steady him. He notices and looks over his shoulder.

"Hey," he rasps. "My date didn't go so well."

"You think?" I smirk. "I know you didn't want to spend time with Samantha, but this is a bit extreme."

He gives me a tight smile. I try to return it, but my face fades into seriousness. "I'm sorry," I whisper. "This is all my fault."

He barely shakes his head. "It's not."

It is. If he had just stayed with me...I clear my thoughts. Now's not the time to assign blame. "Can you stand?"

"I'll try."

Madeline and I help him to his feet. This makes him dizzy and he leans against the wall for balance. While he gets his bearings, I look around the room. It's rectangular with four walls and a ceiling made of coal. The glow from the light door illuminates the space. There's nothing in here but four Guardians and us.

A young girl stares at me. Her caramel colored eyes are panicked and stand out against her red hair. I read her thoughts. *"Now what? You came through the light. How will we get out?"*

"What do you mean?" I ask.

Her eyes grow wide. "It's true."

"What's true?"

"Garrett said you were Charmed. He told us what happened and about the La..Lav..." she can't say the word.

"Larvatus," I say.

"Of course it's true," Meg says to the red-haired girl. "Garrett wouldn't lie." She leans forward. "Do you remember us yet?"

She knows about my memory loss? I guess they have had a lot of time to talk in here. I shake my head. "I don't."

"I'm Meg." She points to herself and then around the group. "This is Jenna, Joss, and Thomas." They all give me warm smiles.

"Got it. That's Madeline," I say and look toward her. She flashes a quick smile our way as she tends to Garrett. "As soon as we get out of here we'll join James and Ash."

I can help but notice Meg's reaction when I say James' name. She lights up.

"Jenna," I change tack, "what did you mean about my coming through the light?"

"Only The Allegiant can come and go," she says. "We can't pass through."

My face twists. "It's a one-way door? How did Jack visit you?"

"He didn't come all the way through," Thomas says. "Lucas told him to not to."

Frowning, I walk around the Guardians toward the light and step through to the other side. I have no problem going back and forth. I reenter the room and look at Madeline.

"It's an Allegiant creation to contain Guardians," she says. "They didn't count on us."

I stare at the light. How can we get everyone to the other side? I push and pull my hand back and forth through it. It's so bright. What is it made of? The only other light I've seen remotely like this came from James' palm.

"That's it." I turn toward Madeline who is still holding on to Garrett. "We have to deflect it."

She reads my mind. "I think you're right." She hands Garrett off to Thomas and moves to stand beside me. I stare at her and ask, *"Is he going to get any better?"*

"I hope so," she shoots back to me. *"Or we'll have to carry him."*

That won't go unnoticed.

I pull my anlace from my belt and Mad does the same. "Try once first?" I ask. She nods.

With all the strength we have, we thrust our weapons into the light and draw them to the side, like we're cutting a piece of fabric. My anlace vibrates in my hands almost uncontrollably, and I have to set my feet to remain standing. But it works. A dark space forms between our knives as if Madeline and I are drawing back a curtain.

The Guardians don't hesitate; they know we don't need another trial run. First Jenna and then Meg sprint through the space. Thomas needs a little help with Garrett and Joss assists him. Once everyone is through, Madeline and I follow. I look behind us and the curtain of light has fallen back in place. No one will ever know.

"This way." Madeline steps to the front of the group to lead us out to the waterfall. I relieve Joss of Garrett and pull his arm around my shoulders. He leans against me as he tries to walk; his legs are like jelly. Thomas supports his other side as we practically drag him along. "I'm glad we're not in a hurry," I try to joke.

All Garrett can do is snicker. His breathing is labored even with our assistance.

We make it to the waterfall, and Madeline changes places with Thomas at Garrett's side. She asks us all to join hands. "We need your help to manifest out," she says. "Emma and Garrett can't do it alone. From there you can disappear to wherever you see fit."

"If it's all the same," Thomas says, "I'd like to stay near you three."

The other Guardians murmur in agreement.

"That's fine," Madeline says. "Just try to look inconspicuous when we get out of here."

The effervescence of manifestation builds inside my body and evaporates. I'm getting used to this. I feel Garrett's weight against me and open my eyes. We're outside on the museum steps. Time to move.

"You're going to have to try and walk," I tell Garrett. "We need to get across the street."

He gives me a frantic look. Apparently, he hasn't acquired the full use of his limbs.

"Forget it," Madeline says. "Let's just go."

Garrett tries to stand upright and walk between us, like he has his arms casually draped around two girls. I doubt it looks anything but awkward. The ladies move a few feet to our right and act like they are in the middle of a conversation. Thomas heads off on his own independently, but still within earshot. We begin to descend the staircase. No more than three steps down Jack appears in front us, startling me.

"You have to get out of here!" he hisses. "They know!"

How is that possible? I read his scattered thoughts. *"Too many Allegiant! James and Ash forced back! They're heading to the arch!"*

I nearly drop Garrett. "We have to help!"

"Get to the arch!" he says through gritted teeth.

My mind races. Garrett is too weak. We can't bring him to a fight! He'll be picked off for sure. I look around. We can't leave him here on the stairs, either. He's too sick; he needs to get back home *now*. I look between Jack and Mad. They're the only ones who can get him there. I shout my thoughts at Madeline. *"Use Jack and manifest Garrett home! I'll help James and Ash!"*

Her eyes widen. *"They need both of us!"*

I'm already several feet from her. *"That's not going to work! Just do it!"*

I run in the direction of Central Park, blowing past other Guardians without a second thought. After I cross the street, I sprint toward the bridge with the arch underneath, then scramble down the hill beside it. I pause on all fours near the base and listen. I hear grunting and scuffling, then a blast, and then the sound of rock scrabbling to the ground. How many Allegiant are there? I pause. Does it matter?

Clutching my anlace, I launch my body off the hill and land with my feet shoulder width apart. Fully exposed to the entrance of the arch, I quickly assess the situation.

There are two Allegiant engaging James and Ash. They dance around one another in a flurry of body parts and light. James trades beams with his attacker while the other dodges Ash's knife. I move into his line of vision. *"I'm here!"*

"Move behind us!" he silently shouts.

I do as I'm told, and I instantly know what he's trying to do. He wants to back his attacker into my blade.

"Watch out!"

I duck. A beam of light sails over my head, outside of the arch, and singes a few leaves off a nearby tree. My face twists. I'm not in the mood to be incinerated today. I jump to my feet and race up behind Ash's assailant. Unfortunately, he turns and catches me with his elbow – in my throat. I stagger backward, but stay on my feet and focus on breathing. In, out, in, out. My windpipe feels crushed.

The attacker gives me a curious look and moves toward me, but not before Ash catches him. He wraps his arms around the

188

Allegiant's chest like a vise from behind. I shake off my pain as the enemy struggles against him, realizing this is my shot. I take it, running toward him, and driving my anlace straight into his gut. He looks at me with wide eyes, his mouth forming an O, before bursting into dust.

The space that separated Ash and me becomes vacant, and I gaze at him in shock. *"I just killed someone."*

He gives me a curt nod. *"You sure did."*

Our attention turns to James; he is still dodging his assailant's attempts to kill him. Ash and I move in unison, parallel to one another, in an effort box them in.

"Get out of here Emma!" James shouts.

I shoot him a confused look. Did he not just see me take out that other guy? I have no qualms about hurting this one either; in fact I'm looking forward to it.

Suddenly, the remaining Allegiant's arm shoots to the left, changing direction and catching Ash off guard. He tries to dodge the beam of light, but he's not quick enough and it slams him against the stone wall. I see red and spring into action, heading for the enemy's arm. I want to rip it off.

Before I can get there, the Allegiant releases Ash and he crumples to the ground. My mind scrambles. Oh shit oh shit oh shit! Half of me wants to check on him while the other half wants to continue the attack. Ash's eyes flutter and they catch mine. *"Give me a minute. I'm all right."* I center myself and focus.

James runs up on our attacker and barrels into his waist, shoving him back and sending them both to the ground. I jump out of the way as they roll. They tumble near Ash, fists flying. It's hard to make out who has the upper hand. How am I supposed to get a clear shot? One punch lands with a sickening thud and I wince. James lies motionless on the ground as the Allegiant pushes off him. My chest constricts as I stare at James. How badly is he hurt?

"Get away from him!" I yell.

The attacker stands and I crouch defensively. He turns and gives me a sick smile, allowing me to clearly see his face for the first time. Why does he look familiar?

"Emma," he sneers as he advances. "It's so nice to see you again."

He knows me? My mind reels. Think, think, think! I stare at him in confusion and not fear. "Who are you?" I snap.

He stops in his tracks. "You don't remember?" He looks pissed. Super pissed. "Allow me to jog your memory."

He charges at me and I put my arms out to block him, catching his shoulders and pressing him back with as much strength as he exerts against me. A look of shock flashes across his features. Is he surprised I'm fighting back? I push forward, our faces inches apart. A vision returns to me from when my bracelet left my wrist. It clicks. Blond hair. Distorted left eye. But where are his glasses?

It's Patrick.

I shove against him with everything I have and he stumbles. "Don't touch me," I snarl.

He laughs. "So you do remember." We begin to circle one another and he gives me a superior glare. "Don't worry. I won't have to touch you to hurt you like before."

He unleashes a beam of light from his hand and I fall to the ground against my stomach to avoid it. He jerks his palm toward me, and I roll then jump to my feet. I need to work my way into him to have a chance at hitting him with my anlace. In my periphery I see Ash move to his knees; he's coming around. I need to distract Patrick and buy time.

"When are you going to give this up?" I spit. "Attacking me this summer wasn't enough?"

"No," he growls. "Kellan found me and made me immortal for one small price. I merely have to work for him and kill you and your friends. I told him I wouldn't mind; it's an easy price to pay."

Kellan turned him Allegiant to make him his lackey? To what levels will this man stoop? I'm sure he assumed my seeing Patrick would make me vulnerable. Little does he know I have virtually no memory of his assault. Seeing Patrick doesn't faze me. It only fuels my desire to eliminate him.

"I'm sorry to disappoint you." I give him a wicked smile. "But your debt will remain unpaid."

"I beg to differ," he says and charges.

I allow him to come at me and then spring to the side at the last second. I need to turn us around, so I can back him up toward Ash. I dodge his punches and attempt a roundhouse kick. He grabs my ankle and twists my leg causing me to fall and land hard against my shoulder. Pain sears through my back and I gasp.

"I figured you'd be more scared of me," Patrick gloats as he grips my leg. "I have to admit this is kind of fun. You're not the same Emma from months ago."

I grimace. "No shit Sherlock! When do you figure that out? When I showed up in the Intermediate or when I kicked your friend's ass?" I'm not backing down.

"He wasn't my friend," he says referring to the dead Allegiant. "Just another piece in Kellan's game."

I twist my body and move my arms, which makes my shoulder throb. I set my hands and push my upper body off the ground, yanking my foot from Patrick's grasp. I scramble backwards and get to my feet. My eyes sweep under the arch for James and Ash. Ash now stands, but James has disappeared. Where did he go? My heart starts to pound.

"Push him outside!" Ash sends me his thoughts.

Patrick comes at me again. I grip my anlace and ready myself. I take a swipe at him and he jumps out of the way. I circle around him and try again. He dodges. He throws a beam of light and I weave to the right. Another beam, another swipe. After a few more attempts I've worked Patrick outside the arch. Now what?

Suddenly, James drops from above, landing on Patrick's shoulders and smashing him to the ground. He must have crawled to the top of the bridge while we fought. He wraps one arm around Patrick's neck and the other around his chest, pulling his body back and jerking Patrick to his knees. He holds him in place as he struggles and shouts, "Emma now!"

In two strides I stand directly in front of Patrick. I raise my anlace in both hands and a look of terror crosses his face. I imagine it's the same look he saw in my eyes this summer.

I bring my weapon down.

He explodes into nothing.

Chapter 17

We appear in a room that overflows with concerned faces. Madeline and Dane. Matt and Shel. Thomas, Joss, Jenna, and Meg. Jack looks less impressed.

"Thank God," Madeline sighs. She sprints to Ash, weaves her arms around his waist, and buries her head against his chest. He lets go of my hand and envelops her.

James releases my other hand and makes a fist. "Nice job, Donohue."

I smirk and bump my fist against his. "Ditto, Davis." This is a much more subdued celebration than the one we had after Patrick's demise. James gave me a hug so tight it put pressure on my heart. Then he laid a kiss on me to match.

"Hey there, kid." Thomas approaches us and gives James a hearty slap on the shoulder. Meg, Joss, and Jenna are right behind him to greet their friend and I step aside, allowing them to get reacquainted. From what I've been told they haven't laid eyes on each other in two months.

My attention is drawn across the room and meets Dane's gaze. Relief visibly washes through him and he stands. I notice he's still wearing his tux; although, his tie and jacket are gone, and his collar hangs open. My eyes bounce to Matt and his outfit is the same; Shel has changed and must have borrowed something from Madeline to wear. I immediately make my way toward them and Dane meets me half way. He wraps me in his arms and I try not to wince.

"What's wrong?" He steps back, tentatively holding my shoulders.

"Nothing," I lie. Now that I'm not distracted by fighting Allegiant ex-lab partners, my injuries are starting to show. My throat aches with every swallow and my shoulder has decided to lock up. "I'm just a little sore."

"From what?"

"What do you think?" I smile. I don't want to worry him; the tender muscles will heal within days. It's a Larvatus perk.

"This one," Ash appears by my side, "is one tough little fighter. She took an elbow to the throat and remained standing. I know guys twice her size that move would've laid out."

Dane's eyes grow dark and his jaw tenses. He looks at me. "You call that nothing?"

"I..."

"The blow to your shoulder was probably just as bad," Ash continues. "We should really look at it. Even though it will heal quickly, ice may help the swelling."

"What kind of blow?" Shel steps beside me, her medical training kicking in. "Was the joint dislocated? Can you move it?"

I roll my eyes and raise my left arm up and down even though it kills me to do so. "Yes, I can move it. Relax."

"What happened?" Dane asks.

"I got tripped up," I sigh. "I tried to kick Patrick, but he caught my ankle and I fell on my shoulder."

"Patrick?" His eyes grow wide. "How in the hell is he involved?"

"Kellan turned him Allegiant to aggravate Emma," James says from behind us.

Dane's eyes dart to him and back to me. I set both hands on the sides of his face while a self-satisfied smile plays on my lips. "Don't worry. We took care of him."

"*You* did," James says. "I only held him down."

I look at him over my shoulder. "I wouldn't have been able to do it alone."

"Yeah, yeah, you two make a great team," Dane mutters under his breath. He hands me off to Shel who winds an arm around my waist. "Let's get you checked out, okay?"

I know I'm fine, but I allow them to dote on me. This night has been rough on everyone, and I'm sure they want some semblance of control. Matt and Shel have to be so confused and Dane is just straight up worried. I walk next to Shel as she steers us toward the hallway off The Larvatus' great room.

"I'll come with you and check on Garrett," Madeline says and starts to follow us.

How could I have forgotten about Garrett? I stop walking. "Is he all right?"

Madeline turns her big green eyes on me as Shel responds. "He's stable."

I frown. "What does that mean?"

"He's unconscious," Madeline says as she reaches my side. "Your friend can explain more. We're lucky to have her."

My eyes swing to Shel. "C'mon," she says and pulls me forward. "Let's look at you first. He's not going anywhere."

We make it to a spacious bathroom where Shel closes the door behind us. "Take off that mess." She indicates my shift.

It takes me a minute, but I do as I'm told. My shoulder is throbbing. I pull the green top over my head to reveal the white tank underneath. Shel steps behind me and gasps.

"Jesus Emma!" She gingerly slides the left strap off my shoulder. "Your skin is a rainbow."

"Not a pretty one?" I smirk in the mirror.

"These particular shades of green and yellow are never a great combination." I see her brow furrow over my shoulder and feel her trace the outline of my injury. "Move your arm," she instructs me and I do. "Now try to roll your shoulder."

OW! I bite my lip to keep from cursing. "That hurts."

She steps around me. "I figured as much. You've sprained it and given yourself one heck of a bruise; although, the coloring indicates it's already healing. It should be gray and purple for having just happened."

"See? It'll be fine in a day or two."

She squints at my neck. "You've got another one there from the elbow."

I lean forward and notice my throat is faintly yellow. "No one will notice."

She sighs. I can see her eyes begin to tear in the light of the bathroom fixture as she says, "Let me get you some ice."

She starts to walk away and I grab her wrist. "Are you okay?"

She looks at me and tries to blink away her tears. "Yes...no. I'm not sure."

I pull her further into the bathroom where I lower the toilet lid and have her take a seat. I set myself next to her on the edge of the tub and grasp her hand. "Talk to me," I say quietly.

"You're hurt and you don't care," she says. "You should care."

"Trust me, I do," I say to reassure her. "But, I know I'll be better soon, so it's not a huge deal."

"It is so a huge deal!" she exclaims. "You could have been killed! Someone – Patrick of all people – tried to kill you! That's important. It's *serious*," she emphasizes. "You cannot die on me." Tears trickle down her cheeks.

"I know this seems scary, but it's who I am now." I clutch her hand. "Did Dane talk to you? Did you ask him questions?"

She nods as she looks down. "He said he told us everything he knew."

"Do you believe him?"

Her head snaps up. "How can I not? I saw you evaporate in front me! Then, I saw you reappear. And James is alive," her voice breaks on the word alive. Suddenly, her expression morphs into one of concern. "How have you been dealing with this for so long?"

I shrug my good shoulder. "I don't know. I can't remember anything Guardian related past a month ago. Did Dane tell you about my memory?"

"Yes." She looks at our hands. "He told us your bracelet blocks it for some reason. He also said it gives you your abilities. I guess I know why you won't take it off now."

"What happened saved me, Shel. Without it I'd be dead."

She takes a shaky breath. "I know." A tear winds its way to her chin and she wipes it away. "Dane said you saved his life."

"So I've been told." I give her a tiny smile. "And I'd do it again in a heartbeat. For any of you."

She studies my face and then pulls me forward to wrap her arm around my neck. "When did you get so brave?" she whispers.

That's easy. "Since the people I love were threatened."

She squeezes me. "This is amazing, but really messed up. How am I supposed to be a medical professional when I know people can be resurrected from the dead?"

I laugh against her shoulder. "That is twisted."

She leans away. "Your erratic behavior is more easily explained now."

"I'm sure." I smile. I look at her and a calm feeling settles over me. I have someone to talk to about this. An outsider to give me perspective. My best friend. "I'm so glad you know," I say, relieved. "And Matt, too. I won't have to lie anymore. And James needs his friends. I'm sure he's ecstatic to have you guys back."

"Speaking of," she clears her throat and raises an eyebrow at me. "What in the world is going on? You're seeing Dane *and* James? That's...it's..."

"Crazy, I know." I let out a heavy breath. "My feelings for both of them are trapped in my memories. We're trying to build new ones."

She gives me a sly smile. "How's that working out for you?"

I playfully swat her leg. "It's a day by day thing."

"So, what are you going to do?" she asks. Leave it to Shel to get right to the juicy stuff. "Do you have a chart where you compare them against one another? A column for personality, a column for looks, one for kissing, one for..."

"No!" I laugh. "We have rules."

"What?" she giggles. "Tell me!"

"I won't do with one what I won't do with the other."

Her mouth falls open, and I know what she's thinking. "No clothes come off *ever*," I stress. "Making out is as far as it goes."

She makes a face. "I was joking about the kissing! They're okay with this?"

"Should they not be okay with it?"

"Emma," she chastises me. "The James I know would never let another guy come within a ten mile radius of you let alone touch you! And Dane...he's head over heels in love! You two, you know, in St. Thomas..."

I gape at her. "He told you about that?"

"You both did! I mean neither of you denied it while feeding me that story about needing a vacation."

My face turns red. "I don't remember any of it."

"You don't remember sleeping with him?"

I shake my head. "Or James."

"Wow." Her mouth forms a huge O on the *ow*. "I thought you'd at least remember Dane. He's not a Guardian."

"But, all of our time together is due to Guardians," I explain. "Our whole relationship is wrapped around them."

Her eyes search my face and she tilts her head, propping her chin on the heel of her hand.

"What?"

"I'm curious," she says slowly. "Do you think you guys would still have a connection if you eliminated all the supernatural stuff?"

I blink at her. That's an excellent question.

A knock interrupts us and my body jerks. "Everything all right?" Dane is on the opposite side of the door.

"Yes," I automatically respond. "Can you bring us some ice?"

"Sure thing." I hear him walk away.

"So?" Shel asks quietly.

It's true she's given me something to ponder. I'm not going to figure out my romantic life in the next five minutes, so I concede. "I'd like to think we would. He's a great guy."

She pats my knee, and I stand to open the door so Dane can enter when he returns. As we wait, I think. Would Dane want me if I had just been a normal girl when we met? If he didn't help free me from – what did he say? – a protective shell? My demeanor this summer should have been a turn off except he's proven over and over again that he enjoys a challenge. Is that what I am to him?

Moments later, he appears with a plastic bag full of ice. "Which shoulder?" he asks.

I turn and point to my left. He steps toward me and grimaces. "Damn," he mutters. "Are you sure it's not broken?"

"Dr. Moore says it's only a sprain and it's healing." I wink at Shel.

He places the bag against my skin, and I reach up to hold it in place. "Thanks."

"Have you seen Garrett?" he asks.

"Not yet. Let's go."

I follow Dane and Shel a few steps down the hallway to a bedroom. When I enter I'm not prepared for what I see, and the bag of ice slips from my hand. Dane catches it.

Garrett lies pale and motionless in the middle of a twin bed. His head is propped on two pillows and his arms lay outside the blankets that are pulled to his chest. A bedside lamp provides the only light in the room; it casts eerie shadows across his body and face. One of those shadows looks like an IV pole. Wait. It is an IV and it's dripping into his arm.

"Where did you get that?" I ask.

"Matt's clinic," Shel answers as she rounds the bed. "It's the best I could do on short notice. Tomorrow, I'll head to the hospital and get him some TPN."

I stare at her confused.

"Total parenteral nutrition," she clarifies. "He's extremely dehydrated and malnourished." She gently picks up his wrist and checks his pulse. "His heart rate remains steady," she says almost to herself as her fingers travel to the side of his neck. "If I could get him hooked up to a monitor I'd feel better about keeping tabs on him."

"He won't wake up?" I move to stand beside her. "He was talking in the Intermediate."

"He collapsed as soon as he arrived with Madeline and Jack," Dane says.

"I didn't have to do CPR, so I don't suspect any brain damage," Shel continues. "But I'm not a doctor yet. I know he needs rest and fluids. Without taking him to the hospital, we'll just have to wait and see."

"Why can't we take him to the hospital?" I look from her to Dane.

"If we register him as a patient Kellan can easily find him. At least that's what Madeline said."

"Then we use a fake name," I say adamantly. "He needs our help."

"Em," Dane says. "He can still search who was admitted and on what date."

I let out a frustrated sigh and reach around Shel to grasp Garrett's hand. He feels cold to me. "Do you think he needs another blanket?"

Shel looks around the room. When she doesn't immediately find more bedding she opens the closet to search.

"Garrett?" I lean over him. "Can you hear me? Are you cold?"

Nothing. No response. An ache in my chest starts to build over the one in my shoulder. What if he doesn't wake up? I think of Jack. He must be livid. He said he'd hold me responsible if anything happened to his brother. In all honesty, I will hold myself responsible too.

"Garrett," I say again, "we're going to get you some type of food soon. Stay strong. You've come too far to give up now."

"I don't think he has any intention of giving up," Dane says, suddenly behind me. "He just needs time to heal. He's still turning human after all."

This is true. It makes sense his body would be overwhelmed by all the stresses on it. That wouldn't be easily explained to a doctor or a surgeon.

"Here." Shel pulls a blanket out of a dresser drawer. She unfolds it and I grab one end. Carefully I place it over Garrett, lifting his arms and tucking it around him. "Better?" I ask as if he'll respond.

He doesn't even twitch.

Dane gently touches my arm. "Let's get you home. You need to rest."

"No." I brush him off. "Someone needs to stay here in case he wakes up." I glance around the room and notice an overstuffed armchair. "I'll sleep here."

"You will not," Dane's tone is stern. "You can't sleep in a chair with your shoulder the way it is."

"Watch me." Why is he giving me a hard time?

"Guys," Shel interrupts. "When I told Madeline I'd have to leave to get supplies she volunteered to keep an eye on Garrett. I think he's in good hands." She eyes me. "Go home and get some sleep. I know I have to if I'm going to be of any use tomorrow. There's nothing anyone can do until I get the TPN anyway."

I sigh. I don't want to leave Garrett. He looks awful. But, I trust The Larvatus. Besides, they can reiki him, or Pax him, or whatever if necessary. Not that it's helping now.

"Fine, but I'll be back," I say stubbornly. "What time do you think you'll be here?"

Shel thinks about it. "I'll call you. It depends on how long it takes me to *borrow* what we need."

Great. I realize Shel can get into some serious trouble over this and suddenly I feel tired and defeated. "Be careful. Don't get arrested for stealing."

Her expression twists as she walks toward me. "You do remember who you're talking to, right? I don't get caught doing anything." She grins.

As we leave the room, I give Garrett one last glance. *Please be okay,* I silently pray. *Please.*

When we make it back to the living room, we catch Ash in the middle of describing what took place in the Intermediate. Madeline sits next to him, and I catch Matt standing near the corner. I break my own rule and read his thoughts.

"When can we get out of here?" he mutters. *"This is too much for one night."*

My heart goes out to him. I glance around the rest of the room and find the other Guardians standing about sporadically, except for Meg. She's sitting conspicuously close to James on one of the couches, and her hand rests on his knee. I can't help it and one eyebrow shoots up. Really? She doesn't waste any time does she?

James jumps to his feet when he spots me and everyone turns my way. "How's your shoulder?"

"Fine." I take the bag of ice from Dane and set it back on my skin. "Garrett's the one you need to worry about." I glance at Ash. "What did I miss?"

"I was saying that we'll need to regroup and strike again to retrieve Lucas. It shouldn't be too hard if we're not separated. I think we took out the majority of the new Allegiant we came across tonight."

"How many were there?"

"James and I encountered six. We barely took out two before realizing how outnumbered we were. I demanded James abort the mission and then two of them followed us to the arch. You know what happened after that."

"So when do we go back? We can't allow Kellan much time to create more." If we do we'll just end up in an endless cycle of cat and mouse.

"Our good friends over here are going to make sure where we stand." Ash glances toward the other Guardians. "They'll let us know if Kellan has anymore Allegiant hiding in the wings. Once we know exactly what we're dealing with, we'll return. Today was a close call. I don't want that happening again."

I couldn't agree more.

Ash stands and addresses the group. "I believe everything we need to talk about has been discussed. Mad and I are ready to call it a night; we need to keep an eye on Garrett. You're all more than welcome to stay here if you'd like."

James looks at me expectantly. Is he kidding? I'm sure Meg would rather I didn't. My eyes dart to her, and my mind hears her southern twang. *"Please say no."*

Her comment tips my mental scale, and the weight of everything that's happened today settles on my shoulders. My friends know everything. I killed two people. One of them was Patrick. I got a little beat up. Garrett is really sick. Meg wants time with James. And we still have to rescue Lucas.

I need to be alone.

"I'm headed home." I take a step. "For someone who doesn't tire easily my bed is calling."

James stops me. "You can't go home."

"Why?" Dane and I give him confused stares.

"When we were in the Intermediate I managed to get some information out of Patrick. I read his mind, but it wasn't giving me what I wanted to know. I demanded he tell me how he got there and of course his smug ass told me."

"What did he say?"

"That Kellan found him through Garrett's memories. Remember how Jack told us Garrett's mind had been read?"

My eyes dart to Jack and I nod.

"Garrett knew about Patrick because he tried to help me over my guilt from your attack. Kellan tried to use Patrick to get under your skin. Think about it. If he knows all about you from Garrett's memories with me then he knows where you live. How many times have I been to your house? How many times did Garrett pull me away from you this summer?"

I can't answer him because I don't remember. All my body registers is the feeling of an invisible elephant sitting on my chest. "I need to get my parents out of there," I whisper. "If he used Patrick then what's to stop him from using them?" I'm terrified. What am I going to do?

Instantly, Ash is at my side. "It doesn't work that way," he calms me. "He can't turn the living without their permission. The only reason it worked with Patrick is because his mind was sick and he had no better option. I doubt your parents would agree to die and become one of Kellan's minions."

I give him a wary look. "He can't force them?"

He shakes his head. "There are rules they have to follow, too. Safeguards. The position holds great responsibility; they wield a lot of power. We wouldn't want a rogue Allegiant getting a big head and trying to rule the Intermediate *and* world now would we?" He attempts to smile.

Relief floods my body. Thank God.

Ash isn't finished. "I do agree with James, however. It's not safe for you to be home alone. At least one of us should be with you in case Kellan sends multiple Allegiant."

Not this again!

"She can stay with me," Dane volunteers. "Garrett has never been to my place."

"You cannot defeat an Allegiant," James says, his jaw tense. "Kellan has read Lucas' mind. Obviously, he knows who you are. Your potential father-in-law never visited your apartment?"

Dane looks irritated. "Physically, no. But he does know my address. It's in my employee file."

Well that screws that. "I guess I'm staying here then." I look to Madeline. "Which room would you prefer I take?"

"Wait a minute," Dane stops me. "How are you going to explain moving out to your parents? 'Hey, by the way, I don't want to live with you anymore? I'm moving out with some random people you don't know?' Come on, Em." Clearly he doesn't want me staying here.

"I could stay at your house invisibly for most of the time," James pulls my attention from Dane. "That eliminates the moving out problem."

It's too late for this insane Ping-Pong of arguments. I look at Meg. She's not happy. I look at Dane. He's not happy. "Enough!" I step away from them. "I'm staying with Shel for the night." I glance at Matt. Now he's unhappy. Ugh! "Never mind," I sigh. "The easiest thing is for me to stay here for now. We'll figure something out in the morning. Mad?" I glance at her again.

"You know," Ash says, "not that it will help immediately, but moving in with Dane isn't out of the question."

What? My eyes flash to James. Now he's pissed.

"What do you mean?" Dane asks.

I stare at Ash and read his thoughts. He can't be serious!

"Mad and I could Gift you," he says aloud to Dane. "We always need more Charmed, and I believe you're worthy of The Larvatus. What do you say?" he asks. "Care to join our team?"

Chapter 18

"Absolutely not!"

Dane looks at me in shock. "Excuse me?"

I slap my hand over my mouth. Did I say that out loud? His eyes bore into mine, hard and intense. He's angry.

"Perhaps this is a discussion for another time," Ash says diplomatically.

"No, it's a discussion for now." Dane's neck flexes. "In private."

My stomach twists into a hard knot. I've truly upset him, and I wasn't trying to. I turn my weary eyes to Madeline and she reads my thoughts.

"There are four bedrooms upstairs," she says. "Take your pick."

I start to walk away, and James grabs my arm.

"You don't have to explain yourself to him," he says. He turns and shoots daggers at Dane. "I think it's clear how she feels. Leave it alone."

Dane's eyes flash. "Let her go."

The grip on my arm tightens.

Have these two lost their minds? Everyone in this room must think we're nuts! "James, let go." I brush his hand and it falls from my arm. "I don't have a problem explaining what I said."

Dane looks vindicated as I step around him, and I sense him follow me as I head up the stairs. I don't bother to say good night, or nice to meet you, or see you later to anyone. I just head to the first empty room I find.

Dane shuts the door behind us. "Why did you say that?" he demands.

"I'm sorry. It was a gut reaction."

"To what? The idea of my being like you? Why is that so repulsive?"

I frown. "It's not repulsive. It's uncalled for."

"How so?" He takes two steps to stand directly in front of me. "I could protect you; we could protect each other."

"I know."

"You know?" He scowls. "Then give me a good reason not to march back downstairs and demand to be Charmed tonight."

I stare at him wide-eyed. "You would do that?"

"Hell yes I would do that! If it means protecting you. If it means we could spend more time together. I'd do it in a second."

My face pinches. I try to speak, but my thoughts won't form sentences. He shouldn't want to drastically alter his life for me; he should want do it for himself.

"Say something," he says and grasps my arms. "Give me a good reason not to do this."

I stare into his hazel eyes, the flecks of green burning bright with his intense words. I say the first thing that comes to my mind. "I don't want you to change your life for me."

His eyes narrow. "Or is it that you don't want me cutting into your time with James?"

What? I shake my head violently. "No! That thought never crossed my mind!" No wonder he's so angry. "I simply don't want you to become something you're not because of me! You should want to do it for yourself. What if you hate it? I don't want that guilt."

He gives me an uncertain look. "So it's all about you?"

"No," I sigh as I remove his hands from my arms. "It's entirely about *you*. If you choose this life you should do it because you want to live it. Not because you felt compelled to do it for me. I would never ask you to give this much of yourself. I *won't* ask you to. This shouldn't be a rash decision."

He studies my face and then the floor, hopefully digesting my words. After a few moments, he looks at me again. "And if I decide I want it? Would you be upset?"

"No," I admit honestly. "Not after you've spoken to Ash about what it involves and given it some real thought."

He sighs, rubs his tired eyes, then reaches for me. "Come here."

As I walk into his arms, I wrap mine around his waist. He pulls me to his chest, and I bury my head under his chin. "This is not how I hoped this night would end," he says against my hair. "Some New Year's Eve."

My embrace tightens. "I think its New Year's Day now."

He nods in agreement. "Being stuck here with Matt and Shel drove me out of my mind. All I kept thinking was that you should be safe with me and wearing that amazing dress."

I lean away from him. "If I recall the evening correctly you wanted me out of that dress, mister. I don't know how *safe* I was."

He smirks. "Your memory has suddenly become infallible."

I laugh as his hands start to move against my back.

"Do you think I could get that kiss we missed at midnight?"

"Sure," I say and then arch a brow. "As long as you promise not to make any hasty decisions when it comes to your humanity."

He pauses to consider my request. "Will dwelling on it for a couple of days suffice?"

"Make it a week and I'll give you more than one kiss."

He doesn't hesitate. "Done."

An exasperated sigh escapes me. "You give in too easily."

He lowers his gaze and holds his lips centimeters from mine. "When are you going to figure out I can't resist you?"

"So what did you tell your parents?"

I slam the car door behind me. "That I'm a supernatural force of nature and I have to save our little piece of the world from impending doom."

Shel gives me a sarcastic stare.

"They told me to have fun and be careful," I tease.

She groans. "I still don't think any of this is funny."

"You need to lighten up," I tell her and turn the key in the ignition. "I told them we're on a pre-semester vacation just like we talked about."

A few days, and several discussions later, I find myself faking a girl's trip because I'm stuck with The Larvatus for the foreseeable future. Rather than making up daily lies to feed my parents about why they never see me, Shel and I came up with the idea for a faux winter trip. Supposedly we're headed to her aunt's place in Traverse City while, in reality, I'll be fifteen minutes away practicing defensive maneuvers and keeping vigil at Garrett's bedside. My lie buys me one week of time; after that, I'll have to come up with something else.

"I'm surprised Matt didn't ask you to watch the game with him," I say as we back out of her driveway. "He misses you."

"How do you know? Did you read his thoughts?"

"Maybe."

"You're such a freak!" she laughs. "He did ask, but I really have no interest in sports. Besides, I need to make sure both you and Garrett are still in one piece."

Her concern makes me smile.

"So," she pauses to pop some gum in her mouth, "have you seen Dane? Or is he still working ungodly hours?"

"Still working." I frown. "This year-end financial stuff is no joke when it's never been your responsibility before."

I haven't seen Dane in days. As soon as he got back to work, Teagan gave him the task of reviewing the reports for Legionnaire's annual audit. He's nervous he is going to miss something important, and he's been putting in extra time. When he gets home he calls, usually after ten o'clock. Last night all I got was a text:

Finally home. Management is not my calling.

I'm sure you're doing great.

We'll see. I miss you.

Miss you too.

"He won't change his mind about moving in? Even for a little while?" Shel asks.

"I told you," I say as we stop at a light. "He can't stand James. You saw how they acted the last time they were together. Dane says he doesn't want to fight and he's sure he will, given how stressed he is. He was kind of embarrassed about it the last time." Dane told me he felt like an ass getting into it with James in front of The Larvatus and every Guardian we know. While he's not happy about my living situation, he understands why it is the most logical choice for me. It's just not the best choice for him.

"Has he mentioned which way he's leaning on the Charmed thing?"

He hasn't, and I secretly hope he'll forget the whole idea. He's been too preoccupied to consider it for the right reasons. "No, and I haven't brought it up. He has enough to deal with."

Shel stares out the window and chews. "You've got that right. Working with Teagan would suck the life out of anyone." She turns to me. "You don't think she's keeping him late at the office on purpose do you?"

I shoot her a confused look. "How do you mean?"

"What do you mean how do I mean?! She's his ex-fiancée that has yet to get over him. You don't think she might be creating more work than necessary to worm her way back into his life?"

The idea sounds foreign to me. "I hadn't considered that, no."

Shel crosses her arms. "You can be so naïve sometimes."

"Thanks a lot!"

"Have you forgotten who you're dealing with? This is the woman who held Dane's job over his head to make him marry her. The same person who let herself into his place and waited for him *in his bed* after he broke it off with her! She is the evil wench who anonymously sent you an article about her return to town and upcoming wedding. It was how you found out about Dane's engagement in the first place."

Is she kidding? He didn't tell me about the engagement himself?

Shel takes in my bewildered expression and her eyes grow wide. "Of course you don't remember! It's all blocked."

She's got that right. "Is there anything else I should know?"

"She's frickin' gorgeous." Shel scowls. "Why is it the pretty ones are always so mean?"

I shrug. From the brief absence of my jewelry, I remember Teagan's appearance; she was dressed as Dorothy from the Wizard of Oz. Even so, I have to agree she is beautiful.

"That girl doesn't play," Shel continues. "Last I heard she still refuses to take off Dane's ring. You might want to pay an unannounced visit to the office to check her, to let her know you're still in the game."

My face twists. I don't play games. "Do you think Dane would go back to her?"

"Do I think he would give up on you for her? No. Do I think she will try everything in her power to convince him otherwise? Yes."

A vision of them staying late at the office, sharing takeout, jumps in my head. My mind sets a scene where she blatantly reaches across the desk in front of him for some papers, her low cut top and barely work appropriate skirt advertising everything she has to offer. Things I don't own and aren't willing to give up. A sour taste appears in the back of my throat.

"Are you trying to make me sick?"

Shel's expression turns sympathetic. "I'm not," she sighs. "If it makes you feel better our waitress was flirting with Matt during dinner yesterday and I wanted to slap her."

"Was he flirting back?"

"Of course not. He's oblivious to that stuff most of the time. I just don't get why people can't let other people be. If it's clear someone is in a relationship just *walk away*."

I murmur my agreement.

"Take Meg for example. She knows you and James are still involved; she's known about you from the beginning. Do you think she could tone down the flirting a little? Holy cow."

I know what she means. "She is really obvious, isn't she?"

"You think?!" Shel scoffs. "That girl has an agenda. She's just waiting for you to make up your mind. You can see it in her eyes."

I let out a heavy breath. "Did I tell you she kissed James?"

Her eyes get big. "In front of you?"

"No, months ago. Before I left for the island. James told me."

"How do you feel about that?"

"At the time I didn't know her; I couldn't remember anything except her face. And now, seeing them together makes me uncomfortable. I'm not going to lie; whenever they're together, I leave the room."

"Are you sure you want to stay here?" Shel indicates The Larvatus' house as we pull up the drive. "Maybe you should get a hotel room or something."

I smile. "It's free to stay here and I need to keep up with my training. Besides, I really like most of the company, and I want to be around when Garrett wakes up."

I park my car in front of the garage and then get out to retrieve my suitcase. Even though I've been spending the majority of my time here, it's never been overnight. Plus, I needed to put on a show for my girl's trip ruse.

"When will Matt be by to pick you up?" I ask as we head to the door.

"My guess is around eight or so. You never know when he gets together with his cousins."

"Great! You can work out with me."

Shel groans. "Do I have to?"

The door unexpectedly opens before us and Madeline stands there smiling. "Guess who's awake?"

Shel and I look at each other and then sprint over the threshold. I abandon my suitcase and we head straight to Garrett's room. When we enter, I find Joss and Jenna sitting on one side of the bed and Meg on the other. I mentally blanch at her presence, but then my eyes fall on Garrett and I break into a smile. How long have I waited to see those eyes?

"Oh! You're here," Joss says as she notices me. "He's been asking for you."

"Really?" I round the side of the bed and tease Garrett. "Don't you have more important things to worry about?"

He gives me a tiny smile. "I thought it was weird you weren't here." He doesn't sound like himself; his voice sounds rough and stuck. "I know you've been reading to me."

"I have. How are you enjoying *Pangalax* so far?" I downloaded the book to my iPad last week.

"It's confusing," he says honestly. "I think I'm missing some parts."

"You probably are."

Joss gets up, so I can take her spot. I collect Garrett's hand and squeeze it. He still feels cold and his overall complexion remains pale. "You scared the hell out of me. Don't do it again."

He rolls his tired eyes. "My apologies."

My attention is pulled away from him as I catch Shel changing his fluids on the opposite side of the bed. "You've given my best friend some real hands on experience. You're lucky I have connections; Shel is studying to be a doctor."

He turns his head against the pillow. "So I've been told."

He tries to extend his hand to Shel, but it takes a great deal of effort. She grasps it instead. "It's nice to meet you and a relief to hear you speak. How are you feeling?"

"Exhausted and thirsty," he rasps.

"Madeline? Could you go get Garrett a glass of ice please?"

Mad nods and leaves the room while Shel checks Garrett's pulse. "Where is everyone?" I ask Jenna. "Do they know he's awake?"

"James and Ash were here and they left to give him some space," she says. "Thomas went to find Jack."

Some weight leaves my shoulders at the mention of Jack's name. Surely he won't dislike me as much now that his brother has regained consciousness.

"Joss says I've been out for almost a week," Garrett croaks.

"Just about," I confirm. "Today would have been the sixth day."

Madeline reappears with a glass filled with crushed ice from the refrigerator. She hands it to Garrett with a smile and Shel speaks up.

"That's the first thing that's gone down your throat and landed in your stomach in over a month. It might feel a bit weird. Promise me you'll take it easy, okay?"

"Whatever you say," Garrett says with a tired smile. "Thank you for everything you've done."

She pats his arm in a very doctor-like manner. "Well, thank you for waking up."

Out of the corner of my eye I see Jack materialize with Thomas and I stand. "Your brother is here. I'll get out of your hair and let you two talk."

"You'll come back later?" he asks. "I've appreciated your voice."

"Absolutely. We have to learn the truth about the Eridanis, right?"

He gives me a confused look. He must have missed that part.

I release his hand and head out of the room with the ladies on my heels. As we walk down the hallway, Joss says, "I'm so relieved!" Murmurs of agreement surround me. I'm more than relieved. I'm ecstatic. I can't wait to tell Dane the news.

Once I'm in my room I text him and then unpack my stuff to find some workout clothes to lend Shel. She's exercising with me whether she likes it or not.

"Hey."

I look up to find James in my doorway. "Hey. What's up?"

"Great news about Garrett, huh?" he asks as he enters the room. "I think I can breathe a bit easier now."

"Tell me about it. I'm so glad he's all right. Now Jack can back off and stop giving me the stink eye."

James smirks. "What?"

"I read Jack's mind when we were in the Intermediate. He said he'd hold me responsible if anything happened to his brother. I'm pretty sure I dodged a bullet today."

"Why would he say that? It's not your fault Garrett was captured."

"It kind of is," I remind him. "I'm the one who forced him to spend time away from us, remember?"

"Yeah, but your heart was in the right place. Knowing what we know about Kellan he could have nabbed us at any time if he truly wanted to. He still can."

"I guess," I sigh, "but I don't think Jack sees it that way. He was upset that I delayed the rescue because I was at the party, too."

James takes a few steps toward me. "Trust me. Jack is hard to please. You've done nothing wrong."

I shrug. I hope he's right.

"Listen." He pauses and shifts his weight. "I came to ask you something."

"Shoot."

"Will you give me an honest answer?"

I hesitate as I take in his uncertain expression. It makes me wary, but I still respond, "Yes."

"Are you avoiding me?" he asks. "Because, lately, every time I enter a room you leave it. And, we've only practiced together twice in the last week. What's going on?"

My chest tightens. He's noticed my disappearing act around Meg. As much as I don't want to discuss her there's no time like the present to air my feelings.

"It's not you," I say and sit down on the edge of the bed. "It's Meg. She's everywhere you are and it's obvious she really likes you. It's hard to watch, you know?"

He takes a seat beside me, his hip touching mine. "Kind of like when I see you and Dane together?"

I totally deserve that. "I'm sorry for the double standard. I'll try to be better."

He stares at me for a moment and then cradles my face with his hand, running his thumb over my cheek. "Spend some time with me tonight," he says quietly. "Not here in this room, but at my place."

"Are you sure?" I ask, cautious. "I don't want to make enemies of Meg."

James frowns. "Why do you care what she thinks? This is about you and me. Period."

He's right. Why am I tiptoeing around her? "I promised Garrett I would read to him later. I'll come by afterward, okay?"

"Okay." He smiles and leans in to kiss my forehead. When he moves back he notices the clothes I laid out on the bed. "Headed to work out?"

I smile wickedly. "Headed to torture Shel you mean."

His eyes light up. "Can I join you to egg her on?"

I laugh. "We'll meet you in ten."

When Matt came by to pick up a sore Shel she wasn't very happy with me.

"Friends don't do this to friends!" she shouted as she went out the door. "But I still love you!"

After they left I went to visit Garrett. I brought him up to speed on the story we're reading after he asked some questions about what happened in the Intermediate. Even though everyone has been filling him in he wanted my perspective. He looked genuinely excited when I explained my battle with Patrick, and I got a little overly animated in retelling it. It was good to hear him laugh; although, he ended up having some sort of coughing fit. I brought him some more ice, checked his IV the way Shel taught me to, and managed to read through one chapter before he drifted off to sleep. Once he was tucked in to my liking, I left his room to find James.

As I walk through the house, thoughts of Garrett's homemade meals dance through my mind, making my stomach gurgle. I laugh at myself. What I wouldn't give for some of his lasagna! Is it selfish to want him to get better quickly in order to cook?

When I arrive at James' door I grab the handle to let myself in. Thank God for my amplified hearing because I catch myself before I interrupt. Voices can be heard on the other side, and I pause to lean closer to the wood. James and Meg are having a conversation and all thoughts of eating leave my mind. I really shouldn't eavesdrop, but it's way too tempting.

"...you know why."

"That's not what I'm saying," Meg says quietly. "I'm asking if you have any feelings for me."

James sighs, and I picture him holding his head in his hands. "I think I could."

My breath hitches.

"I don't understand," Meg says and I envision her gently pulling his hands from his face. "Are you saying you don't feel anything for me or you won't allow yourself to?"

He releases a breath. "What I'm saying is I can't. What if she remembers? I still love her and I've caused her so much pain. We can be together again and if she wants me I *will* give myself to her. I owe her the future we were supposed to have."

They fall silent and my heart wants to beat out of my chest. I should walk away, but I don't.

"James," Meg says, "I know you care about her. My presence won't erase that, and I'll never be able to replace what you two had. But, you have to realize you'll never be able to have the same relationship as before. Too much has happened. Not only between her and Dane, but between us."

She pauses and I imagine her holding his hand.

"Ever since I've known you, you've been sad or angry or jealous. I understand those feelings; I went through them all when it came to my David. That's why I wanted to help; I saw myself in you. When we were together, it seemed like I relieved your burdens; I know you made me forget mine. Then, you would go to Emma and come back a mess. Remember when you found out you couldn't be human? How upset you were? And then we kissed and it was like a weight had been lifted. I'd never seen you anything but sad, and I finally saw a light in your eyes. I care about you, and I want to give us a chance. I think I could make you happy."

It's silent for a few moments and I find myself holding my breath. I hate that James was miserable. I hate that he feels obligated to me. And I hate that Meg sounds so sweet right now.

"I'm sure you could make me happy," he admits. "I wish I could reciprocate what you feel, but I can't. I have to focus on Emma. You have to understand why."

A mixture of emotions swirls in my chest. I don't want to hear anymore. I command my feet to move and they carry me back to my room. I can't spend time with him right now; I'd be distracted trying to pretend I didn't hear what was said. I find my phone and text James.

I can't come by tonight. I'm sorry.

Chapter 19

James hits the floor hard. *Smack!* Before he can blink, I straddle his waist and pin him to the ground, pressing my forearm to his throat.

"Christ! Take it easy!"

I release him and his expression twists.

"What's gotten into you? I take it your headache's gone?"

After receiving my message last night, he promptly appeared at my door. I told him I wasn't feeling well and my head was killing me. It wasn't far from the truth. He left me alone, but asked if we could train today. So here I am. Training. And literally kicking his ass.

"Yep," I say and spring off him. "What's that now? Five for five? Care to go again?"

He stares at me like he doesn't know who I am and pushes himself off the mat. "I'll think I'll grab a drink instead."

He walks away and I wander to where my water bottle sits. Picking it up, I head to the wall to stare at the television. Ash was listening to CNN earlier as he hit the punching bag. Nothing goes with sweat quite like politics.

It's hard to focus on the program and I find my thoughts turning to last night. I couldn't sleep with my mind running in circles. I kept hearing Meg's voice and her words; I kept replaying James' response. When I finally forced them from my psyche it immediately turned to Dane. It was then that I realized I hadn't heard from him at all – no phone call, no text – and I cried. I actually *cried.* I can't remember the last time I was upset enough to cry. I mean, a few tears of pain trickled out when my bracelet came off, but this was a steady stream. I didn't even cry when I killed two people! My mind then started to create scenarios involving Teagan and, when I couldn't block them out, I got up and took a hot shower. I tried to wash away everything that was bothering me.

If only it were that easy.

My assumptions are implanted in my brain; my feelings are trapped in my chest. I'm pretty sure I'm trying to release them by beating on James.

Feeling a tug on my braid I turn around. "I didn't know you were so interested in foreign policy."

I give James a blank look. "What?"

"You're staring at Anderson Cooper like you want to throttle him. Did he piss you off or something?"

"No. I'm just distracted."

"By?"

I want to say a conversation I can't unhear and assumptions I can't unassume. But, instead, I say, "It's nothing."

"Are you sure you're all right?" he asks, concerned. "You're not acting like yourself."

"I'm fine."

Movement catches my eye as I catch a glimpse of Meg across the room. She materializes, all long tan legs and cute white sundress. Her face lights up when she spots James, but as soon as she finds me her body stiffens. As quickly as she appears she evaporates.

James notices my body tense and looks over his shoulder. "Did I miss something?"

Yes, I think to myself. *You're missing something huge.*

He turns back to me, confused, and I swallow. "We need to talk."

I reach for his hand and lead him back to the mat where I sit cross-legged. He follows me, mirroring my pose, and rests his knees against mine. There's only one way I'm going to stop this inner dialogue and trying to ignore it isn't the answer.

"I have a confession," I sigh. "I came over last night, but you had company."

He looks alarmed. "I wasn't expecting anyone but you. Why didn't you knock?"

I take a deep breath. "Because I decided to eavesdrop instead."

His eyes grow wide and he searches my face. "What did you hear?"

I hesitate and study our knees to gather my thoughts. It's not long before he places his fingers beneath my chin and gently lifts my gaze. "I love you," he says.

"I know you love the old me." I curl my hand around his wrist. "But I'm not that person anymore."

His hand falls from my chin. "What are you saying? Do you think I'm lying?"

"Not at all." I shake my head. "I'm saying Meg's words made me realize that you and I...we've changed."

His eyes lock on mine as he tries to figure out where I'm headed with this.

"I love you to death," I say honestly. "Just not in the way you deserve. You deserve to be happy and I'm making you miserable."

He takes my hands. "You do not make me miserable!"

"Yes, I do. Meg said you've been sad most of the time she's known you. I heard you say you owe me the future we were supposed to have. I don't want you to owe me anything! You are not obligated to me."

"Of course I am! I don't know life without you," he protests. "We've known each other since we were ten years old; I was your first love and you were mine. We're forever connected."

"We always will be." I clutch his fingers. "But Meg is right; we're different people now. Things will never be the same. I don't want you wasting your time waiting for the old Emma to return because I don't know if she exists."

He abruptly pulls his hands away from mine and my heart jumps. He grips my shoulders and looks me dead in the eye. "So you think we should give up? After all we've been through to be together this is how it ends?"

And with those words, everything becomes crystal clear. My vision shifts and our future stretches before me.

"No." I give him a small smile. "Don't you see? This is how it begins. We're Larvatus and Allegiant, enemies by nature who defy the supernatural to remain soul mates. You can't kick me out of your life just as much as I can't kick you out of mine."

He stares at me as he digests my words and I continue. "I will always have your back as long as you'll have me. But, romantically...you need to let me go." I can't deny him a chance at happiness with Meg; he said last night that he could have feelings for her. My heart pounds as I utter my next sentence. "I need to let you go."

He blinks like I've stung him. "What if I don't want to be let go?"

I give him half a smile. "I think you know that you do."

Minutes of silence pass. I'm beginning to think he'll never say another word to me when his eyes soften. I breathe a sigh of relief.

"You'll have my back?" he asks. "Until the end of forever?"

Why does that ring a bell? A sense of déjà vu overcomes me and the sentiment sounds perfect. "Until the end of forever."

He removes his hands from my shoulders to cradle my face. "I will always be here for you. For whatever you need. For anything."

"I believe you."

He kisses my forehead and his lips linger against my skin. When he releases me, I throw my arms around his neck and hug him tight. He crushes me to his chest and his hands travel up and down my back.

"Damn it, Emma," he says against me. "I will never get over you. You know that, right? No matter how much we change you will always own a piece of my heart."

I squeeze him tighter.

When we pull apart he looks tired. "Breaking up with you wasn't what I expected to do today."

I smile and shove his shoulder. "We're not broken up. We're a team, dumbass."

He shoots me a sardonic look. "Dumbass?" He springs forward and pins me on my back against the mat. "Who's the ass now?"

"You," I laugh and he smirks.

"Why are you still here?" I chastise him. "You're a free man and there's a beautiful girl out there who adores you. I suggest you go find her before she realizes what she's getting herself into."

He smiles. "What about you? Why aren't you running off to Dane?"

"It's complicated."

His eyes grow dark. "What happened?"

"Nothing," I protest. "He's just been busy with work and I haven't seen him in awhile. Days, actually. He usually calls, but he didn't last night."

"Did you call him?"

"Well, no. I was a little preoccupied with spying and then thinking about everything and..."

He pushes himself off me. "Go call him. Now."

"Wow. That's quite the attitude change."

His expression turns serious. "So help me Emma if he ever hurts you I will hurt him. Got it? Go find out why he's ignoring you and then just say the word."

"Okay." I stand. "Calm down Hulk."

"Just because we're not sleeping together doesn't mean I don't love you," he says. "Always remember that."

By the time I reach my room, I'm anxious to talk to Dane. Why didn't he call? It couldn't be Allegiant related; if anything had happened in the Intermediate our Guardian friends would have let me know. That leaves a few options: work, Teagan, or he's hurt. My stomach clenches. Would the universe be that cruel?

When I find my phone, I'm relieved to see I have a missed call, although it's from a strange number. I dial my voice mail and hear Dane.

"Grace? It's me. I'm so sorry I didn't call last night. I crashed on the couch with a beer in my hand, and I woke up this morning with the damn thing spilled all over. My phone is fried. The company is express shipping me a new one today. If you need to get a hold of me call the office at this number. Actually, call me anyway. I miss you. And I have news. Okay. I'll talk to you later. Bye."

Relieved, I immediately hang up and return his call.

"Grace?"

"The one and only."

"Hey." I can sense his smile through the phone. "I was starting to think you weren't speaking to me."

"I could say the same about you. You ruined your cell with a beer?"

"Along with the couch and the floor."

"Geez," I laugh. "The audit is that bad? Were you drinking a Forty?"

He chuckles. "I haven't hit the brown bag yet, but it's getting close."

I take a seat on the bed. "So, what's your news?"

His voice lightens. "I put my foot down. No more overtime. Tonight's my last night; it's back to my regular job and normal hours in the morning."

Could my smile get any bigger? I let out a quiet "yay."

"That's it? That's all you've got for me?"

I reassure him. "You should see the size of my smile right now. It's hard to speak."

"Excellent," he says and I imagine him grinning. "You can plan on seeing me tomorrow."

"I can't wait." Butterflies instantly appear in my stomach. I have news for him, too. Tomorrow is going to be huge. I'm quiet while I think about it. Should I try to make things special?

"Em?" he asks. "Are you still there?"

"Yep, I'm here."

"What are you doing?"

"Thinking."

He lets out an overly exaggerated sigh. "That's never good."

"Hey! Be nice! It just so happens I have something important to tell you, too. I'm trying to think of the right way to do it."

"Really?" he voice rises. "Are you headed back to the Intermediate? Tell me."

He has no idea this is about James. The thought of surprising him almost makes me giggle. "No; don't worry. This is something good." At least I'm pretty positive he'll think it's good.

"So tell me."

"Not over the phone. This has to be done in person."

He's silent for a second and then I hear his breath hitch. "I'm coming over tonight."

"No!" I blurt out. I need time to plan something other than just telling him face to face. "I need...I want...just trust me," I sigh when I can't think of anything to say. "It'll be worth the wait." Now I *really* have to come up with something good! Damn it.

I can almost hear him smirk. "I know what it is."

"You can't possibly."

"Wanna make a bet?"

Here we go. He knows I can't resist competing with him. "What are the terms?"

"When I show up tomorrow and I'm *right*," he emphasizes, "you have to do something for me. Anything I ask."

I let out a sarcastic laugh. "What? I'm not agreeing to that! There are a million inappropriate things you could ask for! No dice."

"The rules are still in place are they not?" he questions me. "I wouldn't ask you to do anything that violates our terms."

Hmmm. Now I'm intrigued. "Anything you ask, huh? And what do I get if you're wrong?"

"Simple. Whatever you want."

It sounds too easy. Thoughts of making him my man slave and watching him paint my toenails nearly makes me choke with laughter. "I'm in."

"I knew you'd cave."

"That's because I'm going to win," I say arrogantly. "What time is this little bet happening?"

"How's seven-ish sound?"

"Perfect."

"Emma?" Madeline interrupts from behind and I turn to face her.

"Yeah?"

"Garrett's asking for you. He says it's important."

"Oh, okay." I smile. "I'll be right down."

"Who was that?" Dane asks.

"Mad. She says Garrett needs me."

I hear papers shuffling. "How's he doing? I got your text."

"Great," I tell him. "Well, at least better than he was. He's still sleeping a lot and he's not eating solid food yet, but he'll get there."

"Good. Go check on him," Dane says. "I need to get lost in these payroll reports to keep my mind off tomorrow."

"Prepare to lose," I taunt him.

"Never."

We say our goodbyes and I head downstairs. No, I skip downstairs. I feel giddy. Elated. Super fantastic. Okay, that's enough. Even I'm annoying myself.

"Hi." I peek around Garrett's door. "You wanted to see me?"

He smiles. "Yeah. Can I talk to you for a minute?"

"Sure." I round his bed and pull the armchair close to the side. It's then that I notice his overall complexion appears better, like his skin has seen the sun. "It looks like you've regained some color."

He examines his hands. "It does, doesn't it?"

I smile. "So, what's up? Hungry for more *Pangalax*?"

He shakes his head. "Hungry, yes. But not for the story."

"Hungry for real?" My eyebrows shoot up. "That's great!" My expression turns sheepish. "I miss your cooking. When do you think you'll be back in the kitchen?"

He gives me a weary smile. "I don't think I'll be back in the kitchen."

My face falls and I pout. "Why?"

He eyes the open door. "Do you mind closing that?"

I shoot him a puzzled look, but comply with his request. When I sit back down, he takes one of my hands. "What I'm about to tell you I don't want anyone else to know. Okay?"

My heart begins to pound. "What's wrong?"

"I've been having dreams," he says. "Actually, I've been having the same dream. Over and over since yesterday."

"Is it bad?"

"It's Amelia," he says and a wistful expression clouds his features. "She's beautiful. Gorgeous. She's an angel."

I'm confused. "Amelia is?"

"My first love. The reason I chose to be a Guardian."

My expression melts. "That's a lovely dream. Does she say anything?"

"The same thing each time. She tells me everything's going to be all right. She says she's waiting for me."

"That's sweet." I squeeze his hand. "Have you ever dreamed of her before?"

"Never until now. That's how I know she's real, and I'm not pulling her from a memory. She's really there."

My face twists. "You mean she's actually visiting you in your dreams? Are you sure?"

"I'm positive."

He can tell I'm having a hard time believing this, and he meets my eyes. "Emma." He pauses. "I'm going to die."

I feel like I've been slapped in the face. "You are not going to die! Why in the world would you say that?"

"Because she told me."

"That's not possible," I reason with him. "Your mind is playing tricks on you; you've been through a traumatic experience."

He places his other hand on top of our already joined fingers. "No."

The intensity of that one word and his stare convinces me he wholeheartedly believes Amelia. "Then let's stop it," I say, adamant. "Let's get you out of here and to a hospital where we can find out what's really wrong with you." I stand and start to pull back his bed sheets.

"Don't," he says and tries to pull the blankets from my hand. "A doctor won't find anything wrong. It's turning human that's killing me."

I freeze. "What?"

"Trust me. I asked the same thing," he says. "I asked her how and why and to explain. She said what happened in the Intermediate weakened my humanity, essentially killed the human inside me. When all of my Guardian traits leave my body – when I'm completely Reborn – I will die."

I feel like I've been punched in the stomach and I can't find air. My eyes frantically comb over him. I notice how healthy he looks, how he no longer needs the IV. I recall how much he's sleeping and how he said he was hungry. My eyes land on his and a hard lump forms in my throat. His eyes are completely brown. Not a shade of turquoise remains.

"When?" I whisper as my body sinks to the chair.

He doesn't answer. He looks down and clears his throat. He adjusts the sheets and when he looks at me his eyes glisten. "Soon."

"I'm going to get Ash," I decide and stand again. "You can be Reborn Larvatus."

Garrett lets out an exasperated sigh. "Has anyone ever told you you're stubborn?"

"All the time." I cross my arms. "I'm not going to stand here and do nothing while you fade in front of me! I'm getting Ash."

"I can't be Larvatus," he says. "I need to be a Guardian to be Reborn or I need to be human to be Gifted. Right now I'm neither. I'll never be a Guardian again; I'm Lost like you. And when I finally do turn human..." he drifts off and swallows. "I'll be gone."

This is not happening. Tears sting my eyes, and I try to blink them away so I can see. It's hard to talk around the lump in my throat. "Why are you telling me this?"

"Because you are the one person I cherish in this life."

I close my eyes and it forces a few tears to fall. They wind their way to my chin before I look at him again. An inexplicable laugh escapes as I see Garrett holding out a tissue for me. "I'm supposed to be comforting you."

He gives me a tiny smile. "I was hoping you would feel that way."

I take the tissue from him and wipe my face.

"Do you think you could do something for me?" he asks.

"Anything."

Sadness creeps into his eyes, and I've never seen anyone so vulnerable. It's easy to imagine him as the little boy he once was and my heart begins to ache.

"Will you stay?" he asks nervously. "My first death was so sudden; I wasn't expecting it. But this...the waiting..." He looks down and then at me again. "I'm scared."

It's as if my heart is in a vise; it strains to beat. I'm not sure I can breathe. There's no stopping the tears now and I manage to nod. I'll do whatever he wants.

He reaches for me and I take his hand. Absentmindedly, I rub the back of it as I sit next to his bed. I find myself looking everywhere but at his face so I can try to keep some semblance of composure. My breaking down and wailing will be the opposite of helpful, but it's exactly what I want to do.

"You look terrible," he says.

"Well," I run my fingers over my cheek, "what did you expect? Tap dancing and rainbows?"

He chuckles. "Not the rainbows."

I roll my eyes at him and sniff. "I'm falling apart."

"Me, too."

Silence reigns and after a moment he tugs on my hand, pulling my arm. He moves to the side of the bed to make room for me, and I read his mind.

"I'll hold you together if you hold me."

I crawl beside him to lie down, tucking my body along his, and laying my head against his shoulder. Our arms wind around each other and he rests his cheek against the top of my head.

"I'm going to cry all over you," I warn him.

"That's all right. At least I won't have to watch you do it."

I snort. "This is messed up."

"All the best things are."

I bury myself against him. "Why won't you tell anyone else? They're your friends; they deserve a chance to say goodbye."

"Losing my second life is hard enough without a pity party." He adjusts his arms. "Besides," he adds softly, "you're the only one I care about."

His words give me pause and I'm afraid to ask what he means. Instead, I lift my head and give him a questioning look. His quiet answer confirms my suspicions.

"Maybe in another life?"

My throat feels thick. How long has he felt this way? "Maybe," I whisper.

Time passes and evening fades into night. Exhausted from the day's emotions, I find myself nodding off. Each time I do I catch myself and jerk awake, my body tensing and startling Garrett. I lose track of how many times I do this before he tells me to relax and go to sleep.

"I'm tired, too," he says.

I adjust my hold around him. "But if you sleep you might not wake up."

His voice cracks. "I know."

I cling to him, as if I can will his heart to keep beating, as if I can give him some of my strength.

"Promise me you will live a full life," he whispers.

It's all I can do to nod through my tears.

In the early gray of morning my muscles scream. I've been locked in the same position for hours; my entire body aches. I stretch my legs to release some tension and freeze.

I can feel the difference under my arms, and I start to panic. Garrett feels cold; it's as if I'm wrapped around a piece of granite. I can't bear to look at his face, so I raise a shaky hand and press it to his chest, over his heart.

There is no beat.

My entire body shakes. Loud, ugly sobs build inside me until I can no longer contain them and they rip through my throat. Tears pour from my eyes and soak Garrett's clothes as I bury my face in his shoulder and twist his shirt in my fist. It won't take long for everyone in the house to come running.

Minutes later, I hear a gasp and force myself to lift my head. The eyes that meet mine burn with such intense hatred that I cower against Garrett's body. I search for my voice and will it to speak, to try and explain. All I can rasp is his name.

"Jack."

He doesn't stay. He vanishes from the foot of the bed and fear seizes my heart.

Chapter 20

Steam rises from the mug Madeline offers and I shake my head to refuse it. She kneels, lowering her pleading eyes to my level.

"Please drink something."

Reluctantly, I take her offering. The heat from the tea warms my hands and I know it will warm my body. I wish it would warm my mind too, and unlock its frozen state.

For hours I've done nothing but sit on the couch with my knees pulled to my chest, replaying every Garrett memory I have. The current image behind my eyes is of him curled around LB as they slept at my place. I remember how he would let her get away with anything, even lying across his neck. Unfortunately, the memory doesn't stay; it's replaced with one of me wrapped around his lifeless body. I search for something happier and find the sound of his laugh when we discovered I could bench 300 pounds. I close my eyes and concentrate. I want to pull that sound out of the other noises around me.

"We should call Shel," I hear Madeline say.

"And Dane," I hear Ash add.

The Larvatus were the first to find me. I was such a wreck; I couldn't explain what happened. Between Madeline and Ash deciphering my thoughts they put the pieces together. I'm not sure when James appeared, but he was the one to lift me from the bed. He carried me out of the room, so Ash could tend to the body. Garrett's body. I have no idea what he and the other

Guardians did with it. Is there a morgue on the property I don't know about?

A few moments of silence pass until I hear Ash ask "Have you been able to locate Jack?" My eyes fly open and I see James and Meg have entered the room.

"The Intermediate is a big place," James says. "The others are still looking; we came to check in. How's she doing?"

By she he means me.

Ash frowns. "We got her to hold some hot tea, but I've yet to see her drink it."

Meg sends me a sympathetic expression. "Poor thing."

For some reason her words stick. I don't want to be considered a "poor thing." I'm not the one something tragic happened to – Garrett is. It's then that I decide to sit up and cooperate.

Madeline notices me stir and helps steady the tea while I sit. I take a sip as she wraps an arm around me. I wish my friends would focus on their grief. If anything, they should be mad I allowed Garrett's capture in the first place.

"No one blames you," Mad says quietly.

"That's a lie." I stare at her. "Jack does."

"We'll find him," she assures me. "Don't worry."

James hears us talking and crouches in front of us. "Are you all right?"

I nod and he sighs. "Em. Don't lie."

I clutch my mug. "What happened hurts, but I'm not ready to jump. A friend just died. Give me some time, okay?"

He searches my face and his pinched brow smoothes. "Okay." He gently tucks some hair behind my ear then stands to rejoin Ash and Meg.

As they talk I stare into my tea. "Mad?"

"Yes?"

"Did you know Garrett had feelings for me?"

She squeezes my shoulder. "I did."

"Since when?"

"Since we met in Hope Mills."

I close my eyes and swallow. How did I not see this? It's frustrating to know I have memories of him I can't find. I pray I never led him on in any way.

"He asked us to protect you should anything happen with The Allegiant," Madeline explains. "Of course we questioned his request. We don't run around Gifting humans for fun."

I open my eyes. I remember her saying something similar when we discussed my being Gifted before, something about him wanting me safe. "So he told you?"

"Not in so many words." She removes her arm from my shoulders and taps her temple. "We read his thoughts. They revealed how much he cared about you. He was sorry for the hurt he caused when he assigned James; he didn't want to bring you anymore pain. Your friendship was special to him because you never treated him like a Guardian."

"But why didn't he tell me?"

She gives me a knowing look. "Did he really stand a chance? What good would it have done to make things awkward? He settled for what he could be. A friend."

Frowning, I look away from Madeline. She's right; he wouldn't have stood a chance with all the James and Dane drama. I still feel bad, though, for not recognizing his feelings. His asking for my protection is the main reason I'm alive, and I allowed him to be captured resulting in his death. Some great friend I am.

"You've had a rough night." Madeline rubs my arm. "Why don't you take a bath? It'll make you feel better."

That does sound like a good idea. Not to mention I was wrapped around a dead person.

"Then I'll make something to eat. Are you hungry?"

I say yes to appease her, but I doubt I'll be able to taste anything. I hand her my tea and stiffly walk upstairs.

After I get some fresh clothes, I make my way to the bathroom and fill the tub with the hottest water I can bear. I find some bath soap under the sink and pour a few capfuls. It smells like vanilla and cinnamon, and the scent consumes the tiny room. It relaxes me enough to stay afloat in the water, but not enough to keep my morose thoughts at bay. I can't stop thinking about death.

When my skin wrinkles and my thoughts are sufficiently somber, I get out of the tub and get dressed. I braid my hair again and find my way back to the bedroom to deposit my dirty laundry. When I'm headed out the door, my phone chimes alerting me to a text message.

Excited about tonight. Can't wait.

It's Dane. I forgot all about his coming over and our little wager. How am I going to make anything seem special now? I stare at the phone feeling drained and numb. All I want is the warm comfort of his arms and for him to tell me everything will be okay.

"Important call?"

My head snaps up to find Garrett standing a few feet away. I gasp and drop the phone.

"Surprise." He smiles warmly at me.

Oh my God. Is this really happening? My eyes double in size.

He looks anxious. "I didn't mean to scare you."

"I..." I stutter. How is this possible? He's wearing jeans, a t-shirt, and tennis shoes just like any other day. His eyes are a soft caramel brown, his hair looks neatly cut, and his skin looks like it's glowing. Adrenaline soars through my veins. "Are you an angel?"

He laughs, the sound echoing the one from my memory. "Far from it."

"How...? Did Ash...?"

"Turn me Larvatus?" he guesses. "No." He extends his hand toward me. "See for yourself."

I take his hand, and he gently pulls me toward him. I can't believe it. He's human. He *feels* human. "Is this some sort of miracle?" I ask in awe.

He shrugs. "Depends on how you look at it."

I turn his hand over in mine and glide my fingers over his palm. I stop at his wrist and feel his pulse there, steady and strong. My breath catches as tears prick my eyes. He's alive.

"Hey," he says softly. "Don't cry yet."

I blink my tears away. He's right. This is a cause for celebration. Excited, I meet his eyes. "We have to tell everyone!" I pull him toward the door. "They're going to be so happy to see you!"

He chuckles as we head into the hallway.

"Let me guess," I ask excitedly. "Amelia made this happen?"

His eyes dance. "Do you believe in karma?"

"Firmly."

"So you believe actions determine fate? That a person is rewarded or punished depending on their deeds?"

"Absolutely."

We make it to the bottom of the stairs, and he abruptly steps in front of me. "Well, I'm here to tell you something."

"What's that?" I smile.

He grabs my shoulder suddenly, painfully, and sneers. "Karma is a real bitch."

Shocked, I wrench his hand away and step back. What the hell? I've never seen him so full of hate. I try to read his thoughts, to figure out what just happened.

And I can't.

"I'm so glad you could join us," a silky voice says from across the room. "Thank you, Jack."

My stomach falls through the floor as Jack's, not Garrett's, eyes lock on mine.

"What goes around comes around," he snarls and turns to reveal four Allegiant I don't recognize. James, Meg, Mad, and Ash are all restrained and panic threatens to overcome me. I can barely breathe as I realize Jack is Allegiant, too.

"How could you?" I whisper.

"Easy," he snaps. "My brother is dead."

I stare at him in disbelief. I know he despises me, but why would he ruin everyone else? "Why would you do this?"

He quickly grabs my arm and twists it, his face hovering inches from mine. "Because there's no other way to kill you."

My heart goes into overdrive and my adrenaline spikes. I'm not scared. I'm furious. How dare he endanger everyone just to get to me! My eyes narrow and I pull myself out of Jack's grasp with such force it surprises us both. Silently, I make a vow. No one in this room I care about will get hurt today. No one.

I back up defensively and search for a distraction to buy time. Ash must read my mind because he tries to offer one.

"Jack!" he shouts from across the room. "What has she done? Think about it! Your grief is clouding your mind!"

Jack scowls and turns on Ash. "My brother is dead because of her! He chose to spend his last breath with *her!* No one knew; not one of us was allowed to say goodbye except the precious *Emma*," he twists my name and faces me. "What makes you so goddamned special?"

I start to protest, but the words get tangled. I want to tell him I'm not special, that I asked Garrett to tell the others. But Jack doesn't want to hear excuses. He unleashes a beam of light from his palm, and I fall to the floor. It misses me, ricochets off the wall, and bounces off the ceiling. He's so new he can barely control his powers.

Meg lets out a strangled cry and my assailant's head snaps around to find her.

"What are doing?" she pleads with sorrow-filled eyes.

Jack stares at Meg, and his features momentarily soften. She tilts her head, as if sending him a silent message, and I read her thoughts to understand her sadness. *"I care about you; I loved you. Please don't do this."*

Her thoughts reveal that she and Jack were passionately in love once; that they had parted ways but remained friends. She asks him why he would do this to her, to any of them, when they are all fighting for the same thing.

Jack's expression hardens once more. "Because we're not fighting for the same thing." His eyes jump to James and back to Meg. "I wanted humanity for *us*," he spits the word. "And you want him."

Meg's face crumbles as he raises his hand to send a beam of light in James' direction. I take the opportunity to launch myself at Jack, connecting with his midsection and landing a quick one-two punch. I then spring back to kick him squarely in the chest. He flies backward into Meg and the Allegiant that holds her, all three of them tumbling to the ground.

"Emma!" Ash yells. I connect with his eyes and read his thoughts.

"Where's your anlace?"

"Upstairs!"

"You need it!"

No shit.

"Tell Meg!" he silently shouts.

My eyes search for Meg, and I find her separated from her captor due to the fall. "Meg! Upstairs! My anlace!" I yell.

She instantly vanishes.

Jack scrambles to his feet as the Allegiant he hit gives him a hard stare. "Stay here," he growls at Jack then advances toward me. He's tall and muscular with blue eyes and sandy brown hair. I quickly retreat and take a defensive stance, putting the couch and coffee table between us. The objects won't stop him, but at least something is in the way.

"I killed you once," he sneers. "Let's make sure it takes this time."

This must be Kellan.

He comes at me, leaping over the couch and landing on the table so hard that the wood splinters and shatters. Is this supposed to intimidate me? It doesn't. It just pisses me off that he ruined Mad's furniture.

He glares at me, and I decide out-maneuvering him is my best option until my weapon arrives. Despite my strength, I doubt I'm a good match against his height and weight. If I can work us around toward The Larvatus maybe I can free them like Meg. In a flash, his palm radiates light at my head and I duck, rolling and tucking my body behind a chair. The furniture explodes, the cushions blasting into a cloud of white fluff. The intense heat attached to his attack singes my skin through my clothing, and I inwardly cringe. Is he trying to incinerate me? I guess that's one way to go.

My eyes search for something to throw, and I spy an armrest no longer attached to the chair. I grab it and whirl around on my knees, throwing it at Kellan with all my strength. It misses him by inches, but manages to hit James in shoulder. Shit! I said I'd have his back, not break it! I quickly look for something else and find a decorative serving tray that used to sit on the coffee table. I heave it at Kellan like I'm throwing a Frisbee and it connects with his neck. I take advantage of his two-second distraction to sprint behind the couch.

"Ugh!"

Unexpected arms catch me from behind, and they pull me back against my will. I thrash against them, managing to free one arm. I elbow my assailant in the ribs and hear him grunt as he loses his breath. He adjusts his hold to wrap both arms around my chest, to pin mine to my sides, and fully expose my body to Kellan. I can tell from his shirtsleeves that it's Jack, and I struggle against him as Meg materializes in front of us. Kellan unleashes a blast of light in our direction, but Meg blocks it, unaffected. She thrusts my anlace into my right hand.

An eerie confidence surges through me, and I almost laugh. I wrench my body away from Jack, raise my weapon, and spit, "I thought your boss told you not to move!"

He looks at me with wide eyes causing me to pause. Damn it if he doesn't look just like his brother! I have to remind myself that this is not Garrett; it's Jack. And he wants me dead. He wants us all dead.

"Do it," he sneers when he senses my hesitation. "Kill me just like you killed Garrett."

His words sting and the pain unleashes an anger inside me I didn't know I could carry. I would never intentionally hurt Garrett, but Jack will never understand that. My heart will ache from his loss for a long, long, time, but I will choose to honor his memory. I would never soil it like Jack has; I would never endanger innocent lives with wrongful vengeance. I may need therapy after this, but I glare into his eyes and utter one word. "Gladly."

Jack bursts into a cloud of dust under my weapon, and I turn to face the remaining Allegiant. Meg is acting like my human shield as Kellan tries to reach me around her. Why is she not hurt by his attempts? It must be a Guardian thing; she's the only one here. Across the room, I see James and his captor are engaged in a full fight, and he seems to be holding his own. There's only one direction for me to go.

"Meg! This way!"

I want to sprint toward Madeline and Ash, but I need Meg's blockade. As we get closer to The Larvatus I see fear in the eyes of the Allegiant who holds Mad. I scoff. "First day on the job?"

He stares at me with large brown eyes, and I swear he trembles. Do I scare him? The thought that I might actually be a badass flits through my mind. I like it.

"Let her go," I demand and to my amazement he releases her. He shoves her toward me and evaporates into oblivion. I hope he's truly a coward and not playing a trick.

Madeline meets my eyes, and I scream my thoughts.

"Your anlace! Go!"

She disappears, and I zero in on my next target – Ash's Allegiant. He tries to use my friend's body as a shield, even though Ash is doing his best to pull away and give me a clear shot. As Kellan's attacks continue behind me, I realize we're getting nowhere fast and I place my weapon in my mouth, grasping it with my teeth to free my hands. I drop to my knees, grab Ash's legs around his calves, and pull him forward with all my might. Briefly, he's a rope in a tug-of-war before the Allegiant's grip slips, and he's holding Ash by his armpits. Instantly, I release his legs and crawl beneath him, between his body and the enemy's. Still on my knees I thrust my anlace into the Allegiant's thigh, and he barely has time to glance down before exploding into vapor. Unfortunately, I don't have time to get cocky about it because his demise causes Ash's body to crash into mine, his weight no longer supported. His upper body hits my neck and shoulders, the back of his head cracks against my skull. *Holy hell.*

I see stars and fall forward, catching myself with my hands against the floor. The impact sends painful jolts through both my shoulders, and I can't keep my arms from collapsing. Crumpling to the ground, I smash my chin in the process. *Oh. My. God.* Pain sears through my jaw.

"Emma!" Ash shouts as his body slides off mine. He peers over me to make sure I'm conscious, and I send him my thoughts.

"You have a hard head."

He nods and jumps away, appeased by my coherent observation. His action reveals Madeline's feet in my peripheral, and relief trickles into my veins. We can end this. Three Allegiant down, two to go.

The Larvatus must relieve Meg because she throws her body over mine, protecting me until I can see straight. Grateful, I whisper, "Thank you."

Her blue eyes send me a serious gaze. *"No. Thank you."*

It takes only minutes for the throbbing in my body to subside, but it feels like longer since I'm stuck motionless on the floor. When I'm ready to rejoin the game, I lift my head to calculate where I can fit in to this supernatural dance. Madeline and Ash have their hands full with Kellan. James looks less taxed; he clearly has the upper hand with his foe. It looks like I get to help take out the big guy. Lucky me.

I begin to sit up and Madeline notices. I focus on her face.

"Stay down!" she silently hollers.

"Why?"

"Let us turn him around!"

I get it. If I act wounded, he'll ignore me, and I can surprise him from behind.

I lie back down, watching their intense exchange, all the while tensing my muscles for the right moment. Kellan's beams of death are on hyper drive as he releases one after another after another. Holes are blasted in the walls, the ceiling, and the floor; a piece of the staircase goes flying. It seems he's learned a thing or two from their last altercation; The Larvatus are forced to spend their time avoiding his attacks rather than working their way in toward him.

The longer I watch the more I get a feel for the cadence of their fight; believe it or not it almost falls into a rhythm. It's then I realize I know when to strike.

Just as The Larvatus unleash another pattern of moves – duck, roll, leap, dodge, retreat, try again – I count to three.

One.

Two.

Three.

My coiled muscles launch my body into the air. I want to crash into Kellan's side to avoid a direct hit while allowing The Larvatus a chance to advance. It's a stroke of bad luck when he turns in my direction as I'm mid-leap. I end up flying at him head on. Time stops as my eyes lock on his. He registers my hurtling body, and I know this can't end well. My mind does the only thing it can to protect me – an image of Dane appears.

My heart burns as I think of him. The Allegiant could truly be incinerating me for all I know, but the only thing I can see is Dane. I imagine him opening his arms, as if he's going to catch me, and to my surprise my delusion allows me to land safely in them. Is this what death feels like? A safe place?

My mind clears, and I'm shocked to find myself in a real pair of arms – Kellan's. He actually caught me. What the hell? He looks stunned, just as I'm sure I do, and I have to force my body to move. I quickly bring my arms over my head, grip my anlace in both hands, and bring it down right between his shell-shocked eyes.

Since I lack the ability to float in mid-air, I come crashing down hard on my tailbone which sends a wave of excruciating pain up my spine. Words can't adequately express the sensation, and I end up spewing a string of obscenities that make me sound like a seasoned sailor. I roll on my side and pant for a moment. *Please stop hurting please stop hurting please stop hurting.*

Madeline kneels to hover over me, and I find her face. "There's still one left!" I wheeze and she smiles. *She smiles.* Does that mean James took care of him?

Moments later, I bite my lip and get to my feet, seriously considering another line of work. My body feels trashed in a way I never thought it could, but I can't stay down. I need to make sure my help isn't needed. When my eyes bounce around the room and find no threat I start to smile, but stop. Everyone is staring at me.

"What?" I ask. "Isn't it over?"

Madeline looks at me with tears in her eyes. "It is," she whispers. "Because of you."

I give her a weary smile and allow my body to sag against one of the side tables that made it through the melee. Her words unlock the floodgates; the realization that we eliminated Kellan and our fight is finished begins to sink in. A surge of relief flows through me as Ash approaches.

"Are you hurt?"

I look up at him. "You're head is as hard as a rock."

He glances at Madeline then smiles at me. "I've been told that before."

I feel a tap on my shoulder and turn to find James. "You're insane, you know that?"

I push myself off the table and into his waiting arms. "How's your shoulder?"

"Nice aim," he teases then kisses my hair. "You are unbelievable."

"Do you mean my cursing or my fighting?"

"Both. You saved us."

That's not entirely true. "I had help."

"Oh, Mad. Look at this mess!"

Meg's voice gives me pause, and I step back from James. Without her I'd be dead, I know it. She protected me when no one else could. I move around James and step up to her. "I owe you," I say sincerely. "You saved my life."

She shakes her head and looks from my face to James, her expression softening to reveal all she feels for him. "No. I owed you."

I give her a tiny smile and almost reach out to touch her. Instead of getting overly sentimental, I thank her again and then turn to ask Madeline where she keeps her pain pills. My back and tailbone are starting to speak. I find her and Ash engaged in a passionate kiss, so I quickly look away. My eyes fall back to Meg who is now facing James and holding both of his hands in hers. Okay. I feel a little out of place.

Suddenly, I know where I want to be. I search the room for the clock that used to hang near the window and find it on the floor. I walk toward it to consult the time. It's almost six and the urge to see Dane overcomes me. What time did he say he would be here? Seven? I don't want to wait another hour; there's so much I need to tell him. Would he mind if I dropped by his place? There's only one way to find out.

I head upstairs to call him.

"Everything all right?" Madeline asks as I pass her.

"I need to call Dane."

"I know where he lives," James volunteers. "Would you rather speak to him in person?"

I'm momentarily confused until he asks Mad to assist him. They take my wrists, and I feel the familiar fizzle of manifestation. This night may turn out to be special after all.

When we arrive, I find myself standing on the sidewalk outside a row of townhomes. I'm familiar with the complex; the buildings sit just outside of town. James and Mad release me and I take a step forward. "This one?" I point to #202, the door directly in front of me.

James nods, and I start up the porch stairs. On the second step, I turn around.

"Thanks for bringing me." I smile at the two of them. "I'll see you later?"

Madeline grins and vanishes while James lingers. "Behave yourself," he teases and his eyes meet mine. They soften, as if he's coming to a conclusion, and then he gives me a small wave and evaporates.

A nervous excitement starts to take over as I make my way up the stairs. I have so much to talk to Dane about; I'm going to have to pace myself. He's going to think I've gone off the deep end if I start talking as fast as my heart is pounding.

I find the doorbell, press it, and then thrum my fingers anxiously as I wait. Would it be too bold to try the knob and see if it's unlocked? I turn my ear to see if I can pick up any sound. Finally, I hear footsteps, and I try to contain the idiotic smile that breaks across my face. I seriously need to calm down.

The door is thrown open and words fall from my mouth. "I know you were supposed to come to me but I couldn't wait and..."

I freeze. The eyes that meet mine aren't expected.

"Well." Teagan sizes me up. "Ding dong the witch *isn't* dead."

Chapter 21

Her statement takes a moment to process. Is it possible she knows what I've been through? Or is this some vague reference to the Wizard of Oz?

I read her thoughts since I don't give two shits about being polite. They tell me I was the Wicked Witch opposite her Dorothy at a Halloween party. They also tell me that I look like a hot mess; I never bothered to check a mirror before I left. Short pieces of hair stick out from my braid in every direction, my clothes are disheveled, and my chin sports a healthy bruise. My eyes also look overly huge from finding her here. I immediately adjust my features to look more confident.

"Who is it?" Dane asks, appearing behind Teagan. Concern darts across his face when he sees me, and he anxiously brushes past his ex. "What happened?"

I take in his appearance and find it a little hard to breathe. Glancing at Teagan, I put two and two together and take a step back. The only thing Dane has on is a pair of jeans. No shirt, no socks. Teagan is wearing a Detroit Tigers tee that's way too big for her. I know it's his; she doesn't strike me as the type who would pair that shirt with slacks and heels. A hard knot forms in my stomach. "I could ask you the same thing."

Dane looks down at himself and then at me. "This isn't what it looks like."

My brows arch skeptically. "Then what is it?"

"She needed a file and spilled her coffee. I lent her a shirt."

"It was a Chai tea latte," Teagan snaps.

I ignore her and focus on Dane. "And you're naked because?"

"I was changing clothes to come see you." He stands inches from me and searches my face. "Are you okay?"

I give him a curt nod, still uncertain about the situation. He widens his eyes giving me permission to read his mind; instead, I turn toward Teagan and read her thoughts. She's thinking about what he said, and I see her replay what happened. She came over for a file all right, one that she purposefully placed in his bag. When he retrieved it and asked her to leave, her Starbucks conveniently slipped and drenched her white silk blouse. Shel was right. This girl is relentless.

"You should go inside," I tell Dane. "You'll get sick." It's January, and he's standing on the porch half dressed.

"Come on." He takes my hand and pulls me behind him, past Teagan and into his place. I hear the door close as he deposits me in the living room and watch him gather the oh-so-important file and Teagan's purse. He balances one on top of the other and hands them to her.

"Here," he says and shoves the items into her hands. "I'll see you at the office."

"You're making me leave?" she asks, her eyes wide with shock.

"Yes, I'm making you leave. I have plans with Emma."

"But I was here first," she pouts. Her eyes land on mine and narrow. "I was always here first."

Is that a threat? The idea to physically escort her out appeals to me. "I'd think twice about what you say," I warn her. "I've had a bad day."

Her eyes rake over my body, analyzing everything in seconds. "Looks like it."

I take a deep breath to steady myself as a new idea comes to mind – strangulation.

"Okay." Dane steps between us. "It's time for you to go."

"What about my shirt?" she asks, her voice morphing from snarky to innocent. "When can I come back?"

Come back? I think. Um, never. "I'll get it for you," I volunteer, sickly sweet. "Where is it?"

"In the bathroom," Dane says before Teagan can answer. His eyes widen and I hear, *"Off the kitchen."* We wouldn't want her to think I didn't know my way around.

I walk further into his place, past the dining area and into a small kitchen. There's another doorway, and I find a tiny bathroom. Teagan's blouse lies across the counter, the bottom half hanging in the sink. It's been rinsed, but I can still see the tea; it's obvious the delicate fabric has been ruined. Picking it up I catch the label. Escada. Expensive. What wouldn't this girl do to spend time with Dane? More than ruin a pricey piece of clothing, I'm sure.

The shirt is damp in my hands, and as I turn to leave an evil thought enters my mind. Maybe toilet water would remove the stain?

Moments later I make my way back to the living room just in time to see Dane push Teagan's hand away from his chest. It irritates me, and I walk faster. He really ought to put some clothes on.

"Here you are." I toss the blouse at Teagan with two fingers, and she nearly drops the file to catch it. She makes a face. "Why is this so wet?"

I shrug innocently. "That's how I found it."

She glares at me.

Dane steps further away from her and gestures toward the door. "Goodbye," he says sarcastically.

She turns to leave with a sour expression. "I expect to see you at eight in the morning."

"Or what?" Dane scoffs. "You'll fire me? Please do."

Teagan's eyes bounce from Dane to me and back again. Her thoughts reveal she'd never do that; she wants him around too much. "Just don't be late," she snaps. She heads to the door, violently throws it open, and then slams it behind her.

Dane is in front of me in seconds, holding my chin with gentle hands. "Why does it look like someone punched you?"

"No one punched me." I wrap my hands around his wrists. "The floor and I had an altercation."

"You fell?"

"It's more like I knocked heads with Ash, saw stars, and my jaw met the floor."

He stares at me, confusion and worry etched across his face. "You were fighting again, weren't you? You went to the Intermediate."

"No." I draw a heavy breath. "The Intermediate came to us."

His eyes grow wide with surprise, and he immediately wraps me in his arms. "Thank God you're safe," he murmurs against me.

I press my cheek to the skin of his chest and find his strong heartbeat. My body immediately relaxes; it's as if he is absorbing all of my tension. My muscles feel weak at letting it go.

"You're tired," he observes as I sag against him.

I lift my head. "Not really. Just relieved to be here."

"I'm sorry about Teagan," he apologizes. "I didn't invite her. You know what happened, right?"

"I do. You shouldn't leave your stuff unattended or mystery files will end up at your house."

He groans. "I knew I didn't leave it in my bag. She put it there?"

"Yes. You might want to think about staying dressed in front of her as well." I arch a brow. "That is, if you don't want her getting all touchy-feely. There's only so much a girl can take."

He starts to defend himself, but stops. "Can you take it?" he asks and steps out of my arms.

Now that he mentions it, no. Without Teagan distracting me, I find myself pleasantly uncomfortable in his half-naked presence. I try not to stare at the defined muscles I always knew were there, but kept hidden beneath clothing. I purposefully focus on his face which, lucky for me, is equally as nice to look at. My ears start to burn. "Um..." I stutter. "You need clothes."

He grins and takes my hand. "Walk and talk," he says as he pulls me behind him and up the stairs. "I want to hear all about your visit from the supernatural."

He leads me to his room where he drops my hand and heads to the dresser in search of a shirt. As he finds one and pulls it over his head, I take a minute to peruse my surroundings: unmade king size bed, no headboard; side table strewn with a remote, a watch, and an alarm clock; flat screen mounted in the corner of the room between the closet and the window; and a Papasan chair with a blue cushion opposite the dresser. It strikes me as a typical bachelor's room. I take a tentative seat on the bed as he turns to me.

"So?" he asks and sits down. "Are you going to fill me in?"

I know where I need to begin, but thinking about the event that set everything in motion makes my chest feel hollow. Garrett is dead; my friend is gone. It's such a final thought. Saying it out loud will only make it that much more real.

I swallow and Dane notices. His brow furrows, and he takes my hand. "If it's too hard you don't have to – "

"Garrett died," the words fall from my mouth. I didn't mean to say them so insensitively; I just needed to get them out.

"He what? When?" Dane's face registers shock. "I thought he was doing better."

"I thought he was, too. When I went to see him, after talking with you, he looked like the picture of perfect health. He was even hungry." I give him a weak smile.

"So what happened?"

"He told me he was going to die. He said Amelia, his first love, had come to him in his dreams. She told him his time in the Intermediate killed his humanity, that when he completely turned he would pass."

Dane squeezes my hand.

"He asked me to stay with him." My throat feels thick at the memory. "He said he was scared." Tears prick my eyes. "He died in my arms."

With those words I'm immediately in Dane's embrace. He holds me tight and smoothes my hair. "That's horrible," he whispers. "Why didn't you call me?"

I shrug against him. "Jack found out and was furious; James and the other Guardians went to search for him. I was locked in a haze for most of the morning until Madeline convinced me to take a bath." I'm rambling now. "Jack appeared, pretending to be Garrett, and he lured me downstairs where the other Allegiant were waiting. He'd turned Allegiant himself; he brought them to us. Mad, Ash, James, and Meg – they were all trapped."

Dane inhales sharply. "How –?"

"I took them out," I say, staring straight ahead. "I killed Jack and some nameless Allegiant. I killed Kellan." I sit up straight and my gaze meets Dane's. "I killed three people today."

His eyes search mine. "Are you okay?"

I pause to take stock of my body and blink back the tears that never fell. "My head is tender, my shoulders and tailbone ache. But, it'll pass like it always does." Now that I think about it, I adjust my weight to my hip to take some pressure off my sore bottom.

"That's not what I meant." He moves one hand to cradle my face. "I meant in your heart, in your head. Are you okay?"

"I think so," I say honestly. "I mean, I need to grieve for a lost friend and killing Jack was twisted." I hesitate. "But it's over." A small smile creeps on to my face. "Kellan's gone. Lucas can come home. It's really over."

Dane's eyes light up at the revelation, and he brushes some stray hair from my face. "What can I do?"

"About what?"

"About your pain. Do you need ice or Motrin or food or something?"

I think about it as the throbbing at the crown of my head starts to feel tighter. "This is going to sound silly but...could you rub my head?"

He smiles. "I think that can be arranged. Turn around."

I do as he asks and turn my back toward him, scooting further toward the center of the bed and crossing my legs. This hurts my tailbone, so I end up curling my legs to the side instead. He removes my hair tie with a soft tug, pulls my braid apart until my hair is a crazy mess, weaves his fingers up under my hair, and then begins applying gentle pressure to my scalp. At first I feel self-conscious; I'm sure I look like some sort of untamed wild woman.

But, as the tips of his fingers move in small circles against my tender skin, I want to melt. His hands are magic, and the ache in my head starts to wane.

"I don't like your hair braided," he says as he works.

My droopy eyelids pop open. "Why?"

"Because it's not you. It reminds me of Madeline, and she's not hot."

"What?" I interrupt his work and look over my shoulder. "Madeline is beautiful."

He tenderly moves my head back into position. "In a motherly sort of way."

I sigh. "You don't like it because it reminds you of what I can do," I nearly whisper because his hands are moving again. "You're afraid I'll hurt you one day."

He snickers. "Maybe so. The way you wear your hair should be our code; if you're mad at me, braid it. Then I'll know to stay away."

I laugh which comes out as some sort of weird garbled scoff-sigh. I could fall asleep under his touch. "How should I wear my hair?" I murmur.

"Down," he says immediately. "Down or half-up."

Apparently he's thought about this? "What if it's hot?" I complain.

"Ponytail."

Well, okay then.

We fall silent as he massages my head; I swear I've found some sort of endless heaven. Just when I don't think it can get any better, he moves down to my shoulders and presses his thumbs hard against my shoulder blades, running them in circles. "These hurt too, right?"

I nod and let my chin droop to my chest. He works his way along the tops of my shoulders, my shoulder blades, and then up my neck. Does he have some sort of masseuse training I don't know about? Despite how amazing this feels I can't help myself and find a sarcastic comment. "Are you going to massage my ass next?"

His mouth appears at my ear. "Only if you'll let me."

I wasn't expecting his voice to be so close and it startles me. Or maybe it's the feeling of his breath against my skin. I try to remain unaffected and lift my head. "That might be awkward. I think my tailbone will be fine, thanks."

"Hey, you're the one who asked."

He continues to mold my muscles under his palms, and I glance around his room once more. I look out the open door and into another bedroom that sits across the hall. It's set up like an office, and I can see a desk, a Mac, a file cabinet, and stacks of random papers. But I also see art. Tons of art.

"Can I look across the hall?" I ask.

His hands stop moving. "If you want."

I scoot off the bed and smile. "I want."

When we enter his office, I'm blown away. I know he works for Legionnaire, which is an advertising company, but I had no idea he created anything off the computer. Sure, some of the ads he's created are framed and hung, but what catches my eye are the pieces that are done in pencil or charcoal. Most are on plain paper, only a handful look to be on canvas. His artwork consists mostly of landscapes or a single subject, like a leaf or a gnarled tree. I roam around the room, awed by his talent, until I come full circle. My eyes land on a picture that leans across the arms of an upholstered chair; the canvas is by far the biggest in the room. I move toward it, mesmerized, until I realize what it is.

Dane's hands land on my shoulders from behind. "It's not finished," he says quietly. "You're always a work in progress."

My eyes grow wide as I take in the drawing; it's the only one in the room that's done in color. I walk toward it cautiously, like it might bite me. It's overwhelming to see myself because it's clearly me, yet it's not. This girl is gorgeous.

"When did you –?"

"I started it after we got back from Western." He steps to my side. "It's my favorite memory of you."

I'm lying on my side, asleep. One arm rests beneath my head and the other is bent in front of me, my hand nearly reaching my face. I can tell I'm in bed by the way he's drawn the blanket to hug my every curve; he's given me a waist and hips and long, long legs. My hair flows around me in waves, down my back and across the pillow; he's colored it far more auburn and striking than in real life. Long, full lashes grace my cheeks, and he's made my lips perfect and pouty and pink. All of my exposed skin is sun-kissed, and I know this has to be from our time on the island.

"This is what I woke up to in St. Thomas," he says, his voice low. "I'd wake early each morning just to watch you sleep."

I turn to him, completely baffled and honored at the same time. "You're incredibly talented." I place my hands against his chest. "That's not who I see when I look in the mirror."

His hands wind around my waist, find the back pockets of my jeans, and slide inside. "It's who I see every time I close my eyes."

Oh my heart. It wants to leap out of my chest.

He pulls me to him, presses me against him, and finds my mouth. His kiss is demanding yet soft, and my arms slide up his chest, around his neck, and hold him to me. After a moment, his lips move delicately over my injured chin, travel along my jaw, and bury themselves under my ear. My body starts to warm against him as his hands move to my lower back, slide beneath my shirt, and then out again.

"Stupid rules," he murmurs into my ear.

"Oh!" I step back, startling him. "I forgot!"

"Forgot what?"

"Our wager." My eyes get big. "Our bet."

He gives me a sideways glance then wraps his arms around my waist again. "You're right. We do have that matter to attend to."

"You first." I poke his chest. "What did you think I was going to tell you tonight?"

He smiles. "That you wanted me Larvatus. I thought you were setting it up for Ash to Gift me when I came over."

I bite my lip to stop my stupid grin.

"That's not it, is it?"

I shake my head. "What would you have asked for if you had won?"

He pulls me closer. "I was going to ask if you would consider moving in with me."

I'm surprised. "Really? That's kind of a big step, don't you think?"

He meets my eyes. "I figured if we were both Charmed you might want to. Ash gave me the idea."

Ash did say that. The thought of living with Dane both excites and scares me. I know without a doubt that I want to start something with him, but moving in together is a big commitment.

"So?" he breaks my train of thought. "Don't keep me in suspense. What did you want to tell me?"

Suddenly, I'm nervous. This is huge. This is the official beginning of us.

I take a deep breath. "Yesterday morning..." I pause, my heart beating fast. Geez! It feels like I'm asking this guy to marry me or something. "Yesterday morning I let James go." My words come out in a rush.

His body tenses, and he blinks at me.

"Did you hear what I said?" I ask quietly.

He slowly nods. "Say it again."

"Yesterday morning I let James go."

He moves one hand from my waist to the nape of my neck. "You chose me?" he asks in disbelief.

I smile. "If you'll have me."

His gaze shifts to my mouth and he dips his head, catching my lips in a soul-crushing kiss.

"Is that a yes?" I ask when he rests his forehead against mine.

"That's a hell yes," he breathes against me. "You so win."

"I knew I would."

"What do I owe you?" he asks. "Anything you want."

I lift my forehead away from his. "Well, I had thought about having fun with this and making you my beck-and-call-boy for awhile."

He runs his fingers up my spine and down again sending shivers to my toes. "I'm already there."

"But I'll ask for your patience instead." I try to remain focused. "This relationship stuff is new for me; I don't want to screw it up. I know we have a past, but I don't remember it. I need to get to know you again. Do you think you could start over with me?"

He pulls me close. "I've already told you I can't resist you. I'll start wherever you are."

My stomach growls loudly, interrupting our serious discussion.

"And it looks like we're starting with dinner." Dane smirks. "What do you have in there? Some sort of monster?"

My nose scrunches. "I haven't eaten since yesterday. That's a record, I think."

He laughs, takes my hand, and leads me downstairs where we consult a plethora of take-out menus. It takes us awhile to sort through them because everything sounds so good I want it all, not to mention Dane keeps stopping to kiss me. Finally, we ditch the take-out plan and head to the nearest restaurant, Kentucky Fried Chicken. We order an eight-piece meal and polish it off when we get back to his place.

"I'm not the only one who was hungry," I note as I wipe my greasy fingers. "You ate just as much as I did."

He grins while finishing a honey covered biscuit.

"Sweet tooth?" I ask.

"Guilty," he says, his mouth so full it comes out more like "gilfy."

I laugh. "I'm learning things about you just by having dinner." Pulling my legs from beneath me, I leave the living room to throw away our trash. When I come back, an idea strikes me.

"Let's play Truth or Dare," I suggest.

He looks at me suspiciously. "Why?"

"So I can learn more about you." I sit next to him on the couch and lean back against the armrest, throwing my legs over his lap. "You game?"

"You have to promise to do the dares," he challenges me.

"Of course." I roll my eyes. "I'm not going to welch on my own suggestion."

"Remember that." He winks at me.

"You first," I say. "Truth or dare?"

"Truth."

"What's your favorite color?"

He rests one arm along the back of the couch. "It used to be blue, but now it's green."

"Why'd you switch?"

"Look in the mirror."

My cheeks flush. My eyes are green.

"Your turn," he says. "Truth or dare?"

"Truth."

"What did you think the first time we kissed?"

My forehead pinches. "I don't remember the first time we kissed."

"I mean when we got back from the island. Our experiment."

I tilt my head. "I thought it wasn't very hard to kiss you and it was really nice."

He gives me a stale look. "Nice? That's it?"

I place my hand on top of his. "Not long after, I was trying to figure out how to make it happen again. Does that count?"

Apparently it does because his eyes light up.

"Now you," I tell him. "Pick one."

"Dare. Read my mind."

His thoughts ring clear. *"Dare me to kiss you."*

My eyes get wide. "I have to dare you to do that?"

"Never." He braces his arms, hovers above me, and zeroes in. His kiss is all consuming, illegal even, like he's claiming me as his own. After a minute or two, when he moves back to where he was sitting, my lips feel swollen.

"What did you think that time?" he asks, cocky.

I narrow my eyes, refusing to admit that he's an amazing kisser. I don't want to start a discussion as to how he refined his skills. I smirk. "You taste like honey."

He rolls his eyes. "Your turn."

"Truth."

He hesitates over his question. "How did James take the news?" he finally asks.

I frown. We just went from carefree to serious in seconds. "That's heavy."

"I need to know if I should watch my back."

I shift my weight. "It went okay. We're still friends; we'll always be in each other's life. He's Allegiant, I'm Larvatus. We're a team."

Dane's brow furrows and his hand tenses around my knee. I can tell something's wrong; he doesn't like my answer.

"Truth or dare?" I ask quietly.

"Truth."

"What's bothering you?"

He lets out a resigned sigh. "I don't like that you're still involved." He looks at me. "Will I ever have you to myself?"

"It's not like that." I sit up straight. "James is with Meg. I overheard them talking; I found out he was repressing his feelings for her out of some misconstrued obligation to me."

Dane frowns. "He said that?"

"Well, yeah."

"I thought he was fighting for you."

"He was. He told Meg he would give himself to me if I wanted him, no questions asked. I had to think long and hard about that." I pause. "In the end, I had to be the one to make the decision for both of us. I made the choice that would make us both happy."

Dane leans toward me, concerned. "How much more do you think you can bear?"

"What's that supposed to mean?"

"In practically one day you've broken up with your long-time boyfriend, watched a friend die, and killed your mortal enemies."

I look down. Yeah, yesterday and this afternoon sucked. I'm not going to forget what happened anytime soon. But....

"You're forgetting the best part." I look up and run my knuckles down his cheek. "I have you."

His eyes flash and his shoulders relax. "Truth or dare."

I'm feeling bold. "Dare."

"Stay here tonight."

I lean forward and hold my face inches from his. "You couldn't pay me to leave."

He quickly reaches for his phone, pulling it from his pocket. He glances at the screen then holds it out to show me the time. "Is 8:01 too early for bed?"

"Not on a school night." I'm being sarcastic, but it is Tuesday.

He swings my legs off his and stands, then pulls me to my feet. He busies himself turning off lights and making sure the front door is locked. As he moves around the room with newfound energy, I realize I should have been more specific. I'm afraid he's expecting more than I can give.

When he reaches for my hand and tows me toward the stairs, I say, "Slow down! We need to talk about – "

He abruptly stops walking, and I bounce off him. "Sorry," he apologizes. "I'm not expecting anything from you tonight, if that's what you were going to say. Waking up next to you is enough for me."

I exhale. "Okay. Good." This is new, and I don't think I'm ready for absolutely *everything* yet. "Can we still play Truth though? So far all I've discovered is your favorite color."

"Sure."

When we make it his room, he moves to the dresser and finds me a shirt to wear before changing himself. "Here." He tosses me a white undershirt for bed.

I hold it up. "This thing is practically see through," I chastise him.

"So?" he asks over his shoulder.

"Are you trying to make things difficult for yourself?" I raise my eyebrows and think of his earlier words. "Can you take it?"

A slow smile spreads across his face. "I can. I'm sorry you couldn't earlier."

I purse my lips. "Fine. Don't say I didn't warn you." I turn my back, although I still don't completely get what he sees in me. I quickly remove my shirt while simultaneously pulling on his, revealing nothing in the way that girls do; we're masters at getting dressed in front of people. His shirt falls almost to my knees, so I slide out of my jeans, also revealing nothing. I move my arms beneath the shirt to take off my bra, sliding it off and tossing it on the floor, again, completely covered.

"Do they take you aside and teach every female how to do that?" Dane asks from behind me.

I turn around. "It's an age old secret, the result of being forced to undress in crowded locker rooms for gym," I explain.

"Ah." He pulls back the sheets.

"You know," I can't help but comment, "if you keep giving your shirts to random girls you won't have any left."

"Funny. Would you rather Teagan stayed naked?"

"I'm sure that was her plan." I don't like that she was wearing his clothes now that I'm doing the exact same thing.

"I'll burn that shirt if she ever gives it back to me," he mutters.

I crawl on to the bed and sit. "Which side is yours?"

"The middle," he responds. "Take your pick."

I decide to head to my right, crawling under the sheets, and busying myself with fluffing the pillow. Dane is changing and he's not being very secretive about it; although, he just pulls on sleep pants over his boxer briefs. He hits the light and joins me, sliding beneath the blankets. We reach for each other, and I wind my body against his. Immediately, I know there is no place I'd rather be.

We're silent for a few moments until he kisses my forehead. "Ask me truth," he says softly.

I lift my head off his shoulder to look at him. "Truth?"

"I love you."

My breath catches, and he feels it. This is only the second time he's told me this that I can remember, the first being when he explained why he wasn't with Teagan anymore.

"You don't have to say it back," he says as he runs his fingers through my hair. "I just wanted you to know."

I swallow. "I feel like I should say it."

His hand stops. "Do you want to?"

I don't know if I'm ready to say this. He told me I said it before, right as Kellan blasted my memories away. I know I'm leaning in that direction, but this feels like a giant step. We're supposed to be starting over, not leaping off a cliff all crazy-like.

My mouth opens to rationalize my decision to wait, but my eyes catch his and I know I'm a goner. The way he looks at me, even in the dark, is insane. Has anyone ever looked at me this way before? I doubt it. I still don't understand why he feels the way he does about me, but I'm not about to question it now. For the first time since this Guardian mess started I realize how truly lucky I am. Garrett made me promise to live a full life. It's time to start living it.

I pull myself higher and bring my eyes level with Dane's. "I love you," I whisper, and lean in to show him how much.

Chapter 22

Dane's body shifts beside mine as he silences his ringing phone. I roll on to my stomach to stay buried in the bed; it seems way too early for the outside world. I drift back to sleep and wake some time later to the delicious smell of breakfast. My stomach is ecstatic at the promise of bacon.

Stretching my arms over my head and my feet in the opposite direction, I take inventory on how I feel. My tailbone remains unhappy yet improved; my head and shoulders no longer ache. I move to my side and run my hand over the spot where Dane slept, a slow smile spreading across my face. This is really happening for us.

Over the course of the night I learned several things, some from our Truth game. Dane's middle name is Ryan, he played baseball in middle school, graduated college a semester early, and his favorite cartoon as a kid was X-Men. His all-time favorite food is a rib eye steak, preferably grilled, and he had one steady girlfriend prior to Teagan. It was a sweet, eighth grade romance.

The other knowledge I gained wasn't spoken. It was felt. Last night was the most peaceful night I've spent in a long, long time. There's no question that I feel content in his arms; I feel safe. Now that I've let my guard down, I can't believe how blind I was to my attraction to him. I'm sure all the making out probably reinforced those emotions, but damn! I've never felt this way; at least not that I can recall. My eyes land on my wrist, on my bracelet, and I wish there was another way to reclaim my lost memories. I want to remember every single moment with him.

Dane's phone vibrates against the bedside table, and I snap to. It's time to get up and get moving. I scoot out of the bed, careful of my sore behind, and decide to get dressed in what I wore yesterday. As much as I like being here, a change of clothes and my toothbrush would be nice. Should I ask him if I could leave some of my things here or would that be too forward? He said he wanted me to consider moving in, but that was before he knew of my decision. I'm curious if the motivation behind that thought was to get me away from James at any cost. Now that he has me, would he really want me around all the time?

As I head to the bathroom to throw my hair up in a ponytail, Dane's phone vibrates again. Someone is really trying to get a hold of him. I decide to grab his cell and take it with me, to give it to him downstairs. Unfortunately, the text message received is prominently displayed.

It's because of that bitch isn't it?

Okay, what? Those are fighting words. I know I shouldn't, but I slide my finger across the screen to unlock it. Dane's cell opens to a text thread with Teagan. Only the last few messages are visible, and they're all from this morning.

8:08 Teagan: *You're late.*

8:09 Dane: *I quit.*

8:10 Teagan: *You can't do that to me.*

He didn't respond.

8:42 Teagan: *Can you at least tell me why?*

Then, five minutes later, the message that degrades me appeared.

I set the phone back on the table because I'm tempted to scroll through their prior discussions. Nothing screams "I don't trust you!" like snooping through someone's cell. I decide to leave the device behind as I leave the room; I don't want Dane to know I purposefully read his texts. In the bathroom, as I pull my hair back, the thought of Teagan makes my skin crawl. I understand why Dane quit his job *again*. How could I subtly hint to him that he should also change his number?

266

When I find him in the kitchen he's scraping scrambled eggs out of a pan and on to two plates. I walk up behind him and wrap my arms around his waist.

"Good morning," I say against his back.

He looks over his shoulder and smiles. "Hungry?"

"Starving. I didn't know you could cook."

"My repertoire is limited," he says as he focuses on the task at hand. "How much bacon do you want?"

"Did you seriously ask me that?" I sound surprised. "Like, all of it."

He laughs and places a few pieces on one plate and then sets the rest on the other. He picks up both dishes, and I release him so he can turn around. When he looks at me his face falls. "Shouldn't you be wearing my shirt?"

I look down at myself and back at him with a smirk. "Shouldn't you be at work?"

"I quit," he says like it's an everyday thing to do.

"Why?" I manage a confused glance. "Teagan's going to be pissed."

He shrugs and moves past me to the small dining table where silverware and orange juice wait. "That's not my problem. Lucas will be back soon; she doesn't need me."

Following him, I take a seat. "But what will you do?" Don't get me wrong; I'm happy that he won't be around his gorgeous and annoying ex. But, I don't want him broke either.

"My resume is ready to go." He stabs his eggs. "All I have to do is send it out." He smiles at me before taking a bite. "No worries, Grace."

I smile at his nickname for me and pick up a salty strip of bacon. "Well, since you have nothing better to do," I pull the meat in half, "can you drop me at Ash and Mad's? I need to shower and brush my teeth. I feel kinda gross."

Dane swallows his food. "You can use my toothbrush."

"Ew!" My face contorts. "That's nasty."

He grins. "You didn't have a problem with my tongue in your mouth. What's the difference?"

My face flushes. "You did not just say that."

"It's the truth."

I concentrate on eating, unable to look at him. It may be true, but do we have to discuss it?

"You're cute when you're embarrassed," his voice is playful. "What else can I tease you about?"

"I'm sure you'll think of something," I say sarcastically. It doesn't bode well for me that he has a memory bank of us that I don't have access to.

After a few more bites, he changes the subject. "So, I've been thinking."

I shoot him a questioning glance.

"Aren't you supposed to be vacationing with Shel? When do your parents expect you back?"

"Saturday," I answer. "My internship begins next week and so does my class."

"What would you say if I asked you to stay with me for the next few days?"

I pick up my juice. "Like live here?"

"Just until you have to be home."

"Don't you think you'll get sick of me? We just got together."

He smiles. "I lived with you in St. Thomas for almost a month. I think I can handle it."

I look down to think it over, but who am I kidding? His proposition sounds perfect. Except... "What will we do all day? Stare at each other?"

His eyes light up. "I have some ideas."

Butterflies instantly appear in my stomach.

Dane stands and approaches me, setting one hand on the table and the other on my chair, boxing me in. "Let me romance you." His eyes soften and search mine. "At Western I promised we'd date and so far I've only managed to take you to the Bay Woods employee party. When you start working you'll be busy what? Twenty? Thirty hours a week? Let's enjoy this time while we can."

Now my heart starts to flutter. Am I turning into some sort of lovesick mess? "You want to wine and dine me for the next three days?"

"Amongst other things." His expression turns wicked. "The harder you fall the easier it will be to get you naked."

My mouth falls open as I blush. "That's what this is about? You're expecting the Big Event before Saturday?"

He laughs. "The what?"

"You know what I mean." I cross my arms. "I thought I won your patience from our bet."

He shakes his head. "I'm teasing you, Grace." He plants an innocent kiss on my forehead. "I don't expect the Big Event before Saturday." He looks into my eyes again. "What do you say?"

Of course I'm going to say yes; I'm not stupid. But, I feel like he's going overboard and it isn't necessary. "I'll stay but on one condition." I hold up my finger. "No fancy stuff." He's not working and he doesn't need to spend a bunch of money on me. "In fact, let me make you dinner tonight. Then you can have the other two days."

"Agreed." He leans back and moves around the table to finish his breakfast. He picks up his fork with a gleam in his eye. "Hurry and eat so we can go get your things."

"Welcome back," Ash greets us as we enter the house. He's wearing splattered coveralls and holds a spackling knife, his hands covered in white paste.

"What are you doing?" I ask.

"Fixing the damage."

He smiles like he's having fun, and I read his thoughts. He's relieved everything is over even if it means major home repair.

"Let me help you," Dane murmurs as he looks around the living room. His eyes land on mine, and he frowns. "You downplayed the fight a bit don't you think?"

I glance around. There are sporadically spaced gaping holes in the drywall, only about a quarter of which are patched. You can see where part of the staircase railing was blasted away and the remaining spindles stand cut off and sharp. Scorch marks grace the floor and ceiling, and minimal furniture remains in the room.

I turn to Dane and shrug. "You didn't ask for a play by play."

He takes off his coat and starts to roll up his sleeves. "What can I do?" he asks Ash.

"I'll help too," I volunteer, "after I take a quick shower." I'm literally craving hot water and deodorant; I hope I don't come across as yucky as I feel. I make my way to the stairs, take one last look at Dane, and read his mind. *"Don't forget to pack."*

I can't help but smile.

When I'm clean and comfortable, I round up the few things I brought with me to stay with The Larvatus. It all fits in my suitcase with no trouble. Seeing the bag reminds me that I need to call Shel and fill her in on everything that's happened. She's going to be disappointed that Garrett didn't make it; I hope she won't blame herself in any way. There was nothing any of us could have done. Which reminds me – where *is* his body? I involuntarily shudder.

"Are you leaving?"

I look up to find James in the doorway. "Yeah, Dane asked me to stay with him for a few days."

"That doesn't surprise me."

I smile as I mess with my suitcase. "So how are things with Meg? Good?"

"They're decent," he says and tries to suppress a grin.

My eyes light up, happy for him. Any rational person would be upset that their ex found happiness with someone else so soon. Not me. I'm excited for him because I can relate to what he's experiencing. Plus, Meg isn't all that terrible; she helped me tremendously during the fight.

"I'm glad." I set my suitcase by the door. "I'm headed to help Ash and Dane. What are you up to?"

"Fetching you," he says. "We brought Lucas here last night. He'd like to talk to you."

This is news. "How is he?"

"Still weak, but better. He's disappointed that Garrett suffered and angry about what we had to go through. He feels he owes you an apology."

I grimace. The bad guys are gone; it's time to move on. Let's stop rehashing the past and move forward already. "I'm not in the mood to discuss anything depressing."

James shrugs. "Better now than later."

I sigh and start out the door.

"Em, wait," he says and gently pulls me back. He catches my hand and runs his thumb across my knuckles. "I need to tell you something."

I give him a curious look and his cerulean blue eyes focus on mine. "Meg is great, and I'm excited about what our future may hold. But, I want you to know she will never replace what we had. I don't want you to think that I'm moving on easily, as if all our time together meant nothing. Because it means everything. I'll never forget what we shared."

Why does it sound like he's saying goodbye? I frown. "Are you going somewhere?"

"Nowhere unfamiliar." He gives me half a smile. "Lucas has asked me to accompany him to the Intermediate to keep things in order. We're the only two Allegiant left that can be trusted."

I recall the fight and the one Allegiant that ran away. "Do you think the other could be a problem?"

"Depends." James weaves his fingers through mine. "He could reveal what happened here which wouldn't be good. As far as the Intermediate is concerned nothing has changed. The Guardians still think the same Allegiant watch over them and humanity is not an option. Once word spreads who knows what will happen."

I recall the story Ash told when we first met, about The Larvatus and when they were first created. If unhappy Guardians find out The Larvatus exist, how many will leave their Wards, search out the Charmed, and ask to be Reborn? "Mass exodus," I murmur.

James nods. "Possibly. We need to sit down and make some decisions. And soon."

"Like what?"

"We have to figure out how many Allegiant to create and who is worthy; we need to decide how to work with the Charmed now that we know they still exist. The Larvatus have agreed to spread the word that any Guardian who seeks them out should not be automatically Reborn, but we still need to figure out how to organize our efforts."

A slow smile breaks across my face. "See? I told you we were a team."

He returns my grin.

"And look at you, helping to rule the Intermediate. That's quite a promotion."

He sighs. "It's a job I never signed up for."

"But one you'll be amazing at." I step closer to him. "What you've experienced will prevent what happened to us from happening to other people. Maybe this was your calling all along."

He pauses to consider my thoughts. "You could be right. I just wish I didn't have to hurt you so much in the process."

I push his hair off his forehead and out of his eyes. "I won't forget what we've shared either," I tell him. "But I will miss my friend. Are you planning on having a human life too?"

"Absolutely," he says without hesitation. "I'm not giving up you or Matt or Shel."

"Good." I step forward and wrap him in a hug. He holds me tightly and when we step apart he smiles. "So, you know my plans for the foreseeable future. What about you?"

"Besides staying with Dane it's the same old, same old." We exit the bedroom and head downstairs. "My class and internship start on Monday."

"I'm proud of you," James says as we walk. "You could have easily given up with all that's happened. You'll have to let me know when graduation is; I want to be there."

I smile.

When we reach the living room, I find Dane and Ash still hard at work; although, Dane is talking to Lucas over his shoulder. His boss, Teagan's father, sits on the couch, and I remember his black hair and moustache from the brief absence of my jewelry.

"There she is." Lucas gives me a genuine smile and rises to greet me. He appears shaky, so I pick up the pace so he won't keel over. He extends his hands and I take them. "I've heard some amazing things about you."

I blush. "I'm sure whatever you've heard was exaggerated."

He sits down on the couch and pulls me to join him. "You wiped out a room of Allegiant," he says. "That's no small feat."

I shrug. "My friends were in danger. There was no other choice."

Lucas grips my hands and looks me in the eye. "I owe you so much. Thank you."

I'm confused. He owes me nothing. What I did was second nature; anyone in my position would have done the same. My response comes out more like a question. "You're welcome?"

He chuckles. "You have no idea, do you? You've saved me in more ways than one."

Now he's really lost me.

"Not only did you get rid of the person that was trying to eliminate me, you convinced my best employee to return to work and save my company. We're talking about my family's livelihood here. I love my daughter very much, but there's no way she could have done it alone. That was incredibly selfless of you seeming as how you and Dane are involved."

Oh. Does he know I didn't remember his daughter enough to worry?

Lucas looks at Dane, who has his back to us. "I've been trying to convince him to stay on with the promise that Teagan will not."

Dane ignores him and continues to patch the wall.

"Anyway," Lucas focuses back on me, "please accept my thanks and an apology. If I had known the Charmed still existed I would have sought them out. Garrett would never have assigned

James to you; you wouldn't have had to run away. You wouldn't have lost your memory, and you wouldn't have become Larvatus."

I open my mouth to tell him I enjoy my new abilities, but James rounds the furniture and asks a question before I can. "Garrett once said that his being Reborn was part of your plan, something you were working toward to benefit humanity. What were you trying to prove?"

As Lucas gives James a defeated look, I realize our conversation now has the attention of everyone in the room. Ash and Dane have focused on us, as well as Madeline who just rounded the corner from the kitchen.

"I'm afraid my plans weren't that original," he admits. "The Larvatus have been doing what I envisioned for years." His eyes land on Ash. "Decades ago, I stumbled upon an old text written by Xavier himself. The book was hidden behind some thick volumes in The Allegiant's library. His writing documented his experiments with his previous Ward; I believe her name was Catherine."

"Let me guess," Ash says. "She wanted to be human."

Lucas nods. "He analyzed everything in excruciating detail. Why Guardians existed, how they are created, what can they do, it went on and on. Then, when he started to explore why Guardians were released, he found his answer. Catherine assigned her Ward to his true love, and she became human again. She was Reborn."

I want to ask how that works, but I'm not sure if it's my place. Ash reads my mind and asks for me. "How does that act restore humanity?"

Lucas looks around the room. "What's the one thing that releases a Guardian into eternity?"

Do I know the answer to this question? It feels like I should.

James speaks. "Love," he says quietly. "True love is the only thing that can release a Guardian from their duty."

"Precisely," Lucas says. "Love is a powerful force. When a Guardian assigns a Ward to their beloved, what they feel for one another is released. The Guardian absorbs the couple's connection and their love gives him life."

My eyes lock on James as this information settles over me. Our feelings for each other gave Garrett life. What we had must have been incredibly strong.

Lucas redirects my attention. "Xavier's writings ended there. If we look back at history, we can assume he took his findings to the other Allegiant, who then condemned him for his curiosity. I think we all know what happened next, except I was under the impression that none of The Larvatus remained. I thought the method he discovered to create the Charmed was lost long ago."

He pauses and rubs his palm over his tired eyes. "Once I stumbled upon the method to being Reborn I couldn't shake it from my mind. It had to exist for a reason and what better reason than to guide humanity from the Intermediate *and* below? I convinced myself that my idea was progressive, beyond Xavier's original vision, and I took my thoughts to my brothers. Of course they didn't agree, so I set out on my own to prove them wrong. I recruited Garrett and Jack because I knew they were unhappy. If one of them could be Reborn, I could support the possibilities."

"But, you knew it would ruin Emma and me," James says. He steps closer to Lucas; his eyes hard, his jaw tense. "It's forbidden to assign a Guardian to who they love. You knew it would ruin us, but you made Garrett do it anyway."

Lucas sighs. "You know The Allegiant are full of themselves to a debilitating extent. I regret my arrogance; back then, I felt the experiment was worth the risk. All the things that have happened...the attempt on my life...everything...all I have learned has been humbling to say the least. I should never have discounted how hard this would be on the two of you." He looks between James and I, then offers James his hand. "Search my memories. I want you to know I'm telling the truth."

James eyes his hand suspiciously and doesn't take it. "What good would it do?" He steps away angry. "It won't change anything."

But I can see that it will. "Do it," I tell James. "The two of you rule the Intermediate now; you have to rely on each other. Your partnership won't work without trust."

"She's right," Ash agrees. "Last night you said you wanted to work with The Larvatus for the greater good. I can't agree to that if you don't have faith in one another. Our kind needs to trust you." He looks pointedly at Lucas and then at James. "Show us you want this alliance."

I read Ash's mind, and he silently hopes that James will cooperate. He needs reassurance to partner with our former enemy. If James can demonstrate he's willing to try and move past what Lucas did – if Lucas' thoughts ring true – then Ash can move forward with a clear conscience.

James hesitates, and I silently plead with him. *Do this and don't be a stubborn ass!* I'd like to make sure Lucas isn't inherently evil as well. The man knows all about me, and he's still holding one of my hands. James finally relents and takes Lucas up on his offer, grasping his hand and closing his eyes in a determined concentration.

Several minutes pass and tension fills the air. I look at Madeline, who gives me a small reassuring smile. I look at Ash, who waits patiently, yet taps his fingers against his crossed arms. And I look at Dane, who looks a little lost. Finally, when James opens his eyes and blinks to focus, his expression is dazed, but confident. What must he have seen? He gives Ash a curt nod. Lucas checks out.

Ash steps forward and extends his hand to James. "I trust you," he says with confidence. They shake and then Ash repeats the gesture with Lucas. "Let's learn from our past and move forward, shall we?"

Hours later, as I busy myself in Dane's kitchen, my mind wanders through the events of this afternoon. A supernatural alliance was created before my eyes with a simple handshake. You would think a partnership of that magnitude, one that eradicates thousands of years of hatred between groups, would have called for some sort of ceremony. Maybe a chant or a sacrificial toast or the signing of a document. None of that happened. I almost volunteered to be their scribe, to record this event for future generations, but I got sidetracked. For one, Madeline presented me with Garrett's ashes. And for two, Meg, who appeared shortly after the Declaration of Codependence, apologized for her Ward's behavior.

Finding out Garrett was cremated was the first big surprise. Madeline produced a small gilded box with more reverence than what was afforded our new other-worldly alliance. She told me she and Ash gently took care of his remains with an enchantment, and they agreed I should be the one to decide his final resting place. Whether that be with me or somewhere else she didn't know, but The Larvatus felt strongly this is what Garrett would have wanted. The news garnered confused looks from both James and Dane, and I didn't feel like explaining Garrett's feelings for me. I really don't understand them myself and, for whatever reason, I felt the situation was too personal to reveal. I simply accepted the box as graciously as I could, and it now resides on the front seat of my car. I know that's tacky, but what am I supposed to do with it while I'm at Dane's? I'll give it a place of honor when I get home, somewhere nice while I decide what to do.

After that, I worked side by side with Dane patching holes. It was fun. He made the mistake of trying to spackle me instead of the wall, which left me no choice but to demonstrate my Larvatus badassery. Later, as I was trying to leave for the store to get dinner supplies, Meg pulled me aside for surprise number two. She offered her apologies for Teagan's antics; apparently I knew Teagan was her Ward prior to my mind wipe. She said she's been trying her best to guide her, but to no avail. Teagan is strong willed and her feelings for Dane run really, really deep. Meg thought I should be warned, and I thanked her for the heads up.

Now, as I check the potatoes to see if they are soft enough to whip, I silently remind myself to prepare my arsenal of verbal assaults.

The oven dings, and I turn off the timer while simultaneously opening the door to check the meatloaf. It may seem like an odd choice for a dinner date, but it's one of the few dishes I know how to prepare because it's my Grandma Ethel's recipe. I know it tastes good and I don't want to embarrass myself and make something that turns out awful. Plus, it's really cold outside, so I felt comfort food was in order. Coupled with mashed potatoes and asparagus, I think this is one hell of a delicious meal.

I look around the corner and see Dane sprawled on the couch watching TV. I asked him to stay out of the kitchen, so I could surprise him with what I was making; he didn't join me at the store because I needed my car.

"Hey," I call to him, "you might want to turn that up. I'm getting ready to use the hand mixer."

He glances at me while raising the remote. "You'd better hurry up, Grace. I'm starving. Keeping a man hungry and waiting isn't the best way to start a first date."

I'm instantly challenged and move my hands to my hips. "This isn't our first date and if you keep it up there won't be any more."

"I doubt that." He wiggles his eyebrows at me.

Damn. He's right.

After another ten minutes, I call him into the kitchen to make his plate.

"What? You're not serving me?"

"Uh, no." I hand him a dish. "I don't want you to get the impression that I'll wait on you hand and foot. Besides, I don't know how much you want."

He peruses the food in front of him and points. "Is that meatloaf?"

"Yeah. Why?"

He tries not to smile. "You made the one thing I refused to eat as a kid."

It's hard to hide my disappointment. "You're kidding me."

He shakes his head.

"Aw, man! It's my grandmother's recipe. You'll at least try it, right?" I make an uncertain face. "They say your taste buds change every seven years."

"Who says that?"

"I think I heard it on Dr. Oz."

He wraps his arm around my shoulders. "For you, yes, I will try the meatloaf." He kisses the top of my head. "But, I want it noted that meat should never be in loaf form."

I roll my eyes. At least we'll have enough leftovers to keep me fed while I'm here.

Dane manages to eek the thinnest slice of meat out of the pan, then heaps a mountain of mashed potatoes on his plate and a pile of asparagus. He takes his dinner to the table, and I'm not far behind. I refrain from eating and purposefully prop my chin on my hand to watch him take his first bite.

"Oh my God," Dane says as he chews. "This is really good."

I try not to look smug. "Seriously?"

He nods and takes another bite. "What is in this?"

"It's a Donohue family secret." I pick up my fork.

Dane finishes his tiniest piece of meatloaf ever, and I'm curious to see if he'll go back for more. He eats half of his potatoes before making a trip back to the kitchen. When he reappears the size of his helping is much larger. So much for leftovers.

"Save room," I tell him. "I have a surprise for dessert."

He stops mid-bite. "Does it involve you wearing it?"

"No," I laugh. "I could feed it to you though."

He raises an eyebrow. "Sounds promising."

After we finish, I instruct him to stay put, so I can get our last course. Yesterday I learned Dane has a thing for sweets, so I went a little berserk. There's this great bakery in town, and I got the biggest box of assorted desserts I could buy. I swear there has to be fifty pieces of goodness in there.

Emerging from the kitchen, I carry the box to the table, set it in front of Dane, and promptly take a seat in his lap.

"Well, hello," he says as he wraps his arms around my waist. I curl one hand around his neck and give him a slow kiss before flipping off the box top with my other hand.

"Behold sweet tooth heaven." I gesture in a very *Price is Right* hostess sort of way. "We have everything from chocolate covered strawberries, to bite size cheesecakes, to lemon squares, to fudge bites. Take your pick."

His eyes grow wide as he leans forward and looks over the selections. "You got all of this for me?"

"Yes, but I was hoping you'd share."

He gives me a sly smile. "Which is your favorite?"

I look into the box. "Has to be the strawberries."

He picks one up and holds it to my lips. I take a bite, and it tastes like perfection.

"Is it good?"

"Very."

He finishes the rest of it.

"Your turn," I say. "What's your weakness?"

"You won't find it in that box."

My face falls. "Did I screw up again? There has to be one thing in there you like!"

He turns me by my hips, forcing me to bend one leg and let the other fall to the side, so we're eye to eye.

"What I like is in my lap," he says and smiles before kissing me. His left hand leaves my side, and I can feel him reach into his pocket. When he leans back, he holds a silver key in the space between us, and I shoot him a questioning look.

"This is to my front door," he says. "I want you to have it."

I'm confused. "For what?"

"For whatever you want. For whenever you want. Come and go as you please."

I eye his gift, uncertain. "I would never just show up unannounced. What if I interrupted something?"

He smiles. "Never, huh? That's exactly what you did last night."

Shoot. He's right, but I had big, exciting news to share. "I won't do it again. I promise."

He groans. "You're missing the point." He turns my hand over and presses the key to my palm. "I *want* you to show up. Announced or unannounced. And frequently." He widens his eyes for emphasis. "I still can't believe yesterday happened. You picked me. *Me,"* he squeezes my waist, "and my ex was here to ruin it. You could have easily walked away. I want you to know I have nothing to hide; I don't have any secrets. I don't care what I'm doing or who's here. There's nothing you can't see."

I fold my fingers over the key. "It's hard to keep secrets from the girl you love when she can read your mind," I tease. "Are you sure you want me to have this?"

"Yes," he says as he searches my face. He gives me a crooked smile and my heart melts.

"What if I come by and you're not home?"

"Make yourself comfortable." He kisses my nose.

"What if you're taking a nap?"

"Join me." He kisses my chin.

"What if you're in the shower?"

"Definitely join me." His lips find mine.

The wants of my body start to take over the longer we stay connected. All logical thoughts scatter except for one.

Things can't get any better than this.

Chapter 23

The activities for the next two days were Dane's responsibility. I was curious as to what he could come up with to romance me – his words not mine – on such short notice. My stay at his place wasn't exactly planned and I requested we do nothing fancy. What could be simpler than sharing a meal? I expected two more dinners.

I greatly underestimated his creativity.

On Thursday, he informed me we were going to the movies and to be ready by six. Assuming this was a typical no-frills date, I readied myself in jeans, a sweater, and a ponytail; not a speck of makeup graced my face. However, as soon as we set foot in the theater lobby, it was obvious this wasn't a normal movie date, and I should have tried harder.

The cinema manager was waiting when we arrived. He introduced himself as Ben and gave "Mr. Walker" a hearty smile and handshake. He led us through the building and into the last movie theater, where I quickly observed we were the only people in an empty room. Dane had rented the whole theater just for us, complete with a private concession stand. Next to speechless, I stupidly asked what we were seeing. Dane escorted me toward the delicious smell of popcorn and casually informed me that we were seeing an advanced pre-screen of Channing Tatum's new movie *Side Effects*. It wouldn't be out in theaters for another month.

Once seated, I smacked him in the arm and told him this was way too overboard and how did he know I liked Channing Tatum anyway? He laughed and revealed our discussion in the

Caribbean, about how I thought Channing was hot because he could dance and that he would look good in a Speedo. I must have flushed a million shades of red. Dane then innocently asked me what was so "overboard" about going to the movies. All I could do was give him an incredulous stare. No one I know goes to private advanced pre-screenings of yet-to-be-released films. No one.

After that surprise, I had no idea what to expect on Friday. Dane disappeared mid-afternoon to run "errands" and, shortly after he left the apartment, I received an unexpected delivery. Opening the package, I found an outfit and a note from Shel. The note read:

"Shut up. Put this on. Do you hair. Paint your face. Love you!"

I did as I was told.

Around five o'clock I sat anxiously in Dane's living room. The clothes Shel provided were not my regular style. I was dressed in tight, hip-hugging, low-rise, black leather pants; a glittery tank top covered in gold sequins; and high heeled, open-toed, black sandals with a gazillion straps. Not your typical January attire. I curled my hair and wore it down, remembering Dane's preference, and made up my face like a good girl following my mother's orders. When the doorbell rang, I pulled open the door to find an impeccably dressed handsome man standing on his own front porch.

It was hard to resume breathing after taking in Dane's sexy grin, perfectly fitted open-collared black button-down shirt, dark denim, and tousled hair. But I did it. I accepted the red rose he offered, grabbed the small clutch that Shel graciously provided, and allowed him to escort me to the sleek black limousine waiting in the parking lot. *A freaking limo!* Once inside, I opened my mouth to rip into him about going overboard again, but he stopped my words by kissing them away. He told me I looked amazing, said we were just going to dinner, and asked what was so over-the-top about that? I gave him a playful shove and caved in to his charm. If he wants to go bankrupt it's on him.

Our destination was the MGM Grand in Detroit; specifically, a private table at Wolfgang Puck Steak. After dinner, we moved on to V Nightclub, also inside the hotel/casino, where I soon discovered I love apple martinis a bit too much and that Dane can really, really, dance. We stayed out until the wee hours of the morning. The last thing I remember is crawling into the limo to leave and snuggling up next to Dane. When my eyes opened the next morning, I was in his bed with no recollection of how I got there.

And now, a week later, I'm still dwelling on it. I hate that I fell asleep at the end of our date! Especially after all the effort he put into it and, especially now, that I'm back home with my parents. As I sit behind the reception desk at my internship, I stare through the computer screen in front of me recalling his words.

"I don't care that you crashed in the car. I got to carry you inside and tuck you in. You're adorable when you sleep."

Gah! What can I do to make it up to him?

"Emma? Are you in there?"

I snap to and focus on Sheila's puffy face. The poor woman. Her baby was due yesterday – literally. I don't understand why she continues to come to work; her feet are so swollen she can barely wear flip flops. The woman visits the restroom every ten minutes, and she's exhausted. I told her that as much as I like her, my internship duties do not include delivering babies on the Randall Veterinary Clinic floor.

"Sorry," I apologize. "Entering these invoices is riveting."

Sheila smiles. "I just wanted to tell you I'm headed to the bathroom *again*. I want to get another trip in before you go to lunch."

I laugh, yet sympathize. "I feel so sorry for you. Why don't I skip lunch today so you can take off early? It's not a big deal."

"No. If I'm home I'll just keep cleaning until my fingers go raw. I've been nesting for weeks. Work occupies my mind and keeps it off the fact that I'm still obnoxiously pregnant."

I give her a wary look. "If you say so." I silently reassure myself with the fact that I researched the quickest route to the nearest hospital in case her water breaks.

Sheila waddles away to the employee restroom and I hear my cell chime. I grab my purse from below the desk and check my phone. I have a message from Dane.

Guess what? I love you.

I can't keep the stupid grin off my face. I text back. *Love you too. How did your interview go?* He has two job interviews today; one was this morning and one is later this afternoon.

Good. It's an easy drive and the people seem friendly. An offer from them would be nice.

The first advertising agency that responded to his resume is near Lansing, which is an hour travel time one way. The second company, the one he just interviewed with, is closer to Pontiac and only a half hour drive.

I can't see why they wouldn't. I saw his portfolio; they'd be crazy not to hire him.

My phone vibrates in my hand. *Are we still on for tonight?*

Why would you even ask that? I send my obvious response – *YES.*

Every night for the past week we've spent a few hours together, but I don't stay very late. I have to be at work early and, since Matt's dad is doing me a favor by sponsoring my internship, I want to be a model employee. Tomorrow is Saturday though, and I don't have to be anywhere, which means I plan on staying out most of the night.

;) I'll call you when I'm on my way home. Use your key.

I smile. This will be the first time.

The door to the clinic glides open, and I set my phone down to greet the customer. When I stand and make eye contact, I freeze. It's Teagan.

"You've got to be joking," she sarcastically spits. Her almond eyes narrow as she approaches the desk. "Since when do you work here?"

My jaw tenses, but I manage a professional tone. "Since Monday."

"Perfect. Now I'll have to find a new vet," she sniffs.

Ugh! I want to strangle her. Instead, I conjure up the most courteous smile I can muster which turns out to be a lame smirk. "You know you won't find anyone better than Dr. Randall," I say like the good employee I'm trying to be. I break her evil stare to consult the appointment log and see "Molly" at one o'clock. "The doctor will be right with you and Molly." I glance at her. Where is her pet?

Within seconds, I see a tiny tan head pop out of her bag. Of course Teagan would have a purse dog. Even though the puppy is cute, I can't help myself. "Oh! What a cute rat."

Teagan's eyes flash and she hisses. "She's a Yorkie you twit!"

I shrug. "Sorry."

Her eyes shoot daggers. "No one disrespects me and gets away with it. You have no idea who you're messing with."

"Oh, I think I do," I say confidently and lean toward her. "You don't scare me," I whisper.

She glares at me as I redirect my attention to messaging Matt's dad that his appointment is here. He instantly responds that he's ready and to send her to exam room two.

"You'll be in room two," I inform Teagan sweetly. "Would you like me to escort you back?"

She huffs and marches away without another word, bypassing a slow moving Sheila. Apparently, Teagan is self-sufficient when it comes to finding the exam room.

I shake off her ridiculousness as I leave for lunch. Sitting in the drive thru line at Subway, I come to a conclusion. I'll never be able to stop myself from making snide comments when she's around, so I shouldn't even try. If she would just shut up when we run into each other we wouldn't have a problem. What did Dane ever see in her anyway? I mean, she's pretty; I get that. But was he ever that shallow?

When I return to the clinic, I park in my usual spot behind the building. My stomach rumbles and I grab my food, focused on making it to the break room. I hear a car door slam.

"We need to talk."

I turn to find Teagan approaching me from her Lexus. Fabulous. She was lying in wait for me? I shoot her a confused look. "What could we possibly have to talk about?"

She stops about a foot away, crosses her arms, and sets her jaw. "Don't play dumb. You may have fooled Dane, but you haven't fooled me."

What in the world is she talking about? "Are you off your meds?" I ask sarcastically. "I haven't fooled Dane about anything."

Her nostrils flare and she points to herself. "I'm not the one who's mentally unstable here. You are."

Okay, whatever. If she keeps this up I'll be forced to physically put her in her place. You don't mess with a hungry Larvatus. "Teagan," I take a deep breath, "I barely know you and you hardly know me. Let's just stay away from each other, okay?" I take a step toward the building.

She reaches out and grabs my shoulder, stopping me and turning me around. "No one turns their back on me."

She did *not* just touch me. Adrenaline courses through my veins. I glare at her, wrap my fingers around her wrist, and remove her hand from my body as calmly as possible. "Well, get used to it, because it's going to happen again."

I turn away, take two steps, and stumble. Did she just shove me?! That's it! I have never been involved in a catfight before, but I guess the time has come. I turn on my heel and on her.

"What is your problem?" I snap.

"My problem is you." She moves closer. "The only reason Dane left me is because you put on a good show. We'd still be together if it weren't for your little depression routine this summer. The only reason he's with you is because he feels sorry for you."

That can't be true, but her words still sting. My eyes narrow. "You couldn't be more wrong."

"Really?" She raises her brow. "Then what is your relationship based on? You haven't even known each other a year. I was with him for a decade!"

I smirk. "I'm sorry you wasted your time."

She steps closer and we're nearly nose to nose. "You think you know everything, don't you?"

I stand my ground. "No, but I know this. Dane and I love each other." I pause. "So build a bridge and get over it."

Teagan tries to slap me, but I drop my lunch and catch her wrist, stopping her hand in mid-air. "I wouldn't do that if I were you." Little does she know I could toss her into next week.

I feel her arm relax and let her go. She jerks away and steps back. Because I feel my point's been made, I bend at the knees to pick up my Subway, but maintain eye contact. "I'm going back to work now. I suggest you do the same."

She surprises me by stepping forward and kicking my lunch under the nearest car. Does she have a death wish? "What is with you?" I spit. "Are we in kindergarten?"

"I'm not through with you yet," she sneers.

"Well, I'm through with you." I stand. "Let me know when you're ready to act your age. Maybe then we can talk."

I start to walk away, and she catches my forearm. Seriously?! I haven't touched her once! "Let me go." I try to pull away without ripping her fingers off.

"I said I'm not done with you," she hisses.

This is ludicrous! I tug my arm harder, and her grip slips to my wrist. Forcefully, I yank my arm free and her hand leaves my body – taking my bracelet with it.

Instantly my eyes are on fire. The blinding light is back as memories start to flood my brain. I try not to cry out; Teagan can't see me like this. Pain sears though my skull, and I bring my hands to my face to block my expression. How long will this last? How can I get the jewelry back? The visions start to come in rapid succession. James. Dane. Garrett. Dane. James.

"Look at me!" she shrieks. At least it sounds like she's shrieking.

I try to pull my hands away from my face, but it's as if they're locked. A memory of James asking me to prom morphs into a memory of Dane kissing me in Matt's backyard.

I feel Teagan's hand around my wrist again. It pushes me over the edge, and I lash out. "Stop touching me!"

My fist connects with her nose.

"Argh!" she screams. My hand feels wet, and I know I've made her bleed. I peel my eyes open and see her stumbling backward, her hands cupped over her face. There's blood on her fingers.

"You broke my nose!" she yells.

Shit. I know she's right.

I slam my eyes closed and will everything to stop. As much as I loathe Teagan I need to get her to a doctor. More scenes play behind my eyes, and I lean against the hood of the nearest car. I'm fighting the pain as hard as I can, but it's not making things go any faster.

"You're such a bitch!" I hear Teagan snap. "All I was trying to do was talk to you!"

If I could roll my eyes I would. Who had their hands all over who?

Temporarily distracted by Teagan's rant, I find that the pressure behind my eyes lessens and the memories start to fly. Despite the chaos that surrounds me, I have a brilliant idea. I've been fighting the pain. What if I willingly accept it? Take my focus off it? Maybe things will go quickly. I try to relax and open my mind despite Teagan's whimpering and how much my head hurts.

"Are you just going to stand there?" she demands.

I want to tell her to fuck off, but I focus on breathing instead. To my amazement, the memories feel like they're falling into place, like they're physically filling the holes they left behind. It's as if they're being vacuumed into my brain and the pain lessens as they find their place. Within minutes it's over.

I open my eyes and blink rapidly. I did it. I have my memory back.

And a different pain surrounds my heart.

Three hours later another doctor comes in to review Teagan's x-rays. I stare at the wall from an uncomfortable plastic chair as his words mirror the first two physicians statements. She won't need surgery because they were able to realign the breaks, but she will have a swollen face and some serious black eyes for a while.

That's right, I said breaks. I broke her nose in two places.

No words have passed between us since we left the parking lot. I believe the last two sentences uttered were mine, "Get in the car!" and hers, "I'm pressing charges!" I know she's a witch and she deserved what she got, but I do feel bad about what I've done. That's why I haven't left. I need to make sure she's okay and give my statement to the police when she calls them. I hope she does it soon because I really do need to go. My recovered past keeps surfacing in waves, and I have to consciously push it back. Every time a memory plays, my throat tries to close and my eyes prick with tears. I can't break down in the hospital; I just can't. I need a private place to let out an ugly cry.

As the doctor reviews the discharge papers with Teagan and demonstrates how to replace the gauze packed in her nose, my phone rings. I pull it from my coat pocket and answer Dane. "Hey."

"Hey! Listen, my interview ran long and I'll probably get stuck in rush hour traffic. I don't want you to worry when I'm late."

His words resurrect the anxiety I felt in St. Thomas when he returned late from planning our fishing trip. He wants to make sure that doesn't happen again. Before I can respond, the doctor attending Teagan is paged over the loud speaker.

"Where are you?" Dane asks.

"In the ER."

"ER? As in emergency room?" Dane's voice raises an octave. "What happened? Why didn't you call?"

"Because I'm fine," I say. "I'm not the one who's hurt."

"Who is?"

I close my eyes and wince. "Teagan. I kind of punched her in the face."

"You *what?*" I can hear the shock in Dane's voice. "Why? How bad is it?"

I open one eye. "Bad. I broke her nose...in two places."

The line goes silent, and I glance at Teagan. She's watching me intently from her sterile bed.

"Don't move," Dane growls. "I'm coming to get you. Which hospital are you at?"

My stomach drops. He's mad. I don't want to fight in a public place, especially in front of his ex. "You don't need to come here. Teagan is being released, and I'm only waiting for her to file charges. Then I'll head home."

"She called the police?!" he nearly shouts. "Why is she involving the police?"

"Because I broke her face."

"It was an unprovoked attack I'm sure," he says sarcastically. "Put her on the phone."

"Dane, I..."

"*Put. Her. On. The. Phone,*" he demands.

I turn to Teagan and hold out my cell. "He wants to talk to you."

Arrogantly, she holds out her hand and I set my phone in her palm. She raises it to her ear and her demeanor instantly changes. "Bear," she whimpers, "your girlfriend hit me!"

I bite my lip and stare at the floor. What could he possibly want to say to her? I know I shouldn't, but I try to listen. All I can hear is his muffled voice growing louder and louder in between her attempts to explain.

"No...I...wait...just stop...you don't...I'm the one who's bleeding!" That's all she can get out.

After a minute or two her shoulders slump. "Fine," she snaps. She eyes me with disdain and holds out my phone. "Here."

I cautiously bring it to my ear. "Hello?"

"If she even breathes at you wrong call me," Dane says, adamant. "Promise me you're still coming over."

I'm stunned. What did he say to her?

"Grace?" he asks, worried. "Promise me you're still coming over."

"I...I promise."

"Good. I'll get there as fast as I can."

Does he think I'm hurt or something? "There's no rush."

He chuckles. "I don't know. Do you think you can keep your hands to yourself, Ali?"

I roll my eyes. "Yes. I won't pummel any innocent strangers."

He laughs. "Get out of there and away from her, okay? I'll see you soon. I love you."

I swallow at his words. "Love you, too," I whisper.

When I turn around I see Teagan pulling her bloodied shirt from the plastic bag the nurse put her belongings in. She reaches for the tie on the back of her hospital gown, but can't reach it.

"Do you want some help?" I ask.

She frowns, but nods.

I move around the bed and untie the top of the gown. She immediately steps away from me and pushes it to her waist while pulling her shirt over her head.

"Are you going to press charges?" I ask quietly.

She shakes her head no, refusing to make eye contact with me. "Didn't Dane tell you? He doesn't want me involving the law."

I blink. "You're going to listen to him?"

She pulls her pants from the bag then shoves the hospital gown to her feet. "I love him. Of course I'm going to listen."

Her admission takes me by surprise. I stand there gawking as she pulls on her pants then reaches into the bag and produces my bracelet. She hands it to me without a word. I gingerly hold it between my fingers; it's encrusted with the blood that was on her hands. I put it in my pocket.

"I'm sorry I hit you," I apologize. "It was a reaction; I didn't mean it."

"Yes, you did," she snaps and tosses her shoes on the floor. She focuses on tying her laces and, when she's finished, she gives me a hard stare. "Look. We're not friends."

I nod.

"For whatever reason Dane loves you and there's nothing I can do about it. I've apologized, I've begged, I've connived, I've lied, I've *bled*," she emphasizes the word. "And he still chooses you. So, if you don't mind, I'd like you to get out of my face."

I take a step toward the door. "Well, for what it's worth I really am sorry."

"Stop trying to be nice to me!" she spits. "Just go!"

I leave without saying another word.

When I reach Dane's place, I sit in the parking lot and stare at his front door. I remember when he brought me here for the first time, after he rescued me from James' psychotic mother at the grocery store. We almost kissed that night. I remember when, just hours after James was assigned my Guardian, I came here so Dane could help heal my heart. He took me to the batting cages so I could take out my aggressions, we raced Go Karts, and I challenged him to a game of mini golf. He had no clue what I was going through, but he didn't ask questions. All he did was unconditionally offer his support.

I let myself into his place and shut the door behind me. Immediately, I'm confronted with the stairs. Those steps have new meaning now. As I take them one by one, I recall my body wrapped around Dane's as he carried me. When I reach his room, I run a tentative hand over the bed as I remember what almost happened that night. His patience astounds me.

Unfortunately, those thoughts lead to memories of betrayal, and I mechanically shrug out of my coat. It lands on the floor and I land on Dane's bed, curling on my side as tears start to fall. It's not as ugly of a cry as I had feared, but it's all consuming nonetheless.

James. Holy hell. Could he have been a bigger part of my life? Could I have loved him more? Not possible. My love for him was my world; he *was* my life. And that part of my life is over.

Years of memories flood my brain. Some make me smile through my tears while others give me pause. But, when the images play of James' death, of what he looked like when he died, I physically get sick. I pull myself to the edge of the bed and dry heave over the side; thankfully nothing comes out. Its no wonder the bracelet blocked my Guardian memories. Who would want to remember this? The images The Allegiant projected into my brain are horrid; it becomes clear my mind wanted them erased to protect me. To keep me sane. Who would want to remember my behavior at his funeral? Or his mother's anger? Or our powerless efforts to hang on to something that wasn't ours to have anymore?

I right myself and lie on my side again, realizing the memories are playing like I'm watching a movie. It's like I'm a spectator watching my own life. It gives me a perspective that I never would have had otherwise. I close my eyes, focus on breathing through my stuffed nose, and allow myself to process what my mind is showing me – because it shows me the truth. Despite everything that we did to stay together, we still would have fallen apart. That is how it was supposed to be. Death separated us. It was a fate we couldn't accept, but one we should have. It would have saved us both unspeakable heartache. The knowledge is heavy, yet liberating at the same time. We're both where we should be. It just took us a minute to get there.

Speaking of where I should be, I open my eyes and find the clock. Dane will be home soon, and I'm sure I look like hell. I sit up and scoot off the bed, headed to the one place that always erases the evidence of my sadness – the shower.

As I leave the bedroom, I almost step on my bracelet; it fell outside my coat pocket. I pick it up and set it on the side table. I'll wash it in a minute; it needs to be handled delicately. I may need a brush to remove all of Teagan's residue from the crevices. Gross. I still can't believe I punched her. A slow, evil smile spreads across my face. Today has been full of liberating moments.

The hot water and the steam soothe my sore throat and free my sinuses; the heat relaxes my stiff neck and evenly reddens my splotched skin. As I reach for the soap and lather it in my hands, more lost memories return. Will I ever be able to switch them off? Turn them to mute? Over time, I suppose, but I guess not in the hours immediately after retrieving them.

Visions of the things Dane has done for me and with me bombard my thoughts. They're good memories. Really good. There are a couple of shady ones too, like when we fought before I left for school and when I found out he was engaged. That one hurts. Another not-so-pleasant one is when I tried to push him away after the hospital charity dinner, but it's quickly replaced by the discovery that he gave up everything to fly me away to the Caribbean. Then his explanation of why he loves me quickly becomes a favorite. It's because I accept him for who he is and not who he's expected to be. Mystery solved.

Turning off the water, I step out of the tub and wrap a towel around myself. I open the bathroom door to head back to my clothes and jump. "Holy...! When did you get here?"

Dane is standing directly in front of me, filling the hallway and blocking my exit. He holds up my bracelet with a worrisome stare. "What's going on?" he asks almost inaudibly.

"Oh." I reach out and take the jewelry from him. "Teagan pulled it off. It's why I hit her."

He swallows and eyes me cautiously. "Do you remember...everything?"

I turn and set the bracelet next to the sink behind me. "Yeah, I'd say so."

"Then why are you still here?"

I whip around and shoot him a confused look. "Where else would I be?"

His face relaxes slightly, but his eyes remain sad. "I guess part of me figured you would leave. If you ever took that off, I mean."

My eyes lock on his. "You thought I would change my mind and leave you? For James?"

He shrugs one shoulder. "It's always been in the back of my mind. You two have a past I can't compete with."

I step back and bump against the bathroom counter. Has he lost it? I take in what he's wearing and stop short. He's all business in pressed black suit pants, a white dress shirt, and black necktie. This is probably not the time for inappropriate thoughts, but I remember what's beneath those clothes. I shake my head to clear it.

"Is your tie cutting off circulation to your brain? I said I loved you and I meant it. I'm not going anywhere."

His eyes light up, and he lets out a relieved sigh. "You don't know how happy that makes me, Grace."

"I have an idea." I smile and reach for his tie. I tug on it, pulling him to me, and find his mouth with mine. "You can't get rid of me that easily."

He wraps his arms around my waist and looks down, focusing on my face. "I love you. You know that, right?"

"With everything you've done for me there's no way I could doubt it. I remember it all, and I'll never be able to make it up to you."

He frowns. "That's not what our relationship is about. I do things for you because I want to, because it's the right thing to do. Not because I want something in return. You do things for me all the time that you're not even conscious of."

"Like what?"

"Like when you smile at me a certain way. It melts my heart. Or when you let me kiss you in ways that should be illegal and you don't protest. Or when you let me dote on you without saying anything, even though I know you're silently reaming me out in your head. And like right now. You're standing here in a towel wearing nothing beneath it, but the bracelet I gave you for Christmas. That does about a million things for me."

"Like what?"

He laughs. "Are you stuck on repeat?"

I decide to loosen his tie. "Tell me. If I don't know what makes you happy how can I make sure to keep doing it?"

"Fine." He smiles. "Right now you're the Emma I fell in love with this summer. I don't have to share you." He eyes the jewelry by the sink. "No supernatural stuff."

I make an impressed face, pull his tie from around his neck, and loop it around mine. I start to work on the buttons on his shirt. "Keep going."

He gives me a knowing smirk. "Standing the way you are right now reminds me of St. Thomas. When you would get out of the shower, run to the dresser in a towel, and change in front of me because you thought I was asleep."

I stop unbuttoning. "What?" I ask him incredulously. "You were spying on me?"

He bites his lip and smiles.

"Incorrigible," I mutter as I go back to unfastening his shirt. When I get down to where our bodies meet, I can't go any further. "What about this?" I ask indicating my handiwork with my eyes. "What does this do for you? Anything?"

"Maybe," he says, teasing me.

I can't believe I'm going to do this. But today has been full of liberating moments, and I know what I want to happen. Now that I have my memory back, I can't believe I've waited this long to try.

I place both hands on his chest and push him away from me. He takes a step. I reach for my towel and Dane stills my hands, his eyes questioning.

"Wait. Are you sure?" he asks, his voice low. His tone says he wants this as much as I do, but he's trying to be a gentleman and give me an out. "You've had a rough day."

I tilt my head. "In case you haven't noticed, I'm a little stronger than I used to be." In one swift movement my towel puddles around my feet.

In another, I'm in his arms.

Chapter 24

Three months later

"In conclusion, I'd like to leave you with one last thought. May the world be as ready for you as you are ready for the world. Savor the feeling of this day, of this moment. Hold it close and never forget. Apply this experience to every opportunity that comes your way. For if you do, I guarantee each and every one of you will find success. Congratulations graduating class of 2013. Job well done."

Whoops and hollers follow the college provost's final words and the graduation caps go flying. I toss mine into the air with my classmates, several hundred people who I don't know and will never meet again. But, in this one moment, we're all connected. The girl next to me hugs me like we've been roommates for the past four years. I just met her today. It's odd how I can tell we're feeling the exact same things – relief, pride, and a sense of accomplishment. Hope for the future.

I look up into the auditorium seats and find my parents and Dane, Mike and Kate, and even Matt and Shel. They're all on their feet with the rest of the place, clapping and cheering us grads like we just won the Super Bowl. I smile and wave enthusiastically. I love those people. So much.

As the crowd begins to disperse, I search for my cap. I made sure to put my initials in huge letters on the underside. I frown as the hunt takes longer than I anticipated. I tossed the thing straight up for crying out loud! Where did it go? I head to the end of my row.

"I believe your looking for this."

My head snaps up. James casually leans against the wall directly below where my family was seated. He smiles, holding my graduation hat in his hands.

"You're here!"

"Wild Allegiant couldn't keep me away," he says as I reach him.

He wraps me in a hug; then I take the cap from his hands, plopping it on my head. "What do you think?"

"It's hot." He grins.

"I know, right?" I make a face. "Have you been here the whole time?"

"Yep. Invisibly watching as you begin the next phase of your life."

"Don't be so dramatic." I roll my eyes. "You sound like my dad."

He laughs.

"Walk with me." I loop my arm through his as we make our way to the back of the auditorium. No one here cares enough to pay attention to us, but my family is waiting in the lobby. We'll have to stop by the doors. "Thanks for coming. It means a ton to me. It wasn't too hard for you, was it?"

"You mean watching you graduate without me?"

I nod.

"No, it wasn't that hard. I mean, I did silently announce my name where it should have fallen in the program, but – "

"I did the exact same thing!" I clutch his arm and smile.

"Daniels, Daughton, *Davis*," he repeats, lighthearted. "But, I was so proud of you it really didn't matter." He pulls my honors cords. "Miss Magna Cum Laude."

"Ugh," I groan. "I was so close to Summa. Stupid online Econ!"

James raises an eyebrow. "Sure. Blame economics. Your extracurricular activities had nothing to do with it."

I slug his arm. "Listen. I passed every test with at least a ninety percent. I can't help it the final slipped; I was busy with work."

"Work as in Dane, you mean."

"Don't be a jerk," I scold him. But, I know it's true. Every free minute I have is dedicated to that man. It's not hard to do when he makes me as happy as he does.

We reach the auditorium doors and I stop walking. "My family's out there. You're coming to the party later, right? At Ash and Mad's?"

"Wouldn't miss it," he says. "Congratulations Em." He gives me a quick kiss on the cheek and starts to fade. "I'll see you tonight."

I smile as he disappears.

Opening the doors, I look for my family and friends. I spot them congregated in the back corner of the lobby. Why doesn't it surprise me that my dad would find the free coffee?

"Congrats!" Shel comes running. She hugs me then asks to see my fake diploma. We'll be attending her ceremony next weekend, even though she has another four years ahead of her.

Matt steps around Shel and hands me a bouquet of lavender tulips. I give him a one-armed hug. "Aw, thanks."

My brother and Kate find me next, followed by my parents. They give me a huge bunch of yellow roses and then, as I balance all the flowers, Dane's hand slides into mine. He whispers in my ear. "I plan on giving you my gift later."

"It is inappropriate?" I ask quietly.

"No!" he whispers. "You have a dirty mind."

I shrug then turn my face away from my family and over his shoulder. "We've done a lot of dirty things. It's a fair question."

He squeezes my hand to silence me, but his eyes dance.

"Ready for dinner?" my father asks as we all head out to celebrate.

Since WMU is so far from home, we stop part way into our drive to eat at an Olive Garden. My parents graciously pick up the tab for everyone and just as we were finishing up, my dad proposes a toast with what's left of his beer. I inwardly cringe. My dad isn't a toast kind of guy.

"First off, I want to say I'm not very good at this, but we have a wedding coming up, and I need the practice."

He eyes Mike and Kate as everyone chuckles. They finally set the date for August where I'll be my brother's Best Woman. He said he didn't trust any of his guy friends with the role, but I secretly think Kate's behind the decision. She's the one who doesn't trust his frat brothers.

"Emma," my dad turns to me, "you are, and always will be, my Em Bug."

My face turns crimson. The last time he called me that I think I was four. Okay, maybe not. Maybe fourteen. Wait. It was last week.

"Words cannot express how proud we are of you. The things you've faced this past year," he frowns, "would drive any good person to drink."

"Dale!" My mom slaps the table.

"What? It's true! She's probably tossed back a few due to the circumstances. I know I have."

Good God! He only knows about James and Patrick. What would he think if he knew everything that's happened to me? I glance around the table and everyone looks amused. I sink in my chair, but my dad still finds my eyes.

"I'm sure every father feels this way, but you, Em Bug, deserve everything good life has to offer. I can't wait to see what amazing things your future holds." He raises his glass. "To my baby girl."

My friends and family smile, clinking their glasses around me. I do the same, but avoid eye contact because my dad's words have caused my eyes to tear. I don't want to cry.

"And you," my dad addresses Dane, "keep in mind what I said."

Dane sits up straight. "Yes, sir."

I feel my face start to turn red again. "Dad..."

"Just because I like you doesn't mean you can get away with anything," he says to Dane. "I just want to put it out there. Emma's my baby. Remember that."

"Dad!" I say louder. "Now's the time you bring this up? Really?"

"I have to take the opportunity when it presents itself." He swallows the rest of his drink. "I never see him. You're always at his place."

Matt and Shel decide now would be a good time to snicker – loudly. Okay, it's time to go. I love these people, but I've had enough embarrassment for one day.

We say goodbye to my parents, Mike, and Kate before following Matt and Shel to the Larvatus' house. Late last week, Madeline approached me about having a grad party with our Guardian and Allegiant friends. At first I told her it wasn't necessary, but Ash pulled me aside and asked me to please allow her to do this. He confided that the two of them felt somewhat paternal toward me since they hadn't been successful in having children of their own. This was huge news and, of course, I couldn't say no.

As we drive, Dane takes the opportunity to tease me about my nickname. "Em Bug! That's great. I'm going to stop calling you Grace."

"Like you have room to talk *Bear*," I exaggerate Teagan's name for him. "What's that all about anyway? Were you unnaturally hairy at some point?"

"Haha. Very funny. It's short for Teddy Bear."

"Teddy Bear?" I scoff. "How very unoriginal."

"I don't see you coming up with a cutesy nickname for me." He pouts. "What about Hot Stuff? Or Stud Muffin? Oh! I know. Sex God."

My mouth falls open. "How about Conceited Ass?"

He drops my hand. "That's it. No graduation gift for you."

"I'm kidding!" I try to grab ahold of his hand again, but he keeps moving it, flailing it around the cab of the car. "Stop doing that! We're going to crash!" Finally, I catch it. "I'll come up with a cute nickname for you; I promise."

"You just want your present."

"Um, yeah." I smile. "Because your presents rock."

My compliment makes him grin. "They do, don't they?"

I think about that. He's right. I have no originality when it comes to planning dates or giving gifts. Don't get me wrong; my gifts are always thoughtful, but never one-of-a-kind. "One day, I'm going to outdo you," I tell him. "I'm going to get you something so fabulous you'll never be able to top it."

His lifts his eyebrows at me. "Challenge accepted."

I take in his look and get the distinct feeling that my graduation gift is spectacular. Great. I'd better start planning for his birthday now – six months in advance.

The night is unseasonably warm for the last weekend in April, and when we arrive at Madeline and Ash's the party is in full swing. So much for waiting for the guest of honor.

On the back deck, Matt, Shel, Dane, and I find Thomas, Joss, Jenna, and Meg. They're all in swimming suits, sitting around a fire. Drinking. How is this possible? James is in the hot tub with Ash and Mad, and Shel, taking in the scene, immediately switches to party mode. "I didn't know we needed suits!"

"Don't worry." Madeline jumps out of the water. "I have suits for all of you. Once the weather changed I took the liberty of getting some. They're in the guest room."

She towels off and starts to head into the house with Matt, Shel, and Dane at her heels. She turns and finds me. "I have cake and ice cream." Her eyes light up. "I'll bring it out after I get them settled."

"Aren't you coming?" Shel asks me.

"In a sec," I tell her and move toward James and Ash. I feel majorly left out. I know I've been tied up with my internship, class, and graduation, but it's not like I don't own a phone. "What's going on?"

Joss stands and comes over to congratulate me. "Emma," she says, excited. "Today was a big day. How do you feel?"

"Good." I eye her suspiciously. She reaches out to rub my arm in a motherly way and a flash of light reflects off her wrist.

"You're Larvatus!" I exclaim and point, smiling. "When?"

"Last week." She beams. She looks over at Thomas and he raises his fist in the air. He's Charmed, too.

Immediately, I hug her. "I'm so happy for you." Both Joss and Thomas are so sweet. I don't know anyone more deserving of a second chance at humanity.

My thoughts immediately turn to Meg and Jenna, and I peer around Joss' shoulder. If they've changed clothes too...

Ash reads my mind. "They're Allegiant," he says and answers my unasked question.

I step away from Joss and turn on James. "Really? Why didn't you tell me earlier?"

He shrugs. "It wasn't the time." He pulls himself from the hot tub. "I'm starting to get lightheaded." He grabs a towel and I follow him over to the fire pit, where he sits next to Meg.

"Hi!" she says to me as she wraps an arm around James. "We were wondering when you were going to get here."

"So, how...when?" I ask the two of them. "This is huge!"

James smiles. "It didn't take long for Lucas and I to figure out who was worthy of being Allegiant. Who better than the Guardians that experienced everything firsthand? The Guardians that understand The Larvatus best?"

"Plus, they needed some women on the team." Meg bumps her hip against James. "Jenna and I are the first female Allegiant since..." She pauses. "Since forever."

Jenna gives me a shy smile.

"That's amazing," I say. The Allegiant have probably needed that balance for a long while. "So, it's the four of you? You two, Jenna, and Lucas?"

Meg and James nod.

"Do you guys plan on staying in the Intermediate most of the time or..."

"For the immediate future, yes." James rests his elbows on his knees. "But, when we visit, we'll stay here to take care of human business."

"Until we find a place of our own." Meg takes his hand.

I can tell she's excited to start a human life complete with a white picket fence. Turning to Thomas, I tap his wrist. "How come you chose this?"

"We decided it would be best if we evened out the ranks. Since we're working with The Larvatus now we thought it would be wise to bring our experiences to both sides."

"Well," I say arrogantly, "I think you chose the better of the two."

He laughs and gives me a high-five as Joss joins us. "What about you Emma? When are you going to rejoin the team?"

I glance down at my empty wrist. I've only worn my amulet a few times since I cleaned it after the fight with Teagan. It still works; every time I slide it on my abilities return and my memory stays. But, without any danger and my busy schedule, it's become more of an accessory than a way of life. I need to burn the excess energy that comes with being Larvatus and it's been tough to find time to fit in workouts. Plus, my parents haven't been complaining about the grocery bill, which is nice.

I smile at Joss. "Eventually. Lately, I think of myself as more of a second string player."

Eyes focus on me and I look over to find James intently staring at me. I keep forgetting that everyone can read my mind now that I'm not wearing the bracelet. I remember explaining to him that we were a team and would always be in each other's lives. I'm not holding up my end of the deal. I send my thoughts to him. *I'll find my way back. I just need to be regular old me for awhile. Okay?*

He gives me a half a smile.

Dane, Shel, and Matt reappear through the sliding door clad in swimsuits. Mad follows with a ginormous sheet cake in her hands, and I stand to help her set it on the picnic table. It says "Con"grad"ualtions Emma" and an owl, piped in icing, wears a graduation cap and takes up most of the left side. "He's too cute." I hug Madeline. "I don't want to cut him."

I'm forced to hack into the adorable student owl because the Larvatus around me are starving – as usual. I finish my piece of chocolate cake then head inside to change because of everyone's ribbing. Why isn't the guest of honor living-it-up in the hot tub? Because the guest of honor can't hold her liquor and being drunk in a swimsuit is most likely a recipe for disaster.

As I'm leaving the guest room in a purple one-piece, Dane stops me in the hall.

"I can't wait anymore. I want to give you my gift." He takes my hand and pulls me back into the bedroom.

"Here?" I ask, shocked. "Don't you think we should be alone?"

He shoots me a confused look. "We are alone."

I need to get my mind out of the gutter. He said it wasn't inappropriate.

He sits me on the bed then finds his leather jacket, searching the pockets. He produces a plain white business envelope and hands it to me. "Your present, Madame."

I turn it over in my hands. There's nothing written on it. "Gee, you shouldn't have," I say sarcastically, remembering our gift challenge. "It's gonna be hard to top this."

"Don't be a smart ass," he says as he sits next to me. "Open it."

I'm surprised to find my fingers shake when I tear open the paper. I pull out a neatly folded letter:

6 am
May 25th
Pack light

My forehead pinches. "Are we going somewhere? Why couldn't you give me this in front of my parents?"

His eyes light up. "Because I didn't want to answer questions and ruin the surprise."

I'm confused. "So, I don't get to know the destination?"

He shakes his head. "Just be ready on that date at that time. I'll pick you up."

A trip? This is over the top. Should I be surprised? No, Dane does everything big. "You really shouldn't have done this. It's going to be crazy expensive, isn't it?"

"Actually, it's not," he says, grinning. "Besides, what does it matter? I'm working."

I keep forgetting that Dane's idea of crazy expensive and mine are vastly different. It is true he has a great job; he got hired the week following his interviews. Both companies offered him a position and luckily he got to choose the place he liked best.

"Well, how long will we be gone? I'll need to let Dr. Randall know."

Yes, I'm asking questions to figure out the surprise. And yes, my internship turned into a full time job. Once baby Sophie was born, Sheila decided her calling was to be a stay at home mom. Working at the clinic isn't what I want to do for the rest of my life, but I have a great boss and it will do for now.

"Just the weekend," Dane says. "Through Memorial Day."

I give him a suspicious look; although, inside, I'm practically jumping up and down. A weekend getaway with him? Yes, please!

I wrap my arms around his waist and sigh. "You know, a simple card and a kiss would have been enough. I don't want you to think you have to lavish me with gifts. I'm not that high maintenance."

"Well, the kiss I can arrange." He leans in and plants one of those all-consuming lethal ones on me. "I'll remember the card for next time."

"Next time?" I smile. "I'm not planning on graduating again."

"This trip is about more than graduation," he says, clearly pleased with himself.

"It is?"

"May 25th is the day we first met." His arms tighten around me. "Did you think I would forget our anniversary?"

I stare at him in shock. Yes, I would expect him to forget! I forgot!

"I plan on spending the rest of my years with you," he says gently. "That means a lot more anniversaries."

My heart starts to race. "Then you better buy stock in Hallmark," I tease, trying to make light of his very serious statement. We've never discussed the future past a few weeks at a time.

He cradles my face and gives me a soft smile. "One day, when the time is right, I will propose to you, Grace. I'm warning you now, so you can prepare a proper response. One *without* sarcasm."

Now my stomach has clenched itself into a knot, and I swallow at his admission. I hadn't thought that far ahead. I hadn't pictured the white dress, and the house, and the kids. There's probably a dog involved somewhere, too.

"Em?" Dane studies me. "Why do you look pale?"

"You want to marry me?" falls out of my mouth.

He chuckles and drops his hands. "Yeah. In case you haven't noticed I'm kind of in love with you. Is that surprising?"

I shake my head to clear it. He hasn't had the best track record when it comes to engagements. "No. I mean yes. I mean, I didn't realize you'd want to go through that again."

"Through what? I've never been married."

"But you had a crappy engagement. I hadn't considered that you considered..."

He cuts me off. "The past is the past. You remember why I proposed to Teagan and it was for a million wrong reasons. What we have is different; it doesn't touch that disaster of a relationship. We're the real deal."

My heart melts and puddles in my chest. "You think we're the real deal? To death do us part?"

"We've already beat death once," he says and runs his thumb over my cheek. "You saved me and I saved you." He eyes my empty wrist. "I say the odds are in our favor."

I can't help myself as I throw my arms around his neck. "This probably isn't the right time to say this, but I never imagined marrying anyone but James. When that option left, I think the whole idea of marriage left, too. You'd be able to put up with me? My sarcasm? My connection to the supernatural? My past weirdness? Everything?"

He laughs. "In small doses your sarcasm is cute. Your past weirdness is part of what attracted me to you, and I'm still hoping you'll cave on the whole Larvatus thing and let me join the club."

I lean back and plant a full kiss on his not-ready lips. He laughs against me.

"So I take it when I do propose you'll say yes?"

I kiss him again.

"What are you doing in here?" Shel appears in the doorway. "Can't you two keep your hands off each other for a minute? Jesus!"

"Like you're one to talk," I chastise her as I stand.

"Hey, I don't get much time with you Ms.-I'm-Graduated-and-My-Best-Friend-Isn't. Come celebrate with me! I leave tomorrow." She pouts.

I smile and drape my arm around her shoulders. "Fine, let's go."

As we leave the room, I wink at Dane over my shoulder.

Chapter 25

My mouth falls open as I stare at the sleek ship. "You bought a yacht?"

Dane laughs and then pulls me toward it. "No."

"You rented a yacht?"

He clutches my hand as he tows me toward the back end. "No."

When we get to where we have a full view of the back of the boat, he makes me drop my suitcase and turns me by my shoulders. "What does that say?"

I read the boat's name. "Evelyn Grace."

His mouth appears by my ear. "Whose name was Evelyn?"

"Your mom."

"And whose name is Grace?"

"Mine," I whisper.

From behind, he wraps his arms around my waist and sets his chin on my shoulder. "This was my mother's boat. She inherited it from her father, my grandfather, when he passed. And when she died, I inherited it from her. Along with a few other things."

I stare at it in awe. "Was her middle name Grace?"

"No." He squeezes me. "It was Anne. I had the boat lettered. What do you think?"

My voice is lost behind the lump that's formed in my throat. I'm beyond flattered, beyond touched. However, instead of expressing my gratitude the stupidest thing falls out of my mouth. "Won't your dad be pissed?"

Dane kisses my cheek. "It's not his boat. Come on." He releases me and grabs my hand, towing me up the small gangway.

"Mr. Walker, sir." A gentleman tips his naval cap to Dane as we step on to the main deck. "It's nice to see you again."

"It's been a few years, hasn't it Greg?" Dane smiles and turns to me. "Emma, this is Captain Travis. He'll be with us for the next few days. Greg, Emma."

"It's a pleasure to meet you." He extends his hand.

"Um, likewise." I give Mr. Travis a tiny smile and a tentative handshake. I'm failing miserably at pretending I belong here.

He turns his attention back to Dane. "I'm sure you'll find everything in order below deck. We'll be underway in, say, fifteen minutes?"

Dane nods. "Sounds good." He pulls me toward a set of stairs. "Let me show you around."

When we make it to the bottom of the staircase I yank Dane's hand hard. He stops in his tracks. "What?"

"I understand the boat is free. I'll even accept the plane ticket to Miami. But a private captain? Is there a maid, too?"

He smiles. "Relax, Grace. Do you think I can drive this thing? Greg is a family friend; I've known him since I was five. He's doing me a favor. Sailing is his hobby, but doesn't have his own vessel."

I'm speechless.

"And no, there's no maid." He winks at me. "You'll have to pick up after yourself for the next three days."

He continues through the ship, pointing out the stocked galley, full bathroom, master suite, small living area with flat screen, and the captain's quarters. They look more like a closet.

"Are you going to make him sleep in there?" I ask. "It doesn't look very comfortable."

"We'll be docking off the coast during the evenings. He'll stay ashore." He winds his hands around my waist and pushes me back against the wall. "Because there's no way in hell we're not fooling around."

Okay, now I can't breathe. The promise of sailing off the coast of Florida, relaxing in the sun by day and sleeping with Dane at night is causing me to have a mild asthma attack. And I don't have asthma.

As we kiss, I mentally high-five myself. I knew this trip would be beyond words because that's how Dane operates. But, I've made preparations to give him some of his own medicine. He loves to surprise and pamper me because it gets a reaction. He likes to watch me squirm even though he knows I'll love whatever he's done. Well, now it's my turn.

It took me nearly three weeks to come up with and execute the perfect plan. It's his anniversary too, so I don't deserve all the gifts. I was a little nervous about my idea at first, but as I thought back on all the things he's done for me, all the things he's said to me, I knew it was the only thing I could give him that made sense. I'm about one hundred percent sure this gift tops all gifts, and I pray he likes it.

The boat motor starts with a loud rumble and it startles us both. We pull apart, laughing, and Dane urges me back upstairs to sit on the deck as we head out to sea. He helps a random deck hand with the moorings as I find a nice sunny spot on one of two small lounges. When we're completely detached, Captain Travis gently glides the Evelyn Grace away from the dock, away from the marina, and out into the crystalline blue water.

Dane finds me minutes later and sits behind me on the lounge. He pulls me back against his chest and wraps his arms around me. I sigh as I relax into him.

"I figured we'd do a lot of this," he says into my ear. "Is that okay?"

I nod enthusiastically. "I'm definitely down for a lot of this." Pure relaxation. Who could ask for more?

Hours later, after we've napped, ate, and basically putzed around, we dock for the night. Captain Travis bids us farewell till morning, and I can't help but feel a little embarrassed by his leaving. Surely, he knows we want privacy. In reality, I'm probably feeling more nerves than embarrassment. I'm about ready to reveal to Dane that I got him something, and it has to happen tonight if it's going to be any kind of surprise.

"So," I try to be nonchalant. "I'm going to need you to sit right here," I grab him by the shoulders and move him to the foot of the bed, "and wait."

He takes a seat, looking bewildered. "For what?"

"It's *our* anniversary," I stress *our*, "and I got you a present. But," I hold up one finger, "there are a couple of rules."

He smirks. "I kind of like where this is going. Continue."

"First rule, no laughing."

He immediately tries to hide a smile. "Okay. Why would I laugh?"

"Just work with me." I hold up another finger. "Two. When I come back out here, you have to *find* your gift. I'm not going to show it to you."

He looks confused.

"And rule number three. You have to be honest. If this gift outdoes all others you have to admit you can never top it."

He mulls over the last rule, or at least pretends to. "Agreed." He grins and shoos me away. "Get to the gift giving, woman."

I smile. "Okay." I make a brief stop at my suitcase, clutch a couple items to my stomach, and head to the bathroom.

As I change, I start to second-guess my plan. It sounded great in my head; I was even confident I wouldn't feel stupid wearing what I bought with his blasted gift card from Christmas. The girl at Victoria's Secret assured me my purchase was classy. The lingerie looks just like a bikini and covers just as much. It's black lace, and a delicate green ribbon, Dane's favorite color, is woven into the waistband and around the bottom of the bra. It's cute. So why am I starting to sweat? The other part of his gift is much more permanent, and I didn't bat an eyelash when I got that. I take a deep breath. I'm so glad I came up with the no laughing rule seconds ago.

When I reach for the door handle, I literally feel like the biggest ass on the planet. Who do I think I am? Gisele Bundchen? Kate Upton? Not! I open the door a crack. Dane remains where I put him except, now, he's leaned back to lounge on his elbows. Attempting to keep whatever shreds of dignity I have together, I open the door all the way and walk out to stand a few feet in front of him. I have to concentrate really hard to keep my arms at my sides and not cross them over my bare stomach.

As soon as he sees me, Dane is no longer lounging. He sits up straight and has to blink a few times to focus. I actually look behind me to see if there's something I missed.

"Um..." He clears his throat. "I think I found my gift." His voice is raspy.

I meet his eyes and they're huge. This gives me a little more confidence, and I push my hair over one shoulder. "You said you wanted to see what I bought," I remind him of our Christmas deal, "but this isn't your present. It's kind of..." I search for words. "The wrapping paper."

He looks even more stunned which makes me smile. I can do this! Although, I'm still a little shaky. Yeah, he's seen all of me before. But it's usually dark, and I'm not normally on display.

He swallows. "So, what do I do?"

I reach for his hand and pull him off the bed. "Find it."

He stands directly in front of me and his eyes bore into mine. "How long do I have?"

"As long as it takes." Which wouldn't be very long if he would concentrate.

He leans in to my ear. "I'd prefer a time limit. I don't know how long I can last."

I almost fall over. "Cooperate and start looking."

He circles my body slowly, and I swear I can *feel* everywhere he looks. It's like every nerve is on hyper drive.

"Why are you making this so difficult?" he asks. "What am I looking for? I like what I see and I'm tempted to tell you this outdoes everything right now. If I do will you –" He stops in his tracks. "No way."

I arch a brow. "See something different?"

He drops to one knee by my left hip where half of a wing is exposed above the waistline of my fabulous underwear. He hooks one finger over the material and edges it down just enough to expose my butterfly tattoo.

The light dawns. "This is why you wouldn't let me touch you last week. You lied."

"I had to! It was tender, and I wanted it to be a surprise." I had told him I wasn't feeling well. "Do you like it? You know why I chose a butterfly, right?

His soft eyes jump to mine. "Because I compared you to one."

I smile and nod as he goes back to examining my body art, tracing the outline with his finger. My tattoo is drawn from a side view; my butterfly has a thin body and delicate antennae. Her wing curls off into dainty tendrils at the top and the bottom, and it's filled with swirls that flow around one another. They conceal, to the untrained eye, the best part of the whole piece.

Dane smiles. "I love this. I'm the only one who gets to see it."

"You're also the only one who knows what it means. You're the inspiration. That's why," I hunch over a little to trace my finger deliberately over the swirls, "your name is right here."

He does a double take and focuses on the pattern. Woven into the design are his initials DRW.

Instantly, he's on his feet. One hand wraps around the back of my neck while the other wraps around my arm, pulling my whole body forward and crushing my mouth to his. He spends a minute there then moves, kissing the corner of my mouth, then my cheek, then my temple. He finds my ear. "I can't believe my name is forever on your body. Why would you do something like that?"

I lean back a bit. "I wanted to show you I'm yours."

"I told you I'd propose one day."

"A ring can be taken off." I trace his bottom lip with my thumb. "This way you're permanently a part of me. Not that you weren't already, but this makes it visible."

He searches my face. "What if...God forbid...anything happens? How will you explain my initials to someone else?"

I cover his mouth with my hand and give him a stern look. "Don't ever say that again."

He kisses my palm and I remove my hand, placing it against his chest. "What did I ever do to deserve you?" he asks.

"Gee, let me think." I overly exaggerate my eye roll. "You stood by me last summer without question. You saved me from a psycho. You abandoned your life to take me to the Caribbean. You forced a bracelet on my wrist that saved me from death, and you never gave up on me throughout my memory loss. Did I leave anything out?"

"Only one thing," he whispers in my ear. "I'm madly in love with you."

"I figured." I smile. "You put my name on a boat."

"You put my name on your body." His lips find my neck; they leave a hot trail down one side and up the other. "Now what happens?" he asks suggestively.

"Now you tell me you can never top my gift."

"I'll never be able to outdo this gift." He leans in close. "But, I'll never stop trying."

"I hoped you would say something like that," I tease, but then turn serious. "I love you. Thank you for accepting me, imperfections and all."

He shakes his head. "You chose me. I'm the one who's honored." He steps back and his eyes rake over my body from head to toe. "Plus, I see no imperfections here." He takes a moment to brush his fingertips over my tattoo. "I don't think I'll ever get tired of looking at this. You may have to stay naked the entire trip."

I laugh. "I don't think Captain Travis would appreciate that."

"He'd appreciate it too much, I think." Dane's expression turns dark as he steps to me again. "Can I show you how much I love you now or should we talk some more?"

My heart pounds. "What's left to say?"

He wraps me in his arms and everything around us evaporates into oblivion. The reason we're here, the fancy yacht, past choices, everything. It's just him and me and our future. I don't have all the answers to what it holds, but that's the amazing part. If I've learned anything over the past year it's that nothing is guaranteed.

The best laid plans change. People change. Sometimes they change for the worse, sometimes for the better, but there's a method to the madness. All I know for certain is that, whatever comes our way, Dane and I will face it together.

And it's going to be fantastic.

The End

Acknowledgements

First and foremost, I cannot believe I wrote a trilogy. A trilogy! Me! Where the heck did that come from? Talk about a hobby spiraling wildly out of control. What started out as simple fun to entertain friends has quickly grown into something I could never have imagined. With that said, there are a few people I feel the need to publicly thank (and possibly embarrass):

My Beta Readers. I've said it before, and I'll say it again: to Koz, Aubs, Bree, and Abbie Gale. Thank you for living in my fictional world. Without you, these books would not exist. You know it's the truth, so stop blushing.

My Family & Friends. I kept the secret that I was writing until I pushed the "publish" button on Amazon. For some misconstrued reason, I thought they would think I was devoting too much time to a simple hobby. Well, I was wrong. *So wrong.* From my husband shooing the kids out of the bedroom so "mom can write," to my parents, in-laws, grandparents, aunts, uncles, cousins, co-workers, fellow hockey moms, and mothers of my kids' friends; even my brother (hint – that scene where Mike proposes to Kate? Yeah, he needs to get on that), it makes my heart want to burst with how much encouragement they have for me. To hear my kids tell their teachers that "my mom wrote a book" makes me think I'm doing something right and showing them that they can accomplish big things. I want everyone to know their enthusiasm feeds mine. Especially my Aunt Gloria's. If you ever run into a lady handing out random *Guardian* promo cards at Home Depot, that's her.

The Indie Author Community. Holy wow. And I mean, HOLY WOW. I count myself lucky to have connected with so many truly supportive self-published authors and bloggers. I wanted to list everyone and their blogs, and I started to, but the length was getting obnoxious, so I'll cut it short and say this – y'all know who you are because I talk with you just about *every single day.* Thank you so much for your support and promotion. I have to call out one blogger in particular – yes, Ms. Tara, I'm talking to you! Thank you for being the first blogger to take a chance and review *Guardian*. Your love for James nearly made me rewrite my story. Almost.

My Readers. I have a hard time calling you "mine" because I know I have to share you with so many other great writers. Thank you for reading an unknown author's work, and thank you for continuing to support writers like me. Your reviews, emails, and messages on Facebook make me smile – like big, stupid, dorky, idiot smiles. There's no better high than knowing others love the world I've created just as much as I do.

About the Author

Sara Mack is a Michigan native who grew up with her nose in books. She is a wife and a hockey mom on top of being trapped in an office – which now has a window! – forty hours a week. Her spare time is spent one-clicking on Amazon and devouring books on her Kindle, cleaning up after her kids and two elderly cats, attempting to keep her flower garden alive, and, of course, writing. She has an unnatural affinity for dark chocolate, iced tea, and bacon.

Connect with Sara and The Guardian Trilogy:

On Facebook:
www.facebook.com
Search Sara Mack

On Twitter:
www.twitter.com/smackwrites

Blog and Email:
www.smackwrites.blogspot.com
smackwrites@gmail.com

Check out Spotify for the Reborn playlist:
www.spotify.com
Search smackwrites

and Café Press for Guardian, Allegiant & Reborn merch!
www.cafepress.com/IndieFriends